Billy

the

Kid

Billy the Kid

THE WAR FOR LINCOLN COUNTY

RYAN C. COLEMAN

BLACK STONE
PUBLISHING

Printed in the United States of America
Originally published in hardcover by Blackstone Publishing in 2024

First paperback edition: 2024
ISBN 979-8-8748-6382-1
Fiction / Westerns

Version 1

Blackstone Publishing
31 Mistletoe Rd.
Ashland, OR 97520

www.BlackstonePublishing.com

To my mom,
who would have thought this was pretty damn cool,
and to my dad, who does.
Thank you for a lifetime of love,
support, and encouragement.

Part I

Chapter 1

FORT GRANT, ARIZONA TERRITORY
August 1877

He'd never killed a man. Didn't know what it would feel like. Didn't know if it would turn his insides out. Turn him inside out. He didn't know if he'd lay awake long into the night, afraid of what may come in his sleep, in his dreams. He didn't know if he'd forever be followed by that dark cloud, a harbinger of his soul's inevitable damnation.

He'd find out though.

Turns out killing a man doesn't change you.

It just reveals the *real* you.

He checked his cards again, then scanned the men at the table.

Henry "Kid" Antrim was small of frame, with a smooth oval face and two larger front teeth that gave him a boyish quality. It was both a blessing and a curse. His visage left some believing his transgressions were simply those of youth, not the sinister undertakings of a career criminal. But others took one look at the scrawny young'un with the baby face and saw a mark they could bully.

This last year on his own in the unforgiving Arizona Territory had imbued the Kid with a worldliness that far exceeded his seventeen years on earth. All that worldliness, all that maturity reflected in his eyes—a piercing crystal blue, they penetrated when he scowled but glistened when he smiled, as he was doing now. To other men it came across as cocksure. To women, however . . .

Henry leaned back and pulled a ripe peach out of his leather satchel.

"May I?" The prostitute bent over the Kid and seductively guided the peach from his hand. She took a bite and dropped herself into his lap, draping her long legs over his. She played coy as her dress slipped above her knee, and Henry couldn't help but eye the rip in her stockings, leading up, up, up her thigh.

The juice from the peach dripped down her chin into her bosom. She wiped the extract from her mouth with the back of her hand and left the rest for Henry to ponder.

"You really wanna sit around with a bunch of dusty ol' men playing cards?" she asked, twirling a lock of his shaggy, overgrown hair. "We could go upstairs."

"And do what?" Henry asked. "Read the Bible?"

"When I turned thirteen, the preacher took great interest in my goings-on."

"Must be nice to have a man of God looking out for you."

"It wasn't my soul he was after."

The other players, losing patience, implored Henry to bet or fold, but he was enraptured with the girl, who continued plying her trade. "What about you? What do you want?"

"I ain't after your soul either, if that's what you're asking," Henry said.

"Well, everything has a price." She picked up a dollar bill from in front of him.

Henry smiled, seemingly debating, then took the dollar back from her and shoved it into the middle of the table along with the rest of his money.

The two men to his left grumbled and folded. The third tried to get a read on Henry, but the Kid's eyes were transfixed on the sweet, sticky juice sliding below the woman's bodice. Deciding he was showing off, the remaining opponent called.

Henry flipped over his cards—three queens beat the man's two pair.

"Looks like God's good fortune smiled on you," she said and ran her fingers along the back of Henry's neck, sending a shiver of excitement up his spine.

His jubilance was broken by creaking door hinges and the jangle of spurs entering the cantina.

"The nerve you got, coming back around here, Antrim."

Frank "Windy" Cahill was a large, ruddy Irishman with thick, strong hands and barrels for forearms, and when he approached he cast a hulking shadow over the table.

"It's a free country, Windy," said Henry, attempting to show resolve in front of the lady.

"You wasn't free last time I saw you," replied Cahill.

"I've yet to meet the restraints that can hold me."

The other men in the cantina couldn't help but snicker. Young Henry Antrim was indeed the source of some embarrassment for the forty-year-old Cahill.

Henry had been making his living through thievery, relocating horses from the soldiers at nearby Fort Grant. He'd pick off a steed or two at a time and sell them for twenty dollars apiece to local Mexican farmers or travelers passing through.

Then he was caught.

As the colonel at Fort Grant transported Henry to the local jail—a six-by-six cell with a concrete floor and an old, mildewed cot—the Kid kept up his jovial spirit.

"Been a spell since I had a nice, warm bed to curl up on. You got them goose feathers?"

"Government only supplies us with straw," replied the colonel.

"What about the blankets? Señor Villareal has got a nice selection in his general store."

"We ain't looking to make your stay comfortable, Kid."

"Then I must commend you on a job well done," Henry answered.

At the jail, they were met by the blacksmith, Cahill.

"Damn, Windy, they get you for borrowing horses too?"

"You ain't charming," Cahill grunted. He clasped iron cuffs on Billy's hands and feet, connecting them with a vertical chain.

"You do some fine work, Windy," Henry said, jangling the iron. "Maybe the best I've ever seen, save for Crook-Legged Tooley up in Globe."

Henry knew Cahill and Tooley had once been partners in a blacksmith shop, an arrangement that had ended bitterly. Henry got his intended response as Cahill scowled.

"Wiseass cunt," Cahill said before he left.

"He don't like you all that much, Kid," the colonel said after Cahill had gone.

"Shit, you must be mistaken. Everybody likes me."

The colonel went home for the evening, leaving Henry alone in the cell. Henry bounced up and down a few times on the mattress, checking the buoyancy. *Well, this sure as hell won't do.*

He rattled the chains once more, then looped the cuffs around the bottom of his boots and pulled. His hands were slowly slipping free, but the iron chafing against his wrists was excruciating. Henry kept going, fueled by one motive: sticking it to Windy Cahill.

His left hand popped free.

Henry rubbed his wrist, now bright red and beginning to swell, and shuffled over to the lock on the cell. He pulled a thin piece of metal from his waistband—it always amazed him no one bothered to check the lining of his britches—and got to work on the lock, using the trick Sombrero Jack had taught him. A few moments later, he felt the hinge pop up, and the cell door opened.

Henry whistled as he inspected the lone desk in the outer room and found the keys to the leg restraints. He spotted a pencil and ledger. Henry smiled and wrote a note, then walked out the front door into the steamy Arizona night.

Dear Windy,

I stand corrected. You are the best blacksmith in all of the Arizona Territory. It took me almost two full hours to free myself of your handiwork!

Your friend now and always,
Henry Antrim

Now here the Kid was, a mere two weeks later, still in Arizona. It was a slap in the face to Cahill, who'd been the subject of merciless teasing since Henry's self-liberation.

"You're as bent as a dog's hind legs," continued the blacksmith. "I have half a mind to lock you back up myself."

"C'mon, Windy, let it go," said the cantina's owner, who took a cut of each card game. Anything that distracted from gambling was bad for business.

Cahill continued to glare at the Kid but sat down anyway. The chair groaned under his considerable weight. The cantina owner placed a whiskey in front of him and one in front of Henry. Cahill raised his glass. Henry didn't.

"Ain't you gonna give me the courtesy?" asked the blacksmith.

"I'm not parched." Henry rarely drank, and he wasn't about to go hazy-headed now, not with Cahill's ire up.

The sight of the cocksure kid lounging in the chair, the comely prostitute draped over him, further gnawed at Cahill. "Fuzz here get a discount?" he said to the girl. "Ain't gonna take but a few pumps."

The other players chuckled.

Henry could feel the blood rushing to his face, a curse of his Irish heritage.

"Now, now, play nice, Mr. Cahill," she said.

"I am," replied the blacksmith. "I'm negotiating a cheaper price for the yearling."

Henry wanted to tell Cahill to pound sand but held his tongue. Cahill had a good six inches and at least six stone on him.

"I don't do discounts," the working girl replied.

"Not even for a peach-fuzzed pecker?"

"Aww," she said, pulling Henry into her bosom. "He's sweet."

"He is . . . as a peach," Cahill replied bitingly.

"I'll give you this," the Kid said, his lips curling into a smile. "You joke better than you blacksmith."

Henry heard the first of the cackles from the fellow players but then found himself on his back, staring up at the ceiling. Cahill was on top of him—giant, meaty fists pounding Henry's stomach, his arms, his chest, and eventually his face, peppering insults in between blows.

"Git off me, you hog-smellin' sonofabitch!" Henry yelled.

Cahill didn't stop. Henry was pinned by the much larger man, who continued his assault. Henry could taste the adrenaline and bile in his mouth, and blood stung the Kid's eye before it trickled its way onto the ground.

No one stepped in to help. Henry's vision narrowed, and one brutal crack across his face had him seeing stars. He was on the verge of losing consciousness. If he blacked out, he was as good as dead . . .

Bam!

Henry and Cahill both froze.

Sometimes there's a split second after a gun goes off when you don't know if you're the killer or the killed.

Then Cahill's eyes went wide, and he slumped over, holding his belly. His vest was on fire, but the blacksmith didn't even feel his palms burning as he instinctively covered the wound. The only one more surprised than Cahill was Henry, pistol still smoking in his hand.

The cantina owner bent over Cahill in dismay, saying no one needed to get shot. The prostitute ran up the creaky wooden stairs, screaming. And Henry fixated on Cahill—gasping and rasping in pain—but all the Kid could hear was the sound of his own beating heart.

Just get to your feet, Henry thought. *Now, goddammit!*

Henry righted himself and bolted from the cantina.

Outside, a summer windstorm was sweeping through eastern Arizona and kicking up dirt something fierce. Henry shielded his face from the needling sand.

He spotted a lone horse tied to a hitching post: John Thompson's steed, Cashaw. Normally, Henry preferred to practice his larceny against the soldiers at the nearby fort, but he was desperate. Just before he reached the town's edge, he turned back to see if anyone was following. No law, no vigilantes, only a small boy of about six, staring at him. The boy raised a hand. Henry, bewildered, slowly returned the wave, then rode out of town.

Henry fled to the nearby Pinaleño Mountains. He used the steep, rocky cliffs and fir trees lining the path to provide aid from the weather. Every time he wiped the blood from his eyes, it was like sandpaper scraping across his face. When the storm finally passed, and Henry was satisfied no one was trailing him, he led Cashaw to a creek.

Henry cupped the cool water and took stock of his wounds and the dried, sandy blood on his hands, his shirt, his cheek. He scooped up more water and began washing away the blood—some his, some Cahill's. He doused his face and hair and tried to scrub his shirt clean. As Henry watched the blood slither away in the slow current, he was struck by a realization: His hands weren't shaking. No, they were eerily calm.

And that's what scared him the most.

Chapter 2

Spring 1869

Henry witnessed his first killing in Kansas.

He was just ten years old.

His mother, Catherine, took her eldest son into town to purchase seeds.

"But we don't know nothing about harvesting," Henry said.

"Sure we do. Our family comes from a long line of farmers back in Éire . . ."

Then she coughed. Henry had noticed she'd been doing that a lot lately. But his concern was soon broken by yelling in the street.

"Scum-sucking fish!" a voice called out. Henry and Catherine turned to see the commotion.

"It ain't how it happened."

"Liar!" screamed the first man. "You owe me restitution."

"I ain't paying you to fuck your wife, Arthur."

A crowd formed around the two men. Catherine pulled Henry behind her, shielding his eyes from the row.

"Then I'll beat the payment out of her," replied the dishonored husband.

"Now, Arthur, I can't let you lay hands on Millie like that."

"Why? She's *mine* to do with what I please."

Arthur's plan to storm home and punish his unfaithful wife was halted by a gunshot. A woman screamed, and the crowd of onlookers backed away, most turning their faces from the horror before them.

But not Henry. He wrestled from behind Catherine's skirt and poked his head out. He was transfixed by the grotesque disfigurement of Arthur, and the portion of scalp that flapped over, hanging on to the man's head by the slenderest margin.

Henry stepped closer. He peered up at the shooter, who was calmly holstering his Colt Army Model 1860 and walking away, the crowd parting for him.

Most of the town viewed this as a holdover from humanity's archaic, violent past, closer to gladiator combat in the Colosseum than to a society ushering in the Gilded Age, but Henry valued another lesson entirely.

No matter a man's size, or lack thereof, there was one great equalizer: the gun.

SILVER CITY

GRANT COUNTY, NEW MEXICO TERRITORY

Summer 1874

"Where you off to?" Henry asked William Antrim while his new stepfather was dressing.

Henry never knew his real dad. All Catherine had said was he died in the war, but many women used that same reasoning to explain a husband who was there one day and gone the next.

William had been all right to Henry while courting Catherine and even let Henry and Josie take his surname when they moved to Silver City, New Mexico, for Catherine's health.

But Henry's little brother hated William.

"He looks at me funny," Josie would say.

"It don't matter if we like him. Mama likes him. She's happy."

"Nowhere," William Antrim replied to Henry's question.

"That's my favorite place to be," said Henry. "Can I come?"

Henry liked school enough, but he much preferred the outdoors, and by the looks of William's attire—a work shirt, wool britches, heavy boots, and a dusty hat—Antrim didn't plan on being inside any walls that day.

"No."

"Well, if you ain't going nowhere, why can't I tag along?"

"I'm heading off to do men's work. In the hills."

"You're treasure hunting. Like a pirate."

William regretted gifting Henry the dime-store novels about Blackbeard and Long Ben. "It ain't like being a pirate. It's hard labor."

"I'm strong."

"No, you ain't," William Antrim replied.

Catherine coughed loudly in the other room.

"When you coming back?"

"You'll know when I do," Antrim said, then he grabbed a lantern off the wall—despite the sun having just risen—and walked out the door.

Henry didn't know if his stepfather regretted getting married, had soured on the kids, or if greed overtook him, but William Antrim began spending more and more time away prospecting silver in the nearby hills. And just as Antrim began leaving the family for days at a time, Catherine's health deteriorated.

"She's heartsick, what with William being gone all the time," Henry said to Josie, who didn't seem to be paying any attention.

Ever since they had moved to Silver City, Henry had noticed a change in his little brother. Josie was no longer the happy-go-lucky kid from back in Kansas, spending less and less time with friends and more and more time by his lonesome. He wouldn't read or draw or nothing, just stare at the walls or the trees or the sky, his mind lost to another world. Henry had even tried to teach him to play cards—despite Mama saying cards led to gambling, and gambling was the devil's work—but Josie would only concentrate for a few minutes before going quiet again. Henry wondered if it was because they were older now—Henry fourteen, Josie eleven—but he suspected it was something else. Henry believed Josie knew what everyone else in Silver City did.

Mama was dying.

Catherine Antrim was confined to bed and soon slipped into unconsciousness. Henry spent all day and all night watching over her, refusing to move. Frightened by his mother's skeletal visage, Josie retreated further into himself, spending his time in the front room running his nails along the floorboards or out in the yard staring at nothing at all.

William Antrim was in and out, never clear on when he'd be back. He returned one night to find his wife unconscious and Henry in tears.

"Where the hell you been?" Henry screamed. "You're supposed to love her!"

"Trying to provide," Antrim answered.

"You ain't provided shit for this family." Henry charged at Antrim, and the adult man easily held off the scrawny teenager.

"She's here dying, and she needs you!" Henry pummeled Antrim's legs but only left faint bruises. Antrim looked at Henry, then at Josie, who was sitting on the floor in the kitchen talking to himself.

"She needs a priest," Antrim replied, then left again.

One evening, a few days after Catherine had become unresponsive, she opened her eyes and found her eldest son asleep at her bedside, still holding her hand.

"Oh, I love you, Henry," she said, waking him.

Tears began to roll down his cheek. "Josie!" Henry yelled out to the front room. "Come quick! Mama's awake."

But his little brother was outside and never heard Henry calling for him.

"What about William?" she asked.

Henry didn't want to tell her that Antrim was off prospecting, but he couldn't lie to her either. "He'll be back soon."

Catherine coughed, and Henry dabbed her lips and forehead with a damp cloth. She pulled her son closer and used what little energy she had left to smile.

"Please . . . promise me one thing before I go."

"You're going to get better, Mama . . ."

"Henry, stop. Listen." She squeezed his hand and pressed it against her cold, gray cheek. "Above all else, my sweet boy, be good. Be kind. And look after your brother. He needs you."

Henry was sobbing and would never be sure if his mother heard him say, "I promise." She took in one last deep, agonizing breath and slipped away.

"Store these for me, will ya, kid?" Jack said.

After Catherine's passing, William Antrim spent most of his time away from home prospecting. Hell, he hadn't even made it back for the damn funeral. Times were hard in Silver City, and no family could take in both boys, so they had no choice but to be separated. Eleven-year-old Josie earned his room and board at Joe Dyer's Orleans Club by cleaning up around the saloon and whorehouse. Henry was sent to his mother's best friend. But Sarah Brown had her hands full with three kids of her own, so Henry found respite under the tutelage of Sombrero Jack Schaffer. The twenty-eight-year-old Sombrero Jack made his living robbing anything he could, no matter how small or useless. And now here he was, outside Henry's bedroom window, extending two quilts.

Henry looked at the blankets, rolled tightly. "Hell, Jack, why can't you keep them?"

"I ever hassle you, Henry? I ever tell you not to do something?"

"Well, no . . ."

"Don't I share with you?"

"You give me a piece of bread when you steal a loaf, sure."

"I don't steal. I reappropriate. Besides, that ain't what's happened here. I bought these for Miss Anabelle as a gift, and I don't want her to see them should she happen to come by."

"Miss Anabelle ain't ever coming by your room, Jack."

"You'll see, kid." Jack ran off into the night, leaving the quilts on Henry's windowsill.

Henry pulled the clothes from his trunk and was about to store the blankets at the bottom—he suspected Sombrero Jack wasn't being fully truthful about their origins—when he felt something firm in the middle of the bundle. Something hard.

Something metal.

Henry unfurled the blankets to find two revolvers. They were weathered and rusty, and Henry doubted they even worked anymore. He rolled the blankets back up over the guns and stuffed them at the bottom of his trunk.

The next day, Henry returned from school, and Sheriff Whitehill was waiting for him.

"Henry, I was cleaning your room and . . ." Sarah Brown trailed off.

Henry then saw the blankets on a chair. Before he could explain—

"Henry Antrim, you're under arrest for stealing the property of Charlie Sun." Sheriff Whitehill pulled out a pair of shackles and clasped them around Henry's wrists.

"Is that really necessary? He's just a boy," Sarah Brown said.

"A boy who's proven a propensity for gunplay and thievery."

"I've never fired a gun in my life," Henry said. "Please, Mrs. Brown, this is all a misunderstanding . . ."

But Sarah Brown did not stop the sheriff from taking Henry away.

It was Henry Antrim's first time inside a jail cell.

Despite the sheriff being relatively kind, the dank, cold confinement plunged Henry into despair. It was only made worse when the sheriff went home for the evening, leaving Henry all alone. Henry couldn't help but think of what his life would be behind bars. Of not being able to look after Josie again.

Henry had been given free rein to wander the sheriff's office. The front door was locked, so Henry spent the first hour shuffling a deck of cards he found in the desk drawer.

"Goddamn Sombrero Jack . . ."

Henry found a spittoon and set it across the room, by the fireplace. He began flinging cards, trying to land them in the tin pot. Mostly he just heard the clang as the cards bounced off the metal.

"I don't even know Charlie Sun. Now I'm locked up over him?"

Clang.

"Josie's out there by himself at the Orleans Club, hanging around whores and drunkards . . ."

Clang.

Henry's anxiety reached an apex, and he flung the next card—the last in his hand—as hard as he could. It zipped through the air, missed the spittoon, and ended up in the fireplace. Henry began collecting all the cards scattered around the floor. When he reached into the fireplace for the last one, he spotted something: a sliver of light.

Moonlight.

Coming through the chimney. Henry looked up and gauged the sides of the outlet, finally reckoning that yes, yes he could.

It took him all night, but Henry squeezed his slender frame up the chimney and onto the roof.

Then he committed another first—stealing a horse—and headed in search of the only adult family he had left.

William Antrim opened the door bleary-eyed and gun ready.

"I need a place to stay," said Henry.

In the year since Catherine's death, William Antrim had sent Henry and Josie one lone letter, from a mining camp in Arizona. Henry had made the long journey and tracked Antrim down in Clifton.

Antrim wasn't thrilled to see his stepson.

"C'mon," Henry continued. "It was a long ride to get here."

"What's wrong with the Browns?" Antrim asked, letting him in. He set the gun on the table. Henry noticed Antrim's bloodshot eyes, his sunken, hollow cheeks, and suspected ol' Stepdad had taken to the drink, if not worse.

"Unless you divulge what you're running from, I can't help," Antrim continued.

"A friend asked me to hold on to some blankets," Henry said, leaving out the two revolvers.

"What kind of blankets need to be held on to? Who was this friend?"

As Henry told him about Sombrero Jack, Antrim began to understand.

"So you hid these blankets . . . which were stolen."

Henry looked down and nodded.

"I don't house no thieves under my roof."

"You're supposed to look after me."

"You're what, fifteen now? Sixteen? You still need to be looked after like a baby?"

"I ain't no baby," Henry said.

"My pact was with your mama. But she's gone now. As is my responsibility. You can stay till morning, then you move on."

And with that, Antrim retired to bed.

Henry was gutted. His mother was dead, he and his brother had been separated, he was wanted by the law, and now his step-father was casting him out.

Henry didn't wait for morning. Once he heard Antrim snoring, he packed up what he had and went out alone, into a strange land. But before he left, he lifted Antrim's gun off the table.

The gun he'd eventually use to slay Windy Cahill.

Chapter 3

SILVER CITY

GRANT COUNTY, NEW MEXICO TERRITORY

September 1877

"Get the mop."

Josie Antrim looked up at his boss, Joe Dyer, through sluggish eyes.

"Goddammit, were you fuckin' sleeping again?"

Josie shook off the cobwebs, grabbed the mop, and went to the main room. Another satisfied customer had discharged his stomach's contents onto the floor.

The Orleans Club was small, dusty, and on the undesirable side of town, but Dyer treated Josie all right and didn't ride him. When he found out Josie wasn't attending school anymore, Dyer simply said, "I expect you to pick up a few more shifts, then."

Even with the extra shifts, not being in school left Josie with ample free time, and the aberrant, introverted boy found his way to the opium dens just past Charlie Sun's laundry.

The first time he inhaled the mystic drug, Josie felt a

sensation he'd never experienced . . . utter calm. Peace. The anguish over his mom's death, the lonesomeness of being separated from his brother, the hurt over William Antrim not caring enough to take him along to Arizona, it was all washed away. And once he knew that was possible, he wanted to feel that way all the time.

"You gonna get the heavy bits too?"

It took Josie a moment to realize he really was looking at his older brother, that Henry wasn't a hallucination. But the mix of opium and life made it difficult to smile.

"C'mon, I want to talk to you," Henry said.

"Dyer keeps me on a pretty tight leash."

Henry looked at Josie's glassy eyes and sluggish way and knew Dyer wasn't keeping him on any sort of leash at all.

"Okay, when your shift's over."

Josie nodded and went back to work. Henry spent the rest of the evening sitting in the corner, eyeing patrons as they gambled and drowned their misery in booze. Henry was itching to play cards but was absent any cash, so he watched his brother meander around in a fog, wiping down a table here and there, mopping up spilled drinks and the occasional bodily fluids. Henry also knew it was honest work, which was more than he could say about his own undertakings.

Finally, Josie's shift ended and the two brothers headed out into the cool, gray dawn of Silver City.

"Where we goin'?" Henry asked, but Josie just kept walking, his feet shuffling through the dirt, the slow march of the undead.

As they passed the laundry, Charlie Sun was outside. Henry wondered if Sun knew he'd been Sombrero Jack's accomplice. Henry hoped not. He remembered how a couple of years ago Sun's wife gave birth to a child with a considerably darker complexion than Charlie or the mother. Sun scooped up the minutes-old baby girl and, amid the backdrop of his wife's piercing cries, fed the infant to his wild sows.

Josie sensed what was on Henry's mind. "Sombrero Jack skipped town right after you did. Nobody's heard from him since."

"I ain't looking for Sombrero Jack. I came back to see you."

Josie didn't respond. He just entered an unmarked one-story stone building. Henry followed.

The smell was the first thing to hit Henry. A mixture of the bitterest chocolate combined with a tart finish that burned the hairs inside his nose. Henry tailed his brother to a Chinese man in a satin robe with large, open sleeves. Josie gave the proprietor fifty cents and in return was handed a tin can. Henry trailed Josie to one of the bunks lining the wall.

The woman on the top bed raised her arm slowly and pointed directly at Henry. "I've been waiting for you."

Henry looked at her, confused. The way she said it, the creak in her voice, the hollow timbre, made Henry uneasy.

"Fear not, child," she continued. "Someone will come for you too."

Before Henry could respond, Josie waved her away. "Scram, you old kook." Then he turned to Henry. "She's always prattlin' on about death coming to her in the night. Then the next day, lo and behold, she rises again."

Henry looked back at the woman, who was now staring at the ceiling and gliding her hand through the air as if riding a strong headwind.

"I'm hungry. Let's go get some eggs," Henry said, hoping to pry his brother from this unnerving den.

"We gonna have to steal those too?" Josie opened the tin and removed a sticky tar, then loaded it into a pipe.

It dawned on Henry that Josie was a regular here. "C'mon, forget all that. I want to talk," Henry said and grabbed Josie's arm, but Josie shook his hand away.

Looking Henry square in the eyes, Josie lit a match and inhaled deeply, letting the opium swirl inside his lungs before expelling it up into the low ceiling.

Henry tried to clear the noxious smoke from his face, but he could already feel his eyes stinging. It was no use trying to extricate Josie from the den, so Henry took a seat on a rug, as low to the ground as possible, figuring smoke rises.

"What do you want to confer about?" Josie asked.

"Just how you been, is all. Can't I check in on my little brother?"

"I'm hog high . . ." Josie trailed off and took another hit from the pipe.

"I went to see William."

Josie's head didn't move, but his bloodshot eyes shifted, landing on his older brother.

"He said he didn't want nothing to do with me," Henry continued.

"Can you blame him?"

"Sombrero Jack did the stealing."

"Then you broke out of jail and hightailed it out of town. Couldn't take responsibility for what you'd done."

"Is that what you're doing now? Being responsible?" Henry regretted it instantly.

"At least I ain't a thief."

"I couldn't stomach the idea of doing a stretch when I was only helping a friend," Henry answered.

"Be careful the company you keep, Mama always said."

Josie's eyelids were growing heavy. The corners of his mouth turned up into a faint smile. His speech slowed to a crawl.

"Funny part is . . . the sheriff . . . he was just bluffing you . . ." Then Josie's head dropped to his chin.

Henry shook his brother awake. "What do you mean he was just bluffing me?"

"It was . . . a warning. He was going to let you go . . . but the joke was on him . . . you were already gone." As Josie chuckled, he lost dexterity and the pipe slipped to the floor.

Henry looked down at the dingy, tar-stained rug, letting this irony wash over him. He wasn't in trouble with the law and didn't have to escape from jail, but by doing so, he had become an actual criminal.

He felt his brother's hand fall weakly on his arm.

"You was gone . . . and I was all alone," was the last thing Josie said before he drifted off.

Henry's mind was racing. He had hoped to settle back in Silver City, but nothing was as it had once been. It made him wonder if his old life—life before he broke out of Sheriff Whitehill's jail—had really been so swell after all. And what about his brother? It wasn't safe for a boy his age to be out all hours of the night, frequenting opium dens of addicts and hustlers. Josie needed help, but what could Henry do? He didn't have a job, he didn't have money, hell, he didn't even have a place to hang his hat. As Henry watched his brother slumber away in a drug-induced haze, he made a decision: *he'd procure all the things needed to give Josie a chance in life.*

Henry stepped out of the parlor into the bright sun. He had lost track of time and was surprised to find the streets bustling. For most, the day had begun hours ago.

Henry made his way back to the center of town in hopes of finding employment. He didn't have much experience in any particular trade—other than horse thievery—but figured he was sharp enough to get by as an apprentice of some kind, or at least sweep floors and stock shelves in a pharmacy.

Henry was lost in thought when he turned a corner and bumped into a man. He noticed the tin star before he realized who it was.

As Sheriff Whitehill stepped aside to let the young man pass, Henry saw the sheriff squinting to place him. "Henry?"

Henry feigned not hearing the lawman and kept walking. The sheriff followed.

"Henry Antrim?"

Henry quickened his pace, but the long strides of the taller man quickly overtook him. Sheriff Whitehill grabbed Henry and spun him around, and as he did, the Kid's coat flared open just enough for the sun to glint off William Antrim's peacemaker tucked in Henry's waistband. Sheriff Whitehill took a step back, arched his back defensively, and hovered his fingers over the bone handle of his own revolver.

"It's okay, son . . ."

Henry eyed the lawman's posture and his hand idling perilously close to the gun.

Henry could turn himself over right here. But what if the sheriff had heard about Henry's troubles at Fort Grant? Henry had been stealing horses from the army, not to mention the hole he put in Windy Cahill. Maybe Henry could explain himself, explain he feared for his life . . .

Henry looked around at the crowded street . . . and ran.

Sheriff Whitehill gave chase but lost Henry when he disappeared around a corner. The sheriff no longer had the stamina of youth or the stupidity to chase an armed escapee blindly through busy streets.

It wasn't worth risking his life over a kid he was simply trying to teach a lesson.

Henry hid behind a stack of wood behind the general store. He held his breath as two ranchers tied up their horses at the trough and went inside for supplies.

Henry waited until the coast was clear, then untied one of the horses and rode out of Silver City, swearing he'd come back and rescue Josie as soon as the time was right.

Chapter 4

September 1877

Henry stretched out his neck and rubbed the tight knots. He was weary and his body was aching, but he had to keep moving. He couldn't remain in Silver City, he was an escaped convict. He couldn't go to Arizona—they'd want him for Windy Cahill's murder. And Mexico was out of the question.

Instead, he rode a dozen miles southeast to Apache Tejo, the small village and watering stop used by travelers making their way from New Mexico to Arizona and back.

Henry found an out-of-the-way adobe wall in the shade to lean against while he cleared his head. It wasn't his intention, but he was exhausted and soon drifted off into the first deep sleep he'd had in a while.

Henry rarely remembered his dreams. Every so often he'd wake with a vague notion he'd been with Mama or that he and Josie were once again running through the streets of Silver City with their friends, but there was no tactility to his memories, not even an image to hold on to, just an aching in his heart when he woke.

But one dream he did remember, for he'd had it over and over since childhood.

Riding a horse through a field, the bright sun warming his hands and face, every breath inhaling the aroma of fresh grass. Up ahead, lining the edge of the field, is a dense forest, the treetops creating a canopy no light could penetrate. A gust of wind kicks up and the treetops billow, like waves crashing gently to shore.

From the rustle of the swaying leaves comes a sound. A song. A faint chorus sung by schoolgirls. At first Henry can't make out the words, only the high-pitched melody cutting through the air, calling to him. His horse begins to gallop toward the forest, toward the chorus of voices. Henry pulls on the reins, wanting to remain in the bright, open, sunny field, but the horse gains speed, hurtling toward the trees. The closer they get, the clearer the song becomes: "Silver Threads Among the Gold."

Darling, I am growing old,
Silver threads among the gold,
Shine upon my brow today,
Life is fading fast away.

The horse continues to pick up speed. Henry tugs, the leather reins wrapped so tightly around his hands his knuckles turn white and his skin chafes raw. Henry tries to bail from the saddle, but his legs are fastened in, unable to get free. He's at the mercy of the beast under him. The horse is sprinting, faster and faster . . .

But, my darling, you will be,
Always young and fair to me,

> Yes, my darling, you will be
> Always young and fair to me.

They dart into the thick, black forest without breaking stride . . .

Henry startled awake. It was now morning, and he took inventory of what he had.

Not much. Less than a dollar in coins in his satchel, the dusty clothes on his back, and the Colt in his waistband. Winter was just around the corner, and soon it would be far too cold to sleep outside. He needed a roof, and for that he needed money.

Henry first went to the local laundry. He'd watched his mother run her own shop, and he'd learned a bit while tugging at her skirt tails, but the laundry couldn't afford to take him on.

The slight teen was laughed right out of the butcher's shop too.

Henry even went ranch to ranch in the surrounding area to no avail. He had all but given up when he saw the smoke rising in the air. Must be a farm of some sort. As he neared, he realized the smoke wasn't from the chimney of a traditional *white* house, but a wickiup.

Henry studied the small oval hut. It was comprised mainly of brushwood and grass and covered with an animal hide to insulate from the weather, except for the chimney, from which the smoke was emanating. Henry thought of turning around, for he wanted no part of the natives, but then he spied a figurine on the ground and curiosity got the best of him.

Henry dismounted his horse and examined his new find. It was a homemade doll depicting a little girl in traditional Apache dress, small and sewn together, but the edges were frayed and the straw was pushing its way out through the seams.

The animal skin covering the doorway to the wickiup peeled back. The Apache man who emerged stood over six feet—a good six inches taller than Henry—and possessed broad shoulders and tanned skin. His hair was dark black, braided and long, running the length of his muscular back. He looked down at Henry with stern consideration.

"Excuse me, I seem to be lost," was all Henry could muster.

The man grunted a response in a tongue foreign to Henry and stepped forward. Henry took an uneasy step back.

"Now, mister . . ." Henry said, his hand sliding down to the Colt in his waistband.

"He's saying his name," came a voice, small and high-pitched as a mouse. "Bodaway."

A little girl, no more than ten, stepped out from behind her father. She adjusted her tiny buckskin dress, which she was quickly outgrowing, and looked at Henry with curiosity.

"My father's name is Bodaway."

Bodaway relayed another message through the little girl.

"He wants to know why you're here."

The girl's innocent nature and easy manner put Henry slightly more at ease. "You tend all that land yourself . . . Apologies, miss, what's your name?"

"Lolotea."

"It's pretty," Henry replied, removing his hat.

Lolotea blushed and looked down and fiddled with the hem of her dress. Bodaway didn't know what Henry said, but he could see his daughter was fond of this stranger. Henry reached out with the doll, and Bodaway took another step forward, putting himself between Henry and his little girl. Henry, understanding, handed the doll to the father. He then directed his next question to Bodaway.

"You tend all this yourself?"

Henry kept his eyes on Bodaway as the girl translated. "Papa says there's no work."

"It's a lot of land, and I've an able body," said Henry.

Lolotea translated, then laughed.

"What's got you chortlin'?"

"Farming is lady work."

It was Henry's turn to blush. He didn't know Apache divisions of labor. "What about washing clothes? That lady work too?"

Lolotea smiled. "Yes."

"And nursing little ones—I suppose that's only for the women as well?"

"Yes!" she laughed.

"Well, shoot, y'all done took up all the good chores. What's left for the likes of me?"

Bodaway, impatient, grunted once more. Lolotea composed herself.

"Besides, we're being moved to the reservation."

Henry cocked his head and squinted. "Why you wanna do that?"

"They promised us feed and supplies, then we'll be able to harvest again."

"Who promised you?" Henry waited as Lolotea received an answer from Bodaway.

"It was an agreement with the army. They're forcing all our people onto that land but in turn pledge to help us rebuild and start anew." Then Lolotea continued in her own words, no longer translating. "They kept true at first, but each month we've been seeing less and less of what we were promised. We don't even have goats to graze our fields."

Henry understood. Times were hard for everyone. He put his hat on and said, "I won't be of any more bother to you."

Lolotea then spoke to Bodaway, pleading with him, and like most loving fathers, he gave in to his little girl's wishes.

"We'd like you to stay for dinner."

Bodaway's stern expression had not changed since he emerged from the wickiup.

"You sure that's what your daddy wants?"

"It is our custom to invite a parentless child into our home and feed them."

"Even if he's a white man?"

"Yes, even if he's an *n'daa*."

Henry cocked his head curiously.

"A pale eyes." She smiled again, and Henry did too.

Henry looked at the sky. The sun wasn't too long from setting. He should really head back before dark, before it got perilous to travel. "Okay then. At least let me help prepare dinner."

Lolotea let out a giggle.

Despite his protests that he'd spent time working as a cook and waiter at the Hotel de Luna in Arizona—leaving out that his employment came to an end when he was arrested for horse thievery—Henry was not allowed to help. Lolotea and her mother, Onawa, insisted their guest should not be required to engage in chores. Henry suspected they didn't have faith the *n'daa* wouldn't ruin dinner. It left Henry loitering beside Bodaway while the women worked.

Bodaway didn't have much to say. Their only interaction came when Bodaway packed a pipe and offered it to the guest, but Henry politely declined. He didn't know what was in it, and the last thing he needed was to follow the same path to Hades as his little brother.

Dinner was ready, and Henry was surprised at the opulence. The meat—from an antelope felled the day before—was tender and moist and made a fine stew. There were also plenty of nuts and berries to accompany the meal.

Lolotea peppered Henry with question after question about his time in the East. She wanted to know what New York was like. She'd read about streets lined with buildings, buggies carrying the finely dressed to and fro, and a new invention, "electricity," that would be able to light up the whole city every night. Henry didn't have memories from New York, just the sort you think you remember because Mama told you the story so many times over the years.

"How come you speak the King's tongue so well?" he asked her.

Lolotea didn't know what he meant. The Ojo Caliente Apache had no connection to or mistrust of the king of England. To them, their agitators were wholly American.

"Where'd you learn English? And the reading? Awfully skilled for a girl your age."

"I don't know. I've always just been able to speak the white tongue. And reading—it's how you learn things the tribe can't teach you."

Henry smiled. "I got that same ability, picking up other languages."

Lolotea thought Henry was pulling her leg. "Prove it," she said.

"I don't feel like it," Henry teased.

"I knew you were fibbing." Lolotea laughed.

Henry then repeated a sentence he'd heard Bodaway tell Lolotea earlier. He didn't know what it meant—*"If we let a white boy into our home, it will invite their deadly spirits to follow"*—but his pronunciation was solid. If it weren't for his slim frame, sunbaked Irish skin, and "pale eyes," Henry might've even passed for an Ojo Caliente Apache.

Bodaway and his wife, Onawa, traded looks until Lolotea explained Henry didn't know what he was saying. But Bodaway kept a close eye on Henry throughout the rest of the meal.

After dinner, they went out front and rekindled the fire under the stars. The air was crisp but felt good after Henry had gorged himself on antelope, berries, and corn. He inquired about the rest of their tribe and was told they had already relocated to the reservation.

"Father is stubborn, and we're one of the last to go. He still has faith the spirits will save us. And if not the spirits, then the great warrior Victorio."

Bodaway, standing a few feet away, took a long drag from his pipe. He didn't trust any white man, but he also didn't know what his daughter was telling this stranger.

"Victorio?" Henry asked.

"He is the chief of the Tchihende and the leader of all our people. His tribe of Apache have been relocated to the San Carlos Reservation."

Henry knew San Carlos. It was in Arizona, seventy-some miles north of Fort Grant, where he'd had his dispute with Windy Cahill.

"When Victorio saw the accord with the army was not being upheld, he gathered a group of fighters and left the reservation for freedom."

"I'm guessing the army didn't look too favorably upon that."

"Victorio is not content to do nothing while our tribe is confined and decimated. Why do whites think this land is theirs when we've been here for hundreds and hundreds of years?"

"I don't know, but it seems they do. They got the guns and the cannons too."

"And we have Usen on our side."

Henry looked confused.

"God," Lolotea said.

"I'm afraid Usen won't be of much use to you, 'less he comes down from heaven and picks up a rifle."

"That's because you have no *faith*."

"I do have faith. In myself and this here Colt," Henry said, patting the gun on his hip.

Henry had his own suspicions of authority, starting when Sheriff Whitehill had fooled him into thinking he was looking at a lengthy sentence behind bars. He suspected Lolotea's tribe had been fed a plateful by those in power too.

"About fifteen years ago, Kan-da-zis Tlishishen called for a truce. He was promised provisions in return for peace, but when he met with the army, they put him in jail."

What came next was hard for Lolotea to say, and after hearing it, Henry wasn't sure it was the sort of thing a ten-year-old should have in her head.

"Kan-da-zis Tlishishen was stripped of his clothes and bound to the ground. The soldiers placed iron pokers in a fire until they were glowing red, then they prodded and cut and burned him until he was writhing so fiercely he broke free of his constraints. Then they shot and killed the great Kan-da-zis Tlishishen, claiming he was trying to escape. After that, the army increased their attacks on our people. And when warriors like Victorio fight back, they say we're the savages. White men could have had peace that day if they'd only kept their word, but they didn't. And that's why my father will join Victorio in his fight, after he settles us on the reservation."

Henry could see the pain in Lolotea's eyes. Onawa leaned over to her daughter and clasped her hand. Even Bodaway was looking away, into the darkness, for while he didn't know exactly what his daughter was saying, he understood it all too clearly.

The rest of the evening passed mostly in silence, as the

weight of Lolotea's story hung heavy. Eventually, Henry thanked Lolotea and her family for their hospitality and left.

Lolotea woke the next morning to the sound of bleating and went outside to find two goats tied to a tree, absentmindedly chewing grass.

Chapter 5

Henry survived the next few weeks by scraping together work on local ranches, earning enough to pay the $2.25 a week to rent a room at the small boardinghouse, but no job stuck for long. Every day was a hustle, and usually he'd spend a few hours feeding pigs their slop or retrieving an animal who had wandered off in search of freedom. Invariably, he was told his effort was appreciated, but he simply didn't have the strength or know-how for the more strenuous chores required. He'd be given a meal, a dollar for his time, and sent on his way.

Henry was settling in for the evening on his rented cot in a room shared with seven other men when his stomach began to growl. He rose quietly, grabbed his satchel and William Antrim's gun, and tiptoed his way out the door. He didn't risk putting his boots on until he was outside.

As Henry walked to the butcher shop, hoping to find an unlocked door or maybe some scraps out back the coyotes hadn't gotten to yet, he heard a commotion farther down the street.

Apache Tejo was a quiet place and rarely saw activity after sundown. Now, close to midnight, it sounded as if there was a gathering in the plain just beyond town. Out past the general store, the world was usually pitch-black, a darkness only pierced when the sky was clear enough and the moon full enough to provide illumination. But tonight was overcast, and staring past the edges of Apache Tejo meant staring into a dark abyss.

The voices grew louder. Henry squinted. He could make out a glow in the distance. Mama always said nothing good happened after dark, but Henry was dissatisfied and a quiet, settled life wasn't in the making.

He continued past the edge of town, toward the gathering, toward the fire. He slowed upon approach, sensing in his marrow that he was taking a risk. But it also sent a thrill up his spine. He stood fifty yards back, aware the firelight would shield the group's ability to see him.

There were a dozen roughhewn men—all older than Henry and more settled into their weathered, strong frames. He could tell from the way they carried themselves, the boisterousness with which they spoke, that these men were dangerous. One scratched a bow across a fiddle while the rest drank, smoked, and danced. Something else caught his eye—there were women too.

It was a goddamn party.

Henry didn't run at first sight of the men. He didn't step forward either. He was beset with wonderment, excitement, anticipation, and most of all, trepidation.

So he watched from a distance.

As the men and women drank and laughed and danced, Henry became fixated on one particular beauty. She was about twenty years old, and her bright auburn hair gave off sparks as it reflected light from the fire. Her dress was long, and she was fond of lifting her skirt and petticoat, swishing them from side to side to tantalize as she giggled and kicked out one of her legs to the rhythm of the fiddle. She was without a dance partner, enjoying her ability to tease not just a single man but all of them at once. The fiddle faded from Henry's ears and the world tunneled, as if she were alone on a stage, dancing just for him.

Henry's enchantment was broken when he was lifted off his feet and slammed to the hard dirt. The air rushed out of his lungs, leaving Henry gasping like a trout on sand. The figure standing over him was tall and strong, and not since Windy Cahill had Henry been so sure he was about to die.

"What are you peepin' at?"

Buck Morton was almost thirty and would have grown to be handsome had he not been thieving and murdering the better part of adulthood, and all that living had not taken such a toll on his visage. He had noticeable scrapes and cuts that had never mended, including a long scar running under his chin that the sun had healed a bright white.

"I said who you peepin', boy?"

Henry reached for words, but nothing came out. His mouth was drier than the Chihuahuan Desert.

Buck smacked Henry across the face hard enough for his vision to flash white.

"You Treasury?"

"Am I . . . what?"

"You out here checkin' fake bills, huh?"

"Mister, I don't . . ."

Buck slapped Henry again. The sting went all the way past his cheek, through his teeth and gums, and rattled his skull.

"We might just send you back to Washington in a pine box!"

Henry reached for his gun, but Buck was too quick, lifting it from Henry's waistband.

"What were you gonna do with this, huh?" Buck leaned over Henry's reddened face. "Were you fixin' to *shoot* me down?"

"No, I was—"

"You was gonna do it, weren't you?" Buck marveled, almost in disbelief. "You was gonna try to send ol' Buck back to his Maker." Buck's own rationale caused him to pause and ponder who else Henry might be working for. "If you ain't from the Treasury Department, what is you? Some sort of bounty hunter, gonna make his fortune taking out the Boys?"

"I ain't looking to take out no one."

"How do I know one of my enemies didn't send some *child*"—he said it with such disgust—"to cut us down? We'd never see it coming in a frame like yours."

"I ain't a boy," said Henry, his Irish blood beginning to boil again despite himself. "I'm seventeen."

Buck tilted his head and studied the young man, then pulled back the gun's hammer.

"Just old enough that the Secret Service, or maybe even that Pinkerton swine, would send you after us. Slip in unnoticed, everyone thinking you too young to mean harm, then *bam*!"

Buck's holler sent Henry's heart exploding out of his chest, but his face remained still.

"You ain't even crying," Buck continued. "No, you got balls of brass, don't you? The kind you get when you been in dangerous spots before. The kind of moxie they *teach* you to have."

Buck turned the barrel on Henry. Henry had no choice but to stand firm against the abuse or feel a bullet rip through his flesh.

"I ain't no lawman, and I ain't no detective. Name's Henry Antrim. I come from Silver City."

Henry couldn't take his eyes off the gun's hammer, knowing the last thing he might ever see would be the split second it lurched forward and turned his world dark.

"Goddamn, Buck. The hell you doing?"

Henry turned his head toward another man approaching.

"I'm tryin' to suss out whether this foal here means us harm," Buck answered.

"And if he does?"

"Then I kill him."

"And if he don't mean us harm?"

"I swear I don't," said Henry.

"Then I guess I have to kill him anyway, on account of we've been conversing, and I've said perhaps more than I ought to."

The new stranger looked at Buck, then back down to Henry, still lying on his back. The stranger crouched down.

"You know who we are?"

Henry wasn't sure what answer would spare him his life.

"It's all right—you can talk freely," the stranger continued.

"He said his name was Buck and y'all were the Boys," Henry said, finally swallowing dryly. "I reckon that makes you Jesse Evans."

"How you figure?" asked the stranger.

"Buck here, he's a serious sort, the type who probably don't take direction easily. But he listens to you. By way of that, I surmise you're somebody important, somebody folks heed. And who else in the Boys could that be but the leader of the gang, Jesse Evans?"

Jesse Evans studied Henry closely, looking over his ratty boots, tattered clothes, and his smooth, boyish face.

"That's a lot of information for you to be in possession of," said Evans.

"So we kill him, then?" Buck had grown weary of the exchange.

"Kill him or don't—makes no difference to me," Evans said as he stood.

Buck's eyes narrowed, and he aimed the gun back at Henry.

"Of course," Evans continued, "Abigail's not gonna wanna lay with no boy-killer."

"I ain't no boy!"

Evans shut him up with just a look.

"What do you mean?" asked Buck.

"Look at her over there, having a gay ol' time."

Henry and the two men turned their gaze to the bonfire, where the others were unaware of the confrontation in the dark. The alluring young woman with auburn hair continued to dance with an endless amount of buoyant energy.

"Then you're gonna wander back over and she's gonna ask what happened and we're gonna say we had to quiet a mutt who may *or may not* have had it out for the Boys. But Abigail ain't like us. She's delicate. You think she's gonna understand the dangers this here child presents? No. She'll just get all weepy, as women do, and when tears are coming out their eyes, they dry up everywhere else."

Evans casually picked a tobacco remnant out of his teeth and flicked it aside. "But again, kill him or don't. Up to you."

Buck played out the scenario in his head. After a moment, he settled the hammer back into its natural position, tucked Henry's gun into his own pants, and walked back to the fire.

Evans helped Henry to his feet.

"You really Jesse Evans?" Henry asked.

"You really Henry Antrim?"

Evans and Henry walked back to the fire. The Boys were puzzled—Evans didn't customarily allow anyone into the inner sanctum—but most were sufficiently drunk and had other things on their mind. The fiddle was still hot, and Abigail was still putting on a show. Buck joined her in kicking and dancing around, and any tension he felt toward Henry seemed to dissipate.

Henry took a seat on a rock next to Evans, who offered him a drink. Henry shook his head no.

"Henry Antrim don't drink?"

"I tend to keep a clear head."

But Evans's attention was already elsewhere, as one of the Boys stumbled into a woman seated nearby. The woman's companion, a wily cuss named Frank Baker, took offense and a scuffle ensued. Evans didn't so much as stand, but rather with a simple nod of his head had Buck and others intervene.

While Buck was breaking up the row, Abigail approached Henry and Evans.

"Henry Antrim, meet Miss Abigail Mondesir."

"Pleased to meet you, ma'am," Henry said, removing his hat.

Abigail laughed. "How old are you?"

"Seventeen, ma'am."

"And how old you think I am?"

Henry blushed, not knowing what the correct answer should be.

"Abigail!" One of the other women sashayed over, carrying a tin cup with whiskey spilling over the edge. "This is going straight to my head." She bent down inches from Henry and studied his face. "You're gonna be a handsome sort when you grow."

"Henry is grown," said Abigail, winking at Henry. "You've downed a drink too many. Close one of your eyes."

The woman did, then let out a shriek of drunken excitement. "Oh my, you *are* already a handsome sort. Come dance with me, Henry."

Henry looked at Jesse Evans for approval.

"As long as she lays next to me come bedtime," the outlaw said.

Before Henry could respond, the woman pulled him up and whisked him closer to the fiddle. Henry was stiff and self-conscious. The woman placed one of his hands on the back of her waist and held the other.

"What's your name, ma'am?"

"Everyone calls me Minnie."

Then Minnie started to dance, jerking Henry along for the initial few steps. He was a quick study and soon was guiding her to the tune of the fiddle. Minnie squealed in delight as they went round and round, Henry even interjecting a new step or two.

As the song slowed, Abigail appeared over Minnie's shoulder. "May I?"

"Okay, but don't hog him. I want another bite at this apple."

Henry placed his hand on Abigail's waist, just as he'd done to Minnie, and they danced.

"You really seventeen?"

"Yes, ma'am."

"Damn you, Henry Antrim. You're making me feel old. Call me Abigail."

"Yes, Abigail."

"What are you doing hanging around these scoundrels?"

"I just met them tonight," Henry replied.

"You were just walking by, a hundred yards outside town, in the middle of the evening?"

"I heard voices out this way, and I guess curiosity got the best of me. Came upon the fire and the people gathered. And I saw you."

As they continued to twirl, Abigail smiled and looked into his eyes.

"You saw me, huh? What did you see?"

"The most beautiful woman I'd ever laid eyes upon, dancing around a glowing fire, as if just for me."

Henry blushed and looked down, cursing his honest recollection.

"Oh, I belong to you?"

"No, ma'am . . . Miss . . . Abigail. I don't want nothing except to appreciate something beautiful."

Abigail studied Henry, then pulled him closer to her body as they continued to dance. Even with the thick smoke coming off the fire, Henry was close enough to be intoxicated by her perfume. He'd never smelled something so alluring and closed his eyes to let it permeate through him.

They made a few more turns, almost cheek to cheek, until Henry opened his eyes again and caught sight of Buck Morton glaring their way. Abigail noticed it too, for she slowed to a stop, bowed, and extended her hand for Henry to kiss, which he did.

Abigail went back to Buck, and Henry sat back down on the rock next to Jesse Evans. But he never took his eyes off Abigail.

"Careful. Buck's the proprietary type."

"Thought we got rid of slavery."

"I'm not fooling, kid. She ain't worth it. And if Buck gets his spine all askew, I ain't gonna step in. 'Cause you sure as hell ain't worth it either."

Henry peered across the way to see Abigail sitting on Morton's lap, caressing his neck as she chatted with the girls. Buck sensed the Kid's look and cut a steely-eyed glare back at him.

Henry didn't look away. He reckoned she *was* worth it.

"Never know—maybe he'd cut me down . . . but maybe, just maybe, I'd get there first."

Evans took a sip of whiskey, trying to gauge how serious Henry was.

"Maybe," Evans replied. "But you ain't gonna cut down Frank Baker and Tom Hill and Dolly Graham and George Davis and Jim McDaniels and Spawny and Indian Segovia and Nicky

Provencio . . . you see what I'm getting at? When you fight one of the Boys, you fight us all."

Henry stood.

"Kid . . ."

Henry was watching Buck, who was now more focused on maneuvering his hand up Abigail's petticoat. She'd playfully knock his hand away, then adjust her bottom in his lap to titillate, then he'd reach, she'd knock his hand away and giggle, and around they'd go again.

"Henry . . ." Henry felt Evans's hand on his forearm. Not forcefully enough to hold him back, but a warning nonetheless.

Henry paused a moment, then sat.

"Can I give you some advice? Don't get caught surprised because of a filly. Don't give yourself over to one. You can doff your cap, you can pick them flowers, you can fuck 'em till they're screaming for their Maker, but never put a woman above your own self-interests. Never get caught unprepared because your brain is swimming in snatch."

Henry nodded.

"You may not know it yet, maybe you do, but you got a cold streak running through you. Keeps you from being scared when you ought to. Probably gonna save your life, if it hasn't already. It's also gonna find you trouble."

"I don't like being pushed, is all."

"Is that what happened with Windy Cahill? Was he pushin' you?"

Henry turned to Evans, surprised.

"Every outlaw in the territory has heard of Henry Antrim, the kid who cut down Windy Cahill," Evans continued. "Shit, don't think twice. Cahill was a surly sumbitch, and the world is better off. But it's only a matter of time before someone gives up you're in New Mexico and trades your name to save themselves.

Be careful who you trust." Evans stood and stretched. "That's all the learning I can teach you tonight. Now I'm gonna go give myself over to that woman."

He nodded to Minnie, who approached gleefully and wrapped her arms around his neck. Evans reached inside his coat and pulled out Henry's revolver.

"Got it back from Buck while you were dancing. Took the bullets out though. Don't want your *gun* misfiring on accident tonight."

Evans then walked off into the dark, Minnie draped at his side.

Come morning, Evans and the Boys said goodbye to the women. As they saddled their horses, Henry approached. Buck gritted his teeth and was about to send him packing, but Evans spoke first.

"Boys, this is Henry—"

"Bonney," the Kid cut him off. "Billy."

Evans just nodded, then the Boys mounted their horses and rode out for Lincoln with their newest member, William H. Bonney.

Chapter 6

It was almost dusk when Billy Bonney and the Boys, led by Jesse Evans, arrived at Blazer's Mill. The outpost and sawmill was owned by Dr. Joseph Blazer, a former dentist who had reinvented himself as a prominent business owner and citizen of Lincoln County. He was thought of as a fair man and neutral in the ongoing conflicts raging throughout the territory. The title of his business was misleading, for while he did indeed run a profitable sawmill, his was also a place travelers could rest, get a hot meal, and care for their horses.

But more importantly, Blazer's Mill occupied a strategic location. Blazer's land was surrounded by the Mescalero Apache Indian Reservation, and Blazer even rented out a building to serve as the government's agency's headquarters. At the base of the agency office was a restaurant, operated by Major Godfroy's wife, Clara.

The Boys, thirteen in all, tied up their horses and entered. Evans sat at the head of a long oak table that was once a tree out back, and Billy took the seat to his right.

"Your old man around?" Evans asked as Clara Godfroy approached to take their orders.

"I'll wrestle him from his engagement," Clara replied.

A few moments later, Major Godfroy, the Mescalero Apache Indian Reservation agent, approached the table.

"Billy . . ."

Billy gave his seat to the major and took a place against the wall behind Evans, able to hear every word passed between Jesse and the major.

"Good to see you enjoying one of our fine meals, Jesse," Godfroy said.

"I ain't here for your wife's shit stew. You sent word, I showed."

Godfroy peered at two travelers keeping to themselves in the far corner, then leaned in close. "We got a fresh supply just come through. Blankets, wheat, flour . . ."

"What am I gonna do with a barrel of flour?"

"Cattle too. A hundred of them. And about twenty-five horses."

This got Evans's attention. "Processed?"

"Not yet," Godfroy said. "I held them up on account of they need to be inspected for acceptability, then branded."

"How long do we have until they're recorded and handed over to the Indians?"

"If I don't do it by morning, suspicions will be raised."

"By who?" Evans asked. "Look around, Godfroy. Ain't nobody minding the store but you."

"If word gets back to Washington that supplies are coming in short . . ."

"Then get your hide up, go process the horses, and pass them along to the savages."

"I'm trying to make things easy on you, Jesse. I hand

those horses over to the Apache, then you try and reclaim said horses—well, the Apache are gonna put up some resistance to that."

Evans thought a moment, then looked at Billy. "What do you think, kid? Take the horses now or wait until they're branded and in Indian hands, then snatch 'em?"

Billy thought about Lolotea and Bodaway, who would soon be making their way to the reservation. "No need to get in a dustup with Apache if we don't have to."

"See, what Godfroy here ain't revealing is the horses, before they're rationed out to the reservation, are guarded by cavalry soldiers."

"Soldiers I can persuade," said Godfroy.

"What if these soldiers are too stubborn to be persuaded?" Evans probed.

"Then you'll have to take advanced measures."

"Or," Billy chimed in, uneasy in his footing, "we draw them away from the corral and abscond with the horses real casual-like."

"How do you propose we draw the soldiers away from their post?" Evans asked.

"There's thirteen of us and you got what, three, four on guard?" Billy replied. "If a rustler was trying to make off with a head or two, would that be frowned upon?"

"It would," Godfroy said.

"So one man makes like he's stealin' a few steers. The soldiers will ride in hard to stop it, not knowing the real theft is taking place behind their backs."

"You forgot one detail, pip-squeak," Buck Morton interrupted. "The one of us creating the diversion—ain't no guarantee he won't catch a bullet."

Billy scanned the table of hardened men staring back at

him. All of them thieves and outlaws, most even murderers. Then Buck smirked at him.

"Shit, I'll do it," Billy said before he could stop himself.

Evans slammed his fists on the table emphatically and stood. "So there we have it. Billy's got the *huevos*. He'll do it."

Godfroy tried to interject. "Jesse, there's more to—"

"Goddamn it, you puritan fuck," Jesse snapped back. "Ain't no need to overthink things."

As the Boys gathered outside just after dusk, Billy had a fist of nervous energy balled in his gut. He wasn't used to working with a group, and he was taking the most risk. If the soldiers caught him, he'd face the gallows for sure. But Buck's shit-eating smirk had gotten under his skin—Billy cursed his own temper—and there was no going back.

As the men fastened their saddles tight and checked their pistols, fidgeting to stay busy, Buck Morton bumped Billy. "You foul this up, one of us might get jailed. But you—you'll be dead. If not by them cavalrymen, then at my hands."

"You just worry about getting all them horses out before the soldiers realize they ain't gonna catch me and hightail it back to the corral," Billy replied.

"All right, the hour is upon us," Evans said, and the Boys all mounted their horses. "Billy, draw those sons of bitches as far out as you can to buy us ample time."

Billy nodded, then spurred his horse for the Mescalero Apache Indian Reservation.

As he made the short ride in solitude, Billy couldn't get Buck's barbs out of his head. Morton was not a man to scuffle with, but Billy recognized a type too. A bully. Billy had already shut one tormentor up. *May have to do the same to ol' Buck.*

Billy reached the corral and spotted three soldiers lounging by a fire, on guard. Fifty yards to their side was the pen holding almost a hundred head of cattle. Steer were more profitable to steal but harder to unload after the fact. There were only a handful of large operations to sell the livestock to, all of them well known to local authorities.

But horses? Hell, everyone needed a horse.

Billy sneaked his way to the far end of the pen and found the rear gate. He dismounted his mare and lifted the cross-beam to let the cattle out, but the livestock weren't privy to his plan and stayed put. A few softly moaned at the intruder, but not in a manner to draw the attention of the cavalry soldiers. Billy knew Evans and the Boys would be riding up any minute now. If he didn't create the diversion, they would find themselves engaged in a shootout with the soldiers, and the Boys weren't the types to lay down for anybody. It was one thing to make off with some horses, but it was another to gun down US soldiers.

No, Billy needed to liberate the cattle now.

He slapped the rear haunch of one steer. Still nothing. Billy had no choice. He got back on his horse, pulled his pistol, and fired three shots into the air, startling the herd and leading them to stampede out of the gate.

"It's a rustler!" a soldier yelled.

As Billy turned to flee, the soldiers opened fire. Billy felt the air crease by his ear as a bullet whizzed past. He spurred his horse and joined the cattle stampeding away.

The soldiers gave chase.

To Billy's surprise, their horses were *fast*. Faster than his. He had a good lead, and the fleeing herd created a moving barrier, but it was one a pistol shot could easily overcome. The soldiers hadn't seen action in months and were all too happy to chase down a rustler and have a story to tell the others at morning chow.

Straight ahead was the forest Dr. Blazer had been deci-
mating for his sawmill. There were still enough trees to create
difficulty in a chase, but not the same cover the forest would
have provided even a few years ago. To his right, Billy spied
hills he could probably use to lose the soldiers, but there was
no guarantee he'd be able to make it there before they caught
up to him.

Billy cut a direct line to the forest. They were gaining fast
and still firing, bullet after bullet whistling past him.

Billy heard a cow moan and go down, taking a hit to the
neck, which caused the stampeding herd to trip and stumble,
creating more obstacles for the cavalrymen. There was a small
mound to traverse, then the forest. Billy had to make it to the
edge of the trees if he stood any chance. Just as he reached the
crest of the hill—

Thump.

A sledgehammer to his shoulder blade, a blunt force that
knocked him off his horse and sent him tumbling down the
backside of the mound. The dull thud was quickly followed by
a searing, fiery pain.

"I got him," he heard one of the pursuers yell from the
darkness behind him.

Billy didn't have time to assess his wound—he had to will
himself back to his feet and keep going.

The soldiers cut their way through the remaining herd and
came upon the peak of the hill, expecting a rustler's dead body.
Instead, all they found was the edge of the forest. No sign of
the thief. No tracks, no blood.

"If you got him, then where the hell is he?" asked another.

The first soldier, moments ago pumped full of pride, sat
flummoxed. "I knocked him clear off his horse." The soldiers
spent the next hour searching the forest for any sign of the man

they swore they felled, but to no avail. Then they spent the rest of the night wrangling the cattle back into the pen.

It wasn't until they got back to the corral at dawn that they realized all their horses were gone.

Billy passed the better part of the night suspended in a tree, gun cocked, watching the soldiers patrol the ground below. He wedged himself in the crook between the trunk and a thick branch. It was the only thing that saved him from falling when the pain got so severe that his head got wispy and his world turned white, which occurred more than once.

Long after the soldiers were gone, Billy worked his way back to the ground and began the long walk back to Blazer's Mill, his right arm hanging limply at his side. Halfway to Godfroy's restaurant, he heard the unmistakable clopping of horses. Fearing it was the soldiers—or worse, Apache warriors who'd grown tired of life on the reservation—he hid in the brush.

The horses continued getting closer until they were almost on top of him. Billy held his breath.

"Kid?"

Billy peered out to find Evans and Morton.

"Shit, Jesse. You had me in a twist," Billy said, revealing himself.

Evans looked at his sagging right arm, bloodied shirt, and pale, sweaty face. "Took one, huh?"

"Hurts something fierce."

Billy caught Morton smirking again.

"You gonna live?" Evans asked.

"Yeah. Could use a doctor though."

"We'll get you one in town." Then he turned to Morton. "Help him."

Morton took his time dismounting, then begrudgingly lifted

Billy onto the back of Evans's horse, taking great pains to not be gentle about it. As the three men headed out, Billy realized they were traveling east.

"We ain't going to Blazer's Mill," Evans replied. "We're going to Lincoln."

"What's in Lincoln?"

"L.G. Murphy and James Dolan."

Chapter 7

LINCOLN COUNTY, NEW MEXICO TERRITORY

Lawrence "L.G." Murphy took a deep breath, held it as long as he could, then exhaled. When he finished, he unrolled his sleeves, fixed his cuffs, and stood. The other man in the room had his back to Murphy, returning the instruments into his medical bag. He did so quietly and deliberately, biding his time.

"No need for the theatrics, Doc," Murphy said. "Give it to me straight."

The doctor demurred and clasped his bag closed without turning around. "The cancer has spread."

"Given your reluctance to meet my eye, I reckon it's severe," Murphy said.

"The tumor has consumed your bowels."

"Are you gonna have to cut me open?"

"I'm afraid we're past the point of treatment," the doctor answered.

Murphy poured himself a stiff drink, then asked the only relevant question left: "How long you suppose I got?"

"Tough to say." The doctor hated this question. Without opening Murphy up, life expectancy was pure conjecture and varied patient to patient. "Could be six months, a year, maybe a stretch more. Best thing we can do now is make you comfortable." He placed a tiny bottle on the table. "To ease your journey."

There was a knock on the office door.

"I'll check on you in a few days," the doctor said, gathering his things.

They shook hands, and the doctor tipped his cap to the man awaiting entry, then left.

"Tip-top shape, L.G.?" asked James Dolan.

"Riley around?" Murphy deflected.

"Downstairs with a customer. Miguel Arrieta's complaining again, saying he's been on the receiving end of some harassment from the Indians. Seems they think his farm still belongs to them. I told him the same thing I tell everybody. All sales are final."

Murphy barely nodded. "Fetch John."

Dolan went to retrieve Riley. Murphy picked up the bottle the doc had left behind.

Ether.

He rolled the small bottle in his hands, contemplating the supposed miracle pain reliever, then tucked it away in his desk drawer. Murphy took a long slug from his glass, and as he wiped the whiskey from his mustache, Dolan reappeared with John Riley.

"Sit," Murphy said.

Dolan and Riley did as they were told. Dolan sensed a weight. They were business partners, but Murphy, almost twenty years his senior, was more than that. He was a mentor. A big brother. And the consternation on Murphy's face now had him concerned.

Murphy turned to Riley, the loyal clerk for their store. "John, you've been a valuable employee of the Murphy and Dolan Company. You've proven yourself capable and like-minded."

"I appreciate that, L.G.," Riley said. "It means a lot."

"I'm going to be scaling back my role in the business, and someone needs to fill that void."

Dolan raised an eyebrow but stayed quiet.

"John, how'd you like to become an equal partner to me and Jimmy here?"

Riley broke into a smile.

"You'll have to buy in for your share, and we'll figure out an equitable price," Murphy continued. "I want you to take a day before you answer."

"I don't need a day." At twenty-six, Riley was a couple of years younger than Dolan and wanted nothing more than to be seen as a peer to his two bosses.

"You'll share in the profit but also be responsible for any debt incurred."

Murphy failed to mention that considerable debt had *already* been incurred, and the company owed the Spiegelberg brothers out of New York more than $10,000. A portion of Riley's buy-in—somewhere in the neighborhood of $2,000— would be turned over to the Spiegelbergs. The rest would find its way into Murphy's pocket.

"Thank you, L.G. I'll think hard about this." Riley would appease his new partners by taking the obligatory day to consider their offer, but he'd already made up his mind.

"Now Jimmy and I have a few matters to discuss."

Riley shook the men's hands and headed down the stairs two at a time, praising this positive turn in his life. Murphy shut the door behind him.

"Do you reckon he'll accept the offer?" Dolan asked.

"I reckon he's counting his fortune as we speak."

Dolan chose his next words carefully, a discipline he prac-
ticed only with his business partner and no one else.

"Something don't sit right with me, L.G. Sure, we owe
some money to the Spiegelbergs, but they're all the way back
east. When Fritzy's life insurance payout comes in, we'll have
the money to cover our debt. After that, it's clear skies ahead.
Why give up some of our future profit for a short-term fix?"

The mention of Emil Fritz's name still sent a nostalgic rail
up Murphy's spine. It had been three years since his friend
and business partner had passed away, and Murphy, who was
not normally sentimental in any fashion, found he actually
missed the sonofabitch. But like everything with Murphy, it
was self-serving. *If Fritz were still here, I wouldn't be in this financial turmoil . . .*

"Alex McSween is still creating trouble for us on the insurance payout," Murphy answered. "He's taken up Emil's brother
and sister as clients, and he's working overtime to ensure the
money goes to them, not us."

"McSween doesn't care about Emil's family. He just wants
the insurance money for himself," Dolan said.

"True, my friend. And now he and his new partner, that
English rat John Tunstall, are cutting into our business as well.
We're at war, Jimmy, and we're being assailed from all sides."

"We still have enough friends to muck up the judgment
and cause a delay. That'll give us time to reason with Emil's
family—make them see the advantages of joining our side and
disadvantages of not."

Murphy peered out the second-story window to the street
below and the citizens crossing back and forth, going about their
day. In the two short years since they opened shop in Lincoln, the
town had grown considerably, and with a little luck, Lincoln could

become a formidable rival to Santa Fe. And it was all thanks to Murphy, a thanks he felt he was owed but knew he would never see.

"Time is the one thing we don't have," he replied.

The Boys brought the two dozen horses they'd relieved from the Mescalero Apache Indian Reservation to Lincoln. They set up camp just outside the town's limits and hitched the stolen steeds to a tree. They cooked rabbit and beans over the fire and discussed what supplies they were going to pick up from the general store or which whore they hoped to encumber once they unloaded the horses.

Billy sat alone on a stump. His arm was in a makeshift sling and the pain was excruciating. The bullet had gone through his back, near his right shoulder blade, and exited just above his clavicle. He could still raise his wing, which Jesse said meant he hadn't done any real damage, but even the simple act of slightly trying caused Billy to flush and sweat profusely.

As he sat as still as possible, he watched Jesse, Buck, and Frank Baker huddled against a tree. He couldn't make out what they were discussing, but soon Buck became animated while arguing his point. Evans responded firmly, and Buck closed up, but he took to glaring at Billy.

"Hey, kid, come here," Evans said.

Billy rose, adjusted his gun belt—he was practicing keeping the holster on his right hip, easy for him to draw with his left hand if the need arose—and joined the three men by the tree.

Evans reached into the saddlebag hung across his horse and removed a small green plant, no bigger than a fist, with nubs and needles coming out of it.

"That's a runty-looking cactus," Billy said.

"It's not just any cactus. It's peyote. For your pain."

"I don't know, Jesse . . ." Billy had heard of the mystical powers of peyote as well as the uncommon visions that appeared when taken. Stories of men who thought they could fly or were gods on Mount Olympus. The idea of losing his faculties around these men was not appealing. "What I need is a doctor."

"Chew it for just a moment and you'll feel downright splendid. We have business in town, then I'll take you to see the doc."

"We don't need some whiny scamp tagging along," Buck argued.

"Don't worry about me. I'm aces," Billy said, straightening his spine despite yet another streak of pain searing through his neck and shoulder and down his arm.

"Need ain't of no concern here," Evans said. "The kid's coming." He turned to Buck. "Whether *you* tag along or not is entirely your decision."

Evans walked away, leaving Billy with Frank Baker, who seemed indifferent to the whole affair, and Buck, who was anything but.

"I've seen the likes of you before. You'll ride with us until things get tight, then shit your britches and scamper back to Mommy, tail tucked between your legs."

"I don't recall seeing you next to me when I was acquitting myself back at Blazer's Mill," Billy replied.

Buck leaned in, so close Billy could smell the wet tobacco and rot of his breath. "You're prince of the moment, but Jesse'll grow weary of you. When he does and you don't have his coat to hide behind, you'll see me all right."

Buck spat a wad of chewed tobacco on Billy's boots, then prepared his horse for the ride into Lincoln.

Billy walked away holding the peyote plant, still sweating from the pain. He broke a leaf off the edge and sniffed it. It smelled like . . . nothing. He put the leaf in his mouth and gently chewed. The taste was strong and bitter, and Billy instantly had second thoughts, spitting it out. He'd deal with the pain until he could see the doctor in Lincoln. As he mounted his horse, he caught Morton shaking his head and laughing at him.

Billy, Jesse Evans, Buck Morton, and Frank Baker rode the first stretch of the ride in silence. Billy could feel Buck's eyes boring a hole into the back of his head. He turned to Evans.

"This L.G. Murphy some hotshot?" Billy asked.

"Just thinks he is. More like middle management. But Lincoln County is his domain."

"So what's he gonna do with the horses once he buys them?"

"Sell them to the soldiers at Fort Stanton or maybe back to the Indians," Evans said.

"Ain't they gonna know we stole them?" Billy asked.

"Shit, yeah," Buck replied. "But it don't even matter. Who's gonna do anything about it?"

Evans could see Billy didn't understand. "You a part of the New Mexico Chain Gang now, kid."

The other men laughed.

"See us, the Kinney Gang—you heard of them, right?"

Billy nodded. Everyone had heard of the ruthless outlaw John Kinney.

"Us, Kinney, and the Seven Rivers Warriors, we all sorta got a peace accord. Help each other out from time to time. We steal some livestock, maybe we pass it to Kinney, who then passes it along to the Seven Rivers Warriors, who then sell it. We do the same for them. By the time it gets to the final destination, ain't no way for the authorities to know where the livestock origi-nated. Who the rightful owner is."

"No victim, no crime," Buck said.

"Surely someone is onto the scheme," Billy replied.

The men laughed again.

"This is New Mexico," Evans said. "The only authority that matters is the Santa Fe Ring."

"And who the hell do you think Murphy and Dolan work for?" Buck added.

"Everybody's getting paid," Evans said. "Especially the fat cats in Santa Fe."

They reached Lincoln and made their way down the only road that cut through the middle of town. Billy thought Lincoln would be like Apache Tejo, just a couple of shops and services for folks traveling through. Instead, he found a bustling community on the rise.

The south side of Main Street was lined with a courthouse, a few stores, an orchard, a cornfield, a smattering of homes, and the focal point of the community, Murphy & Co., also known as the House. The north side of the street was dotted with more homes, the Wortley Hotel, where one could get decent lodging and a hot meal, and the frame of a new building to be erected, which lacked signage.

"Stay out here, guard the horses," Evans commanded Billy when they reached the House.

Billy took in the town. A few kids—not more than two or three years younger than him—were playing with a ball across the street. He recognized the game. Anthony-I-Over.

Josie's favorite.

One of the children blocked the sun from his eyes and squinted at Billy. Billy slowly raised his good arm and waved. The child cocked his head curiously, then went back to his game.

SILVER CITY

GRANT COUNTY, NEW MEXICO TERRITORY

Fall 1874

Billy hadn't thought about Anthony-I-Over in what seemed like forever. Had it really only been a few years?

He remembered their first day of school in Silver City.

"Hurry along, boys. You can't be late," Catherine said, as if everything were normal. Then she did her best to suppress a cough.

Henry looked down at his outfit, he and Josie dressed in their Sunday best. "I don't know," he said. "I don't think the other kids are gonna be in suits, Mama."

"Sure they will. And besides, you want to make a good impression, don't you?"

Henry was just thankful she was up and about that day and not confined to bed, so he didn't protest. He just put a hand on Josie's back and ushered his little brother out the door.

On the walk to school, Billy could see something was bothering Josie. "Ain't nothing to be nervous about. Kids here are just like kids back in Kansas."

"The kids in Kansas didn't like me," Josie replied.

"What about Colorado?"

Josie shook his head.

"Well, that's what's great about Silver City," Henry replied, putting an arm around Josie. "Fresh start."

They entered the two-story structure, and to Henry's surprise, there were a dozen different rooms, and the kids were divided up by age. Henry led Josie to his class, then his little brother froze.

"It's all right, Josie. I'll be right upstairs."

But Josie wouldn't move. A few other kids had to angle themselves to slip into the room, each giving Josie a strange look as they passed.

Henry leaned down to get eye to eye with Josie.

"I don't know anybody," Josie said.

"That's right! And nobody knows you. You can be whoever you want to be."

Josie peered into the classroom. Two dozen kids around his age, all of them already familiar with each other. And no one else was in a suit.

"Don't fret," Henry said. "Ladies love a sharp-dressed man." Josie still wasn't comforted, so Henry softened his tone. "Give them time, and they'll see how incredible you are."

Josie took a deep breath and went into the room.

Henry always had an easier time making friends. But even as he was impressing his teacher with his reading skills or cracking jokes with the other boys, or when he'd catch a girl looking his way and break into a smile that would make the girl blush and turn away, he couldn't help but worry about Josie.

At lunchtime, Henry sneaked out of the room, went downstairs, and peered into his brother's classroom. Josie was sitting near the back, staring down at his desk. A boy next to him tapped Josie on the shoulder and handed him a note. Henry watched as Josie went to open it and the boy shook his head and indicated to pass it to the girl in front of him. Just as Josie did, the teacher looked up and caught them. She took the note from Josie and read it to herself. The other kids in the class started laughing.

Josie didn't know why, but Henry had an idea.

When the bell rang at the end of the day, Henry raced downstairs to meet his brother.

"How was your first day?"

Josie kicked the dirt.

"Let me guess: 'Do you like the new kid?'"

Josie nodded.

"And someone checked no?"

Again, Josie nodded.

"It's an old prank, Josie. They knew the teacher would catch it. They're just razzin' ya. Happens to everyone. It'll get better."

When they stepped outside, a group of schoolchildren were huddled around. A freckle-faced kid—the one who had passed Josie the note—seemed to be the ringleader and was dividing everyone into two teams.

"What're you playing?" Henry asked.

"Anthony-I-Over," the kid replied.

Henry turned to Josie. "You love this game. And you're great at it. Go show those dillweeds what you can do." He nudged Josie forward.

The freckle-faced kid and the others groaned, but they let Josie play.

Henry sat down on the schoolhouse porch and took a pack of playing cards out of his pocket. Just as he was shuffling, the blushing girl from his class walked by. Henry nodded to her with a twinkle in his eye and a half smile. She pressed her books closer to her chest and bounced down the steps. Her friend, trailing right behind, called out over her shoulder to Henry. "She likes you!"

Henry's smile grew. "Well, y'all can't like me from way over yonder."

The girls whispered to each other, giggling.

"Why, what's over there?" the friend asked.

"Just me and this deck of cards, I suppose."

"Cards are the devil's plaything," the shier one said teasingly.

"So my mama keeps telling me."

The girls whispered to each other again, then started back for Henry. Just as they reached the porch, a loud thud came from the game. Henry looked over to see the freckle-faced kid on the ground and Josie standing over him, a startled look in his eyes. Oh shit, Henry thought, his focus now solely on Josie. Then the freckle-faced kid stood up and shook Josie's hand. The two boys smiled at each other and kept on playing. Henry let out a sigh of relief.

The girls reached Henry and stood over him, blocking the sun.

"Are you going to tempt us into your wicked ways, like Satan in the garden?" one girl asked.

"I wish I had that kind of sway," Henry replied, grinning up at them.

"I'm Delia, and the one who won't speak is Janie."

Henry stood and was about to introduce himself when a voice called out across the street.

"Henry Antrim! Josie!" Henry looked up to see William, his stepfather, marching toward them. "What're you doing? Git your behinds back to the house. Your mother needs you."

"Henry Antrim," Henry said to the girls, bowing teasingly.

"Your mother needs you, Henry Antrim," Delia replied.

"Seems so," he answered. He flashed them another smile, then walked over to Josie, who was in the middle of Anthony-I-Over. Josie caught the ball. Henry looked at him— was Josie actually having fun? Josie threw the ball to another kid, then Henry tapped him on the shoulder.

"Time to go," Henry said. Josie didn't want to. "Sorry, but we gotta head home to help Mama." Henry took one last look at Delia and Janie, then led his brother away.

On the walk home, William continued to scold them. "I'm breaking my back to bring in money and put food on the table. Your mother's home sick, and you're out playing children's games, only thinking about yourselves. And goddammit, Josie, your suit is filthy. You're gonna wash it yourself tonight before bed."

"Don't mind him," Henry whispered to Josie. "You were great out there. Best one by far." He tousled his brother's hair.

But by the time they were home, Henry saw that Josie had slipped back into his quiet, reflective self and was no longer smiling. In fact, Henry couldn't ever remember seeing Josie smile again.

Inside the House, Evans picked through various farming tools hanging on the wall, killing time until Murphy and Dolan came down. Morton and Baker stood by the door, awaiting direction.

"Hey, Jesse, you hear the news?" Riley asked. "Murphy and Dolan are making me partner."

"Congratulations," Evans replied. He always found Riley to be a sniveling twit, nothing but a lapdog to Murphy and Dolan. But lapdogs had their use too.

Murphy and Dolan appeared.

"Jesse, my boy," Murphy greeted him with his thick brogue. "Let's find somewhere quiet to talk."

"I told him about me joining as a partner," Riley said, hoping to edge his way into the meeting.

"That's fine, John. But you haven't agreed to anything yet, remember?"

"L.G. wants me to take the night to think it over," Riley directed at Evans, who was no longer paying him any mind. "Even if we already know the answer."

Murphy motioned to the stairs, and Evans, Morton, and Baker followed him and Dolan to the office on the second floor. Evans took a seat across from Murphy at the big desk, Morton and Baker flanked behind him, thumbs hooked into their britches. Dolan leaned against the window.

"Got us twenty-five new steeds. Major Godfroy's proving to be useful after all."

"I told you—with enough patience, every man sees the light," Murphy said.

"Twenty-five horses, you'll sell them for what, sixty dollars apiece? That's one thousand five hundred dollars. So three hundred dollars to me and my men."

"I think you need to go back to college, Jesse. Fifteen percent of one thousand five hundred dollars is two hundred twenty-five dollars," Dolan pointed out.

"Fifteen percent was the previous arrangement. Economy's inflating, and we've had to acquire some new recruits."

"Your men are your problem," Dolan snapped back.

"There's enough slop at the trough for all of us. Let's split the difference at seventeen and a half," Murphy said.

"That's two hundred sixty-two dollars and fifty cents," Dolan said, helping with the math.

"Do we have a deal?" Murphy asked.

Evans took his time thinking, then stood and shook Murphy's hand. Murphy signaled to Dolan, who opened a safe and took out $262 and two quarters, and emphatically dropped the coins into Evans's palm.

"We set up camp outside town, away from prying eyes. Send some of your men out and we'll hand the horses over, then they can sell them back to Fort Stanton."

The plan was solidified, and Evans exited, followed by Morton and Baker.

Dolan knew enough to keep his mouth shut until he heard the men reach the bottom of the stairs. "Lawrence, what are you doing gifting these bastards seventeen and a half percent? We agreed upon fifteen. It's always been fifteen."

"Jesse is a dangerous man you don't want to get cross with."

"So am I," Dolan cut back. "Just ask Captain Randlett."

"Which is why I always tell *you* the truth, Jimmy. I renegotiated our Fort Stanton contract. We're now fetching eighty dollars per steed. A clean two grand for all twenty-five of them."

Dolan took a moment to calculate the difference, then shook his head in awe at his business partner. They'd just stiffed Evans and the Boys out of almost ninety dollars.

Billy leaned against a post outside the House, making sure not to jostle his arm too much, lest he send another lightning bolt streaking through his body.

Life as a rustler was proving to be more boring than he had imagined. Most of the time he was sitting around waiting to be told what to do. But there was safety in being a member of the Boys. Their reputations preceded them, and he had noticed regular folk—the types who kept their heads down and minded their own business—gave the gang a wide berth.

Billy's daydreaming was broken by the sound of laughter behind him.

He turned to find a group of men loosely affiliated with the House—ranchers, a deputy, a couple of lawyers, and a judge—standing on the porch cackling. Billy followed their gaze to the middle of the street, where a woman's wheelbarrow had tipped over. She was struggling to lift the large, heavy sacks of feed back into her cart. Every time she got one back up and in, the weight of the sack would tip the wheelbarrow over again, much to the delight of the men on the porch.

Billy approached the woman. "Excuse me, ma'am." He grunted and used his good arm to lift a sack back into the empty cart, which began to wobble.

"It's gonna go again!" he heard someone yell in glee.

Billy steadied the wheelbarrow with his knee until the woman took the handles.

As he lifted the last sack, a well-dressed gentleman hurried over. Billy, unused to being rushed upon, was about to drop the goods and reach for his gun, but the woman greeted the man with warm familiarity.

"Oh, honey, this young man was kind enough to help me."

The man aided Billy in easing the last sack back into the cart, but as they did, the corner snagged a nail and split open, spilling feed onto the road. The men on the porch howled again, unable to contain themselves.

Billy started to scoop up as much of the feed by hand as he could.

"Leave it," said the man.

"Most of it can be saved," replied Billy.

"We're prosperous enough that a little spilled feed won't even be of notice," the man said loud enough for the agitators to hear.

"But thank you for your help. It was awfully kind of you," the woman replied.

Billy took his first good look at her. She was in her early thirties, he guessed, and had a sharpness that somehow put him at ease and kept him on alert, like a strict teacher with kind intentions.

A deafening whistle came from the porch. Evans, Morton, and Baker descended the steps and headed for their horses.

Billy tipped his cap to the couple and caught up to them.

"The doc's gonna come out to us tonight," Buck said. "Can you make it a few more hours, or will you succumb to your flesh wound?"

Billy's back and shoulder were killing him, and he'd sweat through his shirt, but he'd never give Buck Morton the satisfaction of seeing him squirm.

The Boys mounted their horses and headed out for camp. Billy sneaked one last glance back at the couple, who had continued pushing the wheelbarrow to its destination, all the while still being heckled by the gallery.

"Being kind to the wrong folks—that's the surest way to get yourself stuffed into a pine box," Buck told Billy.

"And they were the wrong folks?"

"You just met Alexander and Susan McSween, Murphy's sworn enemies."

Chapter 8

Alex McSween cut the slab of meat and pushed the peas around with his fork but never lifted the utensil to his mouth. "I ate earlier," he explained.

Susan didn't believe him. Though he denied it, he had been losing weight recently, and she suspected it had to do with the ongoing conflict between him and the House. "Well, eat anyway. I don't want you to cramp up again."

He took a bite of steak and nodded while he chewed. "It's good."

Now she was certain her husband was lying. Susan McSween was an awful cook, and her raised eyebrow told him she knew it.

"All right, it's not a steak at the Wortley Hotel, but it was made by you, so I treasure it," he said and took another bite.

"Forget the steak, Alex. I'm concerned."

"They're just trying to intimidate us, and you, of all people, cannot be cowed."

"I'm a woman and not even those scoundrels would dare lay a finger on me. But you . . ."

"They're toothless bullies. Murphy and Dolan know a new day is dawning in Lincoln."

"That's what has me scared," Susan replied. "You're putting their backs to the wall, and desperate men do desperate things," she said.

"Like invite me to sit down with them?"

This didn't ease her concern. "Please tell me you're not considering it. Who knows what that crazy Irishman Dolan will do. He tried to shoot an army captain in Fort Stanton. Do you really believe he'd think twice about harming you?"

Susan McSween was right to be scared. Lawrence Murphy and James Dolan were unpredictable men, and Alexander McSween—every bit as ambitious and cunning, but far less violent—had a history of double-crossing them.

Alexander and Susan McSween had arrived in Lincoln two years prior. They had planned on settling in Silver City, but during their stopover in Santa Fe they met a local congressman who advised Lincoln was riper with business opportunity, especially if one took up work with Murphy & Co. Susan wished to stick to their original intentions, but Alex figured what better way to launch his new firm than by working as counsel for one of the largest companies in the county? Susan was not one to normally hold her tongue but chose not to push back. His pride needed it, she thought, so she allowed him to alter their plans.

The work was easy, mainly drawing up standard real estate contracts, which McSween would only later learn were for land Murphy did not actually own.

A couple of months on, McSween procured his second prominent client, cattle baron John Chisum. Chisum was facing stiff fines for not reporting all his income, and McSween helped him navigate the charges, move assets around, and avoid further taxes. Chisum was grateful.

Murphy kept a close eye on McSween at first, and only after McSween had proven himself capable and willing did Murphy reveal his true need for the lawyer.

"Order the turkey," Murphy said as the two men took a seat in the dining hall of the Wortley Hotel. "Just sold them a fresh stock today."

"Now you're in the turkey business as well, Mr. Murphy?" McSween asked.

"I'm in any business that can make me money."

"And I suppose that's why you've requested my services again?"

"Mr. McSween, you've proven yourself an adept lawyer with a knack for worming your way through the legal system."

"Always within the confines of the law, sir."

"Of course," Murphy answered with a twinkle, as he suspected McSween to be every bit the cutthroat as himself. "I received a telegram last evening. Our business partner, Mr. Fritz, has succumbed to his illness and passed."

"I'm sorry for your troubles."

"As am I. And I'm afraid it's brought on more trouble than we anticipated. Mr. Fritz had taken out a life insurance policy from a firm in New York. As a partner in my business, even death doesn't preclude Mr. Fritz—or his estate—from taking on their fair share of our company's debt."

McSween was unable to hide his surprise to learn Murphy & Co. was not profitable.

"It's a simple matter of possessing more goods than we're able to sell this quarter," Murphy explained.

"I'm not an accountant," McSween said.

"And I don't need you to be," Murphy answered. "But it seems when my dear friend Emil drew up his will he didn't specify who should receive the ten-thousand-dollar payout upon his passing."

"Others are trying to stake claim to the money?" McSween asked, the purpose of this meeting beginning to crystallize.

"Fritzy's brother Charles and his sister Emile have a wild notion that the money should go to them and that their brother's business partners should be left twisting in the wind. It is not right, and it is not what Emil intended."

McSween sat back in his chair and ran his hand along the side of his head, smoothing out his hair, a practice he took when in deep consideration.

"I think I can persuade the courts where the money rightfully belongs."

"I don't need to think you can, I need to know you can."

"I was being falsely modest, Mr. Murphy. I know I can."

When McSween had told Susan the news that evening, she was less enthused.

"What if you can't deliver on your promise? Do you think L.G. Murphy and James Dolan will just extend a hand and say, 'Oh well, you tried your best'?"

"Don't you see, Susan? This is what I—we—have been working toward. Murphy is entrusting me with his most pressing legal matter. We're in."

"Have you stopped to think if 'in' is even where we want to be?"

McSween wouldn't listen. He was too preoccupied with visions of the finest things life could offer being placed at his doorstep.

Susan, on the other hand, knew from experience that everything came at a price.

As his wife had feared, McSween's confidence was overstated. Further complicating the issue, the insurance company wanted no part of the dispute and stepped back to let the two sides argue their case in court. Only then would they release the funds.

Susan also began to hear rumors concerning Murphy & Co. Stories of farmers purchasing uninhabitable land where crops wouldn't grow. And to compound matters, local Apache would raid and destroy the homes, claiming the land still belonged to them. After the third or fourth of these recounts, even Alex's conscience amplified, and he looked into it on his own.

Sure enough, Murphy & Co. were drawing up fake deeds and selling land that was not rightfully theirs. What McSween couldn't understand was why no one went to the authorities. Surely a prosecutor and judge would get retribution for the swindled farmers.

McSween soon found his answer. He had to travel to Santa Fe for yet another motion in the ongoing insurance case. Lincoln County sheriff William Brady, who had been appointed an "impartial" administer to Fritz's estate until the matter could be properly sorted, accompanied him.

Brady's lofty public office did not come by accident. He had been a major at Fort Stanton at the same time as Murphy, and their friendship continued after they both mustered out of the service. Murphy needed a sympathetic sheriff to keep Lincoln County in line, and he put his considerable weight and resources into getting his friend Brady elected.

On their trek to Santa Fe, McSween noticed Sheriff Brady wasn't his usual talkative self, a habit boosted even more so when drinking, which was often. On this trip, he was quiet and sullen.

"What's heavy on your mind?" McSween finally asked.

Brady just grunted and took a swig from his flask, then wrapped his coat tighter to protect from the frigid air. McSween didn't know Brady well and certainly didn't want to reveal too much of his own opinions, lest word get back to Murphy. So McSween stayed silent, letting Brady imbibe more and more whiskey, until the sheriff drank himself into verbosity.

"It's Murphy. It's Dolan. It's the goddamn House and the whole fuckin' Santa Fe Ring," Brady slurred.

"Perhaps we can put our heads together and find a solution," the lawyer said.

"I can't do nothing without some peckerwood looking over my shoulder and reporting back. I was a major in the war, for chrissakes. And now men no bigger than my shits, like Jimmy Dolan and John Riley, have taken to ordering me around. I'm the goddamn sheriff, not some whipping boy. I have half a mind to reveal all I know."

McSween let the statement hang, not wanting to push for fear Brady'd clam up again. A stiff, biting wind reminded Brady why he was so pissed off.

"Out here in the fuckin' cold while their fuckin' asses are roasting by a goddamn fire . . ."

McSween prodded gently. "Surely the sheriff of Lincoln can act independent of local business."

Brady took another swig. "You're new around here, McSween. Once they get their claws in you, that's it. They don't let go until they've squeezed out your every last breath." He tossed the empty flask aside. "Murphy, Dolan, the Santa Fe Ring. They control everything."

"Even you?" McSween asked.

The sheriff just took another drink.

McSween, who hubristically fashioned himself smarter than almost all, continued to work for Murphy & Co. over the next few months, but the Fritz life insurance dispute dragged on. The more McSween learned, the more convinced he became that Murphy wouldn't win, for while Murphy may be a faction of the Santa Fe Ring—and the ring *owned* New Mexico—this matter was being handled outside their stranglehold, all the way back east in New York City.

Emil Fritz's brother Charles had finally moved to the States to settle his brother's affairs, and McSween had occasionally run into him and made sure to smile and shake hands and show there were no hard feelings, that he was simply doing his job as Murphy's lawyer.

He also wanted to make sure Charles knew he was doing it well.

One evening McSween found himself alone in a Santa Fe cantina when Charles Fritz entered. The two men once again exchanged pleasantries, and McSween asked if Charles cared to join him.

They dined and spoke of their families and what brought them to New Mexico. Eventually, McSween steered the conversation to the life insurance dispute.

"I'm sorry, Mr. McSween," Charles said in a heavy German accent. "I don't think it wise for me to talk about the case with opposing counsel."

"I understand, Mr. Fritz. Let's have another brandy and talk of more pleasant things."

One brandy turned into four, and by then Fritz was amenable to discussing the case.

"My brother's life is separate from his business. The money is intended to help his heirs, and having no children, that means me and my sister Emile and her children. It's what he would want, and it's what is right and just. I'm sorry if this conflicts with Mr. Murphy's plan, but my brother hasn't been in New Mexico for some time now and any debts Murphy & Co. incurred happened well after Emil had come home."

To Charles Fritz's surprise, McSween agreed with him.

"I believe the money rightfully belongs to you and your family. Truth be told, we don't have much of a case."

"Then why continue? We should bring this to the judge."

"I wish it were that simple, Charles. While the money rightfully belongs to your family, I'm afraid you'll never see one penny of it."

Charles was floored. "How can that be? There are laws. Justice. This is America."

"No, Mr. Fritz, this is New Mexico. And you're up against forces far greater than you can imagine. The judge? He's a friend of Murphy's. Sheriff Brady, the administrator of your brother's estate? He served in the war with Murphy. The only saving grace you have is that your brother took the policy out in New York. But I can help you."

Charles looked up and McSween saw it—Charles now believed his only hope was the one man being honest with him, the opposing counsel.

"I hate what they're trying to do to you," McSween continued. "It's not fair and not what this country is about. I'm going to withdraw as Murphy's attorney and, with your permission, represent you and your sister. You won't pay me until we win. And Charles . . . we will win."

Charles hesitated, but what did he have to lose? He thanked McSween for his help, then left to write his sister back east.

McSween finished his meal and paid the bill, satisfied. Charles Fritz never realized their encounter that day wasn't happenstance, that McSween had meticulously plotted it for weeks.

Murphy was irate when McSween quit. He was further incensed when he learned McSween had left for New York to deal directly with the insurance company.

"A ratfuck Scotsman if there ever was one," he'd say to all within earshot. "And we don't abide rats, do we, Jimmy?" he'd ask Dolan, who'd always smile knowingly and respond, no, they certainly do not.

Susan McSween soon learned everything she thought she knew of decorum and decency didn't apply in Lincoln County.

It was past sunset when she answered the knock on her door.

John Riley, then just a clerk for Murphy & Co., pushed his way into her home. She saw his glassy eyes and ruddy Irish face and smelled the stench of stale ale and weeks without a bath.

"Hello, Susan," he slurred. "Your husband home?"

"You know damn well he's not."

Riley smiled and inched closer. Susan stepped away until she felt the counter hit against the small of her back.

"That's a shame." Riley smirked.

A spike of fear coursed through Susan. She had believed she was immune from Murphy & Co.'s wrath, but now she wasn't so confident. She discreetly reached behind her and ran her hand along the counter, searching for a knife or fork—anything—she could use to defend herself, if need be. Riley inched closer again, corralling her between the wall and the counter, blocking any escape. He smiled, leering at the curvature of her breasts and hips, wrapped tightly under her dress. His hot, stank breath hit her neck as he pressed his crotch into her.

"If you were my wife, I'd never leave you alone in a place like this. A lot of dangerous men 'round these parts."

"If you were my husband, I'd kill myself," she replied.

Riley's smile faded. "I'm trying to say you deserve better and you go and disparage me?"

Susan's fingertips brushed cold metal. She inched it closer

and closer until she was holding something sharp and weighted.

"I mean it. I'd open my veins and let all the blood drain from my body rather than be touched by you."

As Riley stared hard into her eyes, she gripped the object behind her back so tightly her knuckles turned white.

Then he took a step back. "Well, you're a surly cunt, ain't you?"

Riley walked into another room, Alex's office, and picked a book off the shelf. He flipped through it, then haphazardly tossed it to the floor. "Pardon me."

Susan followed and stood in the doorway, the potential weapon cupped discreetly in her hand, as Riley threw every book, every folder, every piece of paper onto the ground.

Then he unzipped his pants.

Susan pulled the item from behind her back and looked down at what she was holding—a roasting spit she'd used the night before to overcook rabbit.

"Don't flatter yourself, hon," Riley said. "You ain't pretty enough to waste my seed on."

He urinated on the floor, making sure to douse every one of the items. Then he shook his member in her direction. "This do get your knickers in a twist though, don't it?"

"I can't surmise if it's the whiskey or if you always have such a limp tent peg."

Riley made it three steps toward her before Susan raised the spit, the razor-sharp point pressed firmly against his chest.

"I can push this right into your heart, Mr. Riley."

"Think you can get it all the way through my breastplate? Takes quite a bit of *oomph*."

Susan pressed harder and felt the tip of the spit penetrate his clothes and pierce his skin. A small dab of red blossomed on his shirt. Riley reached inside his shirt, then pulled his hand out, emerging with a spot of blood. He licked it off his finger. "You got more grit than I gave you credit for. Sorta does stoke my fire after all."

"Best you get going," Susan replied.

Riley held up his hands and slowly backed his way to the door, putting himself away as he moved, then left.

Susan spent the rest of the evening in a chair watching the entrance, the roast spit in one hand, a sharp knife in the other.

While his wife was being intimidated back home, Alexander McSween was in New York working on behalf of his new clients, the Fritz family. His first stop was the office of L. Spiegelberg & Sons, the main holders of Lawrence Murphy's debt.

McSween discovered the Spiegelberg brothers had lent considerable funds to Lawrence Murphy. Despite Murphy's power and influence, he was irresponsible with money, taking out loans and leveraging his business for a quick buck. But not many of his investments turned profitable, and now, despite their monopolistic practices and government contracts, Murphy & Co. was floundering.

"I have a proposal for you, Levi," McSween told the eldest Spiegelberg.

"I assume it is not as simple as handing over the money Mr. Murphy owes us?"

"I don't represent Murphy anymore."

This took hold of Levi's attention.

"His logic is faulty, and thus his case is weak," McSween continued. "I am now aiding Emil's siblings in recouping their brother's life insurance policy."

Levi was shrewd and understood there might be something to gain from this meeting after all. "All this before the courts have yet ruled?"

"Yes," McSween said. "But the matter would be greatly

simplified if the judge didn't believe your firm was the ballast supporting Murphy."

"Our firm has no sway in the fight."

"The court believes you have vested interest in Murphy receiving the insurance claim, for then he would be able to settle his debt to you. I come with a proposal: I'll give you five hundred dollars to stay out of the matter altogether."

"Why would we accept five hundred dollars when we are owed ten thousand dollars?"

"Because you will pocket the five hundred dollars, and Murphy would *still* owe you the ten thousand dollars." McSween could see Levi was not convinced. "All we ask is for you to remain a neutral party to the proceedings. My clients' victory is inevitable, it's simply a matter of time. At least this way, you get five hundred dollars today, all for doing nothing."

"One thousand dollars," Levi replied. He and his brothers had built their company based on their ability to assess risk and read people. He calculated, correctly, that McSween was ripe for squeezing.

"Six hundred," McSween countered.

"Eight hundred."

"Seven hundred is as high as I can go."

Levi put on a grand performance as he thought it over—looking to the ceiling, shaking his head as he "struggled" with the terms—then shook McSween's hand, landing on the exact $700 he knew they would.

McSween went to the bank and took out a loan for $700 with the agreement he would repay $1,000 when the Fritzes received the life insurance payout.

All in all, McSween deemed it a successful trip, even if he was returning to New Mexico with no money in hand and now $1,000 in debt himself.

On the long journey back to Lincoln, McSween stopped in Santa Fe to rest before making the last leg of the trip. He rented a room at the Herlow Hotel on San Francisco Street. The Herlow had substandard lodging and barely edible cuisine, but it was cheap and McSween was not rich. Not yet, at least.

It would prove a fateful decision.

McSween went downstairs for supper and found the restaurant vacant, save for one other diner. The two men nodded hello and McSween took a seat at another table. He removed a pen and paper from his briefcase and set about writing a letter to Charles and Emile Fritz, detailing his meetings in New York and assuring them the matter would settle soon. As he was concluding the letter with his well-wishes, he heard a voice he recognized.

McSween looked up to see Robert Widenmann greeting the other diner in the restaurant before spotting McSween.

"Alex?" Widenmann turned to the other man. "It's okay if Alex joins us, right?"

The man put up no protest and McSween relocated to their table. McSween took his first good look at the stranger. He was young, roughly twenty-four, and his face was sprouting the beginnings of a beard, possibly the first he'd ever grown. He wore a finely tailored wool suit and gold pocket watch. As they shook hello, McSween noticed the stranger's hands were soft and smooth, and his fingernails were void of even a speck of dirt.

"Pleased to meet you, sir. I'm John Tunstall."

The three men spent the next hour trading stories. Tunstall told of his travels from England to Canada to work in the family business, but how he would never be satisfied simply riding his father's coattails, how he then came to America to make a name for himself.

"I spent time investigating sheep ranches in California before I learned of the prosperous opportunities here in New

Mexico. I aim to purchase a parcel of land in Santa Fe and make my name in ranching."

"With what capital, Mr. Tunstall?" McSween asked.

"Money I earned working in Canada."

Of course, McSween thought. Another young man who "made it on his own" after a significant stake from his father. But McSween also saw opportunity. This young man had the drive and the capital and was just ignorant enough of the dynamics at play.

McSween leaned in.

"You could do that. It's a safe bet, sure. You'll most likely be able to eke out a small return on your investment and eventually carve out a peasant life for yourself."

"Don't you mean *pleasant*?" Tunstall asked.

"Of course. Why? What did I say?"

McSween had read the stranger correctly. Tunstall didn't come all the way to America to carve out a "peasant" or a "pleasant" life. He could have stayed in London or Canada for that. No, he had grand ambitions to make a name for himself, and quaint wouldn't cut it.

"I sense you have an alternative idea," Tunstall said.

"The market here in Santa Fe is saturated and under the thumb of Boss Catron and his brother-in-law. But Lincoln . . . Lincoln is ripe with opportunity."

Robert Widenmann cocked his head at McSween, who had failed to mention that the Santa Fe Ring didn't just control matters in the state capital, they controlled the entire territory, including Lincoln.

McSween pressed on, extolling the virtues of Lincoln and explaining the various means in which a ranch could thrive. "I represent a prominent cattle baron. Someone with the resources and know-how we could consort with, if need be."

"We?" Tunstall asked. But before McSween answered, Tunstall's mind was already churning. "Who is this prominent cattle baron?"

McSween had the young man hooked on the line, now he needed to reel him in.

"Are you familiar with the name John Chisum?" Tunstall's eyes told him he was. "He's unhappy with the one mercantile and goods store in town and looking to invest in a competitor."

Whether or not this was true, McSween was confident he could convince Chisum it would be in his best interests.

"You have Chisum's ear?" Tunstall asked.

"More than his ear. He's my client. My partner. My *friend*."

It was all Tunstall needed to hear. By evening's end, he pledged to forgo Santa Fe and move to Lincoln, the land of opportunity.

Within two weeks, McSween and John Tunstall would be business partners.

Within two years, they would both be dead.

Chapter 9

October 1877

After the visit from the doctor, Billy's shoulder was healing, and he and the Boys were on a string of good luck. They had escaped the raid on the Mescalero Apache Indian Reservation without repercussion and continued to impose their will on other ranches and farms throughout New Mexico. Jesse Evans saw promise in Billy and even introduced him to the House. Billy was a fellow Irishman, something the nationalistic Murphy, Dolan, and Riley thought could be of value.

Despite his recent good fortune, Billy still had one contention: Buck Morton. Something about the Kid stuck in Buck's craw. Maybe it was Billy's cocksureness. Maybe it was how quickly Jesse Evans took to the newcomer. Or maybe it was the fact that despite the Kid's involvement outside the confines of the law, most found Billy to be affable and downright endearing.

Including Buck's girlfriend, Abigail.

It wasn't dusk yet when the Boys decided to blow off steam at Francisco Lopez's cantina on the Pecos River, just outside Fort

Sumner. Billy was in a rare sullen mood, but Jesse had insisted he come along.

The sight of the drinking, dancing, and laughing left Billy alienated. He wanted to be alone. To keep occupied, he took a chair in the corner of the cantina and opened a book.

Buck was talking louder and drinking harder than everyone else, and Billy was content to ignore him, but Buck was not content to be ignored. He ambled over to the Kid and snatched the novel out of his hands.

"You spend money on this trash?" Buck smirked, playing to the drunken onlookers.

"Only cost but a dollar," Billy replied.

"You'd be better off using it for kindling." Buck tossed the book on the table and stuck a shot of whiskey in Billy's hand.

"Cheers, *Billy*." Buck raised the cup, then stopped. "Or is it William? Or maybe Henry?"

Billy set his drink down untouched and went back to his book, hoping Buck would get bored and lose interest.

"You got a mean habit of slighting me," Buck said.

"It's nothing personal. I just don't much care for whiskey."

"You're a small cuss, you like to read, you don't enjoy whiskey . . . seems to me you don't fit in well with our outfit."

"Lucky for all of us, you don't do the thinking 'round here," Billy replied.

Buck reddened and lurched toward the Kid, but then felt a hand on his back.

"Hello, sunshine," Abigail said. She bounced to give Buck a kiss on his cheek and took his hand in hers. "Sincerest apologies for my tardiness. Would you be a dear and pour me a drink?" she asked, sending Buck off to find the nearest bottle. She turned to Billy. "Mr. . . . Bonney, is it now? How do you do?"

"I'm swell, Miss Abigail."

"Is that why you're huddled in a corner all by your lone-some?"

"I don't feel much like socializing," Billy responded.

"That's a shame. I have someone I want you to meet."

"This someone anything like Buck?"

"No, she's wrapped in a far more pleasant package."

Isadora Cruz made her way over to Billy's table. She was sixteen, just a year shy of Billy, and had a habit of fiddling with her hands when she was nervous, as she was now.

"I've told her all about you, Billy Bonney," Abigail said. "Handsome but impish, amusing but prone to earnestness, kind but stiff-spined."

"My spine bends just fine for those who deserve it." Billy then stood and bowed dramatically. "Other than that, it seems I have been adequately summarized."

He held out a chair for Isadora. Abigail smiled and left the two alone.

"She really does sing you, Mr. Bonney," Isadora said with a heavy local accent. Just as she prepared to sit, a bottle shattered against a wall, startling her. The men across the room howled in laughter, with no attempts to govern themselves.

"Care for a walk?" Billy asked.

The Pecos River was mud-brown and narrow enough in this region to be crossed easily, but the banks were surrounded by lush green trees and brush that was haloed by the setting sun.

Billy carried his book behind his back while Isadora continued to fiddle with her hands.

"It seems I'm at a disadvantage, Miss Isadora, for you know so much about me and I know so little about you."

She hesitated, trying to find the words, then said, "I am with mi mamá and papá and *tres hermanos*."

"Are you native to these parts?"

Isadora reddened self-consciously. "My English not so good."

"I beg to differ. Your speaking is quite skilled. Certainly better than my *español*."

"My family has lived here *durante muchos años*, having come from Chihuahua."

"This is Pete Maxwell's land, no?"

"Sí."

"Your daddy work the Maxwell ranch?"

"Until he passed on."

"Lo siento. Mi padre murió también," Billy replied. "Eventually Mama too."

Billy kicked a pebble. It had been two years since Catherine passed, and he hoped Isadora wouldn't notice the lump in his throat. He didn't know what compelled him to tell her the next part: *"Hoy es su cumpleaños."*

Isadora stopped fidgeting and looked at him. She could see the earnestness Abigail had warned her about. He was raw and heartfelt.

"I'm . . . sorry . . . as well, Billy," she said in disjointed English. *"Cuéntame sobre."* Tell me about her.

"She was a wonderful mother. Couldn't cook for nothing," he said, grinning. "But she was always smiling and singing. She loved me and my little brother, Josie. We were happy."

Billy liked thinking about his mother when she was alive, *really* alive.

"Was she . . ." Isadora searched for the word. *"Bonita?"*

Billy nodded. "Had her pick of any man in Indianapolis. Dodge City too."

But any time he thought of Catherine, no matter how warm the memory, those final months, weeks, days took over. Not his mom's vivacious spirit or loving embrace. But her hollow eyes, sunken cheeks, and pale skin. The sound of her coughing throughout the night. Changing her bed pan when she got too weak to walk to the privy. So yeah, he liked talking about his mom during the good days. But it was mostly the bad days he remembered.

Billy turned the conversation back on Isadora. "You still live on the Maxwell land?"

"Yes. *Mi madre es* . . . how you say . . . caretaker?"

Billy nodded.

"Caretaker of *la casa*," she continued, "and I am tasked with watching *los niños*. We live behind the, uh . . . peach orchard?"

Billy smiled. She had spoken it perfectly.

"Rumor is Lucien Maxwell once owned more land than anybody in the whole United States—some two million acres," Billy said in wonder.

"Eso es verdad."

"Rumor is he also sold most of it and made himself over a million dollars."

"Sí."

"Gee, I can't wrap my head around a number that big," Billy replied.

They continued along the riverbank. The sun had dipped beneath the horizon, leaving an orange hue in the sky that faded into a deep purple against the backdrop of the mountains.

"It's getting late. I should be home," Isadora said.

"Fue un placer conocerlos." It was a pleasure to meet you all.

Isadora laughed.

"What?"

"There is but one of me," she replied.

"Ah yes, *fue un placer conocerlo.*"

Isadora looked into his eyes. She could see beneath his jovial facade his heart was heavy with thoughts of his mother. And Isadora was in turmoil too. He was a stranger to her. An outlaw. But he was also warm and vulnerable and seemed kind. She wanted to hold him, and she wanted to be held by him.

"*Mi madre está en Colfax con mis hermanos.* It is, uh, *da mucho miedo en casa . . .* all by myself."

Billy didn't know *atteradora.*

"It bring me scary feelings?" she tried to explain.

"Oh, of course. You never know what nefarious sorts you'll meet," Billy said.

"*Necesito una escolta.*"

Billy understood and offered his arm, escorting her home.

John Tunstall had arrived in Lincoln a month prior, and Lawrence Murphy needed to know more about the stranger. Before he made any overtures to the Englishman, he invited the man who brought Tunstall to town, Alexander McSween, to sit down.

McSween was apprehensive. He had recently quit as Murphy & Co.'s lawyer and, worse, taken on the Fritz siblings as clients. Had word finally reached Murphy about McSween's deal with the Spiegelbergs, a deal that kept Murphy in hock for $10,000? Murphy had insisted McSween come by himself. Maybe Murphy was going to make him an offer to double-cross the Fritzes, McSween posited.

Or maybe they were just going to kill him.

No, McSween thought, not even Murphy and Dolan were brazen enough to murder a prominent *white* citizen of Lincoln. Susan urged her husband not to go, but he reasoned this was his best—and likely last—chance to glean useful intelligence from the House.

McSween arrived at Murphy & Co. promptly at ten o'clock that evening. The store was closed for business, which left McSween, Murphy, and Dolan able to convene without interruption.

"Upstairs, to my office."

"After you, gentlemen," McSween said.

McSween was still open to the possibility this may be a setup, and when he reached halfway up the steps he heard the heavy thud of boots behind him. McSween glanced back to see Murphy and Dolan's new partner, John Riley, taking up the rear.

McSween was boxed in, and his mind raced, which wasn't lost on Murphy.

"Alex, my boy, there're easier ways to kill an unarmed barrister than lure him to my office in the middle of the night."

"It's true, McSween. If we wanted you dead, we'd just shoot you whenever we damn well please," added Dolan.

McSween felt comforted he wasn't going to die that night but was still quite discomforted by the fact they might still shoot him anytime they want, anywhere they want. Adding to the apprehension was how much the sight of the third partner rankled McSween. Susan had not been sleeping well ever since Riley's visit to their home.

"You asked me to meet, and here I am. But I go no further with him around," McSween said, gesturing toward Riley. Riley climbed three more steps until they were nose-to-nose, and he could see the sweat dripping down McSween's forehead. Despite the nervousness, McSween held his ground.

"Mr. Riley can get a little overzealous in his defense of the company. No harm was intended. Johnny, warm our seats at the Wortley. We'll apprise you of the details later."

Riley saw Murphy was serious. He disappointedly descended out of view.

The other three men made it up to the office. McSween took a seat across from Murphy while Dolan stood behind his partner, as he so often did.

"I understand you have a new client," Murphy said. "John Tunstall."

"I'm simply advising a new friend."

"Oh, come on, Alex. I have eyes and ears."

Murphy turned and nodded to Dolan, who poured three glasses of whiskey and handed one to Murphy and one to McSween.

"There's no reason things need to be so adversarial," Murphy continued. "What we have here is a golden opportunity, a chance to show there are no hard feelings." He raised his glass and McSween reluctantly mirrored him. "In fact, I have a proposition."

Dolan opened a drawer and removed a large scroll. He unfurled it on the desk, revealing a hand-drawn topographical map of Lincoln County.

"I own a tract of land just west of town," Murphy said, pointing.

"How 'just'?" McSween asked.

"A half-day's ride, maybe less. It's fertile, close enough to fresh water, an ideal plot to build and maintain a thriving ranch."

"You do have ears," McSween replied. "You want me to present this offer to John Tunstall in the hopes he'll take it off your hands."

"I'd like you to do more than that, Alex. I'd like you to *convince* the English novice that it is the optimal location to launch his budding new enterprise."

"Why would I do that?"

"Because for all your ambition and all your hubris, you are not a dim-witted man. Do this and I'd be willing to let bygones be bygones."

"We'll even compensate you a ten percent brokerage fee on that property and any other land Murphy & Co. owns west of town that you can unload," Dolan added.

McSween leaned back and took a sip of his whiskey. It was an attractive offer and a good way to squash the tension between himself and the House. It was certainly what Susan would want him to do, in the interest of peace.

"I'll take the proposition to my client."

"I thought he was just your friend," Dolan said.

"In this corner of the world, men need both. May I?" McSween gestured to the map. "I promise to return it within the week, along with our answer."

Murphy nodded. McSween rolled up the map and took it with him. After he was gone, Dolan turned to his partner.

"You think he'll be able to convince Tunstall to buy the bunk land?"

"This wasn't about the land, Jimmy. This was about information," Murphy replied.

"And what did you discover?"

"That dear Alex McSween is a lying sonofabitch. Tunstall isn't his friend or his client—he's his goddamn business partner."

"How do you come to reckon that?"

"McSween is a greedy opportunist. We dangled a big carrot in front of him, and if Tunstall were simply a client, McSween would have snatched that carrot off the stick and devoured it right here and now. But he didn't so much as sniff at it. No, McSween and Tunstall have something else in store for us."

DOÑA ANA COUNTY, NEW MEXICO TERRITORY
October 1877

It was half past midnight when Billy and Isadora reached her family's home, just behind the peach orchard at Fort Sumner. Billy walked her to the front door and stopped.

"Your company has been quite the pleasure, Miss Isadora."

She studied his face for a moment. She reached up and gently cupped his cheek in her palm, then she went inside. But she left the front door open.

Billy hesitated, then followed her inside.

The home was small, only one large room in the front and one small room in the back. Billy took a seat at the long table. The countertop served as the kitchen, there was a rocking chair in the far corner, and a wood basin against the wall.

And a fireplace. Billy watched as Isadora poured water into a cast-iron kettle and hung it above the kindling. She lit the fire, then turned to him.

"*Quítate la ropa.*"

Billy cocked his head. She had said it so softly he was sure his translation was wrong. She approached him and gestured for him to stand.

He did.

Isadora then slid her hands down to his waist, slowly unbuckled his gun belt, and placed it aside. She looked up at him. Into his eyes. And he into hers. The girl who had been so shy on their walk now seemed so sure of herself. She untucked his shirt and lifted it over his head. Her lips were so close he could feel the warmth of her breath, so inviting . . .

Isadora knelt and removed his boots and socks. Then she ran her hands up along his thighs until she got to the buttons on his britches. She unhooked them and slid his britches off.

Billy's heart was racing. Racing even harder than when he killed Windy Cahill.

She helped him remove his long johns. Now he stood before her, completely naked.

Isadora eyed his body, lean and angular with taut ropes of sinewy muscle. Stronger than his small frame conveyed. She noticed he was flush, the blood having rushed to his face, his neck . . . and below.

She took him by the hand. Billy stepped toward the back room, the bedroom, but instead she led him to the wood basin against the wall. She let go of him, their fingers sliding gently, tenderly as she slipped away and went to the kettle over the fireplace. She took the kettle and poured the steaming hot water into the basin. Then she poured water from a second pot in after it.

Isadora put her hands on Billy's hips and guided him into the tub. He sat down and felt the warm water envelop him. Isadora moved behind him. She massaged his neck, his head, running her fingers through his shaggy hair. Then she took a sponge and dipped it into the water, near his waist, sending another bolt of excitement through him. She used the sponge to dampen his back and neck, clean his shoulders, then his chest. Her hands were soft and inviting. She ran the sponge down his torso to his waist . . . then back up his chest to his neck.

Billy gripped the side of the basin with all his might. He was about to burst.

Next she moved around to the far end of the tub. Billy eyed the way she swayed, so effortlessly enrapturing him. Isadora began sponging his feet, his calves, then his thighs, moving in a slow, rhythmic, circular pattern, inching her way up his body.

Her hand disappeared beneath the waterline, and Billy felt her run the sponge along his erection, then he saw the sponge bob to the top of the water while her hand was still below. She began caressing him, then stroking him. Billy looked into her eyes and she into his.

Just as he was about to climax, she stopped.

Isadora then stood, slipped her shoulders free of her dress, and let it slide to the floor. Billy eyed her soft brown skin. The curve of her hips. Her small but firm breasts.

She stepped into the tub and lay gently on top of him. Her heart was beating as fast as his. They kissed softly. Sweetly. Passionately. Then harder, their tongues finding each other's. She angled her hips, and he was inside her. Slow at first, each of them taking their time. Then she quickened her pace, and he followed.

No words. Just moans and the sound of the water lapping rhythmically to their thrusts.

Billy and Isadora made love all evening, only pausing to eat the occasional snack—peaches they picked from the orchard—or to hydrate.

After their third session, they both needed a break. Isadora leaned over him and picked his book up off the bedside table.

"Are you literate?" Billy asked.

"A little," she replied. *"En español."* Billy put a hand behind his head and she passed him the book, then nestled into the nook between his arm and chest. "I want to lay here, *olvida el mundo*, and just listen to you."

Billy opened the book and found where he'd left off.

"No, *no sabré que pasó*," she protested.

I won't know what happened.

"It's the story of a precocious boy who's always getting into trouble, innocent little things here and there, until trouble starts seeking him out. He has to go on the run to hide from a bad guy and *todas piensan que está muerto.*"

Everyone thinks he's dead.

She hit him teasingly. "Your Spanish is better than you let on. *Comienza desde el principio.* From beginning."

He smiled and flipped back to the front of the book. *"Most of the adventures recorded in this book really occurred; one or two were experiences of my own, the rest those of boys who were schoolmates of mine. Huck Finn is drawn from life; Tom Sawyer also, but not from an individual—he is a combination of the characteristics of three boys whom I knew, and therefore belongs to the composite order of architecture . . ."*

Isadora was sound asleep before he finished the preface.

LINCOLN

LINCOLN COUNTY, NEW MEXICO TERRITORY

"I don't know, it seems like a square deal," Tunstall said, looking over the map McSween had laid out on the dining table.

"Too good. Murphy is up to something," McSween replied.

John Tunstall came from strong English stock. Wealthy stock. He was young and believed he had the world by the tail. But as they sat in McSween's home plotting how to proceed, McSween impressed upon him the virtue of patience.

"We need a ranch out in the plains and a store right in town. Buying Murphy's land solves half of our problem," Tunstall said.

"I don't like how eager he is to sell. Murphy's a bastard, but he's smart and hears whispers under every rock. I believe he's on to our intentions. So why would he aid us in our pursuits?"

"Because he'll make a fair deal of money from the sale."

"Murphy owns tracts all throughout New Mexico, some even legally. Why sell us this one?" McSween asked, playing out the various reasons in his head. "If Murphy wants us to do something, that's the surest sign we shouldn't."

"Then we're back to square one. We still need a ranch to house the livestock before we can build our store in Lincoln."

"I concur. But not from him. There's a large parcel of land—about six hundred acres—twenty-five miles beyond town, out by Rio Feliz. The widow Ellen Casey's property."

"What happened to her husband?"

"Robert Casey was killed coming out of the Wortley Hotel some two years back. Rumor was he got vocal about the House, so Murphy paid a man to gun him down."

Tunstall turned and looked at him, his face paling. McSween realized he may lose his fish before they ever got out of the boat.

"Just a nonsense rumor. Casey was known to stiff his ranch hands and eventually crossed the wrong man. But Ellen Casey's loss could be our gain."

"How much do you think the widow would ask?"

"That's the beauty, John. According to official records, it doesn't belong to her or anyone else. See, Robert Casey never paid for his land, he just set down stakes and declared it his own. We don't have to negotiate with Ellen. We go straight to the federal government and utilize the Desert Land Act."

Tunstall didn't know this arcane law.

"Anyone can file on up to six hundred forty acres of desert land at twenty-five cents an acre," McSween continued. "Then you have three years to make improvements upon the land, after which you'll owe an additional one dollar per acre you've claimed. Ellen Casey's six hundred acres at twenty-five cents will cost a mere one hundred fifty dollars."

Tunstall smiled.

"Once we acquire this land, there's no going back, and there's no hiding our true intentions. Murphy, Dolan, and Riley will fight, and nothing is beneath those scoundrels. We need someone else on our side, someone with deep pockets and deeper influence in Santa Fe. We can't go directly to Boss Catron—he has too much already invested in Murphy & Co. But there is someone who hates Murphy and would jump at the chance to stick it to the House."

"Chisum?"

McSween nodded.

"And the widow Casey? What happens to her?"

"Ellen? She's out on her ass."

Chapter 10

October 1877

John Tunstall and Alex McSween arrived at South Spring Ranch just after one in the afternoon, unprepared for what awaited them.

Most of the ranch hands were still battered and bloodied. Those not injured in whatever hell had rained down that morning were treating the maimed, attending to their wounds. The owner of the ranch, John Chisum, was not in sight, and the only thing Tunstall and McSween were sure of was that whatever took place was pure violence.

Soiled white sheets covered three lumps of flesh just outside the main house. The wind had whipped up and drawn one overlay's corner back. Tunstall could see the vacant, faraway look in the dead man's exposed eye, and half of the deceased's face had turned an ashen gray as the blood succumbed to gravity and puddled in the dirt below.

Tunstall had never seen a dead body before, at least not one outside of funeral services, embalmed and suitable for public viewing. This was an honest-to-God dead cowboy, with half his face blown off and flies beginning to circle. Tunstall's stomach turned.

A spry woman just shy of twenty was the first to address the two as they climbed the steps to the main house. She shielded her eyes from the sun and tilted her head.

"What happened here?" McSween asked.

"Oh, we just had a little row. Nothing too far astray from the usual."

"Men are dead," Tunstall replied.

"Like I said," she answered. "But as you can see, today ain't a good day to be conducting business. Please come back tomorrow. Or don't."

"We rode all the way from Lincoln," McSween said.

"You ain't from First National?" she asked.

McSween and Tunstall traded looks. "No, we're here to inquire about a business partnership."

"What sort of business you gentlemen in?"

"Ranching. And we're opening a mercantile store in Lincoln."

"Ranching? Had me fooled, what with y'all looking more like bankers than the types who toil with their hands."

"We're in transition. I'm Alexander McSween. This is my friend and partner, Mr. John Tunstall."

Tunstall leaned forward to shake the young woman's hand, which she offered without enthusiasm. "Sallie Chisum."

"You're the niece," McSween said.

"You bet your ass I am," she replied, then went inside, leaving the door open for them to follow.

McSween and Tunstall sat in the living room waiting for John Chisum to return. The ranch house was large and in the midst of a redecoration. The sofa was made of a fine leather but differed aesthetically from the French armoire in the corner, which differed from the Victorian settee opposite the sofa, which differed from everything else.

"It's garish, I know," Sallie Chisum said, returning to the room with tea. "I am redesigning the entire home, beginning with this room. It makes me positively ill every time I enter. You gentlemen aren't in need of a colonial chandelier, are you?"

"I'm afraid not, miss," McSween answered. "When is your uncle due to return?"

"Soon. He's taking inventory of what we lost in the raid this morning."

"Might I inquire as to what happened?" Tunstall asked.

"Yes, you may," Sallie answered as she settled into a chair across from Tunstall and McSween.

THE DAY BEFORE

Buck Morton kicked the door open. Billy and Isadora snapped awake, and she pulled the sheets up tight to her chin, covering her still-naked body.

"Let's go, *chico*," Jesse Evans said as he followed Buck into the room.

Billy rubbed his eyes, his senses taking a moment to catch up to reality. Billy looked out the open doorway and saw the sun hadn't fully broken the horizon yet.

"What time is it?" he asked.

"It's time to get your hide up and dressed. We're all waiting on you," Evans answered.

Billy climbed out of bed naked, leaving the sheet for Isadora to keep herself covered. Not long ago, he would have been bashful around Buck Morton, but an entire night with the beautiful Isadora had Billy feeling self-assured. He put on his long johns and britches, then searched for his socks and boots.

Evans drifted over to the basin, still filled with water. He found Billy's revolver laying on the ground beside it, along with a serrated knife, the kind small enough to fit in a pocket or boot.

"What's this?" he asked, picking up the gun.

"My pistol," Billy answered as he located one of his boots under the bed.

"What the hell is it doing here?"

"I take it everywhere, just like you taught me."

"No, I taught you to keep it *by your side* everywhere you went."

"And I do."

"Billy, what if Buck bullied in here meaning you harm?"

Buck smiled. The thought had crossed his mind.

"And you got your gun all the way on the other side of the damn room," Jesse continued. "How are you gonna defend yourself? How are you gonna make sure no harm falls on this pretty little lady?"

"I guess I wouldn't be able to."

"When I say something, I mean it to the letter. Never go anywhere without your iron and never leave it out of arm's reach. Now say goodbye to your girl."

Evans handed the gun to Billy, then exited. Buck followed, but not before sneaking another peak back at Isadora, imagining what was under that sheet.

Billy finished buttoning up his shirt and buckling the holster around his waist.

"Don't go, Billy. *Quédate aquí.*"

"I can't stay, Isadora. I can't. But I'll be back soon."

Billy kissed her on the forehead, then joined the men outside.

It was a full day's ride out to Chisum's South Spring Ranch, and Evans and the Boys were intent on arriving in the middle of the night. Billy spent most of the journey in the center of the pack, repeating over and over in his head the instructions Evans had laid out. Evans had worked for Chisum and knew South Spring and the surrounding land like the back of his hand.

The plan was simple. It always was.

But it only takes one loose thread to unravel everything.

The Boys were thirteen deep and all were skilled rustlers, save for Billy, but even he was careering toward this becoming routine.

They slowed to a trot as they neared South Spring. It was past 2:00 a.m., and Chisum's ranch hands were surely all asleep.

"Remember, we're just after the calves," Evans whispered. "Nothing we can do with them jinglebobs, so let them run around like chickens, creating a mess for the Chisum boys. And watch each other's backs."

Evans had insisted they leave the older cattle be, for those had already had their ears split down the middle in the common Chisum practice, preventing thieves from rebranding his cattle. But the young calves had yet to be jinglebobbed and were ripe for the taking.

Chisum's home was set at the front of the property, surrounded by a white picket fence. The large corral containing cattle lay just behind the home, as was the small boarding room where Chisum's hands rested when not on the range.

The Boys made their way past the house, then Evans gestured to Billy, who continued along the fence line on the edge of the corral. Buck followed and went past Billy—elbowing him as he did so—to the back of the pen, where he was tasked with opening the fence for the cattle to escape. Frank Baker's group legged over the fence into the corral, their job being to usher the cattle to Buck.

Despite his aptitude for rustling and this being his fifth or so raid in the last few weeks, Billy still had a knot in his stomach. It was one thing to rip off a government agency—aided with a wink and a nod from the Indian reservation agent—but it was an entirely different matter going after John Chisum.

Billy squatted, his job to protect the Baker group inside the pen and watch Evans's back.

Owen had to piss. After three weeks of bringing Chisum's cattle from Texas to South Spring, the exhausted young ranch hand had consumed far too much food and far too many spirits. He slipped out of his bunk, careful not to wake the other men.

Owen found the nearest tree, leaning against the trunk as he evacuated his bladder. When he finished, he turned around and stopped cold.

He was staring at the back of a man—a boy, really—a mere twenty yards away. The boy had his gun out and seemed to be peering toward the corral. Who was dense enough to be sneaking around John Chisum's place this time of night?

This could be a good opportunity to prove himself to the cattle king, Owen thought. He pulled his pistol and quietly crept up behind the boy. He got within five yards without notice.

The boy was unaware he was about to meet his fate.

Buck leaned against the back fence of the corral, waiting for Frank Baker's group to usher the cattle his way. All he had to do was open the gate and pick off the calves as they came past. The Boys knew Chisum's hands would spend the rest of the day rounding up the mature livestock, and that would leave plenty of time for the Boys to flee the county.

Buck turned his gaze to Billy, whom he could barely make out in the darkness. But what Buck could see was a shadowed young man in just britches and an untucked shirt, creeping toward the Kid, pistol raised. Buck aimed his gun at the young man and had him square in his sights . . .

Then stopped.

Maybe this could be the solution to his "Billy problem."

Billy was oblivious to the young man approaching behind him. He was too focused on Baker's group in the corral and them quietly beginning to usher the cattle toward Buck. Billy looked over at Jesse, who was keeping his eye on the main house to make sure no lanterns were lit or suspecting individuals emerged.

Owen was within a few yards now. He slowly raised his gun and aimed it at the back of the Kid's head. He'd heard that taking the first life was the hardest but had also been promised it would get easier after that. And Chisum had insisted that bad men who broke the law and threatened their livelihood were deserving of frontier justice.

Buck watched as the young man raised his gun. In a moment, the Kid would be snuffed out and no longer the rat gnawing at Buck.

The explosion just about knocked Billy off his feet. It took him a moment to realize the piercing scream that followed was not his own but from a young man on the ground behind him.

The cattle stirred and grumbled anxiously.

"The hell's going on?" came a gruff voice inside the ranch-hand quarters. The door opened and Evans fired, sending the man scrambling back inside.

Baker and his cohorts inside the pen began whipping the cattle, directing them toward the back gate, which Morton had open and ready for their liberation.

Billy looked down at the young man. He was writhing in pain and using his one good hand to hold the bloodied, charred stump of a mess that used to be his second good hand. The revolver lay in pieces next to him, and the chamber still smoked from the misfire.

The door to the ranch-hand quarters opened again, and this time the men came out shooting. The Boys ducked for cover, save Buck, who was ushering the cattle to freedom. The Boys would have to round up the calves in the fields behind Chisum's place as they escaped.

"I need help," the young man gutted out in between shrieks of pain.

Billy didn't move. The young man's cries were a tinny whinge, and Billy knew the young man had just tried to kill him.

"Shit, ain't you gonna end his suffering?" came Buck's voice. "He was fixing to shoot you right in the head, kid."

Billy turned to see Buck ducking and settling in beside Billy as the shootout still raged.

"And how you know that, Buck?" It had dawned on Billy that while he was watching Jesse's back, Buck was supposed to be watching his.

Buck unloaded a few shots at the ranch hands who were now spread out, using their quarters for cover. One of the ranch hands dropped.

A return bullet whizzed past Billy and Buck and embedded in the nearby fence post.

The young man on the ground was still shrieking in pain.

"You too chickenshit to do it?" Buck asked.

"I just don't see the point, is all. He ain't a threat no more. Hell, he's gonna be a cripple the rest of his life."

"It's about sending a warning to others."

Billy fired over his head at the men engaging with Evans. One fell, clutching his leg. Then Billy spied the Baker group scurrying from the back of the pen and away.

"We done what we came here to do," Billy said, then went to move past Buck and join the others in escaping, but Buck grabbed him with one hand and with the other pressed his revolver into Billy's jaw.

"Maybe we got one more sow to get rid of."

Billy looked into Buck's eyes and saw only a deep, black soullessness. Billy braced himself to fire into Buck's belly, which would provide considerably more satisfaction than what he'd done to Windy Cahill . . .

Buck let him go and crept over to the young man on the ground.

"I want my mom," Owen said, hoping Buck would be his savior.

Buck shot him in the head without a second thought, then fled out with the rest of the Boys.

Billy took one last look at the dead young man, his eyes still open and angled to the heavens for a salvation that was never coming.

John Chisum entered the house to find his lawyer and a stranger sitting on the sofa across from his niece. Everyone had tea in front of them, a practice Sallie had insisted on implementing ever since she took over as "matron" of the ranch.

Tunstall was struck by Chisum's extraordinary ordinariness. Chisum was of average height and build. His eyes were a bland brown, and his mustache was waxed to curl up ever so slightly at the tips, but even that appeared unremarkable upon his face.

Chisum kept his hair longer on the sides to offset his only notable characteristic: his sizable ears.

"Miss Sallie filled us in on what took place. I'm sorry for your loss, John," McSween said.

Chisum nodded but only out of expectation. "I'll have to get more help." He propped himself on the arm of the sofa, nearest to Sallie. "I don't like the cowboys around here, not for this sort of work. It's not in their blood. You can't trust them the way you can a Texan."

McSween let slide that Chisum originally hailed from Tennessee. "Who led the raid?"

"My men got a look at one of the turncoats, a bastard named Jesse Evans."

McSween looked to see if the name registered with Tunstall. It did not.

"Sonofabitch—pardon my language, Sallie—worked for me for some time," Chisum continued. "I even came to like him. Smart. Educated. But had a mean streak longer'n a rail line."

"And what Evans takes, Murphy sells," McSween added. "Which is why we're here. I'd like to introduce you to my new friend John Tunstall."

Tunstall stood and succumbed to his proper English manners, making his way across the room to shake hands with Chisum, who never rose from the arm of the sofa.

"Pleasure to meet you, Mr. Chisum."

Chisum simply nodded, then turned back to McSween. "This is a long ways ride from Lincoln, Alex. The timing a coincidence, or are you here to tell me you've taken up Murphy and Dolan as clients again?"

"No, sir, quite the opposite. I came because I thought you might want to help us drive Murphy & Co. out of business."

"I'm not opposed to Murphy going under. Or his business."

Tunstall bristled ever so slightly. He had not heard McSween put it in such stark terms of opposition and was equally surprised by Chisum's response. Tunstall was beginning to see that the territorial conflict went deeper than just two businesses competing over market share.

"We thought you'd like to help us make it happen. Equal partner. We have purchased a ranch out by Rio Feliz—"

"The widow Casey's place. Shrewd."

"Yes, and construction will begin this week on a store in Lincoln proper," Tunstall added.

"You seem to have it all figured out. What do you need me for?"

"We have most of our funding together, courtesy of Mr. Tunstall. But we need beef. And with us as your partners, you know we won't steal from you."

Chisum stood and walked to the window. The men outside were still repairing broken fencing and boarding up splintered panels on the barn. Three ranch hands were dragging a dead horse around the side of the house to a clearing. Rocks had been arranged in a circle around stacks of wood that would be used as kindling for the pyre.

"Partner, huh?" Chisum said, mostly to himself.

"Silent partner," Sallie chimed in. "Silent partner or no deal."

McSween and Tunstall traded looks.

"Mr. McSween, you barely have a pot to piss in," Sallie continued, "and now you're able to fund a venture and take on the House? Hell, the whole Santa Fe Ring?"

"Sallie . . ." Chisum was simply saving face. His niece was raising good points that required answers.

"I apologize, Uncle. I just believe that the best partnerships are formed when everyone lays their cards on the table. No surprises."

"She makes an honorable case. Don't use the Chisum name to promote the business or rally investors," Chisum said. "Short of that, there is no amount of money I won't pay to help you take down Murphy & Co."

The men and Sallie, who insisted on staying, went over some of the finer points, then McSween and Tunstall thanked them for their hospitality and left.

As they rode back to Lincoln, one issue was still gnawing at Tunstall.

"He'll add money. We can purchase his beef wholesale with the first choice of cattle . . . why be a silent partner? His name alone could add to our bottom line."

"He's scared," McSween replied.

"He didn't seem scared."

"Of course not. The fighting had ceased. The danger had subsided, and he'd refound his mettle. But they come around his ranch again, he'll up and cower once more."

Tunstall didn't utter the next query on his mind, the most important of all: *If Cattle King John Chisum was scared, shouldn't they be too?*

Chapter 11

LINCOLN

LINCOLN COUNTY, NEW MEXICO TERRITORY

October 1877

Once again, Billy was left outside while Evans and Buck went into the House to negotiate over Chisum's cattle.

Billy, restless, wandered down the street into the middle of town. A crew of a dozen men were raising the frame of a new building. Billy watched them pulley the wooden frame up into place. It was going to be a one-story structure, south-facing, with a long porch, when finished. But once the men settled the frame into place, Billy grew bored again and headed for the Wortley Hotel to wait.

Billy grabbed the day's paper and took it under the shade of the porch. Just as he opened it, John Riley came out of the House across the street.

"You that new kid ridin' with Jesse and the Boys, huh?"

"Billy Bonney."

"How old is you?"

"Seventeen and some," Billy said.

Riley gestured to the paper. "You the worldly type, keepin' up with current affairs?"

"Just passin' time."

"Well, I got current affairs for you," Riley said. "I'm a serious man around these parts now too. Been made full partner of Murphy, Dolan, and Co."

Billy looked at Riley, standing with one hand partially tucked inside his shirt like a dusty, haggard Napoleon.

"Such a big deal 'round these parts, why ain't your name part of it?"

"You a smart cuss, huh?" Riley said.

"Just a curious sort, is all. Say, what's the new building going up?"

"McSween and an English tenderfoot think they gonna open up a competing venture."

"Looks like they're well on their way," Billy said.

"What goes up can—and will—come down," Riley replied.

Evans came out of the House pocketing an envelope, trailed by Buck. Evans whistled across the street at Billy.

"See you around, *partner*," Billy said to Riley, then he followed Evans and Buck.

When they got back to camp, Evans opened the envelope and doled out the money Murphy had paid them for the stolen livestock.

"We're taking the cattle to Murphy's ranch, then it's best we lay low," Evans said.

"Chisum'll have another herd within the week. We can hit him again," Buck said.

"Chisum's gonna come after us. And we've been riding for three weeks straight."

"We're leaving opportunity on the table. And for what?

Murphy controls the sheriff, District Attorney Rynerson, and what he doesn't have under his thumb, Boss Catron does. Who'd dare touch us?"

"Chisum's got money, and money can buy influence too."

"Goddamn, I ain't never run and hid from nobody, and I ain't starting now," Buck insisted.

"Let it settle," Evans said. "The stingy bastard'll tire of paying extra men to act as security. Then, when he's relaxed and his guard is down, we'll strike again. Besides, I've got a little surprise for us in La Mesilla."

LA MESILLA

DOÑA ANA COUNTY, NEW MEXICO TERRITORY

La Mesilla was forty miles north of El Paso, and when the Boys arrived, sure enough, a group of white and Hispanic women from Texas awaited them. But Billy was most interested in another woman who'd traveled from another place.

Abigail.

Billy smiled warmly. They hadn't seen each other in weeks, not since Billy's one-night courtship of Isadora.

"Did she travel with?" Billy asked.

"No, I'm afraid not." Abigail could see how disappointed Billy was. "It weren't for lack of want. Isadora is quite keen on you and spoke on and on about your time together. So much so her father got wind of what took place, had some choice words for her behavior, and forbid her from ever seeing you again."

Billy was dumbstruck. "I only have the best of intentions for Miss Isadora."

"I know. She told me all about how caring and lovely you were with her." Abigail's hint of mischievousness made Billy blush.

"What sort of choice words did her daddy levy against her?"

"It's not important. It'll blow over and you'll see Isadora again."

"I don't want her besmirched because of the time we spent together."

"Her father called her a gringo-loving whore."

Billy looked past Abigail to the horizon. It burned him that Isadora had to absorb that kind of insult on account of him.

"Billy, it's okay. Fathers and daughters are complicated. But she'll move into a world of her own making soon enough. Now come on, the music is about to start."

Abigail pulled Billy near the piano inside the saloon, and they went around a few times before she passed him off to another lively young woman, who was instantly smitten with him. Billy soon forgot about Isadora as he twirled this girl and that girl, cracking jokes, and reveling in the much-needed rest and relaxation. After a dozen songs, Billy took a seat. One of his dance partners, Beth, settled onto his lap.

"I feel I could go on twirling you around this room till morning," he said.

"Isn't there some other way you could occupy me till morning?" She fixed his shirt collar, making sure to graze his ear as she did.

They retired to a room Billy paid for with his cut from the Chisum raid.

After a couple of hours of playfulness and two acts of deeper intimacy, Beth fell asleep. But Billy lay awake. He did wish to see Isadora again, but another thing was eating at him. A few hours ago, he was devastated that she had not come along, but now, after bedding the delightful young woman snoring next to him, he found he didn't miss Isadora as much.

He connected quickly and intensely with women, but the magnetism was like a fire that burned too hot too quick. And when a new flame was placed in front of him, that became the burning light to which he was pulled. Billy's attraction to the fairer sex was not rooted in the women themselves, but rather by the fact *they were drawn to him*. Their acceptance of him. Their desire for him.

Beth didn't stir as he lit a candle and placed it on the nightstand. He pulled out the paper and began to read, hoping eventually his eyes would tire and he'd doze off.

The front page was an article on the progress Thomas B. "Boss" Catron was making in Santa Fe. The new rail line was a success, and there was an influx of newcomers to the territory. Billy was smart enough to know "newcomers" meant white folks who would be sympathetic to other white folks, their white businesses, and their white ways. It meant a further purging of the traditions of the Mexicans and Indians who'd made the territory home for centuries. Billy had no dog in this fight. He got along with everyone and figured who was or wasn't running New Mexico—the governor or lawmen or businessmen—had no bearing on his life.

Billy turned the page and fixated on another article. A disease outbreak was ravaging the nearby Mescalero Apache Indian Reservation. Some suspected smallpox, but there was no proof. Either way, a third of the tribe had become ill. The Mescalero Apache Indian Reservation was only a hundred miles away, in between La Mesilla and Lincoln, and the fear among the whites was the disease could easily spread to Anglos. *If the pox is so bad, shouldn't they be worried about the people on the reservation?* But Billy knew that wasn't the way things were, and nothing would be done until the disease breached the white communities.

The article wrapped with a mention of how the Apache

warrior Victorio had led 260 Mescalero off the reservation into the hills. The group had not been heard from in weeks, and speculation was they either succumbed to the disease themselves or fled to Mexico. Billy wondered if Bodaway had been involved. He wondered if Bodaway was still alive.

He wondered if Lolotea still had her doll.

Billy heard a tap on the door, then a whisper so low he couldn't place the voice. He slowly rose from bed. Beth was still deep into her slumber. Billy grabbed his gun off the nightstand, within arm's reach, just like Jesse had instructed.

"Are you awake?" came the whisper again. Billy tiptoed toward the voice and cocked the revolver as quietly as he could. The floorboard creaked as he reached the door.

"Billy?"

The door pushed slowly in, and Billy slipped to the side, so as not to be in the line of potential fire. He raised his gun to head height. A hand reached in, and Billy quickly grabbed it by the wrist and spun it inside.

A scream, which Billy quickly muffled. He looked at who was in his grasp.

Abigail.

"Everything all right?" Beth mumbled from the bed. Before Billy answered, Beth rolled onto her other side and fell back asleep.

Billy could only see half of Abigail's face—the half lit by the candlelight coming from the nightstand—but he could tell she had been crying.

He escorted Abigail into the hallway, and there, by the light of the moon coming in through the window, he could see her eye was swollen, her lips were puffed, and the bottom one bled.

"I'll kill him." Billy started to walk toward Buck's room, but Abigail stopped him.

"You'll only get yourself hurt."

Billy continued to stare down Buck's door at the end of the hallway.

"Billy . . . please." She grabbed his face and turned it toward hers.

"Wait here." Billy went back to his room and grabbed his boots and coat.

Outside, Billy draped his coat over Abigail's shoulders to protect her from the cold, leaving himself in just an undershirt, britches, and suspenders. The town of La Mesilla was quiet, everyone having retired after the evening's revelry. They were alone.

"He's never done this before. Not this bad. He was good and soused. He started pawing at me, but I knew when he gets like this it's a lot of preamble and no finale, and I didn't want to go down that road, because when it came time to, you know, he'd get embarrassed and sore and lash out. I figured it was best to just say I was having 'womanly troubles' and try again the next night when he was sober. But Buck took it the wrong way, started accusing me of being tired on account of I'd spent all my energy with another man."

"You was within his eyeline all night."

"I told him that, but there's no reasoning with him when he hits the bottle. He kept going on and on, and I was getting tired of his abuse and fought back."

"How?"

"Oh, Billy, can't we just forget it? I don't want to think about it anymore."

Billy nodded and they continued in silence for a bit. Billy wanted to tell her everything would be all right, that this was just another hiccup of life, that she would still have a fruitful future. But he couldn't. Not as long as she was with Buck.

Instead, not even realizing he was doing it, he began to

whistle. Softly at first, then with more force. Abigail let it go on for a few minutes before turning to him.

"What is that tune? I've heard you whistle it before."

"'Silver Threads Among the Gold.' It was my favorite song when I was young. Still is, I suppose."

"It's pretty. Whistle some more."

But now he was self-conscious and didn't dare try to whistle in front of her again. Instead, he reached into the pocket of his coat that she was wearing and pulled out a deck of cards. He began shuffling them as they walked.

"Teach me," Abigail said.

"We don't have the table or room for faro or poker. How about incognito?"

"How do you play?"

"Real simple. We each hold a card up to our forehead so only the other person can see it. Then we bet on who has the higher card. If you've got an ace, I can pretty easily bet I ain't gonna beat that. If you got a two, I'm gonna place a healthy wager."

"I don't have any money."

"I wouldn't take your money anyhow. We'll play for pebbles."

Billy and Abigail sat down on the porch of the local store, still a couple of hours away from opening. Billy began sticking the cards on his forehead and making dumb faces just to get Abigail to laugh. It started with the crack of a smile, then she showed her teeth, then eventually Abigail was sticking the cards on her own head, too, and giggling until they were both howling.

After a spell, the sun was ready to break the horizon, and La Mesilla would soon be overrun with people. As Billy gathered up the cards, Abigail turned confessional.

"You know why Buck came after me?" she asked. "When we were fighting, I was mad that he was being such a cad, and

I wanted to stick it to him. I said something I knew would cut him deeply."

Billy stuffed the cards back in the coat pocket and let her continue.

"I told him he should stop drinking, then maybe he, too, would be a great lay. That maybe he wouldn't just stick it in as he saw fit, only concerned how the experience was for him. I told him he should be more like *you*."

Billy arched an eyebrow.

"I saw how much it bothered him and couldn't help twisting the knife. I told him how no one has ever described a lover the way Isadora described you. How even after you'd gone she'd lie in bed smelling the sheets, not wanting to clean them, not wanting to wash the smell of you away. I told him *that* was the measure of a man, and he could never measure up."

When Billy met Abigail, she'd been a bright, shining star, and now she was dimmed by the fragility of Buck Morton's ego. Billy wanted to kill the bastard, but he knew that would not please Abigail, and Jesse and the rest of the Boys would have something to say about it too.

"We should get back," he said.

As they reached the hotel, the sun had dawned and there was activity inside.

"You need to get as far away from Buck as you can. Men like him don't change. He'll never forget what you said and the way he reacted and the shame he now feels."

"I know. But I took a wagon with seven other girls out here. I have no way of getting home. Even if I did, Buck will just come knocking 'round my way again."

"Take my horse."

"Billy . . ."

"I can always find my way to another," he said with a wink. Abigail couldn't help but smile. "All right, gather your things and I'll fetch your chariot."

Abigail went to her room and Billy ventured around the side of the hotel, where the horses were tied. He thought about setting Buck's horse free, but what sense would that make? Buck would just procure himself another one by breakfast's end.

Abigail returned ten minutes later, suitcase in hand.

"Buck was still sleeping off last night. He heard me dragging my suitcase to the door and mumbled an apology."

She seemed to be wavering. Billy had a hard time picturing Buck saying sorry about anything, but men tend to bend to the will of a woman, if she's special enough.

"I told him I forgave him and that I was just heading out to get breakfast."

"He believe you?"

"Enough to let me go. Thank you for being easy to talk to. Thank you for being my friend."

"Tell Isadora I'll come calling."

Abigail kissed him on the cheek, and he felt her warmth returning.

Billy watched her ride out of town, looking forward to the next time he'd see his friend.

Until then, he'd have to deal with Buck.

CHAPTER 12

LINCOLN

LINCOLN COUNTY, NEW MEXICO TERRITORY

Alexander McSween and John Tunstall arrived back in Lincoln and went straight to the postmaster general. Ash Upson had a telegram for them. McSween read it and grinned like a Cheshire cat.

"It came through, John. The insurance company has released Emil Fritz's life insurance payout to me. Ten thousand dollars."

Tunstall, too, was elated. It was a big blow to their rivals.

Ash Upson sat in a chair and listened quietly. He was nearing fifty and well regarded, known for fairness. Tunstall noticed the concerned look on the postmaster general's face.

"Don't you see, Mr. Upson?" Tunstall said. "This is wonderful news."

"Is it?"

"Yes. Now the money will make it into the hands of the family, where it belongs."

Upson just nodded and lit a pipe.

"I don't see how this is anything *but* good news," Tunstall said.

Upson took a long puff and exhaled the smoke to the ceiling.

"Before, the money was an abstract concept. A line on a ledger two thousand miles away. But the abstract has now become reality. A check is on its way to you. So it seems to me placing ten grand in your hands—money that Mr. Murphy desperately needs—puts your life in more danger than if you never took hold of a dime."

McSween would go on to protest, to say even L.G. Murphy wouldn't stoop so low as to maim them over the money, especially since their dispute has been so public, that the insurance company's decision put the matter to rest once and for all.

But Tunstall went quiet and remained that way until they left Upson's house.

Tunstall and McSween walked to the jail. Rumor was Sheriff Brady had locked up a drunkard last night, and McSween and Tunstall had business with the sheriff, so they figured Brady was most likely monitoring his prisoner in the pit.

Finally, Tunstall spoke. "You think Mr. Upson's point has merit?"

McSween's mind was on the task at hand. The money being on its way was but one issue the men had to deal with. The other was keeping their promise to John Chisum. In order for them to become business partners, they had assured Chisum they would report the theft of his livestock to Sheriff Brady and help retrieve it. Now they just had to convince Brady it was in his best interest—and his duty as sheriff—to track down the offenders.

"Alex . . ."

McSween finally turned to his business partner.

"Do you think Mr. Upson's point has merit?" Tunstall asked again.

"I think Ash Upson is a worrywart."

McSween and Tunstall did find Sheriff Brady watching over the prisoner.

When Deputy Sheriff George Peppin built the jail a few years back, Lincoln was a small community with little need for holding cells. Instead, Peppin took the $3,000 and built a two-room home in which the jailer would live. And beneath one of the rooms, only accessible by a ladder that descended ten feet underground, was a dirt pit. The ceiling of the pit was nothing more than logs fastened together with rope and hardened mud. It was cold, dark, damp, and meant for only hardened criminals before their transport to proper prisons.

Yginio Salazar was just thirteen and spent his days working as a ranch hand and his nights blowing off steam dancing and playing music. The music was what had landed him in the pit.

Salazar was celebrating. He had taken a local girl out for an evening stroll, and as he worked the bow across the fiddle he sang her a love ballad that made her swoon. When their evening concluded, Salazar escorted her home to her family, kissed her hand with respect, and pledged to see her again.

Upon leaving, Salazar's heart was pumping and his mind was racing. He was already making plans of asking her to marry him and dreaming of the house he would build outside Lincoln, the children they would have, and the prosperous life they would live. Rather than go home, he stopped off at the Wortley Hotel, fiddle still in hand. As one drink turned into five, Salazar was regaling the other patrons with his plans for the future. Inebriated, he would use the fiddle as dramatic additive to his story, hoping to enrapture the bar.

"If I have to hear that strangled cat one more time . . ." Deputy Sheriff George Peppin said.

But Salazar was young, invincible, and nothing would quell his spirit that night.

Or his fiddle.

So on and on he played, improvising songs about his dear sweetheart, until Peppin could take it no more. Peppin grabbed the fiddle out of Salazar's hand and smashed it against the wall. Salazar leapt from his chair and pushed the deputy sheriff. That was all Peppin needed. He arrested Salazar for assaulting a peace officer. He dragged Salazar to jail, and rather than let him serve out his time in the adjoining room, he threw the Mexican teen into the pit. When morning came, Peppin went to sleep, and Sheriff Brady began watching over their "dangerous" prisoner.

McSween and Tunstall approached Sheriff Brady on the porch of the jail, his feet up on the railing, a cigar smoking between his fingers. Brady, somewhat sober at this early hour and still chagrinned by what he revealed to McSween on their trip to Santa Fe, was not pleased to see them.

"Sheriff, we would like you to issue an arrest warrant for Jesse Evans, Buck Morton, and the rest of the Boys," said McSween.

Brady cocked his head and spit tobacco onto the ground, close enough to McSween that it could be construed as a response.

"They have stolen two dozen head of cattle and three horses from John Chisum."

"And killed three men," Tunstall added.

"Yes, they also took the lives of three Mexicans."

Brady chuckled but let him continue.

"Mr. Chisum and his hands got a clean look at the thieves and can certify that Jesse Evans and his gang were the perpetrators. Mr. Chisum wishes to see the full strength of the law levied down on these scurrilous outlaws."

"You want me to track down Jesse Evans, Buck Morton, and a dozen other dangerous, armed men . . . and then what?" Brady asked.

"Arrest them," Tunstall answered.

"How, pray tell, do you suppose I do that? Alls I have is myself and the good Deputy Sheriff Peppin, who right now, I imagine, is in the throes of a debilitating head pain from last night."

"You took an oath to protect the people of Lincoln."

"And I start with myself."

"Fine, I will get you more men to aid in your duties," replied Tunstall. "Will four do?"

Brady thought about it. If Evans and the Boys put up a fight, no, four lousy men would not do. But if Brady did not go, word would spread throughout Lincoln that he was derelict of duty, then the rumors would start. *Brady's afraid. Brady's corrupt. Brady's not fit to be sheriff.*

"All right, you get me four men, we'll go round up Jesse and his pals."

Billy wanted to see Josie. Silver City was due west, and Billy figured he could make the trek in a day and a half, weather permitting. It had been over a year since they last spoke. He missed that connection to his blood. Billy even let himself daydream that Josie had worked his way out of the Orleans Club, stopped smoking opium, maybe even gone back to school.

Billy also figured this was a good time to put some distance between himself and Buck.

But first he needed another horse to replace the one he gave to Abigail.

As he walked La Mesilla that morning, after wishing Abigail well on her journey, he came across a lone horse tied to a hitching post. The animal was strong and majestic, its coat pure white with nary a speckle, and would easily support him on the journey. As he approached, Billy reckoned if they were hiding in the snow, the only thing that would give them away was the piercing hue of the horse's eyes. They weren't a dark brown or black, like most steeds. Instead, they were a vibrant blue.

He looked around—the post wasn't sidled up to a building or seemingly in the property of anyone. Billy unhitched the horse and rode it back to the hotel.

Billy entered to find most of the Boys eating chow. Everyone except Morton.

"Hey, Billy, you gonna bring that little filly down here so we can get a good look at her in the cold light of day?" Kit O'Keefe said, then chortled.

Shit, Billy thought. Beth was still upstairs. But he had other things to worry about. Other men.

"Anyone seen Buck?" Billy asked.

"He's gathering his things. Says he's gotta head back to Fort Sumner," Evans answered. "And, Billy . . . leave him be. He's in a mood."

Billy nodded and tiptoed upstairs and slipped into his room, where Beth was getting dressed.

"I was ready for another roll this morning. Where'd you go?" she asked.

"Couldn't sleep and didn't want to wake you," Billy said as he gathered his things.

"We have some time now . . ."

"I gotta ride out to Silver City to see my brother."

"Want company?" she teased.

"That's kind, but we have some business to discuss that wouldn't interest you."

Beth shrugged and finished pulling on her dress, then turned around for Billy to tie her up.

"You sure you don't have a few minutes?"

Billy was startled to find her hand caressing him over his

pants. He was instantly set to give in to the temptation until he heard loud banging down the hall. It had to be Buck, hungover to all hell, remembering how things ended with Abigail.

Billy stepped away from Beth, who again shrugged. "When you come back this way, feel free to find me."

He gave her a kiss on the cheek, gathered his satchel and hat, and opened the door. Billy stuck his head out to make sure Buck wasn't in the hallway. The coast clear, he headed downstairs.

"Where you going, Billy?" O'Keefe asked before Billy could reach the front door.

"Gonna ride out to Silver City for a day or two, see my brother."

"Can I come along?"

"No."

LINCOLN COUNTY, NEW MEXICO TERRITORY

Dick Brewer was clearing brush when he first saw them cresting over the hill. Three men on horseback, riding at a steady clip. Brewer wasn't an overly cautious sort, but he was no rube either. Men don't ride that fast unless it's urgent. And when something's urgent, there's a fifty-fifty chance you'll find yourself in the middle of a dustup.

He pulled his Winchester rifle from the long holster affixed to his saddle and waited. As the group neared, he relaxed and set the rifle down. He recognized his bosses, McSween and Tunstall. What caught him by surprise was the third man with them. Sheriff Brady.

At twenty-seven, Dick Brewer was a couple of years older than Tunstall, and he rather liked the Englishman. He found Tunstall's manners and posh demeanor a welcome respite from the uncivilized and crude folks in Lincoln. Not that Brewer himself was any dandy.

Brewer was born in Vermont, and like many Americans he slowly migrated west. By twenty-two, he found himself in the New Mexico Territory and began his life as a farmer. He was successful at first, able to produce enough crops to sell to Murphy & Co., but one bad season wiped away what little fortune he'd built, and Brewer was forced to sell his property.

That's when he met Tunstall.

Tunstall was new to the territory and needed disciplined, knowledgeable hands to work his ranch. Brewer proved himself adept and was soon made foreman, overseeing all the other employees. It didn't hurt Brewer was known for being levelheaded, fair, and skilled with the iron.

"Dick, Sheriff Brady needs your help," Tunstall opened.

Brewer noticed Sheriff Brady wasn't the one asking. Brady simply squinted into the sun and awaited a response.

Brewer was skeptical. He knew Brady was a close friend of L.G. Murphy and often exerted his legal authority to further the House's bottom line. Brewer had been eating supper at Francisco Zamora's home when Brady and eight armed men stormed the house, demanding lease money Murphy claimed he was owed. It was, of course, bullshit. Murphy had no claim over Zamora's land, which had been purchased directly from the government. If it hadn't been for Brewer resting his hand on Zamora's arm under the table, Zamora would have pulled his revolver, a losing proposition when facing nine men.

But Brewer himself had never had a row or disagreement with Brady, so he listened.

"The Boys have stolen cattle and horses from John Chisum."

"That sounds like a problem for Mr. Chisum," he answered.

"Normally, you'd be right. But seeing as Mr. McSween

and myself have just entered into a business partnership with Chisum, the problem has fallen on us."

Brewer and Brady were equally surprised to hear of this new business venture, and McSween wished his partner hadn't said it in front of the sheriff.

"We need you to aid Sheriff Brady in bringing Evans and the Boys to justice."

"What kind of justice you looking for, John?"

"The court of law kind. The kind with due process. This is not an execution."

Well, that's good, Brewer thought. The only chance of anyone coming out alive was the prospect of Evans having his day in court.

"Then what?"

"He stands trial and goes to jail for his crimes."

Brewer looked McSween in the eyes, then Tunstall. They were serious. He turned to Brady, but the sheriff was looking at the ground.

"You have reservations?" Tunstall asked.

"I work for you, John. I follow orders. But it seems to me that even if we get Jesse into the pit and put him on trial, no judge in Lincoln County is gonna convict him."

"Why not?"

"You want to tell him, Sheriff, or should I?"

Sheriff Brady glared at Brewer, but he answered. "District Attorney Rynerson is sympathetic to the Murphy-Dolan faction."

"He's in their goddamn pocket," replied Brewer.

"And the Boys are the strength of that faction. If they stole cattle from Chisum—or from you, I suppose—it weren't on a whim. It wasn't in the *hopes* they'd be able to lay off the live-stock with an unsuspecting buyer. They stole knowing very well Murphy would pay them handsomely. Even if Rynerson decides to try Evans and the Boys, it's only because he knows Judge Bristol will never convict."

Tunstall got quiet as he mulled their options. McSween dug his heels in.

"We made a promise to Chisum. A promise we intend to keep. If the system is corrupt and refuses to put these men in jail, then that's on the system. But at least the people of Lincoln will be able to see the injustice with their own eyes."

"Like I said, I work for you," Brewer replied.

Brewer led McSween, Tunstall, and Sheriff Brady to the next ranch over, owned by two best friends, Josiah "Doc" Scurlock and Charlie Bowdre.

Scurlock and Bowdre had met in Arizona a few years back and opened a cheese factory on the Gila River, but that soon went under. After that, they moved to the New Mexico Territory to try their hand at ranching. Not knowing anyone, or how things in the territory worked, they, too, purchased their land from L.G. Murphy, quickly finding themselves under the thumb of the House. But they put their backs into it, eventually paying off the debt, and now things were looking up.

Despite their jovial nature, the two were serious men when it counted. Scurlock, who earned his nickname "Doc" after studying medicine in New Orleans, had been involved in a number of shootouts throughout Texas, Mexico, and the territory. Five years Scurlock's junior, Bowdre was a simpler man but no less ready for a fight. The two soon garnered a reputation as guns for hire.

Now, Brewer stood before them asking for help capturing the Boys.

Bowdre was in.

Scurlock was more wary. He had worked for Chisum

transporting cattle from Texas to the territory, but after two instances of being attacked by Comanche—in which both times his riding companion had been killed—Scurlock quit. Chisum, incensed, refused to pay Doc for services rendered, so Doc stole three horses, a saddle, and a rifle, and rode out for Arizona. Chisum sent men after him, but when they caught up to Scurlock, Doc explained why he'd stolen the goods. The posse, who knew what a miser Chisum was, let him be.

"Why would I risk my life to help Chisum?" Doc said.

"Because I'm asking. As a friend," Brewer said. "Me and Mr. Tunstall and Mr. McSween."

Scurlock looked sideways at Sheriff Brady, lingering in the back, not saying much.

"And him?"

"Bygones be bygones, Doc. That's all in the past," Brady muttered.

Doc still remembered Sheriff Brady locking him in the pit on some minimal charge, and the three days Brady and Deputy Sheriff Peppin spent tormenting and harassing him, throwing horseshit on him, feeding him pig slop, and cackling all the while. But Brady was still the sheriff, and as long as he was, and as long as he had the backing of the House and the Santa Fe Ring, there weren't much Doc could do about it. His revenge would have to wait.

"All right, Dick, since it's you asking . . ."

BLACK RANGE MOUNTAINS

GRANT COUNTY, NEW MEXICO TERRITORY

Billy was more than halfway to Silver City when he decided to camp for the night. He had passed out of the Mescalero Apache territory of New Mexico, but that just meant he had to be mindful of any Chiricahua and Mimbreño. He didn't much know the difference between the three tribes, only that he didn't want to find out.

Billy located a small cutout on the edge of the Black Range Mountains, a spot he was certain no one could stumble across, and built a fire. He thought of the delicious food he'd eat in Silver City. Hell, maybe he'd even stop by Mrs. Brown's, the woman who housed him after his mother passed, to say hello. Billy eventually drifted off to sleep, warmed by the fire and the hope of seeing his little brother the next day.

That night, Billy had the same recurring dream he'd had since childhood.

Riding that mare through the field, the bright sun beaming down warmly on his face, the smell of fresh grass. And, as always, the dense forest just beyond, the canopy of trees no light could penetrate. The gust of wind, the treetops beginning to sway. And from the rustling of the forest, the faint song, "Silver Thread Among the Gold," sung by schoolchildren.

> Darling, I am growing old,
> Silver threads among the gold,
> Shine upon my brow today,
> Life is fading fast away.

The horse picks up speed, racing toward the thick trees. Billy shouts and tugs and pulls, but the horse doesn't slow. What's beyond the sunlit field? What awaits him in the dark, damp forest? Billy tries to bail off the saddle, but the horse sprints faster and faster . . .

> But, my darling, you will be,
> Always young and fair to me,

Yes, my darling, you will be
Always young and fair to me.

*This time he doesn't wake when reaching the trees. The branches
and thorns slice and cut Billy's hands, his arms, his legs, his face. He
feels blood trickling from his rib cage, warm and sticky. A thunderous
blow rattles his side, sending shooting pain throughout his body—*

Billy bolted upright, holding his midsection. He looked up just
in time to see the boot slam into his rib cage again, and he dou-
bled over, sure he was going to vomit.

Laughter. Sinister. Buck Morton sneering down at him. Jesse
Evans just behind Buck, examining the horse Billy had stolen.
The rest of the Boys standing by, watching.

"What the hell are y'all doing here, Jesse?" Billy asked.

Buck kicked him again, this time in the stomach, then bran-
dished a large hunting knife. Billy had time to scope the sharp
serrated blade just before it was put to his throat.

"That horse ain't yours," Buck said.

"Hell, none of our horses were paid for outright," Billy responded.

"But this horse belonged to a friend of ours, Sheriff Barela.
Worse, it was his daughter's mare. The sheriff is quite fond of
his little girl. Pained him to see her crying all morning that her
best friend was stolen."

"I didn't know. Honest."

Mariano Barela was the sheriff of Doña Ana County and a
friend of L.G. Murphy's. The type of friend Murphy could call
upon to do his bidding. And those types of friends had protection from thieves and rustlers.

Billy had broken the most important rule: do not steal from
the House.

"I'll take her back. Apologize to Sheriff Barela. And his daughter. Hell, it'll probably even make him a hero in her eyes."

Billy looked to Evans, who remained impossible to read. Buck, on the other hand, was more transparent than a freshly cleaned window.

"You the type of cocky sumbitch who thinks the rules don't apply to him. That he's special. That he can do whatever he wants with no repercussions."

Buck leaned down, close enough for only Billy to hear. "I know what you did, Billy. Tellin' my girl she's too good for me. Runnin' her off. I know you stuck it in her too."

Buck backhanded him, and Billy felt his lip swell instantly. He could taste the blood on the front of his teeth. Billy knew he was at a disadvantage prostrated on the ground and worked to get to his feet. Buck didn't make it easy, but Billy pushed past him and stood. He finally got a good look at the rest of the gang. There was menace in their eyes.

"Damn, you scared me good, Buck," Billy said as he brushed himself off. He took a step to move past, but Buck blocked his path.

"Jesus, can't a guy relieve himself first thing? I practically soiled my britches I was so startled." Buck didn't move. "You ain't the type that likes to watch another man shit, is you?"

"Fine, but you go over there." Buck pointed in the direction opposite the horse, not wanting Billy to hop on the mare and make a run for it.

"Ignore what you hear. It's gonna be like the devil himself is coming out of me," Billy said, then disappeared behind a large boulder.

After a moment, O'Keefe said, "Probably had it runnin' down his leg."

Buck looked at Evans, who had taken a seat to warm himself by the dying fire.

"I'm done with this little cuss, Jesse."

"Do what you want with the kid. We just gotta get the horse back by sundown."

"Better righten up your britches, Billy." Buck cocked his pistol and rounded the corner behind the boulder, ready to finally put an end to the Kid once and for all.

But Billy was gone.

Chapter 13

LINCOLN COUNTY, NEW MEXICO TERRITORY

"What if he refuses?"

James Dolan paced the office on the second floor of Murphy & Co. while Riley leaned on the windowsill, his leg vibrating anxiously.

Only L.G. Murphy, sitting behind his desk, was calm.

"We'll make him see how it's in the best interest of all concerned parties, especially himself, to acquiesce," Murphy responded.

This was a pivotal moment for Murphy & Co. Revenue was down, the community was grumbling about how the House conducted business, and the Spiegelberg brothers were growing impatient for their $10,000.

The final stressor was coming from Santa Fe, where Thomas "Boss" Catron, head of the ring, had intimated he was considering washing his hands of the House altogether. The House was but just one spoke in the wheel of the Santa Fe Ring, and the kickbacks to Catron had been getting lighter and lighter until this month, when nothing was sent his way at all. Catron had the finances, power, and influence to take over the business, and there'd be nothing Murphy, Dolan, or Riley could do.

Everything rested on this meeting, if the man even showed.

Just as the clock struck noon, there was a knock on the door. Charles Fritz, older brother to Murphy's deceased business partner Emil, entered meekly, holding his hat.

"Charles, please, have a seat." Murphy smiled warmly. Charles did as was requested. "We are sure this is all painfully difficult for you and your family, and we believe we have a way for you to recoup your money in a more timely manner."

"Thank you for inviting me," Charles said nervously. "You were a great friend to my brother."

"I miss him every day."

"But it is my understanding that we are of opposite opinion as to who is the rightful recipient of my brother's estate, and the life insurance policy."

"Nonsense. That is McSween wedging his way into your head, trying to separate you from your brother's money."

Charles startled as Dolan moved across the room to fix himself a drink. He poured one for their guest as well, and Charles flinched again as Dolan appeared over his should to place it in his hand.

"No reason for frayed nerves. We're all friends here. Something Mr. McSween has no right to claim," Murphy said.

Charles's hand shook as he raised the glass to his lips.

"And as a friend, it is my duty—my *obligation*—to reveal McSween is swindling you."

"That would be news to me, sir."

"Which is how the snake oil salesman wants it. The less you know, the easier it will be for him to abscond with what is rightfully yours. Were you aware Mr. McSween has received an official telegram from the insurance company stating the money is to be released into his care?"

Charles was not.

"Are you aware that the money is en route to New Mexico as we speak?"

Charles was not.

"Ask yourself this: Why are you not privy to this development? How will the ten thousand dollars ever end up in your mitts if you don't even know it has arrived?"

Charles had no good answer for why his own attorney had not relayed this information. But he also couldn't see how aligning himself with Murphy, Dolan, and Riley would get him the money either.

"The local judge, Warren Bristol, is a reasonable man. A friend of ours. He will see that you are done fairly."

Charles wished he would have just stayed home, like their sister had, and forgotten all the troubles Emil had found in the New Mexico Territory. But it was too late now. There was a rising tension that would soon boil over into all-out war.

And he was plum in the thick of it.

DOÑA ANA COUNTY, NEW MEXICO TERRITORY

Billy was on foot in the middle of the desert with no water, no horse, and only the pistol he stole from Antrim to protect himself.

But he was alive.

He figured Morton and the Boys would skin west, knowing he was headed to Silver City.

Josie would have to wait.

Instead, Billy crossed the path of the rising sun and traveled east. His only saving grace was that it was October, which meant pleasant weather during the day and a brisk but manageable chill at night. But he couldn't travel on foot forever. Either fatigue, thirst, or those meaning him harm would eventually catch up.

As he walked, Billy kept his mind occupied with memories of brighter days, wondering what Isadora and Abigail were up to at that moment. If he made it back, he would call on Isadora and convince her father his intentions were good. He had no plans to ask for her hand in marriage, at least not yet, but he wanted her father to see he respected Isadora and would treat her well.

Not like how his stepfather, William Antrim, had done Mama at the end.

Billy's mind couldn't help but wander back to those early days, when things were simpler, when he had his family. But any thoughts of his mother inevitably veered into memories of her death. The once vibrant woman who became a shell of herself, who squeezed his hand and told him, "Above all else, my sweet boy, be good. Be kind," then succumbed to the other side.

It still enraged him how Antrim had behaved in her dying days, not being there as she gasped her last breath, not coming back for the funeral. He couldn't imagine treating a woman that way, especially not someone as lovely as his mother, Catherine.

Billy was fourteen the first time he realized he had a kinship with women. It wasn't simply carnal—it went deeper than sins of the flesh.

It was spiritual.

A few days after his mother's passing, Billy and Josie started the new school year. Billy was staying at Mrs. Brown's, and she thought it would be good for the boy to socialize, learn, and take his mind off things.

Mary Richards had just moved to Silver City. Billy was

enraptured with the twenty-five-year-old teacher who could speak four languages, write beautifully, and was as kind as the day is long.

"Me and Miss Richards, we're related," Billy began to tell his friends.

"You ain't related," fired back his classmate Leonard.

"You ever met someone else who's ambidexterious?"

"Ambi-what?"

"We can both do things equally with either hand," Billy said, then he threw a rock into a horse trough across the street, some twenty yards away.

"That don't prove nothing."

Billy picked up another rock and this time hurled it left-handed into the same trough.

"Ambidex*trous*," Miss Richards laughed as Billy recounted the story to her one day after school. Billy blushed and pulled freshly picked chrysanthemums from behind his back.

"Most students bring an apple."

"I'm not like most, I suppose," Billy answered.

"I suppose you're not."

Mary Richards sensed he was still reeling from Catherine's passing, and as someone who had also lost both her parents at a young age, she was sympathetic.

"They're lovely. Thank you," she said as she took the flowers. "Now how is the book report coming along?"

Billy kicked one of his heels and looked at the wooden floor of the one-room schoolhouse.

"It's a hard one, Miss Richards."

"Perhaps I can help. What are you struggling with?"

"I don't know. The sum of it?"

"Do you have the book with you?"

"No, I left it in my room."

"Why don't you go get it and come back?"

"I have my chores to do around Mrs. Brown's place. But maybe after that?"

Miss Richards thought for a moment, then said, "Yes, I have some time this evening to help you. Come by my home after supper."

Billy practically skipped out of the schoolhouse.

That evening, after he had helped clear the table and wash plates, Billy disappeared into his room. He combed his hair, his clothes were clean and neatly pressed, and he even shined his shoes.

"Well, don't you look like a gentleman," Mrs. Brown said, approvingly.

"Miss Richards is going to help me with my assignment," Billy replied.

Mrs. Brown smiled, understanding he had a schoolboy crush, and let him go.

Billy knocked on the door, and Miss Richards answered. She stepped out onto the porch and sat on the bench, patting the seat next to her for Billy.

"Now show me what you're having trouble with," she said. But as they went over the book, it became clear to her that not only had Billy understood the work, he had already finished the assignment. She closed the book and looked at him.

"I know these last few weeks have been difficult," she said softly.

"I'm doing all right. I miss Mama, but I got Josie to worry about." He tried to stifle the rock-hard lump that formed in his throat any time he spoke of his mother.

"Are you staying on track? Are you minding your manners and doing what Mrs. Brown asks of you?"

"I am."

"Henry . . ."

"Most of the time."

"I hear things, you know. I don't mean to, but I do."

"What sorts of things?"

"Like you palling around with Sombrero Jack Schaffer."

"He's just a friend. I don't get into no trouble with him though."

A look of concern crossed her face. "You have a special quality about you," she continued. "You're a natural leader. But be careful. What is special can be used to excel or it can be used to pull us down an unholy path. Do you understand?"

"I think so," he replied. "I promise to always do good and try my best."

Miss Richards smiled and tapped the book on his lap.

"Very well, then. And you don't need to make excuses to get a word with me. If you ever need to talk, I'm always here."

Billy nodded.

"Now you should get on back before Mrs. Brown starts to worry."

Billy stood to leave and looked back just as Miss Richards opened the door to reenter her home. He spotted the chrysanthemums arranged neatly in a glass vase on her dining table. He smiled and bounded down the porch steps, his heart racing with the joy of seeing her again tomorrow in school.

But that evening he hid the blankets and guns for Sombrero Jack, and everything changed. Billy wondered if Miss Richards ever thought about him. He wondered if she missed their talks, of just being in each other's presence, as much as he did.

He wondered if he had disappointed her.

Billy's mouth was dry, dryer than it had ever been. His throat and lungs stung from the sand that had swirled its way into his mouth. His legs were heavy and sore, and his strides were short-ening. He was unsure how far it was to the next town—if there even was a next town—and if he'd reach it before his body gave out and he was reunited with his mother.

Then he saw the trickle.

A sliver of water, no more than the width of a string, moving slowly in a crevice of the arid land. He knew when water was moving it had somewhere to go.

Billy followed the trickle for another hour before coming upon a tiny pond at the base of the mountain. Night was en-croaching and soon the temperature would drop, but the only thing on Billy's mind was quenching his thirst.

He scooped the water into his mouth, the liquid salvation running down his throat, his face, his arms. He had never been so happy in his life. When he'd had his fill, he nestled himself against a boulder and pulled his coat tight to protect from the oncoming cold.

It took another half hour for Billy's satiation to transform into concern, then another fifteen minutes for it to turn into outright terror.

His stomach began to ache. Aching gave way to a sharp pain. His vision blurred. He tried to stand but stumbled over, cushioning the fall against a rock with his face.

Agua mala.

The water was contaminated.

He was going to die.

As he lay face down in the dirt, unable to move, he once again thought of his mother and brother. Poor Josie. He'd be all alone in this world.

And he'd probably never even know Billy had passed.

Just before he lost consciousness, Billy felt a hand reach down and grab him violently by the hair. *So that's how the reaper comes*, he thought. Not with a gentle ushering off this mortal coil but savagely ripping his soul into eternity.

The last thought he had before his world went dark was to wonder which great beyond would be his final destination.

BECKWITH RANCH

LINCOLN COUNTY, NEW MEXICO TERRITORY

When the Boys arrived at Beckwith's ranch, Buck Morton was still steaming. How could that little pissant have slipped their grasp? Morton blamed Billy for Abigail's departure. He blamed Billy for getting them in hot water with Sheriff Barela.

But mostly, he was just a mean bastard who hated the Kid.

Bob Beckwith had put his stakes down in the Seven Rivers area of southeast New Mexico and spent the last decade warding off Mescalero Apache and Mexicans from Chihuahua who ventured north. He couldn't defend his ranch alone, so he had turned to the Santa Fe Ring for help. Beckwith's ranch became a refuge for the Boys, as well as the Seven Rivers Warriors and the Kinney Gang.

As the Boys ate dinner, they heard a rustling outside.

Horses and men.

Frank Baker rose and cracked the door just enough to get a look at Dick Brewer, Doc Scurlock, Charlie Bowdre, and four others settling in, surrounding the house.

"Looks like Brewer and some fellas mean us harm. And Brady's with 'em."

Sheriff Brady trailed behind the posse, less enthusiastic about the mission.

Buck Morton rose from his chair and pulled his pistols. If he couldn't kill Billy, these McSween-Tunstall sympathizers would have to do. The wisecracking Kit O'Keefe followed suit, ready to prove himself to the older men.

"No need for a fight," yelled Sheriff Brady. "Come peacefully and we won't shoot."

The volley that ensued was expected. The posse returned fire, tearing up the broad side of the house and shattering the windows.

When there was a break in the shooting, Evans tried to reason with them.

"We got a woman in here. Lady Beckwith."

"Then you shoulda come peacefully!" responded Scurlock.

More shooting commenced, both sides firing wildly, no one in any serious jeopardy.

Then Kit O'Keefe, hungry since he didn't get to finish his dinner, shuffled over to the kitchen, passing by the open window. He stayed low to the ground but erred in believing he had completely crossed out of harm's way when he stood.

Scurlock's shot exploded O'Keefe's face and skull into fragments, some of which splattered on Beckwith and his wife, who let out a blood-curdling scream.

"Enough is enough," called out Brewer. "You ain't got nowhere to go. Lay down your rifles and come outside, and we promise there'll be no more death today."

"How do we know we can trust you?" Evans asked.

"Because I ain't a thief, and I sure as hell ain't no liar."

Evans and the Boys still weren't convinced.

"We'll make sure you get a fair hearing in front of Judge Bristol," said Brady.

A minute later the door opened, and a half dozen men came out with their hands up.

DOÑA ANA COUNTY, NEW MEXICO TERRITORY

Billy's eyes opened slightly, or so he thought. Everything was pitch-black. He suspected this was the afterlife—all-consuming darkness, eternally. His stomach still ached like hell. He was weak. He was famished. And he had the impression he had discharged his bowels.

Maybe that's hell too, he thought. *A constant state of shitting yourself.*

He heard a shuffling but was still unable to see. Then a figure leaned within inches of his face. It had long, black hair, high cheekbones, and a square jaw. But Billy was fixated on the eyes. Piercing brown, they had seen death but not cowered in the face of it.

An Apache.

The Apache grunted, and as he stepped away Billy caught the glint of a hatchet in his hand.

Then he disappeared back into the darkness.

LINCOLN

LINCOLN COUNTY, NEW MEXICO TERRITORY

Alexander McSween was furious. He'd been blindsided, and now everything he and Tunstall were building was in jeopardy.

"It's okay, Alex," Tunstall said. "I can write home for more capital."

"It's the principal, John. The goddamn principal."

McSween had just come from court. Judge Bristol began the hearing by asking if Charles had anything to add, and Emil Fritz's brother rose and said, "If it pleases Your Honor, I request that the proceeds from my brother's life insurance policy be turned directly over to me, as soon as readily available."

A reasonable request on its surface, but McSween saw through the statement—his client was turning on him.

Of course he intended to turn the money over to Fritz . . . as soon as McSween had recouped expenses for his time and effort. McSween was $1,000 in the hole—monies he paid the Spiegelberg brothers to drop *their* claim on the insurance payout—not to mention the cost of traveling to New York, a week's stay in a hotel, and journeying back to Lincoln.

"If it pleases the court," McSween responded, "I'm afraid if the payout winds up first in the hands of Mr. Fritz he'll turn that money over to Mr. Murphy and Mr. Dolan, and I will not be compensated for my time and expenses. I am owed twenty-five hundred dollars."

Judge Bristol was unmoved. "Mr. McSween, you have argued before this court that the money rightfully belongs to Mr. Fritz."

"Yes, Your Honor, but—"

"And now that you won your argument, you claim the money belongs to you."

"The largest stake in the policy will, of course, be distributed to Mr. Fritz. But the law is my profession, and my services are not free."

"Is it not true you have another venture, in addition to your legal practice?"

McSween hesitated. So that's what this was all about—his new business with Tunstall, their store opening in a few days, the threat to Murphy and Dolan.

"Mr. McSween, it seems you are attempting to have it two ways, a fact this court finds troubling. It is so ruled that when the monies arrive, they are to be handed over to Mr. Fritz, in their entirety, for him to do with as he sees fit."

And that was it.

McSween had walked into court with Charles Fritz at his side, but by the time they left, Charles was shaking hands and slapping backs with L.G. Murphy and James Dolan.

DOÑA ANA COUNTY, NEW MEXICO TERRITORY

Billy snapped upright, struggling to untangle the blankets and coverings that had been laid over him. He stumbled and fell, his legs weak from inactivity. As he lay on the hard ground, his eyes adjusted to the darkness . . .

He was inside a wickiup.

There was a man in the corner, glaring at him. The same man from his dream of death.

Still holding the hatchet.

The man stood and walked toward Billy with purpose. Billy scuttled backward, but the Apache closed fast. He grabbed Billy and threw him roughly back onto the blankets. The Apache gestured intensely with the hatchet, then exited the wickiup.

Billy felt for his gun, but it wasn't there. His eyes darted around the room, looking for anything he could use as a weapon, but all he had at his disposal were blankets and a pail with a few drops of water left in it. Billy wrapped one of the thinner blankets around his hand the way a rider wraps the reins tightly when on a bronco.

The flap to the wickiup opened and the Apache man re-entered.

"I don't want to hurt you, but I'll defend myself if I have to," Billy said, taking a weak pugilistic stance.

Then the flap opened again and in came another man.

"Bodaway?"

But neither Bodaway nor the other Apache spoke English.

"Victorio," Bodaway said, gesturing at the other man.

Billy understood. He was face-to-face with Victorio, the great Mescalero Apache warrior, the man who had fled the constraints of the reservation and was now leading raids against white settlements in an effort to reclaim their land.

Over the next hour, through symbols and sketches in the dirt, Billy learned what had happened.

He had drank poisonous water and was indeed on death's doorstep. Victorio found him and intended on letting him rot in the earth. But Bodaway, who had left Lolotea and her mother on the reservation so he could take up arms against the US Army, the Mexicans, and anyone else who terrorized their people, had recognized the Kid. Bodaway brought Billy to a healer, who mixed a concoction that drove the poisonous water out and saved his life.

Explains why I shit myself, Billy thought.

The next morning, they gave him a horse, which he rode north, up the same Pecos River as Brewer's posse and the Boys, headed for Lincoln.

Victorio didn't understand why Bodaway cared so much about this white boy.

"That's because you don't have a daughter."

Part II

Chapter 14

October 1877

The last missing piece was the signage. Tunstall had wanted to call their business "McSween & Tunstall Co.," but Alexander had argued against it. It was one thing for the citizens of Lincoln to visit a competing store to the House. It was an entirely other matter if that competing business was named after McSween, now a known enemy to Murphy, Dolan, and Riley. "Tunstall & Co." would be cleaner.

Tunstall heard the ruckus before he saw it. A whispering that rolled like a wave through Lincoln. Sheriff Brady and the posse had captured Evans, Buck Morton, and the rest of the Boys.

Brady escorted the prisoners to the jail. To the pit.

"I'll be back in an hour to feed you supper," Brady said before he left.

Evans took a seat against the wall, closed his eyes, and smiled.

"What are you grinning for, Jesse?" Buck said. He was still

angry they'd surrendered so easily back at Beckwith ranch. He didn't think much of Brewer, Scurlock, or Bowdre and reckoned they could've won that row. Now here they were, stuck in the pit, heading to court the next day, their lives on the line.

"You worry too much, Buck."

"Seems we got good reason to worry. Last time I checked, rustling was a hanging offense. And Chisum won't rest till we're strung up."

"Chisum ain't gonna do shit. He can't."

"How do you figure?" Buck asked, his ire rising.

"What'd Brady say to us?"

"Alls I heard is we're gonna have to go before the judge, which is a helluva lot worse than what I was planning on doing tomorrow."

"*'We'll take you in and make sure you get a fair hearing in front of Judge Bristol.'*"

"So what?" Buck asked.

"Buck, you dumb rube. Who do you think got Bristol appointed judge? Catron. And you do know who Boss Catron is, right?"

"Everybody knows Catron."

"You think the ring is gonna let us waste away in jail or swing from our necks? Naw, rest easy, boys. We'll be escaping real soon—you have my word."

"I'd like to make a toast to Dick Brewer and all of you who brought Jesse Evans and his gang to justice today. Lincoln is safer on account of you, and I am in your debt."

Tunstall was in the mood to celebrate. He was holding a small party at the Wortley Hotel, consisting of McSween, Scurlock, Bowdre, and the other posse members. The only one not present was Brewer, who wasn't one for revelry and wanted to get back to his ranch. Sheriff Brady was invited to join but instead chose to spend his evening at another table, with Deputy Sheriff Peppin and a few members of the House.

"What's Tunstall care about Chisum livestock?" Scurlock whispered to Bowdre.

Bowdre shrugged.

Scurlock couldn't wrap his head around why Tunstall kept toasting them every new round. He wasn't privy to the fact that this arrest solidified Tunstall and McSween's deal with Chisum, that it was a great boon for their soon-to-open company. Instead, Scurlock eyed Brady across the room, sullenly drowning himself in liquor.

"What's stuck in his craw, you think?" Scurlock asked.

"Ain't always a problem, Doc," Bowdre replied. "Can't something good just be?"

But Scurlock kept watching Brady. The more Tunstall toasted Brewer and the posse, the angrier Brady got. Brady was in a tough spot. On the one hand, he went along reluctantly, not wanting to cross Murphy, Dolan, and the House. On the other hand, he was the goddamn sheriff, the de facto leader of the posse, and he's the one who convinced Evans to come out peacefully before anyone else got hurt.

And now Tunstall was giving Brewer all the credit.

Another round for the table and again Tunstall, who was good and wet, raised his glass. By now even McSween had come to realize Brady was fuming.

"John, perhaps we've had enough toasts for one evening."

"Nonsense, Alex. The boys here did a remarkable job and should be treated as conquering heroes and carried through the streets of Lincoln!"

"You son of a bitch, who the hell do you think you are?" Brady slurred as he stood and stumbled over a chair on his way to their table. "I'm the goddamn sheriff."

"If it were up to you, *Sheriff*, Evans and his gang would still be roaming free, terrorizing the good citizens of Lincoln County."

"You saying I been derelict of duty?"

"I'm saying you're a drunken fool, and the only reason those thieves are rotting in the pit is because of good men like these here."

Brady knocked Tunstall's glass away, sending it smashing to the floor.

"You're simply proving my point. A man of the law should be above reproach."

"John," McSween interjected, but Tunstall didn't heed his partner's warning.

"A sheriff should be the protector of peace, not a bagman for the corrupt," Tunstall continued.

Sheriff Brady reached for his gun, and it was only due to intoxication that he struggled to pull it from his holster, giving McSween enough time to wrap his arms in place.

"Sheriff, he's drunk. He's new to Lincoln—he doesn't know the way things work."

"I've been here long enough to see exactly how things work," Tunstall countered. "William Brady, sheriff of this great Lincoln County, intends me harm. Not for any law I've broken or violation I've committed but simply because I dared to call out his failings."

Brady struggled to free himself of McSween's grasp, but by now the other Tunstall men were holding the sheriff as well. McSween knew if Brady got a hand on his pistol that would be the end of John Tunstall . . . and their business.

"Sheriff, please, I implore you. A lawman can't gun down a citizen over an insult. You'll be thrown in the pit with the Boys."

Brady thought for a moment, then relaxed.

"All right, gentlemen, I think that's enough for one evening,"

McSween said to the rest of their group. "Let's all go home and sleep it off."

As Tunstall turned for the door, Brady stepped in his way.

"Maybe as sheriff I can't cut you down right here. But I won't be sheriff forever."

RIO RUIDOSO RANCH

LINCOLN COUNTY, NEW MEXICO TERRITORY

Billy arrived at the Rio Ruidoso Ranch, right on the river, just outside Lincoln. He was thirsty, hungry, and looking for work.

Rio Ruidoso was owned by a trio of cousins: George and Frank Coe and Ab Saunders.

Billy climbed from his horse and removed his hat. "I'm not here for a handout, sirs, but I'd be much obliged if you could help me. I have experience ranching, and I'm good with livestock."

Frank Coe and Ab Saunders, who were less than two weeks apart in age, looked at the rider skeptically. George Coe was the youngest of the group, only a few years older than Billy.

"Well, we don't have much in the way of employment, but how about a hot meal?"

After a dinner of pheasant and potatoes, Billy was stuffed. He hadn't eaten this well in months and had forgotten what it was like to be so full your body slumps into a state of blissful fatigue. The cousins had spent the evening trading stories of their upbringing, regaling each other with tales of shootouts that they'd all heard time and time before.

Billy was enraptured.

George Coe and Ab Saunders had grown up near each other in Iowa, and when their cousin from "back east" joined, the three decided to migrate to the New Mexico Territory. They had heard of the cattle drives and individualism and believed themselves to be the next "John fuckin' Chisum," as George recounted. They spent time working various ranches around Fort Stanton, but it took them half a decade to build up enough capital and the right relationships to lease their own plot. To help make ends meet, they also offered themselves as guns for hire, aiding posses in tracking down rustlers and providing whatever justice they deemed fit. Rumor had it they had been with Scurlock and Bowdre when Jesus Largo was pulled from his jail cell and hanged. Some swore it was just Doc and Charlie. The cousins would never say.

"We could use another hand, at least for a little while, till you get on your feet," George said to Billy.

"I appreciate that. You'll find me a diligent worker and of great value."

"It's hard labor," Frank said, looking the Kid over. "Requires a deal of strength."

"I ain't big, but I got a lot of fight in me," Billy replied as he licked his fingers clean.

Before Ab could offer his own assessment, a voice called out from the night.

"You scoundrel Coes, get your asses out here and fight like men!"

George grabbed his pistol and went to the door. Instead of opening it, he bellowed out a response. "Give it your best shot! We got a dozen in here, all skilled with the iron. You'll never take us alive!"

Billy's back stiffened, and he reached for his revolver.

"All right. We're coming in, and we're coming in hot!"

And with that, the door kicked opened. Billy dove behind his chair, pistol raised. The only thing that stopped him from firing was the laughter.

"Whoa," Scurlock said as he put his gun away. Bowdre followed Scurlock in, cackling.

"Billy, this skinny blond son of a bitch is Josiah 'Doc' Scurlock. This other fella with the funny mustache, that's Charlie Bowdre. They own the ranch next door, and while they ain't exactly nothing to look at, they're all right."

Billy holstered his gun and shook hands with the very men who would pull him into the Lincoln County War.

LINCOLN

LINCOLN COUNTY, NEW MEXICO TERRITORY

John Tunstall blew out the lantern, then he and his ranch foreman, Dick Brewer, locked up the store. It was late, they were tired, and tomorrow was the big day. Tunstall & Co. would finally open to the public.

They headed east down Main Street, Tunstall taking in his new hometown. He had come a long way, but he felt firmly in his gut this would be where he prospered.

As they rode by the jail, they heard voices inside. The men in the pit.

"Let's stop and have a word."

"There's nothing to be gained from that, John," Brewer replied.

"Perhaps I can reason with them—make them see it is disadvantageous to be at each other's throats."

Tunstall had grown up with a privilege that made him naive, and when a question gnawed at his psyche, he did his best to get answers.

"Deputy, would you mind if I had a word with the prisoners?" Tunstall said to Peppin.

"Of course. I'm sure they'd be happy to hear from you," he

replied. Peppin was irked he'd been woken from his slumber and thought putting this English newcomer in front of the Boys would at least provide some entertainment.

Tunstall and Brewer walked into the adjacent room and looked down at Evans, Buck, and the rest in the pit. They were cramped but making do.

"Mr. Evans, I hope you find yourself comfortable," Tunstall said.

"Like a warm cooch," Evans responded. His smile was unnerving.

"I've come to set aside our differences. It is doing neither one of us any good."

"We have differences?" Evans asked. "Seems I'm accused of stealing *John Chisum's* horses. How's that involve you?"

"I've heard rumors you are opposed to my new business venture. I just wish to be unencumbered and let the market decide who succeeds and fails."

"What's your venture got to do with a simple rancher like me?" Evans said, getting a chuckle out of the other Boys. "But from my view, you're sitting awfully pretty. Of course, things in Lincoln have a tendency to change faster than the weather."

"Hey, Dicky," Buck Morton crowed at Brewer. "You got any whiskey?"

"I'm plum out, Buck. You might find some on the end of Evans's prick though."

"Richard, please," said Tunstall. "There is no need for vulgarities or taunts. We all want the same thing—to be able to operate our business and provide for our families without fear of interdiction. Isn't that right, Mr. Evans?"

"Oh lordy, it sure is, Mr. Tunstall," Evans mocked. "I's just trying to provide for my kinfolk, build a nice life for myself and my wifey, and serve the Lord our God and savior."

Tunstall pressed on, hoping he could reach Evans and come to a truce. "If you can inform us as to the location of the livestock you stole from John Chisum, I can perhaps testify on your behalf and garner leniency from the judge."

Brewer mentally shook his head. Tunstall was operating by foreign rules of resolution. He didn't get how things worked in America, and he certainly didn't understand New Mexico.

"You'd do that for us, kind sir?" Evans responded. "You'd get us a lighter sentence, so maybe we would only spend five to ten years in prison? Could you make sure we get fresh lemonade delivered to our cells every day? If you can promise that, maybe I can recollect what happened to Chisum's cattle."

"Let's go," Brewer said to Tunstall.

"Wait, I remember what we did with 'em," Buck chimed in. "We was coming out of church and saw the priest was in need, so we tithed him the livestock. Think he was gonna slaughter them as a sacrifice to God. We was all too happy to help."

"No, that ain't right," said Frank Baker. "We took 'em down to ol' Mexico, 'member? Never made it though. Damn things drowned in the Rio. Guess we didn't get the water horses."

"John . . ." Brewer urged again, and this time Tunstall gave up.

As they left, the barbs and snickering continued from the pit, the Boys floating more theories as to what happened to Chisum's steeds.

RIO RUIDOSO RANCH
LINCOLN COUNTY, NEW MEXICO TERRITORY

It was late as Billy sat and listened to Scurlock and Bowdre filling in the Coe cousins. They left the front door cracked to get a draft of the cool breeze. Billy was intimately familiar with the men Scurlock and Bowdre were describing, but it would have done him no good to weigh in.

Especially since he rode with the Boys when they stole Chisum's horses.

"We shot it out with Evans and Morton, bullets whizzing past our heads. But the thieves gave up when one of their own was felled."

"Who got it?" Billy asked, hoping beyond hope it was Buck Morton.

"Some young fella, O'Keefe-something. Practically took his head clean off," replied Bowdre.

That's too bad, Billy thought. He didn't mind O'Keefe, even if the wisecracks were grating as hell.

"Where are they now?" Billy asked.

"Took them to Lincoln. Rotting away in the pit until trial."

"You get all of 'em?"

"Just a half dozen. But we got Evans. He's the meanest sonofabitch I ever encountered."

Not to Billy. To Billy, Evans was just a typical, cold outlaw. Buck Morton, on the other hand, was the devil.

And Morton was but ten miles away in the Lincoln County pit. Billy had half a mind to storm the jail and kill Buck that night. But Morton had friends, and Billy'd just end up hanged.

"Chisum wants necks in nooses," Scurlock said. "He's threatening to leave the territory if the law can't get the rustlers under control. Folks in Santa Fe need Chisum to stay, say he helps the economy. Chisum's no saint. He's just favored in comparison to the House."

Bang!

The gunshot startled everyone, and Bowdre fell out of his chair. The cousins, Scurlock, and Bowdre all looked over to see Billy, his gun still smoking.

"The hell?" Frank Coe demanded.

Billy stood, opened the front door the rest of the way, and walked outside. The other men followed. He placed a hand on Scurlock's horse and bent down by its back hoof.

"It was fixing to get your mare. One bite from a rattler like this is all it'd take," Billy said, holding up a dead, headless snake.

"How'd you even see that from where you were sitting?" George Coe asked.

"What if you shot my horse by mistake?" Scurlock added, incensed.

The thought never occurred to Billy. "Gun sorta hits where I point it. Never have to worry much about waywardness."

Everyone traded looks. This kid, Billy Bonney, was a sharpshooter.

Chapter 15

It was well past sundown when Evans heard the commotion in the other room.

The Boys were still idling away in the jail. Sheriff Brady was on watch. Once the town had gone quiet for the evening, Brady had opened the pit and allowed them to wander freely in the two rooms. They had a nice meal delivered from the Wortley Hotel and after supper had taken up playing cards, trading matchsticks as currency.

When the front door opened, Sheriff Brady made a big show of raising his hands and stepping away from the men, giving everyone a big laugh. Even the normally contemptible John Kinney, leader of the Kinney Gang and fellow associate of the ring, had to smile.

"Well, Sheriff, I believe this is where we part," Evans said.

"I'll hunt you down, if it's the last thing I do," replied Brady, garnering more chuckles.

The Boys followed their liberator Kinney out the door. They

planned to ride back to the Beckwith ranch, but Evans had unfinished business. Evans and Kinney led the Boys to Tunstall's
Rio Feliz ranch and helped themselves to a dozen horses. As
they were leaving, Morton stopped.

"It's not enough," he told the group.

The rest of the Boys watched silently as Morton pulled his
knife and went to work on one of Tunstall's horses. When he
was through, even the grizzled John Kinney had to look away.

Tunstall woke the next morning to find the steed dismem-
bered, each limb scattered throughout the porch and the head
resting against the front door. There was a chicken-scratched
note, written by Morton, stuffed in the horse's mouth: "The
entirety of Lincoln County is your pit, and we're your execu-
tioners."

RIO RUIDOSO RANCH

LINCOLN COUNTY, NEW MEXICO TERRITORY

Billy's first shot spun the tin can off the fence post. At that distance, in this high a wind, it was impressive. The fact he did it
with his off hand made it remarkable.

"How'd a scrawny kid like you get so handy with a pistol?"
George Coe asked.

Billy shrugged. "Scrawny kid like me ain't got much choice,
not in New Mexico."

Frank couldn't understand what Billy was doing out here. He
was intelligent, learned, and easy to get on with. Frank thought
the kid should be a writer or banker or politician—anything
but a piddly hand on a piddly ranch in a piddly dust patch of
New Mexico.

Billy didn't want to be a writer, banker, or politician. The only things on his mind now were avoiding Buck Morton and maybe, if the waters were calm, paying a visit to Josie.

Or Isadora. But weeks had passed since he'd seen her, and maybe she didn't feel the same way anymore.

George Coe shielded his eyes to spy the lone man approaching on horseback.

Frank Coe smiled. He got on well with Dick Brewer. But Brewer wasn't there to socialize. As Brewer talked, he kept a firm eye on the newcomer, Billy.

"I'm sorry to say I ain't here for frivolities," he said. "You Billy Bonney?"

Billy didn't know this stranger, but any time a man rode up asking if you were somebody, rarely did anything fortunate follow.

"It's all right, Billy. Dick's good people," George said.

"Yeah, I'm Bonney."

"Then I'm afraid I gotta arrest you." Brewer moved toward Billy, but before his first step hit the ground, Billy's revolver was off his hip and pointed at Brewer's chest.

"Whoa, Billy, no need for that," said Frank Coe.

"Need for it so long as he intends on taking me in," Billy said, keeping his eye on Brewer's hands, making sure they didn't so much as flinch.

"I'm sure we can work it out. Dick's a reasonable sort."

"That true, Dick? You good people? You a reasonable sort?"

"That's for others to decide," Brewer replied coolly. "But I promise you'll get a fair shake from me."

"What are the charges?" George asked.

"Got word a Billy Bonney used to ride with the Boys and played a hand in stealing livestock from John Chisum."

"That all?" George said. "Hell, half the men in the county have stolen from one another."

"That ain't all, is it, Billy?" Brewer said, looking at the Kid.

No, it wasn't. Men had died that day too.

Billy squinted, contemplating his next move. He could shoot it out with Brewer, but then he'd likely have to take down at least one of the cousins on account of them being Dick's friends, and he didn't want to do that.

Billy uncocked his revolver. "Hang on to this for me," he said, handing it over to George.

"I appreciate you being square about this," Dick said as he roped Billy's wrists.

Brewer dropped Billy off at the Lincoln County jail and was met by Sheriff Brady. Brady and Brewer loathed each other, but they were both acting as officers of the law.

Billy recognized Sheriff Brady instantly. They'd met on one of the Boys' trips into Lincoln. If word got back to Evans—or worse, Buck Morton—that Billy was locked away in the pit, they'd come calling.

"Dick, I don't mean to be ungrateful, but perhaps you could find me other arrangements?"

"Should have thought of that before you went and stole Mr. Chisum's livestock."

"What evidence you got saying I did?"

It was true. The evidence was scant. Brewer had come into Lincoln the night before to deliver goods to Tunstall and after had stopped at the Wortley Hotel for a bite to eat. There he talked to a couple of townsfolk who'd heard there was a new hand out at the Coe ranch, one who fit the description given of the shootout at Chisum's place. So Brewer had gone to Sheriff Brady and asked if he'd ever heard the name William Bonney.

"The Kid?" Brady asked. "Yeah, he was hanging around Evans and them until he stole two hundred dollars, three horses, and a saddle, and rode off in the middle of the night."

Brewer suspected the story was bullshit, but it confirmed Billy Bonney had ridden with the Boys. And that meant he was most likely there that night at Chisum's.

Brewer didn't care a lick about the shootout. They'd arrested Evans and Buck Morton and the others, and the fact the Boys mysteriously escaped the Lincoln pit was of no concern to him.

Fuck John Chisum.

What did interest Brewer, though, was Billy knew the Boys' habits, where they liked to lay low, what trails they used. Which meant he probably knew where the Boys had taken the horses they stole last night from Tunstall.

Brewer figured the only way to coerce young Billy Bonney into talking was to throw him in the pit. So, for the third time in his life, Billy found himself in jail. He was scared of Evans, Morton, and the Boys learning his whereabouts, but jail itself didn't bother him.

If history had taught Billy anything, there's always an escape.

Billy spent the night in the pit. Unfortunately, Brady was drunk, in a foul mood, and bored, so he took to entertaining himself by hassling the Kid. If Billy started to nod off, a stream of liquid would rain down on his head. Billy was thankful it was just whiskey and not the bodily waste the spirit induces. If Billy tried to talk, the sheriff would drunkenly admonish him for his "thieving ways" and "bad judgment." When Billy got hungry, the sheriff was kind enough to shovel pig slop down for him to eat.

Billy sighed and moved into the far corner of the pit, in the shadows, hoping Brady would forget about him, which eventually he did.

When Billy heard snoring in the other room, he went to work.

He reached up and, quietly as he could, splintered off a piece of the wood logs used for the pit's "roof." The shard was a foot long, and he whittled one end into a sharp point to use as a weapon should Evans and Buck show. It wouldn't do much, but Billy'd be damned if he was not gonna go out fighting.

Then he focused on the shackles. He'd slipped bracelets before—much to Windy Cahill's mockery—and set to work. He just needed to get one hand free, then he could use the pick in the lining of his britches to unlock the pad on the roof of the pit.

He looped the chain in the middle of the shackles under his boots, then began to pull. His hands were chafing and turning purple. He'd have to take a break every few minutes to catch his breath and rest, then he'd get back to it. Billy could feel the iron grinding against his wrist bones, but the Lincoln black-smith's handiwork was better than Windy's.

Billy thought about quitting and letting the chips fall where they may, then he thought about how Buck Morton wouldn't be content just to shoot him. No, Buck would find a particu-larly sadistic way of extinguishing Billy's life.

Back to work he'd go, each time making more progress, but never quite able to wriggle free. He was exhausted, hungry, his eyes were stinging from the mud that had seeped down from his forehead, and he had sweat through his shirt.

But this is life or death.

He bit down on his wooden shank and gave one last ex-cruciating pull.

His left hand slipped out.

Billy had lost track of time and didn't know if it was daylight yet. He guessed not because he could still hear Sheriff Brady snoring and choking, choking and snoring, in the other room.

Billy pulled himself up and peered through the logs of the pit's roof. He couldn't see anything. He felt for the lock that kept the roof latched. Just as his hands touched the cold metal, his fingers were crushed by a boot.

"I'll shoot you myself before I let you escape," Brady said, laughing.

Billy dropped back down to the pit's floor and leaned against the wall, holding his aching hand. Brady mentioned something about breakfast being on the way, but Billy knew that just meant more slop, and he'd eaten enough shit already.

Billy hadn't slept in a few days—was it three or four?—and had grown senseless, so when he heard the arguing in the other room, he wondered if it was a figment of his imagination. Brady had gone home and the deputy sheriff was in charge, and now two men were demanding to see him. Hallucination or not, Billy grabbed hold of his wooden shard, wrapping it to his hand with a torn bandanna, and braced himself for a fight. But Jesse Evans and Buck Morton didn't appear.

Instead, it was Dick Brewer and a well-dressed dandy.

"He's just a boy, Dick." Tunstall had been expecting a more imposing figure.

"I'm seventeen," Billy said.

"He's seventeen, John," Brewer repeated. "I've heard he can handle himself too."

But Tunstall couldn't get past what he was seeing. Just a scared child, down in the pit, face caked in mud and dried sweat, eyes that haven't slept for days. He felt sorry for Billy.

"Do you know why you're here?" he asked.

"Seems y'all think I stole some cattle from Chisum," Billy replied.

"That's what got you in here, but that's not what's going to get you out."

Billy looked up curiously. "Any way I can help, I'm happy to do so, Mr. Tunstall."

"So you know who I am."

"They said he's a smart one," Brewer replied. "Clever. Quick. Not to be underestimated."

"It seems some of your friends stole a dozen of *my* horses the other night."

"I don't have any friends," Billy replied.

The statement struck Tunstall as tragically true.

"Well, some of the men you used to ride with—Jesse Evans, Buck Morton, Frank Baker—they stole from me. And I need to know where they're going."

"If I knew that, sir, you'd see me riding the other way."

"You are not part of the Boys?"

"Only rode with them a couple months. Things ended sourly, on account of them trying to kill me and all."

"Why'd they try to kill you?" Brewer asked.

"Morton thought I was involving myself with his girl."

"Were you?"

"It weren't like that. She's just a friend who was seeking my counsel."

"And what did you advise her?" Tunstall asked.

"All due respect, Mr. Tunstall, that ain't got nothing to do with your stolen horses or why I'm in this here pit."

"So you don't know where they might have taken my horses?"

"No, but I can tell you where those horses will end up though."

This had Tunstall's attention.

"I'd keep my mouth shut, Kid," Deputy Sheriff Peppin warned.

Billy ignored him. "In Murphy's and Dolan's hands, then most likely sold off to the army at Fort Stanton or to supply the Mescalero Apache Reservation."

It was just what Tunstall suspected. Billy sat quietly as

Tunstall pulled Brewer aside. A moment later, the two men came back and hovered over the pit.

"You know who put you in here?" Tunstall asked.

"You did, sir."

"You know who's going to get you out?"

"I'm hoping the answer's one in the same."

After hemming and hawing from Peppin, Tunstall and Brewer succeeded in arguing that the charges—stealing Chisum horses—were being dropped, and therefore there was no justifiable reason to hold Billy in the pit.

Brewer was apprehensive about Tunstall's leniency.

"I see something in him, Dick," Tunstall replied. "Something useful."

Tunstall could talk all he wanted and extol the Kid's promise in life, but Brewer suspected there was another reason to free Billy Bonney.

"Won't hurt that he'll owe you a debt of gratitude for freeing him neither."

Chapter 16

COE RANCH

LINCOLN COUNTY, NEW MEXICO TERRITORY

November 1877

"As promised," McSween said, smiling as he pulled the check from his case.

Charles Fritz hated the position he found himself in. It caused him stomach pains that he was convinced would grow into an ulcer or worse. But he'd come this far to see that his brother's money went to the family.

"This check is for but seven thousand five hundred dollars," he said.

"That's the payout on your brother's policy, minus expenses for my time and effort as executor and your attorney."

Charles wanted the money. His family could use the money. He could go back east and put the rottenness of Lincoln County behind him. He steeled himself, then responded.

"This simply will not do. You have cheated me out of a quarter of what is owed."

"Cheated you? I personally traveled to New York to clear the way for this payment. Were it not for me, Murphy and Dolan would've swept in and taken the whole ten thousand dollars. This required my time and money, which I fronted."

Charles Fritz looked at the ground, somewhat ashamed, but there was no turning back.

"Charles, level with me. Do you really believe I have not been forthright with you? Do you really believe I am attempting to cheat you and your family?"

"This will not do," was all Charles could muster before handing the check back and retiring inside his house. Charles then stood by the door, waiting for the sound of McSween riding away.

After he was gone, Charles poured himself some wine, filling the glass to the brim. He never cared for the whiskey so beloved by the Americans in the Southwest, and the beer here was weak and god-awful, akin to consuming a glass of warm piss.

Charles rehashed how it came to be that he would turn down a check for $7,500—$7,500!—and cross a man who had, for all intents and purposes, been square with him, even if Charles knew McSween had his own motivations.

As Charles downed the glass in one gulp and poured another, he wondered if he'd made the right decision. He wondered if he had aligned himself with the right men.

He wondered how the hell he got himself into this position in the first place.

James Dolan had come to him a week prior looking to make peace. The Irishman, who now seemed to be handling more and more operations for Murphy & Co., said it was an awful shame to see them at disagreement. Charles's brother Emil had been a trusted partner—"a mentor," Dolan had called him—and it would break Emil's heart to know this was happening. Surely they could come together in a way that was beneficial to all parties involved. Dolan also intimated McSween was a swindler who was not to be trusted. Dolan argued McSween was going to find an excuse to keep all the money for himself and leave the Fritz family—Dolan made sure to always discuss things in terms of the Fritz *family*—out in the cold. Why should some criminal pettifogger reap the benefits of Emil's hard work when that money so deservedly belonged in the Fritz *family's* hands?

Dolan offered to help ensure the Fritzes received the entirety of the $10,000 payout all for themselves. It was the least he could do for his old business partner. Charles didn't like James Dolan, he didn't trust James Dolan, he didn't believe James Dolan.

But he was scared of James Dolan.

Charles wasn't a fighter, and he certainly wasn't ready to kill over his brother's insurance payout. Besides, even if he did get the best of Dolan, there was L.G. Murphy, John Riley, and dozens of others he'd have to contend with. No, it was easier to go along with Murphy and Dolan's plan, cross his fingers and pray it worked, then get the hell out of New Mexico.

"But if you really want to get the money, all of it," Dolan had said, "first you have to reject McSween's offer to give it to you."

"If he's offering me the money, why would I reject it?" Charles had asked.

"Because he's only going to offer you a portion of what is rightfully yours."

Dolan had been right about that much.

"It is no longer feasible for me to continue on as partner," Murphy began. "It is time for the two of you to step into your own and take over the store."

James Dolan was coming to grips with a new reality. He

and John Riley sat before their mentor, concerned by the grave look in Murphy's eyes. And on his face. And his body.

"How long?" Riley asked.

Dolan knew it needed asking but still resented Riley for posing the question.

Riley was a relative newcomer, but Dolan had been with Murphy for almost a decade, starting as a stock boy managing the shelves and inventory when the company was still back at Fort Stanton, before their—his—"troubles." Dolan still harbored a tinge of remorse over what had transpired in Fort Stanton and had been grateful Murphy had not cast him out.

"Doctors say a year, maybe less," Murphy answered.

Dolan looked at his feet. He was an emotional man, but that normally manifested in anger and rage. Sorrow was new.

"How does this work?" Riley asked.

"Jesus Christ, John," Dolan replied. "Our friend tells us he has less than a year to live and the next thing out of your ungrateful mouth is how do you get more of the business?"

Riley didn't mean to be crass, and he sure as hell didn't mean to cross Dolan.

"It's quite all right, John Boy. You were right to inquire. It's important we handle the transfer in a timely manner that is agreeable to all sides."

"I don't care," Dolan said. "I've trusted you my whole life, Lawrence, so you just name what you believe is fair and I'll sign." Then he got up and walked out of the room.

LINCOLN

LINCOLN COUNTY, NEW MEXICO TERRITORY

Summer 1873

Dolan was twenty-one years old when he mustered out of the service and began working as a stock boy for the Murphy & Co. store in Fort Stanton. He got along well with L.G. Murphy, both of them from Ireland, their hometowns separated by less than a hundred miles. And like Murphy, Dolan's family had left during the Great Famine.

When Murphy took the young man under his wing, Emil Fritz had suggested caution. He could see Dolan had *impulses* that could jeopardize what they were building. But Murphy vouched for Dolan, so Fritz raised his concerns less and less, until a few years passed and even Fritz forgot about his own unease.

"That ain't right, Johnny," Dolan had said to Murphy & Co.'s newest hire. "You need to hang the valuable goods at neck level so the eye is drawn to it. You understand?"

"But why are we selling shovels for more than wagon wheels?" John Riley had asked.

"People here need shovels more than they need wheels for wagons they don't own."

Riley nodded and moved the store's three shovels higher.

Satisfied, Dolan turned back to a customer, an army sergeant. "So you simply sat around an office, writing reports?"

"I suppose you saw action?" the sergeant asked.

"Me? Shit, I saw all kinds of action."

"Closest you got to battle was fighting the drip," Captain Randlett said from the doorway.

Dolan's jaw tightened. He found Randlett to be a pompous ass who looked down on everyone. Randlett thought Dolan a drunken hothead.

Both were right.

"Look at him," Randlett said. "His little Irish face is all ruddy 'cause it's true. Stuck his prick in one camp follower, then spent the rest of the service buying sandalwood oil."

Dolan glared at the taller, broader captain. Randlett was the number two at Fort Stanton and had a righteous streak. He wasn't afraid of Dolan, Murphy, Fritz, or the Santa Fe Ring.

Dolan casually felt under the counter, where he kept a Winchester, but then Emil Fritz returned from lunch.

"Jimmy, a word?"

Dolan continued glaring at Captain Randlett, then approached the Murphy & Co. partner in a quiet corner.

"I need to go to Santa Fe, and I'd like you to venture with me."

"What's in Santa Fe?" Dolan asked.

"Not what. Who."

Early next morning, Dolan met Fritz outside the store, a trunk at his feet. "Just a few items I'm sending back to Germany," Fritz answered Dolan's look.

On the journey due north, Dolan could hardly contain his excitement.

"I've never met the big man before. I've heard stories, but to meet him in person, this is quite a deal."

"What makes you think so?" Fritz asked.

"You're showing faith in me, bringing me more into the fold."

"With that comes great responsibility."

"I won't let you down," Dolan said.

"I'm not concerned about you letting *me* down, Jimmy. But I need you to look out for Lawrence. Protect him."

"Protect him from what?" Dolan asked. To Dolan, it seemed L.G. Murphy was more than capable of protecting himself.

"From whatever lurks throughout this godforsaken territory."

Once in Santa Fe, they drove the wagon north up Palace Avenue, stopping in front of the headquarters for the District of New Mexico.

"Wait here," Fritz said, then disembarked from the driver's seat and went inside.

Dolan looked around. While not New York, Washington, or Philadelphia, Santa Fe was as cosmopolitan as the West would see. Structures up and down Palace, including government buildings, hotels, and seemingly more churches than there were even residents.

Fritz returned quickly. "Mr. Catron isn't in his office. Well, not this one, at least."

They drove the wagon up a block, then hitched a right over to Boss Catron's other office, the First National Bank of Santa Fe. Again, Fritz commanded Dolan to watch the wagon.

"Am I gonna meet the big man or just sit here babysitting things?"

"If time permits, Jimmy." Then Fritz walked to the rear of the wagon, opened the steamer, and removed a large envelope before heading inside the bank.

Dolan bided his time, wondering why Fritz even dragged him along.

Ten minutes later, Fritz emerged from the bank with a tall, portly man whose suit begged to be let out even more than it already had.

"Mr. Catron, I'd like you to meet one of our valued employees, James Dolan."

"It's an honor to meet you, sir," Dolan said and stuck out his hand. While Catron took it, he was already looking past Dolan to his next destination. "If there's anything I can ever do for you, sir, please don't hesitate to ask."

"Don't worry, I will," Catron said, then walked away.

"What he lacks in affability, he makes up for in other ways," Fritz said. "Come on."

They climbed back onto their wagon, and Fritz drove a

few more blocks to a two-story building, the only brick Gothic structure in Santa Fe. Fritz disembarked and headed to the back.

"I know, I know, wait in the wagon . . ."

"No, now you lift," Fritz replied. Dolan helped him pull the heavy steam trunk from the bed, then Dolan looked up at the building: *Mrs. Krause's Boardinghouse and Hotel.*

"We staying the night?"

"No, no," Fritz said as he climbed the porch steps to the front door, one hand heaving his end of the trunk. "Mrs. Krause is going to hold on to this for me."

"Is Mrs. Krause a friend of ours?"

"An acquaintance. Of mine," Fritz answered pointedly.

"Why not keep the trunk in Lincoln? Lord knows we don't lack the space."

"Because I want it stored here."

"Because you want it looked after by a German. What's a matter, Fritz? You don't trust us Irish no more?"

"I trust my life experience," was all Fritz said.

On the way back to Lincoln, Fritz opened up. "I didn't bring you just to shake hands with Boss Catron or help me lug the steamer," Fritz said. "I wanted time to talk. About life. About how the company operates."

"I know how the company works, Fritz."

"You know what we've told you, what we've allowed you to see. Yes, we sell goods in the store, and we have contracts to supply Fort Stanton. But that's not our bread and butter."

"You're talking about the real estate," Dolan said.

Fritz looked at him with a hint of surprise. "So you have been paying attention."

"I overhear things. Seen a deed or two on L.G.'s desk— items that don't make it into the company ledger."

"A lot of white folks moving to New Mexico and a lot of Mexicans looking to stay. All those people need somewhere to live. We provide that."

"What? You guys buy up a bunch of lots expecting a boom?"

"We *acquired* a significant acreage."

"Acquired from whom?"

"This is America. We saw an opportunity and took it," Fritz said. "We sell land on credit to ranchers and farmers new to the territory."

"That don't seem like something that needs to be kept secret."

"It's not a secret, but we'd prefer if people left us alone to operate how we see fit. The ranchers pledge to repay the loan as they sell off their crops. Sometimes the land isn't quite as fertile as the ranchers had hoped, and they fall behind on their payments. So we let them pay us in crops and cattle, which makes no difference to us since those are the very goods we need to supply Fort Stanton and the reservation. But the next month, the farmers still can't pay. Only now it's fall, the crops are dead, and the ranchers don't have our money . . ."

"So they default on the loan," Dolan replied, piecing it together.

"And we reclaim our property."

"They shouldn't take a loan they can't repay."

Fritz smiled. He suspected that beneath the fiery exterior and glinty eyes little Jimmy Dolan was a lot shrewder than he let on. "And what happens next?" Fritz asked, testing him.

Dolan thought for a moment. "Well, the territory is booming with opportunity and more and more people move to New Mexico, so we always have another client to sell the land to."

"That's right. The land doesn't change. The ownership never

really changes. It's just a carousel of defaulter after defaulter, and our bottom line continues to grow."

Dolan still had one question. "If we bought the land that we're then selling to the new rancher, who then defaults and we take it back . . . how is that increasing our bottom line?"

"Who said we *bought* the land?"

Brilliant, Dolan thought. It was free money, minus what they kicked up to Boss Catron.

"And I have some promising news for you, James," Fritz said.

When they got back to Fort Stanton, Dolan was over the moon. First he rushed to the store to find L.G., but L.G. was away, so Dolan celebrated the only way he knew how.

He got good and proper drunk.

Dolan bought a round for the cantina and sidled up to the bar, bragging to anyone who would listen. "Can you believe that? James Dolan, partner of Murphy & Co."

"Shit, Jimmy, congratulations," Riley said. "You earned it."

"I did, didn't I?" Dolan slurred rhetorically. "Another round for all!"

Captain Randlett entered and took in the revelry.

"Jimmy Dolan keeps buying rounds," said a private.

Randlett looked over to Dolan, and Riley elbowed up to the bar. "Where'd that pissant get so much money he can waste it on you soppers?"

"Don't know, didn't ask. Gift horses and all, Captain."

Randlett cupped his hands and bellowed across the room. "Hey, stock boy, who'd you rob now to get all this money?"

Dolan turned. "Stuff it, Randlett. Offer ain't for you."

"I don't need a simpleton gofer to buy my libations."

"Say that again," Dolan said, adjusting himself to appear larger in the moment.

Randlett laughed. "Which part, Dolan? That you're a gofer or a simple one at that?"

"I ain't no gofer, and I sure as hell ain't simple. In fact, I've just been made partner of Murphy & Co." Dolan closed one eye to reduce the number of Randletts he was seeing.

"I don't care what new fancy title those crooks Murphy and Fritz bestowed upon you. You're still just a simple stock boy not worth the muck on the sole of a boot."

All Dolan saw were hot flashes of red. He was tired of the disrespect. He was a part of the Santa Fe Ring now.

Later, when recounting the story to Murphy and Fritz, Riley explained he wasn't even sure Dolan knew what he was doing.

"Tell me anyway," Fritz had said.

"Well . . ." Riley began, sneaking a look to Dolan, who was sitting on the floor in the one spot still shadowed from light coming in through the window, nursing his hangover. "Randlett called him a gofer, which I didn't take offense to on account of that's what I am, but then Randlett also had some disparaging remarks concerning you and Mr. Murphy . . ."

"Of what nature?" Murphy asked.

Riley shuffled his feet, suddenly unsure of himself. "I believe he called you less than obedient when it came to the confines of the law, sir."

"He called you fuckin' crooks," Dolan said, the movement of each jaw muscle causing a million lightning bolts to rattle around his brain. "So I defended your reputation."

"Not you, him," Fritz said, pointing at Riley.

Riley swallowed hard, then continued. "It really was all a blur . . ."

Murphy slammed his hand on the desk, stilling the room. "Spit it out, John Boy, or we'll bring in someone who is able to speak the truth."

"Yes, sir. Captain Randlett puffed out his chest, said Jimmy weren't worth the muck on the sole of his boot. And he did it real aggressive like, so I don't blame Jimmy . . ." Riley could see the exasperation on Murphy's face and hurriedly finished. "Jimmy pulled his gun—and again, I don't know his intentions in doing so—but I steered his arm toward the ceiling, and that's when the shot went off. Like I said, he may not have been planning to shoot the captain, I can't say, and maybe my deflecting his arm northward is what caused his finger to slip and pull . . ."

"Is that true, James? Did your finger 'slip' and 'accidentally' pull the trigger?"

"No. I was going to shoot Randlett right in his smug fucking face."

"Jesus, Jimmy . . ." Riley said quietly.

Murphy approached Dolan, still sitting on the floor in the dark, then patted him on the head and walked out. Fritz followed.

In the hallway, Fritz stopped Murphy. "Now I'm not so certain."

"Why? Because of this little hiccup?"

"Jimmy tried to kill the second-in-command at the fort, Lawrence. There's going to be consequences for our business."

"Maybe, maybe not. Maybe this is a blessing in disguise. Maybe James Dolan showed true grit and spirit in defense of not only his honor but ours. Either way, it's not your problem anymore, friend."

A week later, the army booted Murphy & Co. out of Fort Stanton, and they relocated to Lincoln.

Two weeks after that, Emil Fritz boarded a steamer to Germany, his homeland, to die.

LINCOLN

LINCOLN COUNTY, NEW MEXICO TERRITORY

November 1877

That was years ago, and now Lawrence Murphy, Dolan's mentor, protector, and shield, was turning the business over to him and Riley. It would be a lot to take on. Murphy had handled the relationships that helped the company thrive. Murphy knew where all the money was, who they needed to keep happy, and at what price. Dolan liked Riley well enough but didn't think the young man particularly bright. The responsibility of keeping Murphy & Co. successful would all fall on Dolan. Hell, Dolan didn't even know how much the company was worth, but he trusted his longtime friend and partner to cut him a fair deal.

He shouldn't have.

SANTA FE

SANTA FE COUNTY, NEW MEXICO TERRITORY

Thomas B. "Boss" Catron, attorney general for the New Mexico Territory and president of First National Bank of Santa Fe, analyzed the chessboard in his head. But rather than rooks and knights and pawns, he had sheriffs and judges and ranchers. And, much to his benefit, the pieces didn't even know they were a part of his grand game.

When Murphy had come to him for advice, Catron saw the opportunity right away. It was seven moves down the line, but if everyone acted according to their nature, Catron could enrich himself and his partners in the Santa Fe Ring.

Catron viewed the Irishman as a medium fish in a small pond who thought he was king of the ocean. But part of Catron's brilliance was letting men think the best of themselves, then exploiting that ego.

"Mr. Catron, I have a little issue arising," Murphy said on his visit to Santa Fe. "I'd be awfully grateful if you could exert some influence and see things work out to my favor."

"Lawrence, you're making a fine life for yourself down in Lincoln. You don't need my help," Catron countered. He didn't offer condolences for Murphy's appearance, figuring Murphy had enough of that already. Cancer was ripping through the man. Anyone could see it.

"I worry your patience will soon run thin. I'm aware I'm delinquent on a payment or two."

Even though Catron knew the exact number Murphy was short, he made a big show of pulling out his private ledger to check. It gave the appearance that whatever monies Murphy owed were so inconsequential that it didn't even warrant space in his head.

"Ah, indeed. I received but two thousand dollars in September and nothing in October or November."

"A competing venture has opened in Lincoln, and they're undercutting our prices. We're losing business we've long counted on."

"This sounds like a problem of capitalism, Lawrence," Catron said, casually lighting a cigar and neglecting to offer one to Murphy.

"We also have money tied up in real estate throughout the territory, but word seems to have spread about the tensions, and white folks are settling in Santa Fe County or Colfax, not Lincoln. It's making it hard to recoup our investments."

"Don't bullshit me, Lawrence. These 'investments' are nothing more than you driving people out of business and snatching up their land at a discount. It's borderline unethical what you've been doing," Catron said disingenuously. "But I've always liked you and thought your heart in the right place, so I've allowed it to continue. But now you're saying you don't have the proper monies to show you appreciate my help."

Murphy fidgeted with the hat in his hand. It was rare for him to be subservient to anyone, but Boss Catron was the exception. One snap of his fingers and all the sympathetic judges and lawyers and sheriffs would turn their back and leave Murphy blowing in the wind.

"What can I do to make this right?" Murphy asked.

The men spent the next hour going over every holding in Murphy's name, and the ones he didn't legally own but controlled nonetheless, then shook hands. Murphy & Co. would turn over the majority of their holdings to Boss Catron's First National Bank, and in exchange Catron would continue to pressure law enforcement and the legal system to work in Murphy's favor.

LINCOLN

LINCOLN COUNTY, NEW MEXICO TERRITORY

Murphy had just come from this meeting when he sat with Dolan and Riley and revealed he was selling them the company. He failed to disclose the new legal obligations they would have to First National Bank. He failed to disclose the crippling debt and dried revenue stream they would be facing. He failed to disclose their business was all but through.

Instead, he took $10,000 from each—arranging their loans through Catron's First National Bank in Santa Fe—and retired to one of the ranches he still owned outside Lincoln.

As he left, Murphy thought about how much he admired their loyalty.

And how much he detested their stupidity.

Chapter 17

LINCOLN COUNTY, NEW MEXICO TERRITORY

Late December 1877

Alexander McSween could see the wariness on his wife's face. Susan had been pushing to return to Kansas. "Was this all worth it?" she'd argued. "There is no good outcome to be had."

Susan loved her husband and admired his ambition but was also keenly aware of what he didn't know. She had seen death and despair up close and didn't relish the thought of searching for conflict, as her husband and Tunstall seemed to be doing.

Now here they were, embroiled in a fight with the most powerful forces in New Mexico.

"Alex, I think it best we leave for a bit."

"This is not a good time," he replied. "I plan to meet again with Charles Fritz and settle the insurance policy dispute once and for all."

"You tried to give him the money once already. Your second attempt can wait a week."

Alex looked up. Her tone, usually smooth and warm even when she was being stubborn, was now coarse and direct.

"This will all be behind us soon. Murphy & Co. is in dire financial straits, and it is only a matter of time before they dissolve. Then we'll have the world at our fingertips."

"I'm going to Las Vegas, then I'm boarding a train to St. Louis, where I will spend a week with my sister clearing my head of all this nonsense. You are free to come with and thus continue our marriage. Or you may stay here and hope beyond hope that I will come back to you, which I will not."

She kissed him on top of his head, then retired to bed.

They left the next morning.

LAS VEGAS

SAN MIGUEL COUNTY, NEW MEXICO TERRITORY

Christmas Eve 1877

John Chisum had business in the capital, just forty miles east of Las Vegas, so he accompanied the McSweens. Chisum was in a rare chipper mood, and McSween once again felt like they were true partners. They discussed how best to deal with the House, if there were any influential people in Santa Fe who may be able to help, and how long they'd have to hold out for Murphy & Co. to go under.

They arrived in Las Vegas on Christmas Eve and sat down for lunch. Their food had barely arrived when Sheriff Romero and four men entered.

"We got warrants for your arrests," Sheriff Romero said. "Embezzlement and fraud as related to your dealings with one Charles Fritz."

Susan looked at her husband. He had told her Charles refused the money. But she was also aware of the $326 a former client in Eureka claimed he was owed just before the McSweens left and moved to New Mexico.

"That money was offered and rejected by Mr. Fritz," Susan said.

"Mr. Fritz claims otherwise," replied Sheriff Romero.

Charles's version of events closely aligned with that of James Dolan's, who in turn had parroted the version put forth by the mastermind of the plan, Boss Catron.

Catron had played the long game and now was going in for the kill. He had "suggested" Fritz file a petition with the Lincoln County district attorney, accusing McSween of embezzlement. The ring-friendly DA was all too happy to oblige.

"What the hell'd I do?" Chisum asked between bites.

"You still owe back taxes to the state, Mr. Chisum." Which was true. He just didn't think the sheriff of San Miguel was the one to enforce such delinquency.

Alexander McSween and John Chisum were placed in the Las Vegas jail.

Susan McSween quickly sent word back to John Tunstall that things were escalating.

"Why must we travel all the way to Doña Ana?" McSween asked.

"I'm just following judge's orders," said Sheriff Romero. Truth was, he had no idea why they were transporting the prisoner halfway down the state to stand trial for something that took place in a third, entirely different county.

But McSween knew why. Because that's where the ring had the most sway.

It would take two weeks for the preliminary hearings to begin, and the traveling group would stop for a week in Lincoln so McSween could get his affairs in order and locate the necessary documentation to build his defense. Chisum would stay behind in the Las Vegas jail, as his charges of unpaid taxes were unrelated to the Emil Fritz life insurance policy.

Meanwhile, Tunstall and Dolan each took to the press to argue their side's case in the court of public opinion. Tunstall wrote a letter to the *Mesilla Valley Independent* accusing Sheriff Brady of corruption and stealing $1,500 that McSween turned over for taxes. Dolan fired back a rebuttal claiming McSween and Tunstall were swindling their clients and the people of Lincoln. It wasn't an accident the letters were written to the paper in La Mesilla rather than Lincoln or Santa Fe.

It was simply to persuade potential jurors.

LINCOLN

LINCOLN COUNTY, NEW MEXICO TERRITORY

The night before they were to depart for La Mesilla, McSween and Tunstall held a meeting in their store. Dick Brewer was there, as were the Coe cousins, Bowdre, Scurlock, and a few of the other ranch hands.

Billy leaned against the back wall.

"We're bringing you along as protection, not aggressors," Tunstall opened. "Dolan and his faction are looking for any excuse to engage. Don't give them a reason. But be mindful."

The House would be in La Mesilla too, a show of force consisting of the Boys as well as the John Kinney Gang, and possibly the Seven Rivers Warriors.

A tinderbox looking for a single match.

"I don't know, Mr. Tunstall," came a voice from the middle of the room. "I know these fellas, and they don't want to end up in a pine box any more than we do."

Like many of the men in the store, Billy had worked both

sides of the dispute. But only William McCloskey seemed to hold any sympathies for Evans and the Boys. McCloskey believed cooler heads could prevail if the two sides just sat down.

Billy thought McCloskey a fool.

The debate escalated into raised voices until Billy ambled over to the door, opened it slowly, then slammed it as hard as he could. The room fell silent.

"They ain't looking for olive branches, McCloskey. They ain't looking for an accord that leaves everyone in charge of their own fate. Jesse Evans and Buck Morton only abide by one rule: brute, lethal force at any cost."

"All due respect, Billy, you don't know 'em like I do."

"No due respect, McCloskey, you're in this room now, with us. After they get finished cutting us down, Evans'll string you up next."

Billy walked out.

The yelling continued as he took a seat on the front porch. He was tired of running, tired of living in fear, tired of looking over his shoulder at every turn. He couldn't help but think back to his days in Arizona, when big Windy Cahill was picking on him. He remembered the taste of bile in his mouth as he cowered, trying to avoid the fight. But he had learned two lessons: don't ever let anyone else make you feel that way again, and if they strike first, you're all but dead. It was only by the grace of God that he had been able to reach his gun and get a shot off on Cahill. It was only by the luck of the stars he'd been able to slip away from Evans and Morton. He'd be damned if he was ever going to let anyone get the drop on him again.

Tunstall emerged and joined Billy on the porch. "I must apologize to you, Billy."

"It ain't your fault McCloskey doesn't know what he's talking about."

"Not for that. I understand it was your birthday a few weeks back."

"And it will be again next year," Billy joked.

"Eighteen now. You've proven yourself capable and loyal and a friend I value."

Billy realized Tunstall was holding a long box. Tunstall handed it over.

Billy opened the box, then looked at Tunstall, who nodded. Billy picked up the Winchester carbine rifle and felt its weight. It was pristine, brand new, and all his.

"Thank you, Mr. Tunstall—this means a lot," was all he could get out. Any more and he might've wept right there.

"It's but one piece, Billy. As you know, I've been acquiring parcels of land throughout Lincoln County. I'd like to give one to you to tend and ranch. You'll provide crops and cattle for the store, and we'll share in the proceeds, but make no mistake—the land will be yours."

Billy felt a lump in his throat. For the first time since his mother passed, he felt acceptance. *Kinship.*

"All right." Tunstall smiled. "We've got an early start tomorrow."

He went back inside.

Billy stayed on the porch holding his new Winchester, practicing pulling it and firing.

Billy remained there all night keeping watch, a sentry guarding the palace.

"This has to be a mistake," Riley said.

James Dolan and John Riley were poring over the ledger, the realization dawning on them. They weren't just broke, they were destitute.

"We can't possibly owe that much."

Dolan knew better. He knew what his old partner, Murphy, had actually left them with.

A goddamn trough of shit.

While they still had their contracts with Fort Stanton and the reservation, business from locals had dried up. When Tunstall & Co. opened, many switched their allegiance to the new store.

And then there was the real estate.

The majority of land the company owned was not theirs. Some was land Murphy had falsely staked claim to with no proof of purchase or deed, which Dolan knew about, but the rest had been funded by Boss Catron's First National Bank of Santa Fe and was in arrears. Catron could swoop in and reclaim the land any time he saw fit.

"I don't get it," Riley continued. "We paid good money for this company and all that comes with it."

"And that's what we got," replied Dolan.

Dolan almost had to smile at the artistry of it. Murphy had gotten out on top, and now Dolan and Riley were boxed into a corner with only one recourse: mortgage the House, and everything else they own, to First National Bank and Boss Catron.

LA MESILLA

DOÑA ANA COUNTY, NEW MEXICO TERRITORY

January 1878

The night before the preliminary trial began, Tunstall and Billy were walking to their lodging in La Mesilla when a voice rang out.

"Tunstall . . . oh, Tunstall . . ." The singsong nature of the call made Billy wheel around and raise his new Winchester.

Dolan approached, loose on his feet and stinking of whiskey, trailed by Evans, Buck Morton, and Frank Baker. "Must we go through all the trouble of a trial?" Dolan asked. "Surely we can find a more . . . expedient solution to our quarrel."

Dolan's eyes were crossed. *No way he could hit the broad side of a barn, let alone deliver a fatal shot*, Billy thought. But Evans and Buck could hold their liquor and were itching for a fight.

"Mr. Dolan, the courts can aptly settle any dispute," Tunstall replied.

Billy was still surprised at the faith Tunstall and McSween were putting in the legal system. A fair and impartial one, sure. But this was New Mexico.

"C'mon, Tunstall, let's have it out. Or are you too rat-livered to handle your own affairs?"

"Good night, James," Tunstall said, then turned his back. Dolan reached for his gun, but Billy's rifle was on him and cocked. Dolan glared, but Billy was eyeing the other three men.

"Don't do it, Jesse," Billy said to Evans, whose hand had dropped to his holster. "You may take me, but not before I splatter Dolan's brains all over the dirt."

"You're not long for this world, Kid," Buck Morton replied. "Every time it gets dark, every time you turn a corner, every time you so much as close your eyes, I'll be there."

"We all gotta go sometime, Buck. But I guarantee it won't be you who puts me down."

The next seconds passed like years, the men all waiting for one twitch, one spasm, to set off a hail of bullets.

"All right, Billy, let's head back," Tunstall intervened.

Billy eyed Buck glaring at him, begging for a fight, and couldn't help himself.

"How's Abigail? I ain't seen her since, shit, last time we was all here in La Mesilla."

Buck flinched for his gun, but Billy was too quick. He

had the barrel pointed right between Morton's eyes. Both were willing to rain hell on each other and let the chips fall where they may, but the local sheriff came out of the hotel and sent everyone away.

As Tunstall and Billy walked back to their rooms, Tunstall had to ask. "Who's Abigail?"

"It don't matter."

"Is she the reason he wishes you harm?"

"The main reason, yeah," Billy replied.

Alexander McSween never stood a chance in court.

Judge Bristol presided and District Attorney Rynerson prosecuted, both part of the Santa Fe Ring.

Rynerson spent the entirety of the hearing peppering his case in between insults of McSween. And when he wasn't having a go at the defendant, Judge Bristol was. With each barb or ruling that didn't fall their way, the McSween side would shout and heckle, which prompted the Dolan clan in the other half of the courtroom to retort. On multiple occasions a shootout almost ensued, until even Judge Bristol had to order no firearms allowed in. At the end of three days, Judge Bristol ruled there was enough evidence against McSween for him to stand trial when the territorial courts resumed in two months.

"I cannot accept that," Rynerson said with more than a hint of glee in his voice.

"The bail was set at eight thousand dollars, and I am here to pay it," replied Tunstall.

"You heard Judge Bristol. There's also an attachment of ten thousand dollars on McSween's property." The amount McSween's been charged with embezzling from Fritz. "For all I know, this money you're attempting to hand over is from what is due Mr. Fritz. We'll have to do a full accounting of Mr. McSween's properties and assets before we can accept any bail."

"Absurd," Tunstall responded. "This is money from my pocket, not Alexander's."

"Which brings us to our second issue at hand. Since you and Mr. McSween are business partners, and that business is a part of McSween's equity, we'll need a full accounting of your property and assets as well. The good Sheriff Brady will be in contact soon."

Tunstall looked over to the doorway, where Sheriff Brady was watching. Brady smiled, happy to torment the man who'd earlier denied him credit for a job well done.

Tunstall had to give it to them. Not only were McSween's assets in jeopardy, now Tunstall's were too.

Chapter 18

February 1878

The race was on.

While Deputy Sheriff Barrier was escorting McSween back to Lincoln, the Dolan faction sped ahead to get Sheriff Brady started on attaching all of McSween and Tunstall's property, effectively shuttering their business. Dolan hoped the sheriff would have everything seized and locked before Tunstall and his group even knew what was happening.

A plan this intricate, this detailed, was not the brainchild of James Dolan or John Riley.

No, this was a Boss Catron play all along.

"They'll kill me," McSween told his escort. "Claim I was trying to escape and they'll shoot me down like a diseased dog." Throughout the journey back to Lincoln, McSween, his wife Susan, and Tunstall had been imploring Deputy

Sheriff Barrier not to hand him over to Brady.

"We'll make sure your men are in the room above the pit to ensure there's no foul play."

"That will only get our boys killed as well," said Susan.

When the group arrived in Lincoln, Sheriff Brady was waiting at the jail.

"Cleaned it nice and good for you," Brady said. "Suitable for a man of your standing."

Brady could hardly hide the gleam in his eye. Brady still harbored shame for confessing to McSween that he was under Murphy's thumb.

Barrier eyed Sheriff Brady and the cavalry of Dolan men milling in the street, failing to look inconspicuous. Barrier was coming around to McSween's theory of execution.

"I'm just letting you know we're here, Sheriff," Barrier said. "But Mr. McSween will not be placed in the pit."

Brady stiffened. As sheriff of Lincoln, he had authority over the entire county. "It's not your place, Adolph. It's not your county. We'll handle it from here."

The men in the street were no longer pretending to occupy themselves. All eyes were on the standoff in front of the jail.

"I have the utmost faith in you, Brady," Barrier lied. "But there are men in this community who wish to do Mr. McSween harm, and to avoid putting you in that precarious position, he'll be placed under house arrest, where I'll watch over him myself until trial."

Barrier didn't wait for an answer. He guided McSween down the street, through the Dolan men glaring at them with hands on their pistols, and into McSween's home.

"Thank you, Adolph. You're a decent man," Susan said, once they were safely inside.

Barrier couldn't respond. He was still waiting for his breath to come back into his body.

"It's a mistake," Billy said to no one in particular as he cleaned the Winchester. Tensions were high inside Tunstall's Rio Feliz ranch house, where Billy, Brewer, Scurlock, Bowdre, the Coe cousins, and a few others were meeting. "We sit and wait for them to come to us, we've already lost. Ain't no sense in a counterpunch if the first wallop knocks you cold."

"That's not the way we do things," Brewer replied. "We're on the side of law and order."

"Where's that gotten us?" Billy scoffed. "McSween's facing trial, the House is trying to take everything we own, and we're playing ostrich, sticking our damn heads in the sand. We might as well make our final arrangements now."

"There'll be a trial and the courts will decide," said McCloskey.

Billy had grown tired of McCloskey's neutrality. "Time's come for you to choose, McCloskey. Either get in line or we'll see you on the other side."

"I don't know who elected you leader, but I take umbrage at you questioning my loyalties."

"You can shove your umbrage up your ass," Billy spat back.

McCloskey scanned the room. No one was jumping in to defend him. "Well, if that's the way you think, perhaps we should resolve this," he bluffed.

"All right." Billy headed for the door.

"That's enough, Billy. We don't need to be cutting each other down," Brewer said.

"You're right, Dick. Let's just sit on our asses and wait for Evans and Kinney and God knows who else to kill us first."

Billy glared back at McCloskey, who simply looked down and started cleaning his gun, hoping Billy's argument would blow over. He got his wish when Scurlock peered out the window.

"Shit. Looks like Evans, Morton, Baker, and the rest."

"Fan out by the windows, rifles ready," Brewer said. The men did as he commanded, then Brewer stepped outside to meet the guests. Just before the front door closed behind him, Billy sneaked through and joined Brewer on the porch.

"All right, but keep your head and follow my lead," Brewer whispered to Billy.

Billy nodded. His nerves were calm, and his hands were steady.

"Got warrants," Evans said as he and his gang stopped at the bottom of the porch steps.

"Yeah, for what?" Brewer replied.

"To attach any and all of McSween's property."

"Then I suggest you head over to his place and do as the law sees fit. But this is Mr. Tunstall's land, and there ain't no McSween cattle here."

"Judge Bristol says McSween and Tunstall are partners, so anything that belongs to Tunstall is part McSween's."

"Bristol's a murderer, just like you," Billy said. "Only he hides under a robe."

Buck spit tobacco juice onto the porch, just short of Billy's feet. Billy looked at him.

"We had some good times, didn't we?" Billy said.

"You were a pissant the day I met you, you'll be a pissant the day I kill you," Buck replied.

"I still have fond memories. Us hootin' and hollerin' by the fire, the girls all dancing around us. The time we got into a scrape over them chickens." Billy cocked his head. "And what is that perfume Abigail wears?"

Buck's jaw clenched, and his hand twitched for his pistol, but he stopped himself.

"If you forgot, I got some letters, might refresh your memory. She likes to dab her scent on 'em now. But you may know that already. Or maybe you don't."

Buck's eyes went dark. His only thought was killing Billy.

"Buck . . ." Evans said, eyeing the Tunstall men standing at the windows, guns in hand.

"I don't care, Jesse. This little fuck has to die."

Billy smiled. "See, Buck, I got this habit of rememberin' when folks do my friends wrong. Abigail's a sweet girl. And you had to go and swell up that pretty face."

"Cool it, Billy," Brewer warned.

"I'm just trying to get to the bottom of something that's been gnawin' at me. Why'd you go and knock that *bonita yegua* around, Buck?"

"Women are like broncos. Got to break 'em in or they think they own you."

Billy laughed, rolling it out hard for Buck's benefit. "Broncos? Break them in? No wonder she ain't want to fuck you no more." Then Billy lowered his voice. "But if you want some tips, I'll walk you through how to keep a woman happy, keep her dreaming about you when you're gone."

"Goddammit, Billy! That's enough!" Brewer yelled.

"Geez, Dick, I was just catching up with my old friend."

"We'll find another time to recollect, Kid," Buck grunted.

"You bet your ass we will."

"There's the matter of the warrants," Evans said to Brewer. "What's Tunstall's is McSween's, and what's McSween's is the courts."

"Nothing is leaving this property, Jesse."

Evans looked at the armed men in the windows again. "We'll be back."

After they were gone, Dick turned on Billy.

"What the hell was that?"

"What are you carrying on about, Dick? They intend us harm. You, me, McSween, Tunstall, and anyone else riding with us. But now they ain't thinking about you or Doc or Charlie or the Coes. I guarantee you all they're talking about is the kid, Billy."

Brewer studied him. "Is this about what's best for all or what's best for you?"

"I'm saving your ass, putting the bull's-eye on my back, nobody else's."

"And getting yourself known as well."

"Shit, Dick, everybody's gotta have their day in the sun," Billy said before heading inside.

Chapter 19

February 18, 1878

It was still dark when the gunshots woke the men. Dick Brewer and the others scrambled out of their beds. Brewer rushed to the window and peered out.

Billy was standing in the light snow, no coat on, firing the Winchester at wild turkeys nesting in the trees some fifty yards away.

"Goddammit!" yelled Brewer from inside the house. The last of the turkeys flew away. Billy turned to the window.

"The turkeys, Dick. You scared them off."

"Billy, why don't you get yourself some breakfast. Godfrey has fixed quite a feast to send us on our way," John Tunstall said as he emerged from the house, coffee in hand. He sensed the nervous energy building inside the men.

"I don't need any breakfast, Mr. Tunstall," Billy replied. He then removed a peach from a satchel he had draped over the fence post and bit into it.

"Very well. Ready the horses, then."

As Billy prepped and checked the nine horses they were going to transport to Brewer's ranch, the rest of the men quickly dressed and ate. The sun would be coming up in half an hour and they wanted to be on the trail when it did.

Their trek began uneventful. Most of the men were still wiping sleep from their eyes, bracing from the morning cold. They rode at a steady pace but slow enough for Fred Waite, who was driving the supply wagon, to keep up. It had been a trying few weeks, and fatigue had set in.

Billy spurred his horse to catch up to Brewer, who was leading the caravan. "What say you, Dick?"

"I say I didn't get enough sleep last night, what with you firing off your rifle before the sun even rose."

"All right, let me take your mind off things," Billy said as he pulled out a deck of cards, ignoring Brewer's obvious annoyance. "Pick one."

"This isn't a time for games, Kid. We gotta get these horses to my ranch before Dolan realizes they're Tunstall's."

"C'mon, Dick, one card. You pick one higher than me, I'll leave you alone."

"And if I don't?"

"Then shit, you gotta play poker with me tonight."

Billy knew Brewer liked to gamble as much as he did, though Brewer was much nittier with his wagers. Brewer never bet what he couldn't afford to lose, and if the stakes got too high, he'd walk away altogether. Billy never understood that thinking. What's the point of gambling if there's nothing really at stake? Brewer would ramble on about not risking his future on a stupid game. Billy had heard stories of the old Dick—including one thirty-six-hour faro spree that left Dick's pockets full—and suspected he and Brewer were more alike than Brewer would ever admit.

But then Brewer began working for Tunstall, and something

changed inside the man. He stopped drinking, stopped gambling as much, and became a responsible type. Billy wondered if Tunstall would eventually have the same effect on him as well. It was hard for the Kid to imagine giving up gambling though. How else could a young man feel that sense of rush and exhilaration, other than from the obvious?

That reminded Billy. When things settled, he would pay that visit to Isadora and Abigail.

Ten miles in, the group got to the base of Pajarito Springs. Pajarito provided a shortcut to Brewer's ranch, but the terrain was too rocky and uneven for a wagon, so Waite would stay on the main trail while the rest split off through the pass.

"Hey, Fred, you see anything moving along the way, you shoot it," Billy said. Tunstall didn't like such proclamations and was doing everything he could to avoid bloodshed.

"Oh, don't worry, Mr. Tunstall. I'm just talking about them turkeys. Fred ain't got the marksmanship to gun down no persons."

Waite shook his head and smiled at the gentle ribbing.

"You be careful, Billy," Waite said.

"Don't worry about me—I can handle myself," Billy replied.

"It ain't you I'm worried about. It's everyone else when you get to firing."

Billy jumped off his horse, Fred from the wagon, and the two wrestled good-naturedly before Brewer broke them up with an impatient whistle.

"Enough. We still got another thirty miles to go."

"Yes, sir," Billy said. He mock saluted, then climbed back on his horse. "But Fred, throw me one of them peaches."

Waite tossed it to Billy, intentionally leaving it short so the Kid had to get back down off his horse. Waite laughed, then slapped the reins, driving the wagon up the safer route.

Billy brushed the peach and blew some of the dirt off.

"You ready, Billy?" Brewer asked, his annoyance growing.

Billy took a bite. As the group headed up the shortcut, Billy spat out the dirt that he'd just consumed and pocketed the rest of the peach for later.

It was hard, uneven ground for the horses, but the Tunstall group had picked up the pace since Fred Waite had split off to the wagon-friendly route. Even so, occasionally Billy and Brewer would have to slow down for Tunstall and the others to catch up.

"How's this all shake out, Dick?" Billy asked on one of their letups.

"I suppose a best-case is we find some accord between the two sides."

"I'm not sure Lincoln is big enough for two stores," Billy replied. He removed the rest of the uneaten peach from his pocket and took a bite. "I tell ya what I'm gonna do when this is all over," he said, wiping his mouth. "I'll settle down with a nice señorita, and me and Fred Waite are gonna be the biggest cattle operators in New Mexico. Bigger'n Chisum even."

The Kid dreamed large, Brewer thought, even if he was deranged.

"Don't you laugh. I'm serious. I'll move them along the Goodnight-Loving Trail through West Texas, up to Fort Sumner."

"And what about Chisum? What about the Santa Fe Ring? You gonna cut them in?"

"Aw, hell no. I'm not scared of Boss Catron. The ring can go fuck itself."

"They didn't gather power by accident. You'll have to deal with them one way or another."

"I choose *another*," Billy said, smiling as he pulled his pistol.

"They have something more powerful than guns, Billy. They have money and the press."

"You gonna give me that old shit about how the pen is mightier than the sword? Tunstall gave me that play too. Can't say I cared for it though." It was but one in a number of reading materials that Tunstall had been lending to Billy in the hopes of advancing his understanding of the world.

Billy saw Tunstall, Widenmann, and Middleton ride over the hill. Widenmann and Middleton kicked their horses into high gear, racing to see who'd reach Billy and Brewer first. Billy took the last bite of the peach.

"Things are changing, Dick. I can feel it," Billy said, then tossed the peach aside. "C'mon, scalawags, last one to us is on hog duty tonight!" Billy hollered out to his approaching friends.

But just before Widenmann and Middleton reached him, Billy saw another figure crest over the hill, just behind Tunstall.

Then another.

Then a dozen more.

"It's Evans!" Billy yelled.

Gunshots rang out, scattering the four. Billy pulled his Winchester, then ducked behind a knoll, followed by the others.

"Tunstall?" Brewer screamed at his employer, hoping for a reply. "John?!"

Tunstall froze, knowing he'd never outrace the coming posse. They stopped firing and rode up on him. They circled around him, the horses neighing and whinnying and bucking.

Ever the posh Englishman, Tunstall remained still, a calm in the eye of the storm.

"We have to help him," Billy said, rising, but he was pulled back to the dirt by Brewer.

"It'll only escalate matters. There must be twenty of them. If we go in firing, they'll kill Tunstall, they'll kill all of us."

"They're gonna kill him anyway," Billy said. Again he tried to rise, and again Brewer pulled him to the ground.

"If they wanted him dead, they'd have done it already," Brewer said. "Tunstall's smart. We hold."

They waited, every second gnawing at Billy like eagle talons shredding apart his insides.

"You got yourself some stolen property here, Tunstall," Sheriff Brady said.

"Those horses belong to James Dolan and John Riley," Evans added.

"These horses are the property of Richard Brewer and have no place in Dolan's dispute with Alex McSween," Tunstall replied.

"Look at this English dandy," Buck Morton said, jabbing Tunstall's chest with the barrel of his rifle. "Daddy buy you this coat too?"

Tunstall tried to keep his cool. "I will not let you provoke me into a fight, giving you reason to gun me down."

Buck laughed.

Evans scowled. "We already got a reason, horse thief," Evans said.

Tunstall's mare sensed the tension and began drifting sideways, attempting to extricate itself from the encircling posse. But as the horse swayed, so did the barrier, until Tunstall and Evans's men had relocated around a boulder, out of Billy and Brewer's view.

"Dick . . ." Billy said, itching to go help his boss.

Brewer's concern was growing too, but there was nothing they could do. Four against twenty, in broad daylight, with no room to shield themselves from the inevitable barrage of bullets.

Only God can save Tunstall now, Brewer thought.

"Seems we're at an impasse. You got stolen property, and when confronted became belligerent and hostile, attempting to harm those trying to uphold the law," Sheriff Brady said.

"I have done no such thing," Tunstall replied. "This is a matter for the courts to decide, not vigilantes who have blood on their own hands. Let's ride into Lincoln and—"

It's doubtful Tunstall heard the shot before the bullet ripped through the back of his head and exploded out his left eye.

"Sons of bitches!" Billy cried out.

"Hush, Billy," Brewer said, not wanting to give away their hiding spot.

"Maybe they just fired a warning shot," Middleton added.

But Billy knew.

They had lost sight of Tunstall and the posse around the curve of the boulder, but in his gut, Billy was sure Tunstall was dead. Tears began cascading down his cheeks, and once again he had to be restrained from going after Evans and the posse. Billy was kicking and punching and trying to wrest himself free, and it took all three men to hold him down.

Tunstall's body slumped over, then sloughed off the horse onto the ground, like skin shedding from a snake.

"I was tired of hearing him talk," Buck Morton said, his revolver still smoldering.

Evans dismounted and knelt by Tunstall's body, examining it. A quarter of Tunstall's head had blown clear off. Evans then took Tunstall's rifle from his horse and fired a shot into the air.

"We shot him in self-defense," Evans said, laying the rifle at Tunstall's fingertips.

Sheriff Brady nodded.

A third shot rang out and Tunstall's horse fell over, almost crushing Tunstall's body.

"Goddammit, Buck. How are we gonna explain three shots?" Evans asked.

"Explain to who?" Buck replied.

"What's done is done," Frank Baker said as he and Tom Hill climbed off their horses. Baker picked up Tunstall's hat, which had flown off, and wiggled his finger through the bullet hole for Hill's amusement.

"All right, that's enough. Let's go," Evans said.

"Just a minute," Baker replied. He and Hill leaned Tunstall's body against the dead horse. Baker then took Tunstall's hat and placed it on the horse's head, cracking Hill up further.

"Fucking dolts," came a voice from the back of the posse. Andrew "Buckshot" Roberts was a quiet, secretive man who preferred solitude, but Dolan had promised him a pretty penny if he joined up on the Dolan side. Even so, he had no patience for frivolity. He turned on his mule and rode away, angry for involving himself with these imps.

"What about the rest?" Buck asked.

"They no doubt scattered back to Brewer's ranch," Evans replied. "Ain't no threat to us now. Gather up the horses."

"And Billy Bonney?"

"You know what an Achilles' heel is, Buck?"

He did not.

"Fixating on little ol' Billy is gonna be your downfall. Leave it be. McSween's going to jail, and Tunstall's dead. It's over."

Chapter 20

LINCOLN COUNTY, NEW MEXICO TERRITORY

It was almost midnight when Billy, Brewer, Widenmann, and Middleton arrived back in Lincoln. They rode directly to McSween's house and pounded on the door with such ferocity that Deputy Barrier, who was still guarding McSween, answered with a gun.

"They've murdered him," Billy said, bursting through the door.

Susan McSween entered the front room, trailed by her husband.

"They murdered Mr. Tunstall," Billy continued. Susan wrapped the eighteen-year-old in a hug.

Brewer detailed the events. When he was finished, he looked to Alexander McSween, but McSween's head was spinning. His business partner was dead, he was about to go on trial for embezzlement, and their third partner, John Chisum, was hiding out in a Las Vegas jail, seemingly washing his hands of the whole affair.

"We kill them," Billy finally answered. "We kill them all."

Susan's heart broke for the Kid. She could see how much

Tunstall meant to him. She could also see the rage inside that, if unleashed, was just as likely to end his life far too soon.

"We need to take inventory," Alex McSween said.

"Who cares about inventory at a time like this?" Billy asked.

"Not of stock, but of men. We need to find out who is on our side and who is in the pocket of the House. We need to know how strong an opposition we can put together. If we get enough people from Lincoln and the surrounding villages, we might have a chance."

"And if not?" John Middleton asked.

"Then we leave Lincoln behind, never to return," Susan answered.

"I'm not scattering anywhere ever again," Billy said. He'd finally found a home, a family, a life he wanted. But first Dolan, Evans, Buck, Kinney—the whole goddamn Santa Fe Ring—had to be driven out of existence.

"And how do you propose to do that, Billy?" Widenmann asked. "We're outmanned, outgunned, outmonied."

"One at a time if I have to," Billy replied. "Starting with Buck fuckin' Morton."

Just past 4:00 a.m., fifty men and women, all Tunstall-McSween supporters, crowded into McSween's home to discuss what to do next. Among the throng was the new justice of the peace, John B. Wilson. Wilson had been appointed just four days earlier, when his predecessor, sensing the growing strife, abruptly resigned. Wilson was an affable man who could be counted on to help a neighbor build a fence or carry goods from the store to a widower's home. Now he stood in McSween's living room being debriefed on what sounded an awful lot like a murder.

"Is anyone willing to sign an affidavit attesting to what they witnessed?" Wilson asked.

Billy and Brewer stepped forward and recalled what happened.

"Signing a piece of paper doesn't change the situation," Brewer said. "Dolan still has the Boys, the Seven Rivers Warriors, and the Kinney Gang on his side, as well as the courts and politicians in Santa Fe."

"I thought I saw Buckshot Roberts riding with them too," Middleton added. The mention of loner Buckshot Roberts riding alongside Jesse Evans and John Kinney quieted the room.

"Who's going to stop them, Wilson? You?" Billy finally asked.

No, thought Wilson. *Not me.* "I will issue warrants for the arrests of the men present and will deputize you to apprehend the wanted."

Billy noticed most of the men suddenly found great interest in the tops of their boots.

"Deputize me," Billy said. "Give me the power to bring these men in and I will, even if I have to do it alone. Because if the good people of Lincoln don't stand up and resist in the face of this tyranny, then there's no hope for any of us."

"Horseshit," Brewer said to no one in particular.

"Something on your mind, Dicky?"

"You going there as defender of public interest is laughable."

"You want to wait and hide behind another knoll until they kill Alex? Or Fred? Or me?"

"No, I'm getting deputized right alongside you, Billy. These men will face justice for what they've done. By the power of the courts and the people of Lincoln. We do this right. It's the only way to end this thing."

The other men weighed the risks of going after the House, if not the whole ring.

Scurlock and Bowdre finally nudged each other forward. "We'll ride with you."

Then John Middleton, Fred Waite, and Robert Widenmann, followed by the Coe cousins, and José Chávez y Chávez. Chávez was a petty thief–turned–constable of the small Mexican town San Patricio, just miles outside Lincoln. He was beloved in his community, and an endorsement from him meant they would have the local Mexican people on their side.

All in all, thirteen men signed on.

"What do we call ourselves?" Charlie Bowdre asked.

"How about the law?" fired back Brewer, who wanted the group to be taken seriously, not just seen as another posse of rustlers meting out their own brand of justice.

"No, that don't have any sort of poetry to it. We need something to let people know we're restoring peace in Lincoln. Making it safe to live and raise their families. Making things regular again," Widenmann replied.

"No one gives a damn what we're called," Brewer answered.

"The Regulators," Billy said. "We'll call ourselves the Regulators."

He didn't see Brewer roll his eyes.

"Who is my point of contact?" Wilson asked.

"Dick," Billy said. "That way you can ensure everything is on the up-and-up."

Brewer glared at him, but the other eleven men nodded in unison, so it was settled.

"Now let's go get Tunstall's store back," Billy said.

Billy, Fred Waite, and Constable Atanacio Martinez walked over to the Tunstall store with warrants in one hand, rifles in the other.

Sheriff Brady was leaning against a post outside Tunstall's store as the men approached.

"A couple hares and a Mexican?" Brady jeered. "To do what?"

"We have warrants for the arrests of sixteen men involved in the murder of John Tunstall, including you, Sheriff," Billy said.

"Me? What for? I've been sitting in this new store of ours for a couple days now, making sure the riffraff doesn't return."

"We have witnesses who say you and your deputies inside have been stealing hay," Constable Martinez said.

"Hay? Well, shit, don't shoot!" Brady replied, laughing.

Billy took one step toward Brady when he heard the unmistakable sound of firearms cocking. Deputy Sheriff Peppin and four other men stepped out from the side of the building.

"The six of us—I myself rightly elected by the good people of Lincoln to maintain law and order—are going to arrest *you*."

"On what charge?" Billy asked.

"I don't know," Brady replied. "Maybe I'll think of something. Maybe not."

Brady let Constable Martinez go, saying he was just doing his job and this didn't involve him. Then they took Billy's and Fred Waite's guns and walked them to the Lincoln County jail.

"This is a nice Winchester, boy," Brady said, goading Billy as he fingered the rifle. "It's a shame you lost it."

Billy felt a fire rise up the back of his neck and his face go flush. Tunstall had given him that rifle. He loved that rifle. It *meant something* to him.

"What's lost can be found again," Billy said, right before Brady closed the roof over their heads.

Chapter 21

LINCOLN COUNTY, NEW MEXICO TERRITORY

"I come to you not as an aggrieved party but rather as an officer of the law. The men we seek to put on trial are a ruthless bunch, and it is not fair to ask the good citizens of Lincoln to help detain them."

Robert Widenmann was in Fort Stanton, hoping his new deputy status would be enough to convince Colonel Dudley to have troops aid in apprehending the wanted men.

"We can't go around locking up American citizens," Captain Purington countered.

"When you joined the army, did you not swear an oath to 'bear true allegiance to the United States of America, and to serve them honestly and faithfully, against all their enemies or opposers *whatsoever* . . .'"

Dudley knew the ambiguity of the word *whatsoever* and could have used it as his out. Half of his men had fought in the Civil War, taking up arms against their fellow countrymen. He wasn't eager to enlist them to do so once again.

"Colonel, please," Widenmann continued, sensing he was losing the argument. "These are the very dregs grifting you and your men here at Fort Stanton. They're swindling from the Mescalero Apache Indian Reservation. Their corruption and lethality is boundless. If you do not help us, there is no hope for anyone."

Dudley looked out the small window and loaded a pipe.

Then he called in his aide and had him ready the troops for a trip to Lincoln.

LINCOLN

LINCOLN COUNTY, NEW MEXICO TERRITORY

"Looks like a crowd's gathering over at the store," Sheriff Brady goaded Billy, who was still in the pit with Fred Waite. "Everyone's got on their Sunday best. Why do you think that is?"

Billy dug his nails into the hard mud flooring, fuming over missing his friend's funeral. It made him feel like he was disrespecting Tunstall.

It made him feel like his stepfather.

"Hey, Kid," Brady continued. "Did someone die?"

"The first of many, Brady."

Brady laughed at Billy, but if he'd seen the Kid's face, he would not have.

Billy had been truthful when he volunteered to be deputized. He had wanted justice, just as Dick had. But as he and Waite toiled away another day in the pit, Billy's mind had nowhere else to roam but to the extremes of his inclinations. Perhaps that's why he tilted his head back against the wall, closed his eyes, and relaxed. He was no longer thinking of justice. His life had purpose again. From here on out, the only thing on his mind was revenge.

And it was freeing.

Colonel Dudley's troops, led by Captain Purington, arrived in Lincoln the following day. Their first act was to follow Brewer to the jail.

"I'm glad you're here, Captain. I was just about to set these boys free," Brady said, eyeing the considerable force standing in front of him. "I believe they've learned their lesson." He nodded to Deputy Sheriff Peppin, who retrieved Billy and Waite from the pit.

The sunlight was blinding to the two men who'd spent the past three days in darkness, and Billy squinted one eye closed as he turned to Brady. "My rifle."

"I don't know what you're talking about," Brady replied.

"Have it your way," Billy said as he and Waite descended the steps.

"I better not see you coming around no more, Billy Bonney," Brady said.

"Don't worry—you won't see me coming at all," Billy replied.

Brady's remaining deputies were still guarding Tunstall's store, claiming it was the ruling of the courts since Tunstall and McSween were partners. Captain Purington gave them two minutes to vacate, or else the army would force them out.

After Brady's men left, Purington addressed his soldiers. "Fifteen minutes to eat or rest, then back to Fort Stanton."

Brewer was stunned. "Captain, the job is not yet finished."

"I don't see how. You have your store back."

"But we need help in arresting Dolan's men. We have warrants for eighteen criminals," Widenmann said.

"I have done what I could, but all other matters in the county of Lincoln need to be handled within the confines of the local legal system."

"Let 'em go, Dick," Billy said. "They were never gonna help us anyway."

Fifteen minutes later, Captain Purington and the soldiers went back to Fort Stanton, leaving Billy and his friends blowing in the wind.

"We're sitting ducks once again," Widenmann said.

"Nah. Ducks don't have stars," Billy replied.

"A badge isn't going to save us. We're farmers and ranchers and doctors," Bowdre answered, nodding in the direction of Scurlock.

"Not anymore, we ain't," Billy replied, spinning the chamber of his Colt, then snapping it into place. "Now we're the aggressors."

While Billy and the newly minted deputies were planning how to serve the warrants, Alexander McSween was writing John Tunstall's father. He got directly to the point, laying out the facts of the morning his son was killed, by whom, and what had transpired since. When he finished the letter, he sealed it, and gave it to Robert Widenmann to mail.

Then talk turned to what McSween and Susan needed to do to ensure their safety.

"You can't stay here," Widenmann told him.

"I won't let Dolan chase me out of town."

"Goddammit, Alex," Susan countered. "You've seen what they did to John. Do you want to be next? And what if they miss you and hit me?"

"Alex," Widenmann interjected, hoping to quell the marital tension. "There's a place in the hills about ten miles outside town. You can set up camp on the bluff, and you'll be able to spot anyone headed your way. We can keep a couple of men with you too."

"Then you go," he replied.

The response hit Susan like a blow to the stomach. "No one will write of your gallantry, only of your pigheadedness," she told him. "I'm going, and if you're not with me, I may just ride right past the hills on to Santa Fe and board the next train back east."

"I'm sure your sister would be happy to see you again," McSween said.

"I won't be going to my sister's, and I sure as hell won't be going back to my family in Pennsylvania. But know this: *you'll* never see me again." Susan stormed out of the room.

A moment went by, then McSween could hear her packing in the bedroom.

"Alex . . ." Widenmann said. "Go be with your wife. Keep her safe. Me and the fellas will clean up around here."

McSween turned to his jailer, the deputy who had been sitting silently. "And you, Deputy? Will you let me leave even though I am under house arrest?"

"My job is to keep you alive until trial. Seems to me the easiest way to do that is if you aren't here," he replied.

McSween scribbled out a last will and testament, then they fled their home.

Dolan returned to Lincoln with a renewed sense of bravado. The first thing he did was go check on the prisoners in the pit.

"What the hell, *Sheriff*?" he said upon seeing Billy and Waite had been released. "You let the prisoners escape?"

"They didn't escape so much as walk out the front door," Brady shot back. "Me and Peppin ain't exactly equipped to take on the US Army."

"Troops were here?"

"A whole regiment out of Fort Stanton."

Dolan's blood was cooling and his mind working hard on how to spin this in their favor. He reckoned, rightly, Dudley wasn't going to send troops *back* to Lincoln when they were just here. And he knew Dudley likely viewed this whole affair in Lincoln as a minor kerfuffle distracting his men from more important matters.

"Let's go get McSween," Dolan said.

"On what charges? He's already under house arrest until trial."

"Don't you see? The army cleared out. Now we can run Lincoln as it was meant to be run."

"Dammit!" Brady yelled out when they peered through the windows of the empty McSween house. "Coward fled."

Dolan smiled. McSween had skipped town. Bad for the prospect of inflicting pain on him.

But good for business.

"You're gonna write a letter, Sheriff."

"To whom?"

"To the only man who matters."

SANTA FE

SANTA FE COUNTY, NEW MEXICO TERRITORY

"Bunny, slow down and chew your food."

Not many people could get away with telling Thomas "Boss" Catron what to do, but he adored Julia Anna Walz and gave her leeway he did not afford others. She was seventeen years younger than him—just two years older than Billy Bonney—and they were engaged. He loved her vibrancy and the way she could tease him gently while still demonstrating how much she loved him.

"Apologies, Miss Walz, but I am running late."

"I know you're all in a tizzy about your meeting tonight,

secret as it may be, but you won't do anybody no good at all if you choke to death during supper. Besides, there isn't a meeting in all of Santa Fe that won't wait on you for it to begin."

Catron pulled the pocket watch from his vest and checked the time: 6:58 p.m. Julia was right—the meeting wouldn't start without him, but he had hoped to arrive early and have a word with one of his fellow lodge members.

An hour prior, a courier had handed Catron an urgent message from the sheriff of Lincoln County. Catron never cared for Brady, or L.G. Murphy and James Dolan. He thought they had a grandiose view of their problems, as if they were the only ones to ever face competition. The Lincoln "disputes," as Catron would often derisively call them to friends in Santa Fe, were but one small issue on his rather large plate.

But now, as he held a letter in his hands from Sheriff Brady, Catron's mind began to whir. There might be an opportunity to further enrich himself and his partners in the ring, even if it meant sacrificing a few lambs like Dolan and Brady. Catron folded the letter into his pocket.

It was a short walk to the northeast corner of the Plaza, where the Grand Lodge of Masons in New Mexico would convene for the first time. The fraternal order included many prominent members of the Santa Fe Ring. Catron was the grand lecturer. Lincoln County DA William Rynerson was the deputy grand master. But the master of ceremonies that evening was the man Catron wanted to speak to: Territorial Governor Samuel Beach Axtell.

Axtell came from a long line of soldiers, and his ancestors had fought in every war dating back to independence. But Axtell had never enlisted, choosing law school instead. Like many, he headed west during the California gold rush, and like many, he struck out.

And like many who failed at their preferred vocation, he turned to politics.

President Grant had selected him to be governor of the New Mexico Territory.

Axtell quickly fell in with the Santa Fe Ring, using his office to accrue power and punish their enemies. Now Catron was counting on the governor to do the ring's bidding once again.

Catron approached the hall and could see everyone inside anticipating his arrival. *Let them*, he thought. It's like his bride-to-be had said. True power is when the meeting waits on you.

He lit a cigar and looked up at the night sky. It was cool and brisk, perfect weather to the stout Catron. After a few puffs, when his dominance had been sufficiently conveyed, he entered.

He spotted Axtell, dressed in a garish robe and apron, a callback to the Masonry of the founding fathers.

"Samuel, a word?" Catron said. Catron refused to grant him the honorific *governor*. It would be ceding power to an inferior.

"In a moment, Mr. Catron. I must prepare my remarks."

Axtell took his Mason duties seriously, perhaps more seriously than being governor. Catron grabbed him forcefully by the elbow and led him to a private area, away from others. Catron locked eyes with District Attorney Rynerson and nodded for him to join.

"I am hearing rumblings of goings-on in Lincoln County," Catron said.

"It's a small dispute, nothing the sheriff and his men can't dispose of," Rynerson replied.

"Cut the shit. If Brady had it under control, he wouldn't have sent me this."

Catron pulled the Brady letter from his pocket for Rynerson and Axtell to read.

"Seems like more than a small dispute," Catron continued. "A skirmish or two we can downplay, but we can't have people afraid to go outside."

"One lecherous man, John Tunstall, was killed in self-defense. If the Englishman hadn't pulled a gun on the peace officers, he'd still be alive today," Rynerson said.

"Gentlemen, I hardly see what this has to do with me," Governor Axtell replied.

Catron looked at him sideways. "There's a band of outlaws running roughshod over the county, looking to lynch any man they perceive as being on the side of James Dolan, the House, or *our friends.*"

"Perhaps we should call in the troops from Fort Stanton . . ." Axtell floated.

"Perhaps we should," Catron answered. He couldn't believe it took this much cajoling to get Axtell to see the light. "Perhaps you should get authorization from the president to enlist troops to aid in capturing these outlaws."

"I'll write President Hayes this evening and have the letter sent."

"Samuel, your political skills and ability to inspire are unparalleled. Now go," Catron said.

"You can lead a horse to water," Rynerson remarked, once Axtell was across the room.

"This idiot doesn't even know he *is* a fucking horse," Catron replied.

That night, Governor Axtell wrote to President Hayes outlining everything that had taken place in Lincoln—from Dolan's perspective, at least—and requested authorization to use the troops at Fort Stanton to "assist civil law enforcement" in maintaining order.

The answer was a resounding yes.

The army was coming back to Lincoln, and this time they were not on the side of the Regulators.

Chapter 22

"Maybe they left the county," Bowdre said.

"Maybe they left the territory," Scurlock replied.

"Hell, they probably ditched the country altogether," added José Chávez y Chávez.

Billy and the Regulators, led by Dick Brewer, had scoured Lincoln County for the better part of a week, and there was still no sign of the eighteen men for whom they held warrants.

"You want to go home, no one's stopping you. But me and Dick here, we're following this all the way through," Billy replied.

Brewer ignored the Kid, knowing Billy liked to lump the two of them together as a show of strength, but even Brewer was having doubts they'd find the men responsible for Tunstall's murder. *If you're Evans or Morton, would you still be in Lincoln?*

But short of evidence the men had vacated the territory, Brewer had no choice but to press on. He owed it to Justice of the Peace Wilson, who had stuck his neck out and deputized him and the rest of the ranch hands. He owed it to his fellow Regulators, who had unanimously elected him leader of their posse. Most of all, he owed it to his friend and employer, the late John Tunstall.

He worried about Billy though. Something in the Kid had changed since Tunstall's murder three weeks ago. Billy hadn't hardened, per se, but rather had become . . . *looser*. Quicker with a joke. Quicker to laugh in the face of absurdity. It was a ballsy way to live, Brewer thought, especially in a territory where anything goes. His newfound fearlessness could be their salvation.

Or it could lead right to their deaths.

The sun was setting as the Regulators continued north toward Tunstall's ranch. Brewer looked at the men. Bowdre could hardly keep his eyes open. Scurlock and José Chávez y Chávez hadn't said a word in nearly two hours. Even the normally vibrant Billy had taken to hunching forward on this horse, resting his head on his arms.

"We should cut wide around Bob Gilbert's ranch," Brewer said quietly to his second-in-command, Frank McNab, who nodded in agreement. Gilbert was also known to be sympathetic to the House, and if he was harboring any Dolan men, now was not the time to engage.

Next to Brewer, Frank McNab was the most levelheaded Regulator. McNab had been a Texas cattle detective, investigating and locating Chisum's missing livestock. But it was hard work and required long stretches away from home, so McNab had resigned, hoping to start a life in Lincoln. He began working on Tunstall's ranch and formed a close friendship with Brewer. So when Dick needed aid in hunting down Tunstall's killers, McNab didn't think twice.

Billy was the first to see the fire. There, along the edge of the Rio Peñasco, men were warming themselves before settling in for the night.

"It's them," he said.

"We don't know that, Billy," Brewer replied. "Why would they be out here instead of inside Bob Gilbert's place?"

"Because they know we're looking for them, and they know we'll check all their usual hangouts. This way they aren't inside the ranch, where they could be cornered, but they're close enough they can pop in for food and supplies."

Shit, Brewer thought. *It made sense.* "We need to make sure these are men we actually have warrants for."

"Only one way to find out," Billy said, then he headed straight for the campsite.

"Aw, damn," Dick said before riding out after him, followed by the rest of the Regulators.

Billy's suspicions were confirmed when the three campers scrambled to their mares.

Billy saw the flash of the muzzle and heard the bullet zip by his ear. He spurred his horse, pulled his Colt Peacemaker, and returned fire, the fleeing men and the Regulators exchanging volleys amid darkening skies.

For five miles, the Regulators didn't seem to be closing the gap, then one of the fleeing horses buckled, sending the rider sprawling to the ground.

As Billy and the Regulators rode up on him, Rich Lloyd covered his head, sure he would be either trampled or shot.

"Who's with you?" Billy said. Lloyd was terrified. "There's about two answers you can give that'll save your life."

"Baker and Bu-Buck Morton," Lloyd stuttered out.

Billy slapped the reins and continued on after his white whale.

"What do we do with him?" Bowdre asked.

"No warrant for him," McNab replied. "Cut him loose."

Rich Lloyd got up and disappeared on foot, never to be heard from again.

A mile on, Billy came upon another discarded horse. Fifty yards beyond that, the third.

McNab was the first to spot the tracks. Two men scrambling into a thicket of bushes.

"Ohhhh Buuuuuck," Billy called out.

"Cut it, Billy. This isn't a game, and they still got guns," Brewer replied.

Billy ignored him. "Bucky, Bucky, Bucky . . . are these your size nines heading straight into the shrubs? Or is that Baker's? Frank, you back there, pal?"

"You sure it's Morton and Baker?" Brewer asked.

"I'm certain, Dick," Billy said, loud enough for Morton and Baker to hear.

"C'mon out, Morton. Show yourself, Baker. We have warrants for your arrest."

"You're just gonna kill us," came a voice.

Billy smiled. "Didn't you hear, Frank? We're the *law* now."

It wasn't of any comfort to Morton and Baker, but they had little choice. Three guns came over the shrubs. Bowdre took a step forward, but Billy stopped him.

"Buck, we both know you still got that peashooter on you too." Sure enough, a tiny revolver, small enough to fit in a pocket, landed harmlessly in the dirt.

"How do we know you won't kill us?" Baker asked.

"Maybe we will, maybe we won't, but some things in life are certain. If you don't come out, you'll die for sure."

Billy took out a book of matches and struck one, then set it against the base of the dry brush. A gust of wind killed the flame.

"Whoo, did you get lucky there," he laughed.

"Quit it, Billy," Brewer said. He didn't like the glee in the Kid's voice.

Billy lit another match, and this time the brush caught.

The fire spread and thick black smoke rose into the night air.

"All right, all right," Baker said, then he skipped out, patting down his pants and boots to extinguish the flame at his cuffs. Buck slowly followed, glowering, his eyes locked on Billy.

Billy raised his Colt. He placed his finger on the trigger.

Five pounds of pressure. One light squeeze. To end Buck Morton's miserable fucking life.

"Billy, we gave our word," Bowdre said.

"He killed Mr. Tunstall."

"And he'll stand trial for it," Brewer replied. Brewer put his hand on the barrel of Billy's Colt and directed the gun toward the ground.

"You gonna give some speech about how if I pull this trigger I'm no different than Buck? What say you, Buck?" Billy asked their new prisoner. "We alike, you and me?"

"I suppose maybe we are," Buck answered carefully.

"You're not a murderer, Billy," Scurlock said. "And that's what this would be. Murder."

Billy continued to stare at Morton, every ounce of Billy's body telling him to cut Buck down just as Buck had done to Tunstall and countless other innocent people.

A slight smirk came across Buck's face.

"They don't know, do they, *Billy*?"

"What don't we know?" Scurlock inquired.

"Billy Bonney may not be a killer . . . but Henry Antrim sure as hell is."

"Who the fuck is Antrim?" Bowdre asked.

"Antrim's the one who shot Windy Cahill over in Arizona," said Brewer, the reality dawning on him. "Billy . . . are you Henry Antrim?"

Billy focused on his hand. It wasn't shaking. On his breathing. Steady and even. His palms. Dry as a bone. The only thing moving at all was his mind, seeping red with hatred for Morton. He could kill Buck and still have a full appetite come dinnertime.

And Buck knew it too.

Billy holstered his gun. "Yeah, Dick. I'm Henry Antrim. Least I used to be."

The Regulators loaded their two prisoners onto horses and started north up the Pecos River, headed back to Lincoln. Billy took it upon himself to be Buck's personal escort, riding behind him, the Colt never leaving Billy's hand.

Billy was studying Buck Morton's and Frank Baker's demeanor. It made sense for Buck to not be on edge, Billy thought. That's just his way. Stone-cold killer. But Baker was more high-strung, the type of guy who would startle and pull if a waiter dropped a pitcher. And here he was, after the emotion of their surrender had subsided, cool as a fall breeze.

"Dick, it ever occur to you there might a party waiting for us in Lincoln?" Billy asked.

It had crossed Brewer's mind, and he'd been twisting himself in knots figuring out how to turn the prisoners over without facing mortal rebuttals from the Dolan faction in town.

"It's late too," McNab added. "South Spring's only about ten miles east. Chisum'll let us rest for the night. He owes us at least that much."

Brewer thought about it. It would give the Regulators a chance to collect themselves and figure out how to get their prisoners back into Lincoln.

JOHN CHISUM'S SOUTH SPRING RANCH
LINCOLN COUNTY, NEW MEXICO TERRITORY

Sallie opened the door in the middle of the night.

"Miss Chisum, we're transporting these men back to Lincoln for the murder of John Tunstall. I promise we'll be back on the trail first thing in the morning."

Sallie looked at the motley crew of dirty men on her porch. But she knew Brewer and McNab a little, and thought she recognized Bowdre and Scurlock.

"I'll make up my room for the prisoners," she said and let them in.

"Miss Chisum," Billy said, doffing his cap as he passed. Sallie just stared back curiously at the strange young man with a crooked smile on his face.

Sallie woke the cook to fix a meal for the visitors. Billy wasn't hungry, and he'd broken bread with Buck Morton for the last time. He spotted the latest newspaper and took it out onto the porch, where he found a bench swing to ease into.

The lead article of the *Santa Fe Gazette* described the Mescalero Apache warrior Victorio and the raids he was leading on white settlers in the territory. Words jumped off the page at Billy: "Terrifying! . . . Savages . . . Criminals . . . Cannibals . . ."

Bullshit, he thought. Lolotea and her family weren't savages or criminals, and they sure as hell weren't no people-eaters.

The front door opened and Sallie exited onto the porch, book in hand, thinking she was alone. She startled when she saw Billy sitting there, then regained her composure.

"Perusing the pictures?" she asked.

"I can read, Miss Chisum."

"I'm sorry . . ."

"Billy. Billy Bonney."

"Mr. Bonney, I didn't mean to imply you were illiterate," she said, looking him over. He was dirty and gave off a stench after more than a week without a proper cleaning.

"Don't worry—illiterate's about the nicest thing anyone's called me in weeks." Sallie couldn't help but smile, which made Billy grin too. "I'm awfully sorry we barged in on you tonight," he said.

"It's no inconvenience, Mr. Bonney. I was getting lonely in the house all by myself."

"You got your cook and the maid."

"They're my uncle's employees, not my friends. Not the types I can actually talk to."

"What about your uncle? He still in jail?" Billy asked.

"No, Santa Fe. He's trying to procure government contracts. He thinks we might be able to supply the beef to Fort Stanton and the reservations."

"Dolan and Riley's contracts? I don't think they'll shed them easily."

"Perhaps not, but they're weakened. They just had to mortgage everything to First National Bank of Santa Fe."

Billy knew of the First National Bank of Santa Fe and its controller. "So your uncle's gonna cut a deal with Catron?"

"He's going to do whatever he can for the business—for this family—to prosper."

"And what about Tunstall? What about McSween?"

"Points that have been raised, Mr. Bonney." She studied him carefully, weighing her words. Something about the way he looked at her, about the way he *was*, turned her candid.

"I have told my uncle that any deal with Catron and First National will reflect poorly on his partnership with Mr. McSween, but my protestations fell on deaf ears."

"Your uncle don't mind you expressing your thoughts like that?"

"I have two brothers and a sister, none of whom have a lick of sense about business. But in me, my uncle sees someone he can lean on."

A man came riding up to the house, and Billy slid his hand down to his side until it was resting on the handle of his Colt. Billy looked the rider over. He had on a clean, finely tailored suit, a vest, and a gold pocket watch.

And he'd properly bathed recently.

"Mr. Bonney, meet Mr. Thomas Roberts, one of my uncle's accountants."

"Business associates, Sallie, please."

"One of my uncle's accountants and business associates," she half-corrected.

"He fuckin' you over too?" Billy asked Roberts.

"Is he . . . no, Mr. Chisum has been quite upstanding. And I'll have to ask you not to use such coarseness in front of the lady."

Billy didn't know why, but he felt an air of competition with this man. "*A* lady, or *the* lady?"

"What are you doing here, Mr. Roberts?" Sallie interjected.

"I got word of a commotion at the ranch and came as fast I could."

"Mr. Roberts has taken it upon himself to watch over me while Uncle is away. And I, for one, am grateful for his mindedness."

Billy recognized Sallie was poking fun at Mr. Roberts, a fact lost on Chisum's associate.

"Miss Sallie, your safety is of the utmost concern. I am glad to see you are well and lively this evening."

"Thank you, Mr. Roberts," Sallie said, then she made a dramatic show of taking a seat next to Billy on the swing. "There is some food on the table if you're hungry."

Billy thought he saw a flash of jealousy streak across Roberts's face. Roberts hesitated, his eyes darting between Sallie and the dirty, strange young man next to her on the swing.

"Thank you, Thomas," Sallie said, emphatic enough to make her point and send Roberts inside the house.

"He's keen on you," Billy said, studying her. "But you knew that already."

"I should. He's proposed a half dozen times already."

"Why ain't you said yes?"

"Because I have ambition."

Billy let that hang in the air for a bit. Ambition. He knew what it meant in theory but not practice. He wondered about his own ambition. Did he have any at all? What did he want out of life? What would he do to get it?

What he wanted most, more than anything in the world, was for his mother and John Tunstall to be alive. An ill feeling formed in the pit of his stomach. Where does that leave a man, when the only things he truly desires are impossible to achieve?

He distracted himself by picking Sallie's book up off her lap.

"What's it about?"

"An enchanting young woman who fends off suitor after suitor, instead relishing her independence and fostering her true passion, overseeing her uncle's estate."

Billy studied the cover.

"*Far from the Madding Crowd*, huh? Then what?"

"I don't know. I haven't finished it yet."

"What would you like to see happen?"

"I would hope Bathsheba Everdene does not succumb to the expectations society has for her and retains her independence."

"So she'll never find love?"

"What is love if not on your own terms?"

Billy didn't have an answer. Instead, he and Sallie spent another hour rocking quietly on the bench, Billy reading his paper while Sallie continued her novel.

Billy didn't remember the last thing they said to each other. He didn't remember the last thing he read in the paper. He didn't remember drifting off to sleep, lulled by the gently rocking swing.

That night, his usual dream of being thrust into the dark void of a forest did not come. Instead, his mind conjured up a pleasant story of a soldier returning from war to find true love. The heroine of his tale shared Sallie's more remarkable qualities.

When morning came, he was still upright on the swing, a blanket draped over him.

Chapter 23

Governor Axtell arrived without an entourage. He went straight to the House—now officially renamed J. J. Dolan & Co.—and found the proprietors, along with Sheriff Brady.

"Morning, Governor. I am pleased you were able to take time out of your busy schedule to grace us common folks in Lincoln," Dolan said with more than a hint of sarcasm.

Boss Catron had "suggested" Governor Axtell survey the goings-on in Lincoln himself and see if there might be an end to the unrest. Any resolution, of course, would have to be cleared through Catron, but that was just the price of governing in New Mexico.

"Perhaps it's best if we get started," Axtell said. He didn't want to be in this hellhole of a town any longer than he had to be.

Sheriff Brady was beginning to question his own role in this entire affair. Moments of reflection and doubt, which used to only arrive after a night of raising so many whiskeys his elbow hurt, now appeared in the light of day as well.

"I'll show you everything you need to know," Brady said, then ambled out of J. J. Dolan & Co., followed by the governor, Dolan, and Riley.

JOHN CHISUM'S SOUTH SPRING RANCH

LINCOLN COUNTY, NEW MEXICO TERRITORY

Billy was still on the porch while the others ate breakfast inside. He was hoping for one more moment with Sallie, just the two of them.

The door opened and he got his wish. Sallie looked at the young man with the blanket still draped over him, then stretched her neck. She'd given up her room to the prisoners and had taken Uncle John's bed, but she wasn't used to his stiff pillow and firm mattress.

"Care for me to rub it out?" Billy asked.

"I'd care for you to keep your hands to yourself, Mr. Bonney."

"My mom had the same issue—never could rest comfortably, especially once she got sick. I got pretty good at easing her pain."

"Your mother passed?"

"Three years ago," Billy said with as much resolve as he could muster. "Consumption."

Sallie winced. "I'm sorry for your loss."

"She'd be mighty sore at me if I couldn't help a lady in need," Billy said.

He cocked his head and gave her another goofy smile, a trait she wasn't sure was for effect or was just natural upon his face. Either way, she let out a snort of laughter, despite herself.

"Whoa, Miss Sallie, I may work with sows from time to time, but that don't mean I speak their language."

She laughed again, which caused Billy to crack up, and before they knew it the two teenagers couldn't catch their breath.

"I swear, Mr. Bonney, I have yet to meet another like you."

"That's too bad. I was hoping someone might be mistaken for me and catch all the heat I got comin' my way."

Thomas Roberts, hearing the laughter, came out of the house and looked back and forth between Billy and Sallie, wondering what he'd been left out of.

"Nothing, Mr. Roberts. I was just thanking Miss Sallie for the hospitality she's shown."

"Well, your men are finishing up their breakfast . . ." Roberts said.

"Then I, too, shall prepare myself for the ride," Billy replied, mimicking Roberts's formal tone, which got another smile out of Sallie.

Billy stood fast, not realizing the blood had left his legs from sitting on the swing all night, and he wobbled sideways. He would have fallen had Sallie not caught him.

"Why, Bathsheba, I do believe you saved my life," he said, then winked. Sallie stifled another laugh as Billy went inside.

LINCOLN

LINCOLN COUNTY, NEW MEXICO TERRITORY

James Dolan, Sheriff Brady, and John Riley stayed attached to Axtell's hip as the governor went door-to-door speaking to various citizens of Lincoln. Most, upon seeing the men accompanying the governor, were struck with fear and had nothing but kind things to say about the House. The only man to speak his truth was Justice of the Peace John B. Wilson.

"I am simply here on a fact-finding mission, Mr. Wilson,"

Axtell said. "My goal is to get to the bottom of the unrest in Lincoln and find a peaceful solution for all."

"Are you looking for peace or for justice?"

"They're one and the same."

"Not in my experience," replied Wilson.

"I understand you were the one to take the accounts of what the men alleged to have seen?"

Alleged to have seen.

"Yes. Richard Brewer, William Bonney, and others recounted in great detail and similitude the events of February eighteenth. Mr. Tunstall and his employees were transporting horses and were just south of Lincoln when a band of twenty or so aggressors rode upon the men, scattering Mr. Tunstall's employees. Mr. Tunstall was not able or willing to flee, and after a brief conversation with the band, three shots were fired—one, then a break, then two more. When Mr. Tunstall's employees emerged from hiding, they found their boss dead in the dirt, his horse expired next to him, and someone had placed Mr. Tunstall's hat atop the steed's head."

Wilson thought he detected a slight flinch at the callousness of the last detail.

"There is a competing account of self-defense, with the accused claiming Mr. Tunstall fired at them first."

"Hogwash, Governor. One man up against twenty decides to pull his pistol? And he fired one shot, then took a break and let them draw on him?"

"Did any of the witnesses see Jesse Evans, Buck Morton, Frank Baker, or any other so-called assailant actually pull first?"

So-called assailant.

Wilson bit his cheek. The purpose of the governor's trip to Lincoln was clear now.

"No, Governor, the men feared for their lives and took cover

in nearby brush, around the bend from where Mr. Tunstall was
so coldly murdered."

"So no firsthand accounts."

"If you're walking down Main Street and step in fresh
horseshit, one can surmise a horse was recently there," Wilson
answered.

"A grotesque parallel when you're talking about trying men
for *murder*, Justice Wilson."

"Due to these factors, along with the coroner's inquiry,
which validated the men's statements, I declared John Tunstall
had indeed been *murdered in cold blood* and issued warrants for
the arrests of the men responsible."

"And whom did you task with carrying out these warrants?"
Axtell asked.

"I deputized Richard Brewer, Frank McNab, William
Bonney, and a small gallery of men to apprehend the subjects
and transport them to Lincoln to face a grand jury."

"So the very 'witnesses' whose friend was found dead—"

"No, sir, not 'found dead,'" Wilson replied with more force
than he meant to. "Murdered."

"Whose friend was *found dead* are now acting as judge, jury,
and executioner?"

"Again, no, sir," Wilson exclaimed, his voice rising. "Their
directive is to bring the warranted in to face the legal system."

"Do you really think these so-called 'Regulators'—some
of whom are known murderers in their own right—will really
bring their subjects in alive?"

"Yes, sir, I do."

"Then you are too poor of judgment to remain in your
position. I hereby am removing you as justice of the peace of
Lincoln County and voiding any and all processes you have
rendered during your tenure."

In Governor Axtell's three hours in town, he had fired Wilson as justice of the peace, and in doing so undeputized the Regulators, rendering them powerless.

That should satisfy Catron, Axtell thought as he rode back to the capital.

Sheriff William Brady was now the only legal law enforcement in all of Lincoln County.

Billy and the Regulators left Chisum's ranch and shepherded the prisoners toward Lincoln.

Buck Morton had a request. "Can we stop in Roswell? I wanna mail something."

"We're not stopping until we get to Lincoln," Brewer said.

"This may be my last chance."

"He's right, Dick," Billy said, smiling. "Buck may not make it back to Lincoln at all."

"Quit it, Billy," Brewer replied. "No harm is gonna come to these men."

Billy looked at Buck and shrugged. *Maybe, maybe not.*

"A letter to my uncle. Just to let him know what's transpired," Buck said.

The Regulators and prisoners reached Roswell just past ten in the morning, and Brewer escorted Buck straight to the postmaster's office. Billy had offered to accompany them but was rebuked. Brewer knew Billy was looking to grind an axe other than just Tunstall's murder, and Billy had said nothing to disabuse him of that notion.

"World ain't gotta be about just one thing," Billy had replied.

Brewer knew the only way they'd get justice for Tunstall's

murder and find peace would be if there was a perception of fairness. If they murdered, or even abused, their prisoners before handing them over to authorities, the Regulators would be painted as just another outlaw posse enacting their own vigilante justice.

Billy had argued, with some success, that once they handed Buck and Baker over, the House and the ring would just find a way to free them. "Hell, look at them, Dick. They ain't even acting scared."

"Maybe it's just false bravado," declared McNab.

"Bullshit. They ain't scared because they know we ain't gonna do nothing, and when we turn them over to be put on trial, nothing's gonna happen to them there either."

"What do you propose we do?" Brewer asked, his patience growing thin.

"I say we adhere to the teachings of the Bible for this one, Dick."

"You ain't a churchgoer," Scurlock reminded the Kid.

"But I've read the Good Book," Billy replied. "And the Lord says you pluck out my eye, I'm sure as hell taking one of yours."

"Come on, Buck," Brewer said, and dragged Morton away.

Marshall "Ash" Upson was leaning on the counter. Buck smiled when he saw the man the postmaster was speaking with.

"Wasn't expecting to see you two palling around," McCloskey replied, grinning back.

"Buck is under arrest for the murder of John Tunstall," Brewer said. "We're taking him back to Lincoln."

"I'm headed to Lincoln myself," McCloskey said. "Maybe I'll tag along with y'all."

Brewer was already worried about one of the Regulators taking justice into their own hands. McCloskey's friendliness with the prisoners would only complicate things.

"C'mon, Dick, it's a long ride, and I'd sure love to have some company along the way."

But Brewer felt McCloskey was harmless. "All right, so long as you're ready to go now."

"First I got to let my people back east know what's going on should—dare I to even think it—justice not prevail and I end up swinging by my neck," Buck said.

He handed the letter to the postmaster.

"Are you expecting harm to befall you?" Ash Upson asked.

"I'll make sure no one gets hurt on the journey," McCloskey said.

"Are forces greater than you at work?"

"Shit, they'll have to kill me first," McCloskey replied, then he patted Buck on the back.

Chapter 24

The Regulators arrived in San Patricio just before dusk. Billy noticed the women were all dressed in their finest, brightest dresses, and the men had dusted off their Sunday best. José Chávez y Chávez was turning twenty-seven, and the whole town had gathered to greet him and the Regulators.

As the Regulators dismounted, Antonia Herrera was tasked with bringing them tin cups of mezcal. Brewer declined his, as did Frank McNab. Doc Scurlock took one but was more enchanted with the deliverer than the drink itself. He removed his hat and held it close to his chest as he gave a slight bend at the waist. Antonia blushed.

"Say, Doc, we need some place to put up our things," said Billy, a sly grin on his face.

"You got two legs," replied Doc, not taking his eyes off Antonia.

"Yours are longer. Maybe the lovely woman can show you our accommodations?"

"Might there be a place for us to sleep tonight?" Doc asked Antonia, picking up on Billy's lead. She just looked back at him, not understanding, but still smiling.

Doc tried again in her native tongue, but his Spanish was rusty and came out as nonsense, which made Antonia giggle.

"Goddammit," Doc muttered to himself. He leaned down to draw in the dirt.

"For the love of all that is holy," Billy said. *"¿Hay algún lugar para que nos quedemos esta noche?"*

"Sí," she replied. *"Te mostraré."* *I will show you.*

"Muéstrale a mi amigo," Billy replied, then left Doc and Antonia alone.

Billy didn't understand why the other Regulators were so sullen. They were in San Patricio, there was a party, and plenty of beautiful señoritas to dance with. He tossed his hat aside and made his way to the music, where he eased himself into a jig, stomping his feet to the rhythm of the band and enticing others to join.

Dick Brewer and Frank McNab wandered away from the throng of villagers, Billy, and the music. Dick removed his hat and thwapped it against his knee, knocking the dust away. McNab took a seat next to him and let out an exasperated sigh.

"Look at him," McNab said, nodding toward Billy, now encircled by a few dozen San Patricians, hopping along to the music. "Not a care in the world."

"I don't want to look at him. In fact, I'd like to rid myself of him altogether."

"This ain't the time to be shedding weight. Still a long row to hoe."

Brewer knew McNab was right, but the sight of Billy having a grand ol' time, after what had just transpired, left a pit in his stomach.

"What do you suppose he's so gay about anyway?" McNab asked.

"I sense things between the Kid and Buck went deeper than we realized."

All Brewer had wanted was a little piece of land to call his own, and tend to it and the livestock. But destiny got in his way.

No, fuck that. People got in his way.

People like Billy.

Earlier that day, the Regulators had been leading their captives, Buck Morton and Frank Baker, back to Lincoln. Brewer was riding point, and when they reached ten miles outside town, Billy galloped to the front to join him.

"Say, Dick, what do you suppose they got waiting for us?" Billy asked.

"I don't know, Billy." Brewer was getting more tense the closer they got to town.

"You think it's apple pie?"

"No, I don't think they have apple pie waiting for us."

"Maybe it's a nice cut of beef—something that melts in the mouth, you know?"

"Can you just shut your trap?"

"Naw, you're right. Most of the good cattle's up in San Miguel or Colfax about now."

Brewer had a headache all day, the kind that even the slightest breeze on the teeth caused to pulsate, and Billy wasn't helping.

"You know what, I think I figured it out," Billy continued. "I bet they got about a hundred men, each with two pistols and a rifle, waiting for our arrival."

Brewer gave him a side glance.

"I bet when we set foot in Lincoln it'll be like Gettysburg, only we ain't Union and we ain't Confederates, which just makes us fodder."

"Get to the point, Billy."

"If you was us, and we are, you'd take this very trail on this very day, at this very time, to transport these very prisoners into that very Lincoln."

"And I suppose you got some way around this predicament?" Brewer asked.

"Seems we might wanna cut through Agua Negra, stay off the main trail, lest Evans, Dolan, Brady, or any other sonofabitch gets a meaning to do us harm."

Brewer slowed to a stop, and the rest of the men did the same. The sun was now high, and there would be little cover once they reached Lincoln. "Goddammit."

Billy smiled as Brewer yanked the reins to lead the men into Agua Negra Canyon.

As the group made their way along the dry creek bed, Billy faded to the rear, next to Bowdre and Scurlock, to keep an eye on the prisoners.

He noticed Buck and Frank Baker whispering to one another. Could be conspiring, could be discussing how bad they had to shit. Billy wasn't close enough to hear. Soon McCloskey joined the two prisoners and threw his head back in laughter.

"Say, McCloskey, what's got you cacklin'?" Billy asked.

"Buck was just telling me about some rustler he and Jesse Evans tracked down this one time."

"Funny story, Buck?"

"About the funniest damn thing I witnessed firsthand," Buck responded coldly.

"Well, shit, I love a good story," Billy said. "Spin us that yarn."

"One time, me, Jesse, and the Boys had this pissant tagalong we couldn't shake free. Followed us everywhere we went, playing the big shot, thinking he was tough 'cause he was riding in our trail dust. Little *bastard* worshipped Jesse like a hero. I swear to you, he'd have sucked milk out of Jesse's teat if he could've. And Jesse, he felt sorry for the scrawny, motherless cunt, so he let him stick around."

Billy leaned forward on his horse, as if in rapt attention.

"We stopped in La Mesilla for a night," Buck continued, "and this young'un starts crying for his mommy, for his family, for his brother in Silver City. It got to be so much the women we were with started asking why we let a baby tag along."

McCloskey bellowed in laughter. Baker let out a small chuckle but kept an eye on Billy.

"So the runt, feeling ashamed of how he comported himself, sneaks out in the middle of the night. But before he does, he helps himself to a horse in town. But it weren't any ol' horse— it belonged to Sheriff Barela."

McCloskey whistled to show his enjoyment of the retelling.

The other Regulators were now paying attention as well.

"And Sheriff Barela, he was quite fond of this mare, for he had given it to his daughter on her ninth birthday. And his daughter was damn near devastated. *¿Dónde está Blancito? ¿Dónde está Blancito?*' She just kept repeating it over and over. So now the sheriff, he's all in a twist because his little girl's in tears. Jesse wanted to let it be, but me, I got a sense of honor, and it weren't right someone had stolen that little girl's best friend. So we tracked the runt down in the mountains. When we came up on him, he shit his britches. Right there, in front of a dozen of us Boys, he soiled himself like a helpless infant."

"Then what happened?" McCloskey asked.

"We took the horse, stripped the little fucker of his wet clothes, and made him walk naked through Apache country."

"You didn't kill him?"

"Naw, it would have been like shooting a puppy. Almost too cruel."

Billy adjusted himself in the saddle, aware Buck's and Baker's eyes were locked on him.

"I heard this story, Buck, but not how you tell it. I heard you were beating on a beautiful young filly, and she tired of you. Maybe if you'd brought the oak in the sheets she'd have put up with your shit, but you was flopping wet rope every night and just weren't worth the hassle."

McCloskey, unaware of the rising ire between Billy and Buck, laughed again.

"And this young fella—what'd you call him? Pissant? Runt? Baby?—he took up her defense, was the shoulder she leaned on, and he helped her escape your clutches. And that just riled you up so much you went to hunt him down, except when you caught up to him, he gave you the slip, and now you're left to cock your own gun every night."

Buck clenched his jaw and gripped the reins of his horse tightly.

Baker had drifted closer to McCloskey, sandwiching the impartial rider between himself and Buck.

"Motherless cunt," Billy said, almost to himself.

"What?" McCloskey asked, slowly realizing he was the only one smiling.

"'Motherless cunt.' That's what Buck called the young man," Billy replied.

Frank Baker saw an opening. He reached over and pulled the revolver from McCloskey's side holster.

Bowdre fired first, putting one in Baker's shoulder and knocking him to the dirt.

Buck Morton grabbed McCloskey's rifle, holstered on the horse's side.

But Billy was already on him, Colt raised, pointed square between Buck's eyes.

"You've gotten faster with your pull," Buck said, dropping the rifle.

"I do some things fast, some things nice and slow. Depends on the situation."

"That badge must feel constricting," Buck said. "Stopping you from unveiling your true self."

"All right, that's enough, Billy," said Brewer. "We've got but five miles to Lincoln."

"What about him?" Bowdre asked, gesturing to Frank Baker, who was writhing on the ground, holding his shoulder.

"We'll get him medical attention in town," Brewer said, hoping to calm the tension.

Buck looked at Billy. "You got me now, but right judge, right DA—I'll be seeing you real soon."

As Billy went to holster his six-shooter, Buck continued.

"Maybe it won't be you I'll come see. Maybe it'll be that slut Abig—"

The Regulators heard the shot before they realized what happened. Buck Morton looked confused, then titled backward off his horse, blood seeping from the bullet hole between his eyes.

Smoke from Billy's Colt wafted away in the wind.

"Goddammit!" yelled Brewer.

"Jesus, Billy, you—you—you shot Buck," stammered Mc-Closkey. "This ain't the way it was supposed to be."

"Why's that?" Billy asked coldly. "Why ain't this the way it's supposed to be?"

"Because you're the *law*. You're supposed to bring them in so they can face justice."

"You think that's what happens in Lincoln?" Billy scoffed.

"Justice prevails? You think Buck and Jesse would treat you any different if they were the law and you were the captive?"

"Buck was my friend!"

"Mama always said choose your friends carefully," Billy replied.

Before McCloskey could respond, another shot echoed through Agua Negra Canyon.

Billy turned to Frank Baker, who slacked limp, McCloskey's rifle at his fingertips.

"He went for it," Bowdre said, a little surprised himself he had just extinguished Baker.

"Aw, hell, Charlie!" McCloskey said. "How are you going to explain this to the justice of the peace? To the judge?"

"What's to explain?" Billy asked. "Buck and Baker stole your guns and opened up on us."

"That's the same sort of load they told after they shot Tunstall," McCloskey replied.

"No way to win if we have to play by different rules."

"Win? This is about right and wrong, not some tally you got running in your head," McCloskey said.

A wind blew through the canyon. Billy looked up at the clouds. The skies were darkening. A rain was coming. He locked eyes with Brewer, then McNab.

"I ain't gonna do it," McCloskey continued. "I'm going to the judge to tell him—"

The rifle shot went in McCloskey's cheek and out the back of his head. He fell to the ground next to Buck and Baker.

"Now there's no one to contradict the story," Doc said, his rifle still pointed at McCloskey's body, waiting for a twitch to indicate the job needed finishing.

The twitch never came.

Chapter 25

Once they had reached San Patricio, Brewer couldn't sit around watching Billy dance merrily, Doc trying to court Antonia, and Bowdre getting soused and trying to chat up Antonia's sister through marbled, drunken slurs. Billy was a pain in the ass, but he wasn't always wrong.

They needed to know which way the wind was blowing in Lincoln.

So Brewer used the cover of night to meet up with one of the few people he could trust. He decided to be mostly honest about what transpired, save the details around McCloskey's demise.

That blame, the Regulators had decided, would fall on the dearly departed Buck Morton and Frank Baker.

Brewer arrived at the town's edge. Lanterns were still lit in the Wortley's dining room, but the hotel was quiet. Across the street, he heard a drunken ruckus coming from the ground floor of the House.

He sneaked behind the Dolan store, crossed the small arroyo

that cut through town, crept through the orchard and corn-field, and knocked on the back door of John B. Wilson's home.

Brewer and Wilson sat in the front room, voices low so as not to wake Wilson's wife.

"We caught Morton and Baker."

"Then you best let them go," Wilson said, cutting him off.

"What would we do that for?"

"Didn't word reach you yet? Axtell was here."

"The governor came to Lincoln?" Brewer asked.

"And spent all day being shown the sights by Dolan and Riley."

"I'm guessing their account differs from reality."

"You guessed right," Wilson replied.

"That don't change anything. We captured and arrested Morton and Baker—"

"Dick, you're not listening. Last thing the governor did before he scuttled back to Santa Fe was remove me as justice of the peace and void all processes."

The news took the wind out of Brewer. "Like me being deputy."

"That was the true goal of the declaration, yes. So let Morton and Baker go and move on with your life."

Brewer's mind was racing. "When did this declaration occur?" he asked.

"Yesterday."

"What time?"

LINCOLN COUNTY, NEW MEXICO TERRITORY

Bodaway looked up at the stars and wondered what his wife

and daughter were doing at that moment. Lolotea was probably putting up a fuss about helping with the chores. She had a
fighting spirit, and when she put her foot down, Usen himself
couldn't move her. *She got her stubbornness from me*, he thought.
At least she got her mother's smarts.

Victorio had asked Bodaway directly to find the cavalry.

"How many men am I taking?"

"None. If you're discovered, too many Apache will create
panic in the pale eyes. If you're by yourself, you can claim in-
nocence, that you were separated from the tribe and making
your way back to the reservation."

"What do I do when I find them?" Bodaway had asked, ignoring the more obvious thought that they won't be any kinder
to just one Apache by his lonesome.

"Track where they came from and where they are headed,
then report back. Nothing more."

Bodaway had felt pride that Victorio had come to him.
Bodaway knew what "reporting back" would mean, but he was
no stranger to violence. And there was no length he wouldn't go
to protect his family and create a prosperous life for his daughter, a life she would lead on the land his people had called home
for hundreds of years, long before the white man came over on
their ships, then their steel horses.

On his fourth day traversing southeastern New Mexico,
Bodaway located the cavalry. He found the band of two dozen
infantrymen near the Beckwith ranch in the Seven Rivers area, pa-
trolling the territory for rustlers, vagrants, and those brown of skin.

Bodaway had been careful not to be spotted as he followed
the soldiers for two days and two nights, mapping their route.
It would take another full day to get back to Victorio and the
other guerrilla warriors hiding in the mountains, then one more
for the Apache to spring their attack on the cavalry.

Good, he thought. *I'm ready for this to all be over.*

The army believed Victorio had led his band into Mexico to either relocate or regroup. In reality, the Mescalero Apache were in the Capitan Mountains, just miles north of Lincoln.

Bodaway made his way back, careful to avoid any areas with settlers. He was hungry. He'd spent the last few days surviving on berries and whatever small animals he could kill, but the legwork was done, and he missed his wife's cooking.

And he missed Lolotea.

Bodaway reached into his satchel and pulled out her small doll.

"It carries Usen's spirit," she had said when she handed it to him. "It will keep you safe, Papa." He had tried to explain it wasn't proper for him to carry a child's plaything, but Lolotea insisted. Onawa had given him a stern look over their child's head, and Bodaway knew it was a losing battle. So he stuffed the doll into his satchel and carried it with him.

It would only be another week before he would be able to give it back to Lolotea. He could already see the smile on her face when he did.

Daughters, he thought to himself.

"Sumbitch ain't nothing but Catron's lapdog," Dolan laughed.

"Still got the boys out there riding around, looking for us," Riley replied.

Dolan emptied the rest of the bottle into his glass and took another swig. He was feeling warm and loose. "What are they gonna do?" he replied. "We have the judges, we have the attorneys, we have the bankers in Catron, and now it's been made more than clear we have the governor too."

Riley wasn't so sure that changed anything, but he was reluctant to argue when Jimmy was in this state. When good and stinking drunk, as he was now, Dolan's jubilance could turn to fury in the blink of an eye. Even at Dolan's most buoyant, Riley treaded carefully around his partner.

Dolan looked around the House. A dozen men laughing too loud, spilling their drinks, and struggling to see straight.

What they were missing were women.

"John Boy, you know who I haven't gazed upon in a while?"

"Who's that?" Riley replied, knowing the answer may dictate the evening's course.

"Ada Hampton. Why's that you suppose?"

"Her pa don't like you much."

"Her daddy ain't nothing but a two-bit farmer trying to sow a dirt patch."

"A dirt patch we sold him."

"Ain't our fault the man don't know ripe soil from worthless desert sand. Let's go pay Ada a visit."

"It's a half-hour ride, and he ain't gonna like you knocking at this time of night."

"Then her pa shouldn't of produced such a fine young lady," Dolan replied before standing and taking one graceless step backward, knocking his chair to the floor.

"Let's call on Ada tomorrow," Riley said.

"She's got a sister for you," Dolan slurred.

"Gertrude ain't but twelve. And she looks more like her pa than she do a girl."

"Old enough," Dolan said, then he stumbled out onto Main Street.

"Late afternoon, 'bout four o'clock or so. Why?" Wilson asked.

The sun was setting when they put down Morton, Baker, and McCloskey. Well past four.

"You sure it wasn't closer to, say, seven, eight?"

"Yeah, I'm sure. Governor made his declaration and was gone before shops even closed. Where're Morton and Baker?"

Brewer chose his words carefully. "I heard a story once about these detainees who didn't want to go to prison, so they got the jump on the deputy bringing them in, and in the course of the row, the deputy had to shoot and kill the criminals. The deputy was hailed a hero."

Wilson understood. "So long as whatever went down happened before four o'clock, one should be just fine in the eyes of the law."

But it hadn't happened before four. Unbeknownst to the Regulators at the time, they were ordinary citizens, like anyone else, and had just committed murder.

"He'll eat his," Dolan said. "I'm gonna get that land foreclosed on and take that pretty daughter too."

Things had not gone as planned at the Hampton home. When Dolan and Riley arrived, loudly knocking on the door well past midnight, Rufus Hampton had opened with his rifle in hand.

"I've come to call on your eldest," Dolan had said as he tried to push his way in.

Rufus didn't budge. "She ain't asking to be called upon," he replied.

"What's a matter, Rufus? You're going to let a little disagreement between us keep your child from happiness?"

"Even if I didn't hate your pig-sucking guts, I still wouldn't let you anywhere near Ada."

"We're runnin' a special tonight. Brought John Boy along to take the homely one off your hands too."

Rufus cocked the rifle.

"C'mon, Jimmy," Riley said. "You can call on Ada in the morning."

"I see you set one foot on my property again, I'm gonna put a hole in you."

Dolan glowered. "That's no way to talk to the man who gave you your opportunity."

"Some opportunity. Sold me a bill of goods on this land."

"Smart businessman always does his due diligence," Dolan replied. "And if you had any sense about you, you'd off-load your daughters to us and maybe find yourself back in prosperity."

Rufus kept his rifle pointed at Dolan. Out of the corner of his eye, he could see his daughter Ada shaking behind the door.

"Like I said, set foot on this land again, it's the last tread you'll make."

"Jimmy, we really should leave."

"No, I don't think so, John Boy. We're the goddamn House. And Rufus here is just a simple farmer, in a simple home, with a simple wife, and two simple daughters."

"Ain't the daughters got me concerned," Riley replied. He was looking to the far end of the porch.

Dolan turned his gaze to eight-year-old Dell Hampton and the thirty-inch, 12-gauge double-barrel N. C. Greenough shotgun the boy was holding. Dell had one eye closed as he targeted Dolan and Riley for the buckshot.

"Perhaps it *is* getting late," Dolan said, then he and Riley had backed away.

Now on the ride back to Lincoln, Dolan was still fuming. "Pull a shotgun on me and think you'll get away with it?"

"I gotta piss," Riley said. He'd been listening to Dolan for fifteen minutes straight, and more than needing to empty his bladder, he needed a moment of quiet from the bitching. Riley was urinating on a brush when the gunshots startled him. He turned to see Dolan firing his pistol in the direction of the Hampton home, which was a full two miles back.

Bodaway snapped awake.

Bang! Bang!

There it was again. Gunshots.

"What you working with there, hoss?" Dolan asked.

"Enough," Riley replied. Dolan peered over Riley's shoulder as he was finishing up.

"Hmmm, maybe we oughta go see that snake oiler—get you a growth potion or something."

"Quit it, ya fuck." Riley nudged Dolan back with his shoulder. The still-drunk Dolan lost his balance and fell to the dirt.

"Aw, shit, Jimmy, I didn't mean to . . ." There was no guessing how Dolan would take this. Riley prepared himself for a series of groveling and apologies until his fiery partner was satisfied. Instead, Dolan was looking at the dirt.

Tracks. Not boots, but a flat-soled shoe. And they were fresh.

Dolan cocked his revolver and began to follow the footprints.

"What you doing?" Riley asked.

Dolan motioned to stay quiet. Dolan walked around the shrubs to find a recently extinguished fire and the remnants of a small meal. Next to the ashes lay a small figure, its edges smoldering. Dolan picked it up.

A doll.

Bodaway hid in the brush, just feet away, and watched the pale eyes holding Lolotea's doll. He could tell the man was drunk but also assured. Angry. A fighter.

Lolotea would be upset, but he wasn't going to kill over a doll. He just wanted to get back to the Capitans, deliver the troop movements to Victorio, then go see his wife and little girl.

Bodaway took a quiet step back, and as he turned to slip away, he found himself face-to-face with another white man. One less assured. Less angry.

A man who was scared.

Bodaway and John Riley stared at one another, neither saying a word. Bodaway didn't reach for his hatchet, and Riley made no move for his gun.

Bodaway's eyes looked at the path behind Riley, the path away from here. He inched forward, and Riley, sensing Bodaway's intention, inched to the side to let him pass.

Bodaway was two steps past the man when the bullet ripped through his shoulder and knocked him to the ground. He turned to see the first man—the angry pale eyes—cocking his revolver again. The second shot missed Bodaway by inches and embedded in the dirt.

"Hey now, Jimmy, we don't gotta—" Riley began to say.

Bang!

Another miss from the drunk Dolan.

Bodaway, with red-hot pain spreading from his shoulder to his arm, got to a knee.

Dolan raised the revolver again and closed one eye, sizing Bodaway up carefully . . .

Click.

An empty chamber.

Bodaway lurched forward and rammed his shoulder into

Dolan's midsection and tackled him, sending the men sprawling over the shrubs back near the extinguished fire.

Dolan's gun slid away.

Riley stood still, frozen.

Dolan punched the Apache's midsection, but it was like hitting a rock.

Bodaway countered with a thunderous blow to Dolan's jaw.

"Hey . . . hey!" Riley said and approached, gun finally pulled.

Bodaway heard Riley's revolver cock and rolled Dolan over, using him as a shield.

Riley couldn't get a clean shot.

Bodaway got Dolan in a headlock and squeezed his muscular arms.

Dolan couldn't pry the Apache from around his neck.

Bodaway flexed harder, cutting Dolan's airway. Dolan's face was turning red, and he tried to scratch and claw at the man behind him.

Riley shuffled side to side, trying to get a clear look.

Dolan's left hand dropped to his hip. He was going for his other gun.

Bodaway used his free arm to hold Dolan's down. Dolan couldn't raise it to get the gun free of the holster.

"Let him go!" Riley yelled.

Bodaway continued squeezing the life out of James Dolan.

"I'm gonna shoot . . ."

Dolan's face was now blue and his eyes hued a bloodshot red.

Gun barrel still in the holster, Dolan squeezed the trigger.

The bullet went into Bodaway's foot. Bodaway loosened his grip.

Dolan fell to the ground and gasped for air.

Riley fired a shot into Bodaway's chest . . .

Bodaway didn't slump over. Instead, to Riley's surprise, he charged at Riley, knocking him down.

Bodaway, his chest covered in blood and the hole still oozing more, got on top of Riley. The Apache held Riley down with one arm and picked up a rock with the other. He raised the rock high . . .

Bang!

This gunshot finally keeled Bodaway over. Riley scrambled out from under him. Bodaway continued to scratch and claw his way along the ground, trying to get to Riley.

Dolan walked up and stood over him.

Bodaway reached out, past Dolan's pant cuff to . . .

Lolotea's doll. Bodaway took it in his hand and held tight.

Dolan fired a bullet through Bodaway's head.

Bodaway lay there, his breath shortening, his vision narrowing, his spirit fighting to leave his body. His eyes landed on the object in his hand, caked in ash and blood.

Stupid fucking doll.

"Protect my spirit, Usen," he whispered with his last breath, but it didn't provide him comfort.

He missed his wife.

He missed Lolotea.

Chapter 26

Billy was sound asleep when the door to the adobe hut crept open. The intruders, two of them, tiptoed across the room, over to the bed where he slept.

Billy snapped awake and grabbed the man's wrist. His Colt was pointed at the intruder.

"Jesus, it's just us," Frank McNab said.

Brewer, his wrist still being held by the Kid, just stared at Billy.

"Damn, Dick, you can't be sneakin' up like that," Billy said as he let go of Brewer.

"We was tryin' not to wake the señorita," McNab replied.

Billy looked over at the girl next to him. Last night Francisca had been playful and quick to smile, but now she was looking back at him in terror.

"It's all right—these are my friends," he said. Billy rubbed her arm, but she did not find it reassuring.

"We got a problem," Brewer said.

Billy sloughed out of bed, got dressed, and followed Brewer and McNab to the hut across the way. Last night it was a saloon. Now it was empty, save for Bowdre, Doc, and Big Jim French. Billy noticed the far-off, pleasant look on Bowdre's face.

"She got you good, didn't she?" Billy asked.

"I think she did, Billy. Her sister done got Doc too."

Doc tried to play it off with a wave of his hand, but no one was buying it.

"What's so serious you pulled us all from the throes of pleasure, Dick? We was celebrating. Buck and Baker—hell, that's two down," Billy said.

"Yeah, only a few *dozen* more to go," Doc said.

"That pep you got, Kid, is about to fade real quick," Brewer answered. "We took out Morton and Baker—"

"And McCloskey. Don't forget McCloskey."

"Last thing we're gonna wanna do is remember that, I promise you."

"Cut to it, Dick, before our girls get lonely."

"Shut your mouth!" Brewer exploded. The room fell silent. "This ain't funny. When you gunned them boys down, we wasn't law no more."

"What are you talking about?" Doc asked.

"Our deputy status had been revoked," McNab replied solemnly.

"Revoked? By whom?"

"Axtell," Brewer replied.

Billy looked around. The men were all trading worried glances.

"Is that all?" the Kid finally asked.

"Is that . . . He's the goddamn governor!"

"So what? He's as crooked as any other ring rat and everyone knows it."

"Don't matter who knows it or don't know it," Brewer replied. "Doesn't change the fact that what we did can now be considered, strictly speaking, murder."

"I say we kick dust to Mexico," Doc said.

McNab agreed. "It's the smart thing."

"I can learn Spanish," Big Jim French said.

"You'll fit into Mexico about as well as you would a lady's carriage boot," Billy replied.

"We've stepped outside the law," Brewer responded coolly. "McSween can't protect us. Justice of the Peace Wilson can't protect us."

"And John Tunstall can't protect us," Billy said. "'Cause we let him get killed. And if we scurry off now, tail tucked high, then he died for nothing."

"He already died for nothing," Brewer answered.

"Then go. Spend all your days letting others step on you and take what's yours. But me? Nah, I'm done running."

LINCOLN

LINCOLN COUNTY, NEW MEXICO TERRITORY

Sheriff Brady woke early. His head was throbbing, and it was only made worse by the pounding on his door.

"It's Peppin!" came the voice from outside.

Brady sighed and opened up to find his deputy out of breath.

"Them boys never made it to Lincoln."

Brady shrugged.

"Morton and Baker. Brewer's gang was taking 'em to Lincoln to face charges for the Tunstall thing. Hindman saw the group yesterday, heading into Agua Negra."

The Tunstall thing, Brady thought. He knew Justice of the

Peace Wilson had deputized Tunstall's employees, including that shit-heel turncoat kid, Billy Bonney, to go after the men who had slain the Englishman. Brady was one of those men. But things had changed in the last twenty-four hours.

"And Hindman didn't think to stop them?"

"He was by his lonesome. One man against a dozen. Besides, they'd been deputized too."

"Current affairs ain't your specialty, is it?" Brady replied. He reached into a bucket of water he kept by the bed and pulled out a rag. He didn't care it was soiled from a week's use and draped it over his eyes. "Those Regulators ain't law no more. And if something happened to Morton and Baker, well, they'll have to answer for it."

"Sheriff, Dolan's insisting we do something."

Brady grunted and wiped the dirty rag over his face, then coughed last night's phlegm into it. "Then I guess we better go look for them."

An hour later, Brady, Peppin, and Hindman reached the bodies in Agua Negra Canyon. Peppin dismounted his horse and Hindman did the same from the coach of the wagon. Brady eyed the sun, still rising. It was only March, but the days were getting hotter earlier.

"What do you suppose happened?" Peppin asked, peering over the three dead men lying by the dry riverbank. Flies were hovering, and an animal had taken a chunk out of Baker's thigh.

"Maybe they was trying to escape?" Hindman suggested.

"See them hands? Still roped. These men were assassinated," Brady said.

As Peppin and Hindman began loading the bodies into the wagon, Brady looked back up at the sky. *It was heating up indeed.*

While Brewer hightailed it for the hills to tell McSween and Deputy Barrier what had happened, Billy had another idea. It had taken some convincing, but he finally persuaded a few Regulators to head into Lincoln and talk to former justice Wilson themselves.

After midnight, when the town had quieted down, Billy, Frank McNab, Big Jim French, and José Chávez y Chávez were standing in Wilson's living room. Wilson's wife served them tea, and on her way out she whispered to her husband, "Don't your friends ever do things normal?"

"They aren't my friends," Wilson said for all to hear. "They're *former* deputies who don't have the first clue what sort of hell they've conspired for themselves." He turned to the Regulators. "You know your deputy status has been revoked."

Billy casually dropped onto Wilson's sofa. "Yeah, by that screw of a governor, Axtell."

"Screw or not, he's within his rights to do it."

"And what say the people?" Billy inquired.

"What people?"

"Not the scumfish on Dolan's payroll, the everyday folk around Lincoln."

"What's that matter?" Big Jim French asked.

"Axtell's only as powerful as his favor."

"This ain't one of the states," McNab replied. "Votes didn't put Axtell in power. He was handpicked by President Grant himself."

"You done much reading about the governor?" Billy asked. The men had not. "Before ruling over this little fiefdom of New Mexico, he was governor of the Utah Territory."

"So what? All that proves is he's liked by Washington."

"That's one view. Another is he lasted but four months before being run out by them Mormons. How many more chances a man like that get? See, if *public sentiment* turns on the dear governor, he'll be cast aside again, in shame, and President Hayes will have no choice but to remove him and install a governor with no ties to Dolan, Catron, or anyone else in the ring."

"You're talking a political game," Wilson said. "A gamble, really."

"What's life if not a gamble?"

"Except you lose this one, you don't walk away broke. You don't walk away at all," McNab replied.

"Wilson, just tell me this—which way is the wind blowing?" Billy asked.

"You out of town, if you're lucky," Wilson answered. "Six feet deep if you're not."

It wasn't daybreak yet when Billy and the Regulators left Wilson's home. The town was still asleep, and the men could slip out of Lincoln undetected.

Then they heard a bark.

Tunstall's Australian shepherd, Hackney, was standing in the middle of the street, wagging his tail at the familiar men. Billy started toward the canine.

"Dammit, Billy, let's go," McNab said. "We best be gone before sunup."

"We at least gotta bring him back," Billy said. "C'mon, boy!" Billy playfully jogged toward Tunstall's house, across the street, and Hackney followed. The other Regulators reluctantly followed, their eyes scanning Lincoln for any sign of movement.

Billy brought Hackney to the small corral behind Tunstall's home. Billy got to one knee, laughing as the dog licked his face.

McNab and French were the first to see it.

"Shit, git down!" McNab said.

Billy and the Regulators ducked behind the wall of the corral.

Sheriff Brady was walking down the middle of the street with his deputies, Peppin, Hindman, and Long. Tagging along was Billy Matthews, another member of the Boys.

"What are they doing up so early?" French asked.

Billy peered through a hole in the stone wall and watched Brady and the deputies make their way to the courthouse. They seemed in a jovial spirit as Brady removed a paper from his jacket pocket and read it aloud.

"Let any and all who can hear know this—there is a warrant for the arrests of Richard Brewer, William "Kid" Bonney, Josiah "Doc" Scurlock, Charlie Bowdre, and others for the murder of upstanding citizens Buck Morton, Frank Baker, and William McCloskey in the Agua Negra Canyon."

Brady made a big show of nailing the proclamation to the courthouse door, then the men turned and walked back west through town. They would pass right by Billy and the Regulators.

"As soon as they're gone, we'll dip out back to the Rio Bonito and slip away," McNab said. The other Regulators nodded.

But Billy kept peering through the hole, watching Brady and the deputies getting closer. His gaze was locked not on the men but on what was in Brady's hand.

Billy's Winchester. The one Tunstall had gifted him.

The gunshot rang throughout Lincoln and right through Brady's chest.

Billy fired again. He was standing now, exposed, shooting at Brady and the deputies.

French and Chávez followed suit.

"Goddammit, Billy!" McNab cried out. But McNab rose and opened fire as well.

The fusillade from the Regulators scattered Brady's men.

Hindman caught a rifle shot in the neck and tumbled over, bleeding out in the Lincoln dirt.

Matthews and Peppin made it to the orchard across the street and lay flat on their bellies, out of the Regulators' view.

Sheriff Brady had taken five bullets to the body and was groaning in the middle of the street. Acting on pure instinct, he still tried to get to his feet but just slumped over again.

Billy hopped the wall and approached him. Jim French followed, gun aimed at the orchard for any sign of movement.

Billy looked down at the sheriff, who was gasping and moaning.

"Shoulda . . . when you was . . . the Boys . . ." Brady struggled.

"Yeah, but you didn't." Billy picked up the Winchester rifle Tunstall had given him. He turned it on Brady. "Just so you know, the gun that ended your miserable fuckin' life came from John Tunstall."

Billy pulled the trigger, snuffing William Brady out for good.

Gunshots ripped out from the orchard. Billy instantly felt the pain in his thigh and dropped.

Big Jim French did too.

The other Regulators opened fire, but the assailants were gone.

Billy slid over to French and helped him to his feet.

"Look at that," he said, showing their matching bullet wounds in their thighs.

"You ain't funny," French said through gritted teeth.

Billy wrapped French's arm over his shoulder, and the two limped to the Tunstall store. Once inside, French collapsed to the ground.

"Can't go no farther."

"Just gotta get to them horses," Billy said. "We'll get fixed up in San Patricio."

French chuckled. "You one of them, ain't ya?"

"One of who?"

"The touched. The blessed. The type who attract the ire but never have to reap the consequences. Bullets whizzing all around and you get a mere scratch."

"A scratch? I'm hobbled too."

"But you ain't bleeding like I am."

Billy looked down and saw there wasn't an exit wound.

"The bullet was meant for you but lodged in me," French continued. "How long until Dolan men come bursting through that door?"

"When they do, all they'll find is an empty room." Billy lifted up the hatch to a secret crawl space below the floor. French looked at him.

"I'll send Doctor Ealy, I promise," Billy said, then locked him in.

Chapter 27

LINCOLN COUNTY, NEW MEXICO TERRITORY

Billy settled into an obscure nook in the Agua Negra Canyon, a spot that gave him a vantage point both west, for anyone trailing him from Lincoln, and east, lest one of the Boys, the Kinney Gang, or the Seven Rivers Warriors were making their way into town.

Billy had an uneasy feeling in his gut, one he couldn't shake. Maybe he was haunted by the look of surprise on Brady's face as the bullet ripped through his chest. Or the gurgling sounds Brady made just before Billy closed his eyes for good.

No, it weren't that. Billy had killed before, and he certainly had no love for the sheriff. Brady had been part of the convoy that killed Tunstall. Brady had tormented him in the pit, made him miss Tunstall's funeral. Brady had stolen his prized possession, the Winchester rifle.

But something still gnawed at Billy. Something had *changed*. Not just on the outside, them being wanted men now. But inside. Would Mama even recognize him anymore? Would Josie?

No. *I'm different now* was the last thought he had before drifting off to sleep.

> Darling, I am growing old,
> Silver threads among the gold,
> Shine upon my brow today,
> Life is fading fast away.

The horse is sprinting toward the thick trees, picking up speed, faster and faster . . .

> But, my darling, you will be,
> Always young and fair to me,
> Yes, my darling, you will be
> Always young and fair to me.

They reach the dense forest. Branches and thorns slice and cut Billy's hands, his arms, his legs, his face. Blood trickles down from his rib cage. Warm and sticky . . .

Then a deep, heavy, thunderous crackle splinters the back of Billy's head into a million tiny pieces. As if time has slowed to a crawl, the small fragments of his skull float lazily, drifting ever so slowly away into the sky. His surroundings, the trees, the branches, the thorns, even the horse under him, fade and fade and fade into a bright light until all he can see is a blinding white . . .

Billy woke. He was dizzy and nauseous. How long had he been asleep? An hour? Ten? It was dark now. Judging by the moon and stars, it was late.

Time to ride back into Lincoln.

Billy sneaked back into the store and looked at the damage. The place was ransacked, and whoever had done so had helped themselves to a good share of the merchandise as well.

"French?" Billy whispered as loud as he could without drawing attention from anyone who might still be wandering outside. "Frenchy?"

Still no answer. Billy made his way to the door covering the crawl space and flung it open. There, shaking and sweating but straining to stay as quiet as possible, was Jim French.

"Doc Ealy came and got the bullet, then had to shove me back in here. They ransacked the place. I thought you were them and had come back to burn it down."

"Naw, it's just me, your guardian angel."

SAN PATRICIO

LINCOLN COUNTY, NEW MEXICO TERRITORY

When Billy and French arrived, the other Regulators were waiting. Billy was expecting to be greeted as a conquering hero, a soldier who had vanquished one of their malevolent foes.

Instead, he got an earful from Dick Brewer.

"You gunned down a sheriff, Billy! In cold blood. In the bright light of day!"

"In fairness, Dick, it was morning. Sun weren't high enough to call it 'day' yet."

"Fuck you, Billy!" Brewer said and started after the Kid, but the other Regulators held him back. Billy never budged. He knew Brewer was the most respected of all the Regulators, but for the first time, he saw something else in Dick.

Weakness. An unwillingness to go the full measure.

"What now?" Scurlock asked.

"Our options are closing fast," McNab said. "Leaving the territory is still one of them."

Billy shook his head. Brewer glared at him, but Billy held his gaze.

"What's your bright idea, Kid, huh?" Brewer demanded to know.

"They think we're weak. They think we're on the run. They think this whole mess is about over, and we're gonna hightail it outta the territory, never to be seen again."

"Maybe they're right," Scurlock said.

"Only if we do what they think we're gonna do."

"What any rational-thinking man would," McNab replied.

Billy leaned against the wall. "What's so wrong with what I did?"

"It's one thing to kill a rustler like Buck Morton or Frank Baker. It's a whole other thing to gun down a lawman," Brewer answered.

"Depends on the lawman," Billy replied. "Brady wasn't nothing but a crook with a badge, surrounded by deputies and allies who walked the same. Stealing from the people of Lincoln. On the payroll of those fuck-rats Murphy and Dolan. Taking bribes, harassing any Mexican or Indian he came across. And he's a fucking murderer too, Dick. Blood colder than a Gila. Don't forget that, because the people of Lincoln sure haven't."

"So what if he was? He's got the backing of Dolan. Of the ring. And you're just some pissant kid who's read too many nickel stories."

"He already murdered Tunstall. You really think he weren't planning us the same?"

"They're gonna make examples of us," Brewer said. "Put us on display for all to see. Then their gonna drop the bottom out from under our boots and cheer as our necks snap like twigs."

"It's just a numbers game," Billy replied coolly.

"We don't have the numbers to go to war against the House," McNab said.

"Give me a day or two."

"Others may forget you're just a kid and don't know shit about the way the world works," Brewer replied. "But I don't."

"Sorry, Dick. But I'm all grown up now."

SANTA FE

SANTA FE COUNTY, NEW MEXICO TERRITORY

Samuel Axtell sat in the guest chair. The governor hated being summoned by Catron. He had tried once to get Catron to the governor's palace up the street. Axtell had spent weeks planning. He'd had a new chair made, one with an opulent purple velvet backing and sturdy oak arms that gave the impression of a king. And he'd had his desk raised six inches so he'd tower over whomever sat across from him in the governor's office.

But after two hours of waiting, keeping himself seated in that illustrious throne, it became evident the boss of the Santa Fe Ring was not going to show. To Axtell's surprise, the moment he stood to stretch his legs, Catron appeared in the doorway and said, "Let's go for a walk." They did, Axtell relinquishing whatever power he'd hoped to hold in his carefully constructed office, and it was the last time Catron set foot in the governor's mansion.

Axtell thought the fact President Grant had personally appointed him governor should have given Catron pause, but it didn't. It wouldn't be until a full year into his tenure that he learned Grant had cleared the nomination with Catron first.

Now Axtell sat in Catron's office, in a chair that was too

small, with armrests that were too low, looking up at the boss of the ring. Another man sat in the corner of the room, observing.

"There's unruliness in Lincoln," Catron began.

"I've heard. A gang of outlaws gunned down the sheriff. We'll have Judge Bristol and District Attorney Rynerson issue a warrant."

Catron removed a cigar. He clipped the end off, making a show of his gold cutter, then lit it. "Samuel, if you were running a race, you'd be so far behind you'd think you were winning."

The governor took a look at the man in the corner, who seemed to be taking notes.

"The warrant has already been issued," Catron continued.

"Then good. Local law enforcement has the situation under control."

"En un grado." Catron liked reminding the governor that he was bilingual and the governor was not. "To a degree. I fear the deceased, Sheriff Brady, is not the most sympathetic of victims, and this could cause the strife in Lincoln to continue."

"And that would be bad for business," Axtell said.

"It would be bad for the innocent, hardworking citizens of the territory," Catron replied disingenuously. "The ones going about their lives honestly, trying to earn a living and provide for their families. This could be the most prosperous region of the whole United States."

Axtell noticed the man in the corner was writing again. "And how can I help?"

"You're the governor, Samuel. Govern." With that, Catron stood and motioned for the man in the corner to approach. "This is Jeremiah Stull, the preeminent journalist of his generation."

Axtell shook Stull's hand, then pulled a handkerchief to try and remove the ink smudges.

"I think he'd very much like to hear your perspective on the scurrilous ne'er-do-wells threatening the future of New Mexico," Catron continued.

Axtell was catching on. "Anything in particular you'd like me to say?"

"Jeremiah has the crux of the story fleshed out. You've been quoted extensively."

Chapter 28

LINCOLN COUNTY, NEW MEXICO TERRITORY

The entire village of San Patricio, close to one hundred in total, gathered in front of Constable José Chávez y Chávez's home. The mood was dour. The jubilant spirit from the baile a couple of nights ago was gone. Now tension was high and nerves were short.

"Why have you gathered us here?" one villager shouted out.

"I have crops to tend," said another.

Chávez held his hands in the air. Everyone quieted. He addressed his neighbors in Spanish. *"We all know what has been transpiring in Lincoln County. James Dolan, John Riley, and the men they employ have declared war on the people. They've stolen our horses and livestock, they've gouged us for supplies, and they've given no reverence to our culture and history on this land."*

There was murmuring.

"There are still good people in Lincoln who want to drive Dolan and his ilk out of the territory. But they can't do it alone."

The mumbling grew louder until one villager, Esteban,

spoke up. *"Why is this our problem? Let the whites fight it out among themselves."*

"A threat next door will soon become a threat at home," Chávez answered. *"And their insistence, their greed, is only getting worse. Soon there will be nothing left for us to defend."*

Ignacio Gonzalez stood quietly in the back. He was an honorable man with a wife and three daughters he adored. He was prone to carrying his youngest, Josefina, on his back while he tended the small farm behind their home. He didn't mind that the five-year-old's extra weight made his job harder. Her giggling and laughter throughout the day kept him going. He looked down the lone street in San Patricio, taking in the fifteen compounds that each housed multiple families. He eyed the thick adobe walls and the portholes on top. Portholes that had been used to rain down bullets on raiding Apache. San Patricio was a community built on protecting what was theirs, defending their families, their way of life.

But the community was still small, poor, and understocked. They could hold off a small Apache raid, but they did their best to avoid any conflict with the whites, who could bring in the heavy artillery and reinforcements.

"You say this problem is at our doorstep," Esteban replied. *"But all I see are rustlers and outlaws who use our village to hide from the punishment they have coming. These men you want us to aid, they are killers too, no? Did they not gun down the sheriff in broad daylight?"*

Ignacio Gonzalez felt a nudge on the back of his shoulder and stepped aside. A ripple rolled through the village and the people parted. Billy made his way to the front, next to Chávez. He flipped a wooden crate upside down and stood on it, allowing the Kid to see over the crowd.

"I hear your concerns," he said in their native language. *"You*

have graciously let us sleep in your village, eat your food, and replenish our resources. But without your help, we are as good as dead."

"Perhaps you should be," someone said. *"That is the punishment for murder, no?"*

"It's true. I felled Sheriff Brady. But he struck first, riding with the men who killed our friend and employer, John Tunstall. And if Mr. Tunstall had lived . . ." Billy took a moment to collect himself. *"He would have outsmarted those bastards Murphy, Dolan, and Riley. He would have driven them, and their thieving, murderous henchmen, out of the county for good. And everyone, including the fine people here in San Patricio, would have prospered. You have been robbed of that chance. I have been too. We all have. But enough is enough. I aim to stop all this. And anyone who wants to join, you know where to find me."*

Billy stepped off the crate and disappeared back into the crowd.

The villagers thought the young man was asking too much of them.

Is he? Gonzalez wondered. He looked at little Josefina, who'd long tired of the adult conversation and was chasing her siblings. He watched as Josefina raised her fingers into the shape of a pistol and "shot" her sister, who fell to the ground, both girls giggling.

"Nice speech," Brewer said sarcastically. "What's your plan B?"

Billy didn't know. They needed the San Patricians to join them to have any chance.

"It's time we think about coming to some sort of truce," Brewer continued.

"Yeah, what's that look like, Dick? 'Golly gee, Mr. Dolan, we sure is sorry for all the trouble we caused and getting all ruffled on account of you murdering Mr. Tunstall. It'll never happen again.'"

"Say we do put an end to the House, then what? You gonna

take on the governor next? Boss Catron? The whole damn ring?"

"If I have to," Billy replied.

The nervousness in San Patricio was palpable. The villagers had turned down Billy's plea for help. The Regulators were taking stock of what they had, and what to do next.

Billy sat alone behind one of the adobes, his back to the wall, shuffling through a deck of cards to help him think. He noticed a teenager, thirteen or fourteen years old, loitering nearby. Every time Billy looked up, the teen looked away and pretended to busy himself.

"You're making it hard to get any thinking done," Billy finally said. "Come here."

The teen approached nervously.

"What's on your mind?" Billy asked.

Yginio Salazar, the fiddle-loving paramour who'd been jailed by Peppin, pulled a newspaper from his back pocket and handed it to Billy. On the front page, above the fold, in bold headlines, the paper accused the Regulators of murdering Sheriff Brady in cold blood. Billy skimmed the article:

Affairs have reached a critical condition in Lincoln County . . . Sheriff Brady was mercilessly gunned down by a party of men posted outside lawyer Alexander McSween's house . . . William Bonney, one of the assailants, ran out to steal the dead sheriff's rifle . . .

"Bullshit," Billy said. "That rifle was mine."

"Mr. Billy, there's more," Yginio said.

Billy flipped the paper over to see another article, then went to find Brewer.

Billy dropped the newspaper on top of Brewer's plate of food.

"Goddammit, Billy," Brewer said, sliding his plate out from under it.

"Read it."

Brewer did. McSween's court date was approaching. "So what? We knew this was gonna happen eventually."

"The court reconvening means *officers* of the court are on the move."

Brewer didn't like where this was headed.

"Maybe we're outnumbered in the streets," Billy continued, "but there's more than one way to skin a foe. We shoot down Dolan or Riley or Evans or Kinney, we still got the justice system to contend with, right?"

"That's exactly what I've been saying."

"But we take out Judge Bristol and that scurrilous district attorney Rynerson, people will start to notice. Start to think twice about coming after us. Maybe even start thinking of Lincoln as a dangerous place to do bad business."

"Catron and Dolan will just appoint another friendly compadre to take their place."

"Then we kill them too. And we keep killing until there's no dishonest men left who want the job."

"You're turning into a real bloodthirsty sonofabitch, Billy. We ain't taking out a judge or district attorney. That's suicide."

"Some things are worth maybe dying for."

Brewer thought for a moment. "Or we have a word with the judge and DA away from the prying eyes of Dolan. Gauge where they're at in this whole mess."

"They're more bent than any two men of the ring combined."

"That's why we gotta reason with them. They got it good right now. Comfort. Luxury. They don't want to disrupt their applecart. We can impress upon them the value of peace."

"Fine. But if your way don't work, I've found my plan B," Billy said, spinning the cylinder of his revolver and snapping it shut.

The sun was just about up when the Regulators gathered in the street of San Patricio. Even George and Frank Coe had ridden in to join them.

Except Bowdre was missing.

"Where's ol' Charlie?" Billy asked.

"Haven't seen him," Big Jim French replied. French was still hobbling on account of getting shot a few days earlier, but he'd be damned if he was going to hang back.

"Well, someone oughta wake—"

"Goddammit, Billy!"

Billy looked up to see Bowdre scrambling out of an adobe, still pulling his suspenders over his shoulder.

"The hell happened to you?" Scurlock asked.

"Goddamn Kid happened to me," Bowdre said, running toward Billy. Billy scampered around, always keeping another Regulator between himself and Bowdre.

"Did you . . . damn, Charlie, looks like you had yourself a little accident," Billy said.

"Did you piss yourself?" Big Jim French asked.

Bowdre continued to chase Billy, who was too quick of foot.

"Woke up with my hand in a bowl of warm water."

"That really works?" Scurlock asked.

"By the looks of him, I'd say it did!" Billy replied, laughing loud enough to stir the village.

"I oughta shoot you dead right here," Bowdre said.

"You couldn't hit a hog at the trough from two feet away!" But the look in Bowdre's eyes told Billy he may have gone a step too far. "Damn, Charlie, ain't you ever heard of April Fool's?"

Bowdre, out of breath, stopped chasing the Kid. "That was two days ago!"

The other Regulators laughed, and even Bowdre finally broke into a smile.

"Enough," Brewer said, breaking the revelry. "We got serious business to attend to today."

"Yes, sir," Billy replied, giving Brewer a salute.

"I'd like to ride with you as well." A man stepped out. He was carrying a rusty old rifle and a six-shooter that had also seen better days. But Ignacio Gonzalez had long ago made up his mind that his only purpose in life was to provide a future for his children.

BLAZER'S MILL

LINCOLN COUNTY, NEW MEXICO TERRITORY

April 4, 1878

They rode out to Blazer's Mill in silence. As they neared, nerves began to set it.

"And you're sure they're gonna be coming this way?" Gonzalez asked.

"Fastest route from La Mesilla to Lincoln," Brewer replied. "Bristol and Rynerson will stop at Blazer's Mill for a meal and rest. We'll meet them there, away from Lincoln, away from Dolan, and have a talk."

"And if they don't share our desire for peace?"

"Then we'll have our answer," Brewer said. He sneaked a look at Billy, who was looking right back at him. Billy dropped a hand to his side and patted the revolver on his hip.

Brewer spurred his horse forward, wanting some separation between himself and the Kid.

They arrived at Blazer's Mill just in time for lunch.

"Sam, Ignacio, sweep the area. Make sure no Dolan men are lying in wait."

There would be plenty of places to hide at Blazer's Mill. In

addition to the main house and office building at the top of the
hill, there was the sawmill, the gristmill, the general store, the
post office, and several one-story adobes to conceal an enemy.

"Tiger" Sam Smith and Ignacio Gonzalez headed out to
patrol the area. The rest of the Regulators tied up their horses
and made their way into the agency building for one of Mrs.
Godfroy's meals. Doc Scurlock would take the first shift waiting outside, in case anyone slipped past Smith and Gonzalez.

"Guns on the table, boys," Mrs. Godfroy said as the other
thirteen men entered. It was her one rule, and all the Regulators
slid off their gun belts and placed them by the door.

They ordered and sat back. No one spoke for a few minutes,
until Billy couldn't handle the silence any longer.

"I had this teacher, Miss Richardson—hoo boy, was she a
beauty. She had a crush on me too. We were both ambidextrous,
and that sort of thing connects people."

Brewer rubbed his temples. The Kid was giving him a headache.

"Ambidex—what's that mean?" George Coe asked.

"Means he can shit out both his ass and his mouth," Bowdre
replied, which got a chuckle from everyone, including Billy.

"Means I can do things with both hands."

"I bet you can," French said, mimicking self-gratification.
More chuckles. The mood was lightening.

Scurlock flew in the door. "We got a lone rider."

The Regulators looked at each other. "You sure it ain't two?"
Brewer asked.

"Just the one. And he's heavily armed."

"Shit, Doc, everyone's heavily armed, even Ma Godfroy,
probably," Billy replied.

Brewer headed outside to get a look. Billy followed. In the
distance was one lone man.

"He's on a mule," Brewer said, then traded looks with Billy. Billy's light mood washed away instantly. "Can't be . . ."

Brewer raced inside to tell the other men.

"Buckshot Roberts." The Regulators stopped eating. Some went pale. "We have a warrant for Roberts," Brewer continued. "He was there the day Tunstall was killed."

"We still pretending?" Billy asked.

"That's how we end this," Brewer replied. "By doing things the right way."

"But we ain't the law no more, are we, Dick? That title has been revoked, and until we get a new DA and a new judge and a new governor, ain't nothing gonna change."

"I'm with Billy," Bowdre said. "That warrant don't hold no weight anymore."

Brewer turned to George Coe. "Think you can talk some sense into him?" Brewer asked.

George owned the ranch next to Buckshot Roberts and knew him a little. "I'll try. He's a peculiar sort though. Keeps to himself."

"Will he come quietly?"

"He's outnumbered sixteen to one. Even the peculiar recognize insurmountable odds."

Brewer nodded. George Coe stepped outside to greet Roberts.

"That old coot ain't ever turning himself in," Billy said. "We should get him now, while his defenses are down."

"No," Brewer replied. "We wait. Give George a chance first."

"You scared of Buckshot?" Billy asked. "Scared he can lick the whole lot of us?"

"Settle down, Kid," Frank McNab said.

"No, I want an answer. What're you so afraid of, Dick? The man's ten feet outside that door. You just swing it open and I'll do the shooting. You won't even have to dirty your hands."

"Billy . . ." McNab said evenly. "Shut up."

Outside, George Coe wasn't having any luck.

"We'll take you in peacefully, then let the legal system run its course."

"Why?" Roberts was a man of few words, even now.

"Because there's sixteen of us and one of you."

"Only counted fourteen horses."

"Got two on scout," Coe replied.

Roberts just grunted and stayed put.

"See that?" Billy said, looking out the window. "They moved over to that table and bench. He's getting away, Dick! We gotta do something!"

No one laughed. Billy looked around the room. The men had tightened up.

"He's a dangerous man, right? All the more reason to take him now while we got numbers. Hell, I could probably pick him off from this window, if George'd move his stupid head."

"Is murder your answer to everything now?" Brewer asked.

"Eat or be eaten. Shoot or be shot. Well, I've been shot, and it hurts like hell. I'd much rather do the shooting. And everyone in this room knows I'm right."

Brewer looked back out the window. He could see George stressing his points, trying to sway Buckshot Roberts, but the grizzled gunfighter wasn't budging.

Billy sidled up to Brewer and whispered so only Dick could hear. "We let him go and he kills one of us down the road, how's that gonna hang on your conscience?"

Brewer hesitated a moment, but Billy knew he'd won.

"Fine, enough talking. But we're gonna *arrest* that sonofabitch."

The door to the agency building opened, and Brewer led the Regulators outside. Bowdre pushed his way to the front.

"Throw up your hands, Roberts!" he shouted.

Roberts was off the bench faster than a rattler strike.

Bowdre and Roberts fired at the same time.

Bowdre's bullet lodged into Roberts's side.

Roberts's shot hit Bowdre square in the belt buckle, knocking his gun belt off, sending Bowdre to the ground. The bullet ricocheted into George Coe's hand, shattering it and severing his trigger finger clean off.

Despite the bullet in his hip, Roberts kept firing.

His next burst hit Middleton in the chest, dropping him.

The rest of the Regulators scattered for cover.

Roberts pumped out shots from the rifle as he backed down the hill and away from the Regulators. Scurlock's leg was sticking out from behind a woodpile, and Roberts put a bullet in it.

The Kid poked his head out from behind a stone pile and nearly got it blown off. Roberts's shot still managed to deflect off a rock and slice Billy's arm open.

Roberts continued down the hill, firing at anything that moved. All the Regulators had found cover.

Billy heard the *click* of an empty rifle. He peered out from behind the stones and saw Roberts take a step for his mule. The Kid fired, cutting off his path.

Roberts dove into a small adobe building and slammed the door shut.

"Bowdre?" Brewer called out.

"I'm here. I'm all right."

"George?"

"He shot my damn finger off! And I was tryin' to help him."

"Middleton?"

There was no answer.

"John?"

Still nothing. Billy spotted Middleton's legs behind a trough. Billy ran across the open area and made it to the trough without taking another round from Buckshot.

"He's out cold but alive," Billy yelled out to the others.

Inside the adobe, Roberts strained to pull the mattress off the bed and leaned it by the door. He touched his belly, then looked at his fingers. A deep red blood. The shot was fatal. There weren't much left to do but fight. He spotted an old Springfield buffalo rifle hanging on the wall. The shells were in a container below. He laid down on the mattress barricading the door and readied himself for a final stand.

"Now what, Dick?" Billy asked.

Brewer had to think. Four of his men were injured. Two more were still on patrol, but they'd be back any minute now after hearing the shots. Brewer surveyed the men he could see. Billy, ducking behind the trough, Middleton still unconscious next to him. José Chávez y Chávez and Big Jim French were using the agency building as cover. Frank Coe was tending to his cousin George, whose hand was soaking blood through the bandanna he'd wrapped around it. Scurlock was behind the blacksmith barn, trying to stop the bleeding from his leg. Frank McNab and two others were hunkered behind a shed.

And Buckshot Roberts was inside the adobe, waiting to die.

"I think I got him fatal," Bowdre said. "He ain't long for this world."

But Brewer couldn't be certain. And he was incensed at the damage Buckshot had done to his men. The adobe Roberts was hiding in had a window opening on the side. If Brewer could flush Roberts out, the Regulators could finish him off. Brewer made eye contact with Billy and motioned he was going to get a better look. Billy nodded and raised his rifle, ready to cover him.

Brewer dashed the dozen yards and ducked behind a log pile. Roberts never fired a shot. Brewer slowly peered over the pile. He could see Roberts's legs on the floor inside the hut. He took careful aim and released one shot, then quickly ducked back behind the wood.

Roberts startled as the shot careered into the wall behind him. He saw the puff of smoke from where Brewer's rifle had just been. He aimed at the pile of logs and waited.

"You get him?" Billy asked.

Brewer took a deep breath, then slowly raised his head for a look.

The next rifle shot silenced the valley.

Brewer's head snapped back and exploded.

"Dick!" Billy cried out.

He was dead before he hit the ground.

"I killed the sonofabitch!" Roberts said gleefully.

Billy took a step toward Brewer's body, but Roberts ripped off another shot, sending Billy scrambling back for cover. Billy looked at McNab, whose face had gone white.

Billy scanned the rest of the Regulators. Most were stricken, their heads in their hands. A few still held their guns, but loosely at their sides. The fight had gone out of them.

McNab, Billy, and Chávez watched the adobe closely, guns raised, as the rest of the Regulators loaded the wounded into one of Blazer's wagons.

Then they headed out, leaving Buckshot Roberts alone to die.

Chapter 29

Billy zipped a card past Bowdre's head, and it fell harmlessly to the ground. Charlie ignored it. Billy looked around the room. The Regulators were all there. The ones who were left anyway. And they were alone. None of the San Patricians wanted to be around the surly, downtrodden men.

The only Regulator not licking his wounds was Frank McNab, who was furious in a way Billy'd never seen him before.

"You know what this means, right, Frank?" Billy asked.

McNab continued to pace around the small fire they'd lit in front of one of the adobe homes.

"Means you're our new leader," Billy continued.

"That so?"

"Unless you don't think you have the disposition for it."

"Is that what you think?" McNab replied. He glared hard at Billy.

"Naw, that's just something Doc raised," Billy said, needling Scurlock, who was lost in his own thoughts.

"We tried it Dick's way, and look where that got us," McNab said. "Three injured and him in the ground."

"They didn't have to bury that bastard Roberts in the same damn coffin," Bowdre said to no one in particular.

"It ain't right." McNab replied. "None of this is. And we're done waiting for the law, or anyone else, to fix things. We're gonna take the fight to them, both fucking barrels."

In a flash, Billy pulled his Colt and had it pointed at the shadows behind McNab.

"¿Quién es?"

Yginio Salazar stepped out of the dark. He had another newspaper in his hand but was shaking too hard to move. Billy lowered the gun.

"Can't be sneaking up on people."

"Lo siento," Salazar replied. "I was in Lincoln earlier and brought you back the paper."

Billy waved Yginio over and took the newspaper from him. "'Kid' Bonney and the Regulators Terrorizing Lincoln County."

"Seems we're the menace now, boys," Billy said. "Blaming us for all the goings-on."

Bowdre took the paper from Billy. "They're calling us murders and outlaws and saying we ain't got no right to go after the people who killed Tunstall. They even got quotes from some townsfolk saying we're the real plague and praising Roberts for his marksmanship. They're making him out to be a goddamn hero!"

"So now we're fighting a war on two fronts," Billy said, slightly amused.

"What do you mean?" George Coe asked, feeling for a trigger finger that was no longer there. He hadn't said much since he regained consciousness. Coe had passed out cold when Billy shoved his hand in the carbolic acid to cauterize his wound.

"There's the war on the ground and the war of public opinion. We're losing both."

"Ain't much we can do about public opinion," McNab said. "But the ground we can control. A few of us are gonna head down to Seven Rivers and see what's what."

"What're you hoping to find there?" Bowdre asked.

"A fight," McNab answered.

"We can't all go riding down to Seven Rivers," Billy said. "That many men, they'll see us coming long before we arrive. But just a few of us? We can pick them off a couple at a time and retreat. Hit a few more, then retreat."

The rest of the Regulators weren't convinced.

"Ain't y'all know your history?" Billy continued. "How we defeated the king's redcoats? They had too many soldiers to fight head-on, so we used what we had—our brains and the land—to our advantage."

"You're not going," McNab said.

"The hell I'm not."

"Read the paper again, Kid. You're famous now. Every rancher and farmer from here to Seven Rivers will spot you coming, and if they do, they might make a pretty penny giving that up to the ring. We gotta take the less recognizable."

Shit, Billy thought. *He's right.*

Then Billy read the article again.

FORT STANTON

LINCOLN COUNTY, NEW MEXICO TERRITORY

"I'm going batty in here."

"Not spacious enough, Counselor?" Robert Widenmann replied.

The officers' quarters were bigger than a cell, and Widenmann was thankful for that, but McSween wasn't wrong. Being held prisoner anywhere, especially Fort Stanton, was a bad sign.

McSween hadn't wanted to turn himself in, but he was tired of living in the hills and eager to have his day in court. So Widenmann had retrieved the lawyer and his wife and escorted them to Fort Stanton, where they'd be safe until trial. But when they arrived, Deputy Sheriff Peppin had Widenmann arrested for "aiding and abetting" Brady's murder. They'd been able to arrange being held in the officers' quarters rather than a jail cell, but that was as far as their negotiations went.

Widenmann leaned against the windowsill and wondered how he got here. He'd just wanted to ranch. Then he just wanted to protect his friend John Tunstall. Then he just wanted to help get justice—through legal means—for Tunstall's killers. But no matter what step or turn he took, he seemed to sink deeper and deeper into the quicksand that was Lincoln. Now his cellmate was going stir-crazy being in a large, comfortable room with two beds, a desk, and a stove.

Widenmann was peering out that very window when the stagecoach entered the fort. He watched as a butler helped a fragile old man out of the coach, where they were met by Colonel Dudley. It was late, and the fort was quiet, so their voices carried.

"I'm being hunted," the old man said.

"Who's hunting you?" the colonel asked.

"McSween and Tunstall's boys. Those killers got it out for me. They'll stop at nothing to put me in the ground. They burned my farm."

"When?"

"Back in the winter . . . winter seventy-five, it was."

The old man seemed lost and confused.

"They're everywhere!" he continued. "Behind every rock.

In every brush. Under every bed, they wait, those goddamn Regulators."

Dudley took the man by the arm and led him inside the main office.

Jesus, they were right, thought Widenmann, watching them go. *Murphy really is dying.*

LINCOLN

LINCOLN COUNTY, NEW MEXICO TERRITORY

James Dolan poured a stiff drink and leaned back in the chair that used to belong to his mentor, Lawrence Murphy. He looked around the second-floor office of the House. He'd made a few small changes since buying the company—new curtains for the windows, a solid-gold bar cart to hold his whiskey and glasses—and now he wished he hadn't. It was time and money he'd never get back.

Court had convened for the spring, and indictments had been handed down. Billy Bonney, Big Jim French, and José Chávez y Chávez were indicted for Sheriff Brady's murder. Frank McNab would face trial for killing Deputy Hindman. Charlie Bowdre was charged with murdering Buckshot Roberts.

But despite the sympathetic Judge Bristol, it wasn't all roses for Dolan and the House. The grand jury had exonerated McSween on the embezzlement charges. They got Jesse Evans and some of his men for killing Tunstall. And they got Dolan and Riley too. "Accessories to the Tunstall murder," they'd called it, even though they weren't there.

There was a knock on the door, and John Riley entered, followed by Boss Catron.

"We appreciate you making the trip from Santa Fe," Dolan

said, and he motioned for Catron to sit. Catron just looked around at the office, unimpressed.

"Just have to dot some i's and cross some t's, then I'll be on my way."

John Riley leaned against the window behind Dolan, the way Dolan used to do for Murphy.

"Do you have the paperwork?" Dolan asked, noticing Catron was not carrying a briefcase.

"It's a metaphor, Jimmy. This isn't the kind of thing we need to solidify in ink, is it? I *can* trust you to be men of your word?"

Dolan was bitter, but there was nothing he could do. He was broke, owed thousands to Catron's bank, and to Catron personally. Now he was under indictment too.

"Yeah, we're honest," Dolan replied.

"Good. When will you be out?"

"Next week all right?"

"Sooner. Best to rip the bandage off all at once and get on with our lives, no?"

Dolan was fuming inside but knew better than to cross Catron. He *needed* Catron. "Anything you can do about the indictment?"

"That's a decision made by the good people of New Mexico, Jimmy." Catron got back to the task at hand. "All the contracts and ownership papers are already at First National in Santa Fe, so you just need to move your stuff out and hand over the keys. Edgar?"

A young man entered: nineteen, rail-thin, and sporting a mustache that refused to fill in. It gave him the appearance of a child pretending to be a grown-up.

"Edgar's my wife's brother," Catron said. "He'll be taking over. Tell him everything he needs to know. You have twenty-four hours. And Jimmy . . . take those hideous curtains with you."

SAN PATRICIO

LINCOLN COUNTY, NEW MEXICO TERRITORY

It had pained Billy he couldn't ride along to Seven Rivers. McNab had taken Frank Coe and Ab Saunders on their hunt for Tunstall's killers instead.

Billy hung back at San Patricio with the other Regulators. He was fidgety. He couldn't relax, couldn't sleep, wasn't hungry. He wanted to sing or dance or fight—just do *something*. He looked out at the stars above New Mexico and wondered what his old friends—friends not involved in this whole sordid affair—were doing. He hadn't seen Isadora in ages. Or Abigail.

Or his brother, Josie. He hoped Josie was okay, but Billy knew that was probably a fantasy. Awfully hard to let go of the pipe. When all this was over, he swore he'd grab Josie and take him far away from New Mexico. Maybe they'd head to California, or even Canada. Tunstall had always spoken fondly of the northern country.

The sun had just set, but the night was still early, so Billy wandered the lone San Patricio street, hoping to find someone to play cards with. But everyone he passed gave him only the mildest of courtesies before ducking back into their homes. Billy didn't want a drink, but he knew the adobe at the end of the village was open to those who did.

The adobe was empty. Not even Arturo was there. And Arturo was *always* there handing out mezcal to the parched.

Billy took a seat and pulled out his deck of cards, practicing various shuffles. Overhand. Riffle. Wash. Faro. The Mexican spiral. He'd become proficient in all of them.

Billy heard the boots before he saw the man wearing them.

"You still serving?" The man was almost six and a half feet tall, with dark hair neatly combed, offset by hazel eyes and a mustache that twirled up at the ends in sophistication.

"Guess Arturo went to bed," Billy said. "Help yourself."

The man made his way to the bar and pulled out a bottle. He then cupped two glasses in his large hand and gracefully poured whiskeys. He set one down in front of Billy.

"I'm not much for libations," the Kid said.

The man downed one glass in a single gulp, then set the other in front of an empty chair.

Billy nodded, and the man sat.

"You a cardplayer?" the man asked.

"I dabble," Billy said.

"I hear you do more than that, Kid."

Billy was at a disadvantage that suddenly put him on edge. He dropped his hand into his lap below the table, near his six-shooter.

"Relax, Bonney. I'm just a simple cowboy passing through. Name's Pat Garrett."

Chapter 30

SEVEN RIVERS

LINCOLN COUNTY, NEW MEXICO TERRITORY

April 29, 1878

It was a moonless night, and visibility was low.

The first shot went through Frank McNab's side and knocked him off his horse.

The next one hit Ab Saunders in the hip, and he, too, fell to the dirt.

Frank Coe spurred his horse, but the mare was gunned out from under him. Coe scrambled to the nearby arroyo for cover. He watched one of the Boys ride up to McNab and shoot him square in the face, killing him.

Wallace Ollinger, leader of the Seven Rivers Warriors, said Coe wouldn't be killed if he surrendered.

His cousin Ab was still writhing on the ground, gravely wounded.

Frank Coe came out with his hands up.

SAN PATRICIO

LINCOLN COUNTY, NEW MEXICO TERRITORY

"No foolin'?" Billy asked.

"No fooling," Garrett answered. "Buffalo."

They were a dozen hands into their game of faro.

"What do you do once you fell the big sonsofbitches?"

"That's when the skinners come in. They take a spike and hammer it through the animal's nose. Then you hook it to a team of horses and rip the hide from the carcass."

"Then you eat the meat?"

"Some do. Me, I was in it for the hides. Got close to three dollars for each one."

"You do them rail huntings?" Billy asked.

"That's for tourists and tenderfoots. A man gets up close to his target, looks it in the eye, kills him face-to-face."

Billy placed a chip on top of a card. Garrett did the same.

"Except you got a gun and the buffalo don't," Billy teased.

Garrett laughed. "Maybe that's why I gave it up, started working as a cowboy for Pete Maxwell."

That got Billy's attention. "You stay out at the Maxwell place? Fort Sumner? You ever come across a sweet little filly named Isadora?"

"I've seen her around time to time. Know her pa a little bit."

"How is she?"

"Betrothed," Garrett said.

Billy leaned back and let out a sigh. "You don't say. Serves me right, not calling on her sooner. Getting mixed up in all this mess."

Billy retreated into himself a bit, his mind on Isadora and what could have been. Garrett let him. They continued to gamble, neither taking much off the other, until Garrett finally yawned.

"Time for me to find a place to lay," he said.

"Another game," Billy replied.

"It's getting late, and I gotta be up early to make my deliveries for Maxwell."

"Just one more, I promise. Then I'll leave you be."

Garrett studied the Kid. He wasn't up or down much. He just seemed to need company.

"What are you hiding from?" Garrett asked. His voice wasn't accusatory, it was almost compassionate.

"Nothing," Billy replied.

"These troubles you boys are in—they're serious, aren't they?"

"Mainly for those on the other side of my gun."

"That fixing what ails you?" Garrett asked.

"I'm all right."

"What about your ma and pa? What do they think of all this?"

"Don't have a pa."

"And your mama?"

"She's gone too. Consumption."

Garrett could see the wound was still fresh. "Was she a good woman? A good mother?"

Billy's eyes dampened. He looked down at the table.

"I'm sorry, son," Garrett continued. "I really am."

Billy just nodded and placed another chip on a card.

"The life of the dead is placed in the living," Garrett continued. "Marcus Tullius Cicero."

"So you don't think anything happens when we die? Just poof . . . we're gone? And it's up to the people left behind to give a shit about us?"

Garrett thought for a moment. "I don't think it's our place to know."

"You believe in God?"

"I guess I do. Haven't seen much of him around lately though."

"So what keeps you going?"

"What other choice is there?"

Billy let that hang in the air. "Is God spiteful or loving?"

"You mean is he Old Testament or New?" Garrett asked.

"I mean, do we have to answer for the things we done, or does intention matter?"

"I suppose it's out of our control. Best we can do is try to live right and have our affairs in order when we go."

"No one's that lucky," Billy said bitterly. "Everyone has unfinished business when they die."

Scurlock, Bowdre, and Waite stormed into the adobe out of breath.

"They got ambushed," Bowdre said.

"Who?" Billy asked.

"Them Seven Rivers bastards lied in wait. Soon as McNab, Coe, and Saunders rode by, they sprung on 'em."

"Ab is hurt bad," Doc added. "They took him to Fort Stanton. They got Coe prisoner down in Seven Rivers."

"What about McNab?" Billy asked.

"Executed on the spot," Bowdre replied sullenly.

The remaining Regulators filed in behind them. Garrett took his glass of whiskey to the bar, giving them space.

"Someone's gotta be in charge," Bowdre said. The Regulators traded looks, no one stepping forward. "Oughta be Doc, seeing as he was McNab's right hand."

Doc didn't protest. He was now the new leader of the Regulators. The group's third in three weeks. But no one seemed keen on being Doc's number two.

"Kinda starting to feel like cannon fodder," Big Jim French

replied when the looks turned to him. "First Dick, then McNab . . ."

"Shit, I'll do it," Billy finally said. "From now on, they take one of ours, we take ten of theirs until only one side is left."

The Regulators headed out, Billy taking up the rear. He stopped in the doorway and turned back to Garrett, who was still sipping his whiskey.

"You want to join us, Pat? Get the blood pumping again?"

"I don't think so, Billy."

"Why? 'Cause them Seven Rivers boys ain't . . ." Billy placed a finger on each side of his head, mimicking buffalo horns.

"No, this just ain't my fight."

"Well, it sure as hell is mine," Billy said, then he followed the Regulators into the street.

Chapter 31

Ab Saunders's hip was killing him. He'd been taken to Fort Stanton so a doctor could dig inside and remove the bullet, which he'd done successfully. It'd be some time before Saunders could walk right again. The stiff cots in the Fort Stanton infirmary weren't helping. But the morphine was. He was feeling that warm, calming sensation wash over him when he heard familiar voices out in the plaza.

"C'mon, L.G., quit fussing. We're trying to make you more comfortable."

"Help! Help! They're taking me! Them Regulators got me!"

"We're not Regulators. It's me, Jimmy. And John Boy's here too."

Saunders limped to the door and peered out. Sure enough, James Dolan and John Riley were trying to coax an addled Lawrence Murphy into a stagecoach.

"Jimmy?" Murphy said. "Little Jimmy Dolan, the stock boy?"

"That's how I started, yeah. But I was your business partner too."

"You still puttin' them shovels on the bottom shelf? You gotta hang 'em high, eye level."

"I hang 'em high now, L.G."

They finally got Murphy into the stagecoach and rode out of Fort Stanton.

The road to Santa Fe was an easier trek than others, but Murphy seemed unaware what was happening and was dissatisfied with everything. It was hard for Dolan to reckon with. He harbored anger that Murphy hadn't disclosed the peril the business was in prior to selling it to him, but he still looked up to Murphy like an older brother. Murphy had plucked him from stock boy to business partner of the House. And Murphy had saved his hide after the Captain Randlett affair. The way Dolan saw it, that made them even, and this was the least he could do for his old friend. Fort Stanton was no place to live out one's final days.

They were an hour from Santa Fe when Murphy turned lucid. "I've done some bad things."

"Nothing the Lord won't forgive," Dolan replied.

"I've cheated, lied, and stole most of my adult life."

"Show me a man who hasn't and I'll show you a failure."

"I'm not saying I have regrets. Quite the opposite." Murphy wrapped the blanket around his shoulders even tighter, even though it was a warm spring evening. "No one ever regrets the things they've done, only the chances they missed."

"We had to sell the business, L.G.," Riley said.

Dolan subtly shook his head. Murphy was dying and didn't need to be concerned with such matters.

"That's for the best," Murphy said. "It ain't worth the headache."

"It's your life's work."

"A life I wasted. No wife, no children, no one by my side when I succumb."

"We're here," Dolan replied.

"In the end, we all go out the way we came. Alone in a mess of fluid." Murphy had a good cough and wiped the phlegm on the blanket. "Do have one regret though. Shoulda killed that cocksucker McSween the first time I laid eyes on him."

By the time they reached Santa Fe, Lawrence Murphy was back to not recognizing Dolan and Riley. They dropped him off at the Santa Fe Christian Hospital, watched a doctor and nurse escort him inside.

That was the last time they saw Lawrence Murphy alive.

SEVEN RIVERS

LINCOLN COUNTY, NEW MEXICO TERRITORY

The Regulators, a dozen men now led by Doc Scurlock, made the trek to Seven Rivers.

They approached the cattle camp close to midnight. The house was quiet, and the sky was moonless, providing good cover.

Billy stopped. Two silhouettes lounged on the front porch, Winchesters propped up next to them. "If we shoot 'em, it'll wake the whole damn county."

Bowdre pulled out a knife. So did Jim French. They moved stealthily toward the side of the house. The two Dolan men on the porch were asleep. They never heard Bowdre and French raise up over the side railing. The Dolan men only woke when the hot, searing pain and shock of their throats being slit left them bleeding out.

Billy and Doc approached the front while the rest of the Regulators fanned out, surrounding the house.

Billy was first through the door, followed by Scurlock. One of Dolan's men was crossing the room in his britches, ill prepared.

Billy's shot went clear through the Dolan man's head.

Rustling in the back of the house. Everyone was awake now. Billy slipped into the kitchen and waited, his gun aimed at the door that led to a hallway. It swung open and Billy fired, killing the second man too.

"They're here!" came a voice from one of the bedrooms. Billy could hear windows being opened and men scrambling out, only to be felled by the Regulators waiting outside.

"Doc," Billy whispered, then motioned with his gun for Scurlock to scour the adjacent living room. When Doc stepped out, a bullet tore through his bicep. Doc spun and fired back, killing the Evans gang member.

Billy crept into the back hallway, going heel-to-toe to make as little noise as possible. A door edged open and a head poked out. Billy shot. The head fell to the ground.

More loud bursts of gunfire outside.

Billy went into the first bedroom. No one was there. The window was open, and a dead body lay outside. Billy opened a closet—empty.

Billy exited the room and continued down the hallway.

"Frankie?" he called out. No answer. He kicked the next door open but ducked back against the wall to avoid any waiting gunmen.

Billy listened intently. It was eerily quiet . . . until he heard a floorboard creak, just on the other side of the wall. Then another creak, moving away from the door, toward one of the back windows. Billy stepped back from the wall, his gun following the creaks. One . . . two . . . three . . .

Bang.

Billy heard the body drop on the other side. He burst into

the room to find Nick Provencio, one of the Boys, writhing on the ground in pain.

"Where's he at, Nicky?"

"Jesus, Kid, you got me good," Provencio said, holding his belly. "I think I'm done for."

"Yeah, you done for. And your last act can be a righteous one. Where is he?"

"Shit, this is really it," Provencio answered. He began whimpering.

Billy leaned down over him. "I can make your exit painless or with great suffering." He poked the barrel of his Colt into Provencio's wound. Provencio screamed out in anguish.

"Who? Who you looking for?"

"Frank Coe. Where you got him?"

Provencio was sweating, and the pain was so intense words were hard to form. He nodded toward the back of the house.

"He back there? Who's watching him? How many?"

When Provencio didn't reply, Billy stuck the barrel of his gun back into the wound, really digging in this time.

"The barn! The goddamn barn!"

Billy stood.

"Hey, Kid, make it—"

Billy shot him in the head.

Billy stepped out back to find the other Regulators waiting. Four dead bodies lay on the ground. Men who had tried to flee.

Billy marched to the barn out back, followed by the other Regulators. Billy opened the door to find Frank Coe tied to one of the support pillars. He looked like he'd been dragged through hell. And then hell had beaten on him too.

"You all right?" Billy asked.

"Where's Ab?" Frank asked.

"Got him in Fort Stanton."

"Better than some of the alternatives, I suppose."

As the Regulators untied Coe, Billy looked at the ground curiously.

"We should get going," Scurlock said. "Before anyone else comes back."

"Hold yourself," Billy said, and began walking to the back of the barn, keeping his eyes on the dirt.

"He's right, Billy," Bowdre replied.

"Say, Frank, were you sleepin' when we got here?" Billy asked.

"They beat on me something fierce," Frank Coe responded. "I was going in and out."

Billy made it to the back of the barn, where hay and supplies were stacked high.

"What is it?" Scurlock asked.

Billy pulled the hay pile down.

Indian Segovia was crouching behind the stacks, shaking with fear.

"Please, please. I'll turn myself in. You can take me to Fort Stanton. I'll tell them everything we done."

"Then what?" Billy asked. "Get yourself in front of Rynerson? Judge Bristol?"

"I'll leave New Mexico and never come back. I swear." The man was trembling so hard snot was forming in his nostrils, and spittle collected at the corners of his mouth. "Have mercy on me, please, Billy. I have a mama."

Billy tilted his head and studied Segovia. "Nah," Billy said, then he put a bullet through Segovia's eye.

Billy walked back to the other Regulators, almost a bounce in his step. "Load up the horses and rig up the cattle. Everything's coming with us."

No one moved.

"You got a quarrel with what I just did?" he asked.

Bowdre was the first to finally speak. "No, it's just, well, it's hard to watch a man die when he's pleading for his mama and all."

"McNab had a mama. So did Dick. Hell, we've all had mamas," Billy replied coolly, then walked out of the barn.

On the ride back to San Patricio, Billy felt good. Renewed. Alive. They'd rescued Frank Coe and made off with Dolan's horses and cattle.

They didn't know Dolan had sold his business—and everything attached to it—to Catron.

They didn't know they'd just robbed the most powerful man in New Mexico.

Chapter 32

Governor Axtell walked into the hall less buoyant than at the lodge's first meeting. The stress of governing the territory was taking its toll. His ambition had always been Washington, DC, and now here he was, under fire once again in his second stint as a governor. But tonight was for celebrating among peers, to take a sabbatical from the mess in Lincoln County.

But it was not to be. As Axtell slapped backs with his fellow lodge members, a slender, fragile wisp of a young man tapped the governor on the shoulder.

"I am fine on libations."

But the young man did not float away. "Someone would like a word."

"I'm the governor. Everyone in the room would like a word."

"My brother-in-law is not the waiting type."

The young man's demeanor was not one of fear or intimidation at speaking with the top government official in the territory. He held eye contact with the governor.

"You're Walz, I presume?" Axtell asked.

"And my brother-in-law would like to see you."

Edgar Walz led the governor to an adjoining room, where Boss Catron and another equally authoritative man waited.

"Welcome home, Mr. Elkins," the governor said. "When did you return from Washington?"

"It's more of a goodbye," Stephen Elkins said. "I'm relocating to West Virginia."

Good, thought Axtell. *One less obstruction here in the territory.* "Money or woman?"

"Getting married. I've come back to close my interests in First National and the territory."

"I wish you all successes in your new endeavors."

"Your wishes are noted, Samuel," Catron said. "But you know what would really aid my friend? You doing your damn job."

Axtell shifted uncomfortably in his seat, aware all eyes and arrows were pointed at him. "I believe I've stewarded the territory quite effectively."

"Then you're a moron," Elkins said.

"I take umbrage with—"

"Shush now," Catron interrupted. "These Regulators are still running rampant through the territory. And what of this William Bonney fellow? How have your men not been able to capture and incarcerate him?"

"Bonney?" Axtell said. "I'm not familiar with this individual."

"Jesus Christ, Axtell, he only shot your sheriff in broad daylight," Elkins replied, throwing a weeks-old copy of the *Mesilla Valley Independent* on the desk.

BRADY KILLED IN STREETS;
McSWEEN-TUNSTALL FACTION TO BLAME

"It details how William Bonney and his band of merry men killed the sheriff in cold blood, then Bonney proceeded to scamper into the street and steal the dead sheriff's rifle. So my question is, why haven't you done anything about this?"

"We are working day and night to—"

"Bullshit!" Catron yelled. "If you were working day and night, then Bonney and his outlaws would not have robbed my horses and cattle!"

"Sir, I'm not aware of any—"

"No shit you aren't," Elkins said. "You're not aware of anything of real import."

"Murdering Sheriff Brady, Buckshot Roberts, those two members of the Boys—"

"Not to mention the mess they left in the Seven Rivers yesterday," Elkins added.

"Now they're gonna steal from *me*? And you're not doing a goddamn thing about it?"

Axtell was at a loss for words. He didn't dare risk further enraging Boss Catron.

"Now," Catron said calmly, "we're willing to give you one last chance."

"I am appointed by the president of the United States—"

"With whom I'm having dinner next week," Elkins interrupted.

"George Peppin will be the new sheriff of Lincoln County. I'll let you tell him. He's waiting outside."

"Are you sure another man so closely aligned with James Dolan is the answer to quelling the violence?" Axtell asked.

"One last burst of violence may be what it takes to end this thing once and for all."

LINCOLN COUNTY, NEW MEXICO TERRITORY

"¿Dónde están todos, Arturo?"

Arturo just shrugged and went back to cleaning a glass with his dirty rag. The San Patricians had mostly been staying inside, avoiding Billy and the Regulators.

Billy had an ease about him. Killing the Boys down in Seven Rivers wouldn't keep him up at night. Those days were over. If anything, he felt more at peace than he had in some time.

Billy picked up the newspaper. The press had made up their mind about Henry McCarty, William H. Bonney, the "Kid." And where the press goes, public opinion will follow.

A second headline on the back page caught his eye:

LONE INDIAN FOUND DEAD, STILL CLUTCHING DOLL
The doll was a child's plaything, its dress frayed and the stuffing protruding out the seams.

The article's writer, Marshall Upson, had an eye for detail. And sensationalism. *Bodaway . . .* Billy's heart moved up into his throat, lumping, and he found himself on the verge of tears.

The faintest rustle and Billy's six-shooter was out. *"¿Quién es?* Who's there?"

The room was quiet. Arturo had retired for the evening.

Billy rose from his chair. "I'll give you until three to—"

"Don't shoot!"

A tall, lanky figure emerged from behind crates in the back corner of the saloon. Despite the layers of dust and mud on his face and clothes, his hair was combed neatly to the side. He was about Billy's age.

"What's your business?" Billy asked, not lowering the revolver.

"What's yours?" asked the young man.

"You're the one in the crosshairs of a Colt."

"Name's Tom O'Folliard," the young man said, brushing the dirt off himself as best he could.

"I don't know you."

"I don't know you either," O'Folliard replied defiantly.

"How long you been back there?"

"Too long, I suppose."

Billy looked the young man over, still undecided on what to do with him.

"You're that Bonney fella, huh?" O'Folliard said and took a step toward Billy.

Billy pulled the hammer back on the Colt, freezing him.

"Okay, not one for pleasantries. But I think our interests may be aligned."

"Yeah, how you figure?" Billy asked, not taking the gun off O'Folliard.

"Made my way over from Texas. Times got a little tight. I may have lifted a steer or two that didn't belong to me. Was gonna take 'em back to Texas, when things got all fouled up."

"And who'd you lift the cattle from?"

"A stiff-shirt type—thinks he's a big shot or something. Goes by Dolan."

"Him I know."

"Bastard sent some of his henchmen after me. Now I'm pilfering through rubbage like some scamp just to eat for the day."

"I think maybe you're right, Tom O'Folliard," Billy said, holstering his revolver. "I think our interests may indeed be aligned."

Tom frowned. "Got anything to eat?"

Billy and Tom stepped out into San Patricio and were met by Scurlock, Bowdre, and Big Jim French. Scurlock carried his typical worried look.

"Brighten up, Doc. Got ourselves a new recruit," Billy said.

"Recruit for what?" O'Folliard asked.

"Our entanglement against James Dolan and John Riley."

"I'm just trying to find something to eat and maybe carve out a home for a few months," O'Folliard replied. "Whatever conflicts you got going on ain't my business."

"That's good, Billy," Scurlock said. "Because we're fixin' to lose some guns too."

"What do you mean? Who's wavering?" Billy asked.

"The men are tired, hungry, and broke."

"Shit, maybe y'all are my type of folk," O'Folliard said.

"Some are thinking of disbanding, getting out of New Mexico altogether."

"Now?" Billy asked. "Just when we got the wind at our backs?"

"That ain't wind," Bowdre said. "It's bullets whizzing past our heads."

"We best move on for a bit," Doc Scurlock said.

Billy looked down the lone San Patricio street. The town was quiet, and everyone was in their homes. "Come morning."

"Long as we been here, hell, Dolan's men could be on their way," Bowdre said.

"Relax, Charlie. Ain't nobody gonna raid San Patricio looking for us. I need a warm bed tonight. Don't know the next time I'll get one."

Francisca was waiting for him in the stables behind the adobe her family shared with three others. She giggled as he approached.

He swept her up into his arms, and they fell onto a haystack. That night, Billy wasn't as tender and compassionate as she'd remembered. She still had a pleasant enough time, but this go-round, it wasn't the same.

Chapter 33

LINCOLN COUNTY, NEW MEXICO TERRITORY

The church service being done in McSween's home was just a bonus in Dolan's eyes. The real purpose was to gather his allies. District Attorney Rynerson was there. As was newly appointed Sheriff Peppin, along with Jesse Evans and the Boys.

But the true guest of honor was John Kinney and his band of cutthroat men.

Kinney, nearing thirty years old, was a ruthless sonofabitch who even hardened types like Evans minded themselves around. The Kinney Gang had been stealing cattle and horses throughout New Mexico for years now, and no one would make them atone for their sins. They didn't even have to answer for killing two cavalry soldiers a few years back.

Dolan stood up and addressed the room. "This affair in Lincoln has gotten out of hand. It's taking money out of our pockets and food off our tables."

Kinney spat on the floor. "What of it? You and the fine district attorney here are still donning three-piece suits and trekking up to Santa Fe to kiss the ring. Seems it hasn't slowed you one bit."

"This suit has seen better days, as have our ledgers," Dolan replied.

"Thought your ledger'd be locked away in Catron's desk drawer by now," Evans said.

"It is true, I have turned over controlling operations of the House to Boss Catron."

"Then what the hell are we doing here? Shouldn't we be meeting in Santa Fe?" Evans asked.

"No, this ain't about business anymore for you, is it, Jimmy?" Kinney said. "It's become *personal.*" The members of the Kinney Gang laughed.

"You're goddamn right it's personal," Dolan replied. "The sunlight on our operation here is illuminating us all the way to Washington. Longer this goes on, more likely President Hayes sends someone to clean up the whole territory. That includes you, Kinney, and you, Jesse."

"So what are you proposing?" Kinney asked.

District Attorney William Rynerson stepped forward and cleared his throat. "I aim to deputize the members of the Kinney Gang, under the leadership of Sheriff George Peppin."

Peppin bowed, and there was more laughter in the room.

"We'll pay each of you five dollars a day to locate the Regulators," Rynerson continued.

"Then what? We haul them to jail and you prosecute them in court?" Kinney asked.

"Whether they make it to court is entirely up to you," Dolan replied.

"Any bonuses for ridding the territory of some of the more prominent Regulators?"

"An additional ten dollars per head."

"Ain't a whole lot of money to get shot at," Jesse Evans said.

Dolan could see the men were losing their enthusiasm for being under his employ. "Five hundred dollars if you kill Alexander McSween."

Kinney looked at Rynerson. "That true, Mr. *District Attorney*? The territory's gonna pay out that kind of bounty?"

"It's from me personally," Dolan replied.

"With what money, Jimmy? You're broke."

"I'll pay you in McSween cattle."

"Bullshit," Kinney sneered. "You'll sell the cattle and pay me in cash."

The Regulators went to the hills outside Lincoln to convene with McSween. They told him about the church service held in his home, and the meeting that had followed.

"It's beginning," McSween said.

"They're just trying to goad you," Susan McSween replied.

"Goddammit, Susan! Don't you see? They're conspiring to confiscate my business!"

Billy stepped forward. "We could place some men around the store."

"I appreciate that, Billy, but you'll just get yourselves killed," McSween answered.

"All the more reason we should leave this godforsaken place," Susan said.

McSween was despondent. "And start over? Everything we have is tied up in the business, in New Mexico."

"Let's take the fight to them," Billy said.

"We've got what, a dozen?" Scurlock said. "Kinney alone drags that many along. Not to mention the Boys."

"And fuck me if the Seven Rivers Warriors join the fray," Big Jim French added.

"And then there's the law," Bowdre replied. "Peppin, his deputies, and all those other jack mules who hang around the House."

"Didn't y'all hear?" Billy said. Everyone looked at him. "Kinney and his gang *are* the deputies."

All the oxygen was sucked out of the room.

"What are y'all so sullen about?" Billy asked. "They're just men, like anyone else. A bullet snuffs them out, just like anyone else."

"It's fifty against twelve," Scurlock answered, saying what everyone else was thinking.

"Then we'll get more men, if you're gonna be a baby about it," Billy said. He was the only one smiling.

"Alex, please, let's just go and never look back," Susan implored her husband.

"No, no, Billy's right," McSween answered, more to himself than his wife. "More men means more money. I'll write to John's father in England, see if he'll aid us in this regard."

"And what do we do in the meantime?" Scurlock asked.

"You wore out your welcome in San Patricio," José Chávez y Chávez replied.

"I know where we can go," Billy said. "Somewhere no one will be looking for us."

FORT SUMNER

LINCOLN COUNTY, NEW MEXICO TERRITORY

Billy led the Regulators out to Fort Sumner, at the northern edge of Lincoln County.

Pete Maxwell's ranch.

Scurlock, Bowdre, and the Coes knew Maxwell personally, the rest only by reputation. Pete was the son of Lucien Maxwell, the richest man in the territory until his death a half a decade back. Pete was struggling to live up to his father's success, but he'd carved out a decent life and managed his family's wealth well enough.

The Regulators arrived weary from travel and looking for rest.

Fort Sumner was alive with activity. The town was host to weekly bailes, and men, women, and children had traveled from as far as fifty miles to attend the evening's dance.

"Well, hell, boys," Billy said. "Looks like we won't have to entertain ourselves tonight."

"I just want to find a bed," Bowdre replied. The rest of the Regulators nodded in agreement. Only O'Folliard, himself as youthful as the Kid, was up for revelry.

"Jesus, Billy," Scurlock said, looking around at the crowd. "Hardly discreet, what with a hundred people gathered. Someone's bound to recognize us, maybe report back to Dolan."

"Aw, Doc, ain't nobody know who you are," Billy teased.

Billy hadn't been fully truthful. He knew about the weekly bailes, and he had suspected Isadora and Abigail might be in attendance.

Billy left his things saddled over his horse and headed to the festivity.

Billy didn't wait for a partner. He walked into the middle of the dance floor and began stomping and jigging along to the band. The clapping and knee slapping. The devilish grin. The pure *joy*. Billy soon lost himself in the music and didn't even notice the row of white, Mexican, and even a few Apache women smiling behind their hand fans, hoping to garner his attention.

Celsa Gutierrez was seventeen and the envy of all the girls in Fort Sumner, mainly because she had the eye of all the boys. She handed her fan to her sister, lifted her hem, and joined Billy in the middle of the floor.

He began twirling Celsa around to the rhythm of the guitars and fiddles. When the song ended, Celsa clapped out a beat, and the band kicked into the next number. Billy had the endless energy of youth. Celsa was right there with him, laughing along like the teenagers they were.

A few songs later, Billy was still going strong when he noticed a shy girl, all of fourteen, watching. The girl looked away, embarrassed. Billy sauntered over, took her by the hand, and pulled her onto the dance floor as well.

Paulita Maxwell was Pete Maxwell's youngest sister. Half French, a quarter Hispanic, and a quarter Irish, she was the new America.

Paulita danced stiffly at first.

"Just do what I do!" Billy called out over the music. He began bobbing up and down, hands on his hips, his feet moving faster than a hare's, keeping time with the music. He took Paulita by the hand and helped her along. Soon she lost her self-consciousness and gave in to the elation, giggling and grinning.

Then Paulita saw her brother, Pete, frowning. She let go of the Kid's hand, curtsied, and walked back to her family.

"Who's next?" Billy said to the crowd.

"What about me?"

He turned around and found himself looking at Abigail. He'd missed her face. Her smile. Her voice. He smiled and went to hug her, but she leaned away.

"I don't feel much like dancing," she said solemnly. She grabbed him by the elbow and led him away from the dance floor, away from the music, away from everyone.

Abigail took Billy out to the edge of the peach orchard and found a tree stump to sit on.

"I thought you'd be more elated to see me," Billy said.

"Should I be?" she asked.

"Sure. I'm always happy to see my friends."

"You're still a vivacious kid." It wasn't a compliment.

"Maybe. But it's the only way I know how to be."

Abigail looked away, out over the orchard, into the night.

"Is Isadora here?" he asked.

"Is that all you ever think of?"

"No. I've been thinking a lot about you too," he said. "I miss my friend."

Abigail let out a heavy sigh. "Well, Isadora won't be here. She's with child."

"So it's true, then," Billy said.

"Yes, she wed. A nice man, one clean in the eyes of the law."

Billy kicked a clump of dirt.

"What did you expect?" Abigail asked. "That she'd sit around pining for you on the off chance you ever showed your face again? That we all would?"

"I didn't expect anything. I don't think that far ahead."

"No, you don't. You never think how your actions affect others."

"You about to scold me, Abigail? Make me do my numbers? Write my name on the chalkboard?"

"I have half a mind to do worse than that," she replied. "You better be careful, *Henry*, or you'll end up like Buck."

Billy studied her. He wasn't sure how much she knew about Buck's demise. "Last I checked, Buck wasn't exactly in your good graces."

"That may be, but life's complicated when you're grown. It doesn't mean I wished him dead."

"But dead he is, all the same." Billy was harsher than he intended to be.

"You have a cold streak in you that I don't remember," she replied.

"I still ain't Buck. Never will be."

"Yeah, why's that?"

"Because I'd never let myself get cornered the way he did."

Abigail looked at him. "What do you know of it?"

Billy tried to deflect. "C'mon, I just got in town. It's a party. Let's go dance."

"I don't want to dance. I want to know what happened."

"I don't appreciate you comparing me to that no-good scoundrel."

"How did he go, Billy?" Her tone was direct. Serious.

"With his boots on," he finally said.

"So you *were* there." It was an accusation.

"My six-shooter still smokin'."

Billy felt the sting of her palm, followed by the flash of heat in his cheek. He looked at her, bracing for another slap. Instead, she began to cry.

"I thought you'd be happy," Billy said. "I saved you from him. Saved you from ever having him hurt you again."

"Who said I needed saving?"

"Some thanks. If it's all the same, I'll go be where I'm wanted."

"Dancing with Celsa Gutierrez?"

"Is that her name?" Billy asked flippantly.

"You're cruel."

"No, I'm *justified*," he said coldly. "Buck, Frank Baker, Sheriff Brady, Indian Segovia . . . I don't regret any of 'em."

In the moonlight, he could see the tears now streaming down her face. And in her eyes . . . she was looking at him like he was a stranger. Or worse. Someone she was *afraid* of.

"What happened to you?" she asked.

"Maybe I'm *not* a vivacious kid anymore."

He walked back to the baile, leaving Abigail crying in the orchard.

The knock on the door startled Billy awake. He pulled his Colt from under the pillow. More knocking before he could get his britches on and reach the door.

"Señor Bonney?" It was a woman's voice. Billy tucked his gun in the back of his pants and opened the door.

Paulita Maxwell blushed at seeing the Kid shirtless, his suspenders hanging off to the side. The bed behind him was empty. Celsa hadn't stuck around to morning.

"Paulita, right?"

"There are some people here to see you."

"What people?" Billy said, looking around.

"They're in the courtyard, by the main house," she said. Paulita eyed his taut muscles, then his boyish face squinting in the morning sun, before she walked away.

Billy dressed quickly and made his way to the courtyard.

A hundred Hispanics and whites—men, women, and children—were huddled together waiting for him. He recognized them.

San Patricians.

He saw Francisca. He took a step toward her, but she started sobbing and buried her head in her mother's chest. He stopped and looked at the crowd. Billy realized all the women were crying. Most of the men too.

SAN PATRICIO

LINCOLN COUNTY, NEW MEXICO TERRITORY

The Night Before

Two dozen horses had stormed into San Patricio in the middle of the night, many of the riders holding burning torches. The Boys and the Kinney Gang didn't even bother hiding their faces with scarves or hoods. They didn't care if the villagers knew who they were. In fact, it had made it easier.

They dragged every family out of their homes and demanded to know where Billy and the Regulators had gone.

No one had spoken up.

Kinney's men began pulling the women and girls, some as young as eight, aside one by one, separating them from their families. When one father lurched forward, refusing to let go of his little girl, he was shot dead. What happened next would remain a nightmare forever.

Meanwhile, Jesse Evans and the Boys went house to house stealing money, weapons, food, horses, whatever they desired. When they were finished, and the Kinney Gang had tired themselves out violating the women, the "deputies" and the outlaws burned the entire village to the ground.

Come morning, nine San Patrician men died trying to protect their families. Four women didn't survive the brutal assaults. Two young girls, not even teenagers yet, never saw the morning.

Billy looked at the crowd. He saw the bruises, scratches, and scars. One young girl, about ten, still had blood on her leg.

Billy was enraged. All the Regulators were. But none more so than José Chávez y Chávez. Chávez was stomping the courtyard in a fury, screaming in both Spanish and Navajo, unable to be controlled by the Regulators. He had been constable in San Patricio. These were his friends.

"Hell was visited upon that town." Billy turned to see Pat Garrett behind him.

They looked at the San Patricians. The only things left were the clothes on their backs.

"You see what kind of evil we're fighting," Billy said. "Offer's still good. Join us."

"You're going to war."

"We're already at war, Pat. I'm talking about one final battle to end it all."

Part III

Chapter 34

LINCOLN

LINCOLN COUNTY, NEW MEXICO TERRITORY

July 15, 1878

Day One

"They're here," Dolan said.

Sheriff Peppin was getting his bearings. The moon still hung high. "What time is it?"

"The goddamn Regulators are here. And they're not alone."

"Rode in overnight," John Riley said. "Got a whole caravan with 'em now."

"Gather your forces and arrest them!" Dolan replied.

"Look around," Peppin answered. "Kinney and my 'deputies' are already scattered throughout the territory hunting 'em. Which leaves just me and Deputy Long. Unless you two are gonna get your guns up and join."

The Regulators and their reinforcements had ridden in from the east, under the cover of darkness, and spread throughout their side of town.

José Chávez y Chávez, Big Jim French, and Tom O'Folliard led Alexander and Susan back to the McSween home, followed by a handful of San Patricians, including Yginio Salazar. Yginio was just fourteen years old, but after Kinney and his men had raped his mother and sister, the youngster could not be talked out of picking up a rifle.

When they entered, Susan was met with a shock.

"Elizabeth? What are you doing here?" Her sister, Elizabeth Shield, was there in the living room, talking to Harvey Morris, a young lawyer.

"Shh, the kids are asleep," Elizabeth replied. "The children and I arrived days ago. Where have you been?"

"It isn't safe for you here," Susan said.

"We've come a long way to see you. This young man too . . ."

"Harvey Morris, ma'am."

Alex had completely forgotten a young law student was coming to train under him.

"You must go," Susan replied. "The children, all of you. Right now."

"I'm not dragging them out of bed at this ungodly hour."

"Come first light," Susan said, then she gave her sister a hug.

Next door at the Tunstall store, George Coe, Henry Brown, and "Tiger" Sam Smith burst in, startling Dr. Ealy, who was reading the paper by candlelight. Ealy's wife, Mary, and their children were asleep in the back bedroom and didn't wake.

Doc Scurlock, Charlie Bowdre, Frank Coe, John Middleton, Fred Waite, and "Dirty Steve" Stephens occupied the Ellis house, the building farthest east. They positioned themselves by the front windows and waited for word.

Juan Patron's home and small store was also on the east side of town. Patron was a Dolan sympathizer who'd grown fearful of the Regulators and had moved his family to Fort Stanton for protection days ago. Twelve San Patricians—now Regulators—took over his property.

Billy, Constable Atanacio Martinez, and two dozen more San Patricians holed up in the Montaño house on the south side of the street, directly next door to Patron's place.

The Regulators, sixty men in all, had successfully sneaked into Lincoln and commandeered the east side of town without a single shot being fired.

Billy was anxious. And when he was anxious, he talked. "Fernando, you really like Doc and Charlie this much?" he teased.

"I love my daughters, and they love their husbands," Fernando Herrera replied, clutching his old rifle.

"Enough to get killed?" Billy asked.

"No lo pensé bien," Herrera replied.

Billy smiled. No, Fernando hadn't thought it through. But Billy was glad to have him around all the same.

The Regulators had the east. The House had the west.

Billy stationed himself in the front room, staring out the window, gripping his Winchester rifle, waiting for whatever hell was about to come their way.

If Sheriff Peppin didn't have his deputies, cavalry soldiers would be the next best thing. He sent word to Fort Stanton that the Regulators were in town, and he needed assistance in issuing warrants for their arrests.

Colonel Nathan Dudley received the note with his morning coffee and furrowed his brow. "What do you make of this, Daniel?"

Daniel Appel was Dudley's most trusted lieutenant. "I think unless cooler heads prevail, we're going to see a lot of carnage," he replied.

"Do you believe I should send troops to Lincoln?" Dudley asked.

"A month past, I would have said yes. But—"

"Posse Comitatus," Dudley cut him off.

Appel nodded. "The army can't intervene in what is essentially a local dispute—"

"Unless provoked," Dudley interrupted.

"I suppose that's true, but we have yet to be provoked by either faction," Appel replied.

"Does Posse Comitatus prevent us from playing peacemaker?"

"It's . . . murky, sir."

Dudley sat back in his chair. Unrest in Lincoln was a distraction for his men, and he was tired of the time and energy being spent handling the Lincoln affairs. On a personal level, he was also offended that outlaws had taken matters into their own hands.

"See if you can get those cooler heads to prevail," Dudley finally said.

Lieutenant Appel found Lincoln worse than he'd imagined. As he rode through town, he could see the eyes peering out various windows, men manning rooftops. Even the torreón was occupied. It was a circular stone structure in the middle of town that had been used as a lookout and protective fortress to defend against raiding Apache. How the Dolan men had slipped into it unnoticed by the Regulators was a mystery.

Lieutenant Appel made his way to the middle of the street and addressed the entire town. "I am here by order of Colonel Dudley, commanding officer of Fort Stanton. Discard your weapons, come outside, and find a truce before any more innocent people are harmed!"

There was a moment of silence, then a window of the Montaño home creaked open.

"Sure thing, Lieutenant!" Billy yelled out. "Just as soon as we see them Dolan boys pack up and duck out forever."

"Eat crow, scamp!" came a voice from the western end of the street.

Appel could see this was going nowhere. "I'm going to approach," he said to Billy.

"Do as you please," Billy replied. "But your guns stay where they are."

Appel removed his gun belt and walked toward the Montaño home. As he climbed the porch, the door opened. He went inside.

Appel eyed the tin star on Constable Martinez's chest. "Are you the man to speak to?"

"No, that'd be me, Lieutenant." Billy sat in a chair in the living room, his Winchester propped up next to him.

Appel looked the Kid over. The slight frame, the boyish but handsome features, the cockeyed grin on his face. "William Bonney?"

"He is I, and I is him," Billy replied. Appel went to sit, but Billy tsked. "Don't reckon you'll be staying long."

"What is it your men want, Mr. Bonney?"

"Our ask is quite simple. For James Dolan, John Riley, and

any scoundrel under their employ to leave Lincoln in their dust."

"They have just as much right to be here as anyone else."

"Wrong!" Billy blurted out. "They lost that right when they pressed every decent man, woman, and child in this county under their thumb."

"And how do you propose to convince them?"

Billy went calm and congenial again. "I got a few friends. Some flesh, some steel," he said, massaging the barrel of his Winchester.

"We cannot abide anarchy."

"Then I guess you better negotiate the hell outta Dolan," Billy replied. "One way or another, their reign of terror is over."

Lieutenant Appel left the Montaño home and walked west to the House. Dolan and Riley were as equally unamenable.

"We've simply tried to operate a prosperous business in the territory, and for that we've been crucified," Dolan said. "And now you want us to negotiate with the very outlaws—the *criminals*—who've persecuted us?"

"You're hardly Jesus Christ, our Lord and Savior," Appel replied.

Dolan held his hands out, palms up, exposing his wrists. "If you believe it's a sin to make money in America, then by all means, drive the first nail," he said, to chuckles from his men.

It was hopeless. As Lieutenant Appel set out back to Fort Stanton to tell Colonel Dudley the bad news, he came upon two dozen men riding fast into town. He clocked their rifles and six-shooters, more weapons and ammunition.

Neither Kinney, Evans, nor their men paid the lieutenant any mind as they passed. The Boys stopped at the House, but the Kinney Gang rode on into the middle of town, hoopin' and hollerin'. They fired an array of shots at the McSween home.

Their assault was met by a return from the Regulators. Kinney and his men laughed and scurried back to the House.

The battle had begun.

"That's John Kinney," Constable Atanacio Martinez said as Peppin's "deputies" fled back to the House.

"Yeah, I see it," Billy said, peering out the window. "I reckon he's got Jesse Evans and the Boys down there too. Olinger and the Seven Rivers Warriors can't be far behind."

Billy looked over to Francisco Herrera. Beads of sweat trickled down the man's face, and his hands trembled.

"There's too many of them," Herrera said.

"Ain't a single one of 'em that can stop a bullet," Billy replied with a smile.

"How can you be so cavalier at a time like this?"

"It's the waiting that makes you fidgety," Billy said. "But the wait's over. Now we dance."

"We can't just let them sit there all night," Dolan said. He turned to Peppin. "You're the law, ain't ya? Go do your fuckin' job, *Sheriff.*"

Dolan picked up the outdated warrants on his desk and handed them to Peppin. Peppin immediately passed them to Deputy Long.

"Why me?" Long asked.

"Because shit don't roll uphill," Peppin replied.

Long reluctantly walked to the east end of town. "I have warrants for your arrests!"

"Got a little waver to your voice there, Deputy!" Billy answered from the Montaño home.

Long tried to steady himself. "Put your guns down and come out."

The burst of gunfire from the Regulators sent Long diving

behind a trough for cover. He felt himself over. Somehow he was unharmed.

"Fuck this," he said to himself, then he cut through the orchard, across the arroyo, and back to the House.

"It ain't funny," Deputy Long replied to Evans's and Kinney's laughter.

"Maybe not where you're standing," Dolan replied. "But now we can say we tried."

Shots would be traded intermittently for the rest of the afternoon.

After sundown, the streets of Lincoln went quiet.

Day Two

Billy spent the night propped up on a chair by the window, keeping lookout. The San Patrician men in the Montaño home were tired from stress and most nodded off. The rest stayed silent. One whispered a prayer over and over.

"Up for some cards?" Billy asked the man next to him. There was no reply. The man's hat was pulled down over his eyes. Billy gently lifted the brim.

The man snapped awake, a look of fear coursing through him.

"Relax, *señor*," Billy said. *"Me estoy asegurando de que no estés muerto."*

"I'm alive," the man answered in English.

"Go back to sleep." When Billy peered back out the window, he saw a shadow lurking behind the McSween's home next door.

The creaking back door woke the man again.

He looked up, and Billy was gone.

Billy made his way carefully out back. Making sure to stay out of the moonlight and away from windows in the surrounding homes, he inched along in step, tracking the moving shadow. The shadow reached the back edge of McSween's property.

McSween's compound was U-shaped, with the bedroom wings pointing north, away from the street. The wing where the McSweens and Elizabeth Shield and her children were sleeping. Just as the man reached for the knob . . .

"Flinch an inch and I'll cut you down," Billy said.

"Please, mister, don't—"

"Aw, Tom, I'm just messin' with ya," Billy said, then lowered the Winchester.

"I'd a shit my britches if I hadn't just unloaded in the privy," O'Folliard replied.

They heard noises at the west end of the street. Dolan men were still awake.

"Get inside."

Elizabeth Shield and her children were asleep in one room, Susan in the next. Law student Harvey Morris was resting on a bench in the hallway. Billy and O'Folliard made their way to the front of the home, where a few more Regulators were scattered on the floor, dozing off.

Only McSween was still alert, holding a shotgun, occasionally peering out his window.

"Got bored," Billy said to McSween. "Saw somebody lurkin', came to make sure you were all right."

"Sorry about that," O'Folliard said innocently. "Nerves got my tummy in a twist."

"Kids, huh?" Billy shrugged to McSween.

Berry Robinson was the lone Black man under Colonel Dudley's command. Dudley sent him to deliver a response. As Private Robinson rode into Lincoln from the west, a bullet whizzed by his head. Then another.

Robinson scrambled into the Wortley Hotel, coming face-to-face with Dolan, Peppin, and a cadre of men glaring at him.

"You bring it?" Dolan asked.

"Why they shooting at *me*?" Robinson asked, trying to catch his breath. "I'm just here to deliver a message and damn near got my head blown off."

Peppin looked out the front door of the Wortley. Robinson had ditched his horse by the front porch. There was no wagon attached to it.

"He ain't bring it," Peppin said.

"Who was shooting at me?" Robinson asked, still trembling.

Dolan looked up to see Jesse Evans walk in the back door, holstering his revolver.

"It's those goddamn Regulators," Dolan lied. "Now you see why I requested the colonel's howitzer."

Once he'd been calmed, Private Robinson rode back to Fort Stanton to tell Colonel Dudley and Lieutenant Appel what happened. Dudley listened patiently, then dismissed the private.

"You know the story is rubbish," Appel said.

"I don't know that," Dudley replied. "All I do know is one of my men was fired upon by the Regulators. A member of the United States Army, for chrissakes."

"Think about it, sir. Private Robinson rode in from the west, which is under Dolan's control. So how would one of the Regulators shoot at him? Why would they shoot at him?"

"Are you calling the private a liar?"

"No, sir. I am saying perhaps James Dolan is the one not being truthful."

"Take some men and find out what happened."

When the sun came up, the guns came back out.

A San Patrician in the Montaño house took a slug to the thigh. He would walk with a limp the rest of his life.

Ricochet from another bullet caused one of Chávez's cousins to lose an eye.

Dan Dedrick was shot in the arm and began to question whether breaking out of the Arkansas prison two years back had really been worth it.

The Dolan side suffered less—a twisted ankle from stumbling over an ottoman inside the Wortley, and one of Kinney's men lost a finger when his gun accidentally discharged.

The greatest casualty thus far was to McSween's house, which had been the focal point for most of the day. Riddled with bullet holes along the walls and roof, the building was still standing, save two side windows that had been blown out.

"You want in, Alex?"

No, McSween did not want to play cards. He had spent the day fighting with his wife, who in turn was fighting with her sister, imploring her to take the children and leave. But Elizabeth was scared they'd be mistaken by Dolan's men, so they stayed put.

Night had fallen again, and McSween was back to manning the window, keeping an eye on the west end of the street.

"What do you plan to do when this is all over?" O'Folliard asked Billy.

Billy shrugged. "I guess meet me a nice lass, settle down, and tend that ranch Mr. Tunstall was gonna give me. If the offer still stands."

"It does," McSween said, still peering out the window. Billy noticed McSween's jaw was tight, like he was chewing his own teeth.

"What about you, Tom?" Billy asked, then he frowned as Yginio won the hand and raked in the "pot"—spent shell casings.

"Guess I'll come work for you," O'Folliard replied.

That sounded all right to Billy. Someone working for *him*. "If you want. But think bigger. When this is all over, we'll have the run of town. Maybe get you your own property."

"I don't have the head for it. Only thing I'm good with is horses and cattle."

"Yeah, taking them," Billy chided. "Speaking of cattle, Alex, any word from Chisum yet?"

McSween shook his head and muttered under his breath. He'd written Chisum five times while hiding out in the hills, asking for his aid, and testing to see if they were still secret partners. Each letter was met with silence.

"Maybe I'll go call on Sallie Chisum, see if we can't work something out," Billy said.

"Work something out for the business or for . . . you know?" O'Folliard grinned.

Yginio, whose English was getting better by the day, smiled too.

"There you go, Tom. Now you're thinkin' big."

Day Three
That night, Billy finally slept, dreaming again. Only this time he didn't snap awake when his horse reached the tree line and his body

and face were cut and scraped and sliced. No, instead he just kept riding deeper and deeper into the forest, until everything faded to pitch-black. The only sound was the beating of his own heart . . .

Dolan was losing patience. So Sheriff Peppin sent five men to the hills behind the Montaño home. The men lay down, steadied their rifles, and opened fire on the house for one full minute. Wood splintered off the walls, windows and glass shattered, and the back door fell off its hinges. When the shooting stopped, two of the San Patricians inside were dead.

As the five Peppin men stood to retreat, Fernando Herrera—Scurlock and Bowdre's father-in-law—fired a lone shot into Charlie "Lollycooler" Crawford. Crawford fell, holding his belly. His four friends ran off, leaving him behind.

Lieutenant Appel, Captain Purington, and Captain Blair arrived in Lincoln close to noon. They were horrified by what awaited them.

Every home and business was now boarded up. Every structure was littered with bullet holes. Debris filled the streets. And the two factions were no closer to an accord.

The shooting stopped. Both sides were wary of invoking the army's wrath.

The silence was broken by a guttural, primitive moaning from behind the Montaño home. Crawford lay where he fell, still alive, begging for anyone to come to his aid.

"No one is to fire!" Lieutenant Appel yelled out. "If anyone shoots, it will be seen as provocation and met with the full weight of the United States Army!"

"Ain't nobody gonna fire," Billy called out from his now-broken window in the McSween home. "Get that man outta here so we can get on with our business."

The cavalrymen could hear Billy chuckling as they dragged the mortally wounded Crawford back to the Wortley Hotel.

Isaac Ellis, who was boarding Scurlock, Bowdre, Waite, Middleton, Frank Coe, and other Regulators, took the momentary truce to step outside and quickly feed his mule.

Two shots came from the torreón. The first whistled past Ellis into the abyss east of town. The second shattered Ellis's windpipe.

Scurlock and Bowdre raced out of the Ellis home and over to Tunstall's store. Dr. Ealy might be able to save the man. Ealy took some convincing—mainly by the barrel end of George Coe's rifle—but when Ealy set foot outside, he was immediately fusilladed by the Dolan men. Dr. Ealy dove back inside, swearing he would not go out there again.

"Chicken liver," Scurlock said with disgust, then he and Bowdre dodged the hail of bullets and dragged Isaac Ellis back to his home.

Inside McSween's, despair was setting in. Susan and Alex had stopped speaking to one another. Her nieces and nephews didn't understand why they now had to hide in the cellar. Harvey Morris tried to talk through some legal strategies with Alex, missing the point that no arcane lawbook would provide the solution out of this.

"He's a decent man, you know," Billy said to Susan as she scoured the kitchen and took inventory of what they had left.

"I suppose he was at one time," she replied.

"He and Mr. Tunstall, they took me in when I needed it most."

Susan turned and looked at Billy. She didn't see the boastful outlaw or the charming scamp. No, she was looking at a young man whose world was crumbling around him. "Is that what you think they were doing, Billy? Taking you in to help *you*?"

"Gave me a roof and food on my plate," Billy replied.

"And what did you have to give them?"

Billy hadn't contemplated it before. "I protect my friends," he said finally.

"I've always been fond of you, Billy. We all have. But at some point you're going to grow up and realize people take and they take and they take until only the shell is left."

"And what's been my reasoning, then?" he asked.

She looked at him in bewilderment. How had he never understood the true essence of himself? "You needed a *place* in this world."

Day Four

The three Hispanic women set out before the sun was up. Juanita Baca and her two friends traveled ten miles on foot to Fort Stanton to get an audience with Colonel Dudley. Dudley tried to ignore them, but they refused to leave until he met with them.

"All three of our homes have been overtaken by both the McSween side and the Dolan faction," Juanita said. "Our children are hunkered under their beds day and night as artillery is exchanged throughout town."

"I assure you we will take every step within our power to quell the unrest and keep you and your families safe," Dudley replied dismissively. He didn't have time or care for the three women.

As they left the fort, the women passed a trio of riders. Juanita Baca hissed at the lead rider, who only laughed. Dolan, Jesse Evans, and John Kinney walked into Dudley's office without knocking.

"It's about time we end this," Dolan opened.

"I was thinking the same thing," Colonel Dudley replied.

Dolan traded looks with Evans and Kinney. This might be easier than they thought.

"Did you see those women?" Dudley continued.

"The three little Mexican *chicas*?" Evans asked.

"Oh, Jesse, they're so much more than that," Dudley replied. "They're your salvation."

After initial reluctance, Lieutenant Appel gave in to Colonel Dudley's pressure and signed the testimony of account.

Private Benjamin, while stationed under the supervision of Colonel Dudley at Fort Stanton, had been fired upon by a faction of outlaws known as the Regulators.

Dudley was sending troops to occupy Lincoln, "To protect the women and children."

Dudley's so proud of his own cleverness, Appel thought. *But what a cost that cleverness will bring.*

The bullet passed through the shattered window, narrowly missing Billy, and lodged into Luke Cullins's skull. It sobered the room in a flash.

"Tom," Billy said as bullets continued to riddle the house and walls. Billy ducked down and reloaded. He eyed O'Folliard, who was fixated on the dead body in the middle of the living-room floor, eyes vacantly staring off into space.

"We'll bury the dead later," Billy continued. But O'Folliard didn't move. "Chávez, Morris, take the body down to the cellar."

"That's where Miss Shield and her children are," Morris replied.

"Whether they stay down there is up to them," Billy answered, then he leapt back up to the window and fired a few more rounds at the west end of the street.

José Chávez y Chávez and Harvey Morris carried Cullins's

body down to the cellar. They had the decency to throw a bedsheet over it before they did, but it didn't make a lick of difference. The Shield children began crying anyway.

This time the shooting continued throughout the night and into the morning and only stopped when Colonel Dudley and thirty-five infantry soldiers rode into the middle of town.

Billy couldn't help but notice they brought the howitzer.

Chapter 35

Day Five

The howitzer could fire over two hundred rounds a minute. And Dudley had more than enough ammo.

Inside the McSween home, despair had given way to outright hopelessness for most.

But Billy was alert again, seeming to find *more* energy. With each shot from his pistol or rifle, he'd snicker and say, "That was a close one, boys," or, "I think I nicked him that time," or, "You see ol' Johnson's hat blow clear off?"

He'd been right about one thing though: one way or another, the troubles in Lincoln were coming to an end.

"Our mission here is to protect the women and children," Dudley told the men inside the Wortley Hotel. "We will treat both sides equally, and if either faction aims one bullet in the direction of me or mine, that entire faction will be wiped clear of God's green earth."

"I thought he was on our side," Riley said after the colonel had departed.

"Aye, he is," Dolan replied. "But once the dust settles, and reports are made about what transpired, he needs history to record him as impartial."

Colonel Dudley did not deliver the same message to the Regulators.

Dudley's men rode confidently east, crossing over the small arroyo, past the McSween house, the Tunstall store, Justice of the Peace John Wilson's place, and the torreón.

The Regulators watched in anguish as Dolan men traveled in their wake, using the ceasefire to encroach farther east. By the time Dudley finished setting up camp, Dolan's side had overtaken most of the town and the stable behind Tunstall & Co.

"What do you reckon they're doing?" Big Jim French asked.

Billy smiled to himself and shook his head. "Don't you see? Now they got us surrounded."

Once the army was settled, two cavalrymen unloaded the howitzer from the wagon and began loading rounds.

Then they wheeled the monstrous weapon of death around and pointed it directly at Jose Montaño's front door.

The Regulators inside Montaño's home didn't wait. They pulled blankets over their heads to hide their identities and ran out the back.

They were met by the Regulators from the Patron house next door. They, too, had seen the howitzer and decided their war was over. The two groups fled east, making it to the Ellis home on the edge of town without being spotted.

"Both dwellings are unoccupied," the soldier replied.

"That can't be. We've been sitting here, right across the

street . . ." Colonel Dudley said, blood rushing to his face. "You mean to tell me they slipped away without us knowing? Without *you* knowing?"

The soldier stayed mum. Nothing he could say would placate the colonel.

"I didn't see them ride out," Captain Purington replied. "Which means they're still here somewhere. In one of these houses."

Dudley scanned the street. Dolan's men had overtaken most of the homes in Lincoln. They had been keeping a close watch on the McSween and Tunstall places, which meant only one thing: the Ellis house.

"Don't fire unless I give the order," he told his men as they wheeled the howitzer east and aimed it at the Ellis home, where Scurlock, Bowdre, the Coes, and most of the Regulators were now holed up.

The men inside the Ellis house didn't even bothering concealing themselves this time. They ran to the corral out back, mounted their horses, and bolted out of town, bullets ripping past their heads.

The fleeing Regulators made it across the Rio Bonito, to the northern hills.

Billy saw their escape. *We're on our own now.*

He looked around the McSween home. French and O'Folliard were still manning the windows. José Chávez y Chávez covered the back. Law student Harvey Morris had picked up a rifle and held it awkwardly. Yginio Salazar and two others had their eyes on the west wing. Susan McSween was in the kitchen, using what little she had left to make food for the men. Her sister and the children were in their bedroom in the east wing, no longer content to be in the cellar with the dead body.

Billy knew Henry Brown and "Tiger" Sam Smith were still hunkered down in Tunstall & Co. next door. But that was it. All the manpower they had.

Twelve men, two women, and five children up against the whole goddamn House and Colonel Dudley's army.

French and O'Folliard couldn't figure out why Billy started laughing.

Sheriff Peppin led his men to the Ellis house. Scurlock and the Regulators had fled. Now the home was ripe for the picking. Peppin and the "deputies" pilfered through everything, taking what they wanted, trashing the rest. They made off with a handful of pistols and a half dozen rifles. From the corral out back, they confiscated twelve saddles and horses, including Billy's.

Bob Beckwith of the Seven Rivers Warriors found the coal oil tucked in the back of the corral and took that too.

"I won't do it," Justice of the Peace Wilson said.

Dudley was impatient. He had figured the Regulators would surrender or flee the moment the cavalry arrived, but Billy and the remaining Tunstall men had proven stubborn.

"You will do it, by order of the US Army," Dudley replied.

"I can't issue warrants for arrests without proper affidavits and testimony."

"These *Regulators* perpetrated an attack on one of my men. It is by the grace of God that Private Benjamin made it out with his life. But an attack on one soldier is an attack on the whole army. There must be consequences."

"Colonel Dudley, I understand the predicament you're in

here. Every moment they remain inside the Tunstall home is a black mark on your leadership. But I still have to abide by the laws, even if you may circumvent them."

"There is another option," Dudley said coolly. "I could write Governor Axtell and explain your dereliction of duty."

"Even if I were to issue the warrants, to whom would I issue them? Who fired the shot at Private Robinson, all the way on the *other side of town*?"

Dudley was beginning to detest the citizens of Lincoln more and more each day. Their sanctimoniousness. Their outsized opinions of their importance to the territory.

"I'll make sure you're placed in irons and answer to the courts for your insurrection."

Wilson knew the threats weren't idle. Dudley would arrest Wilson and figure out the charges later. So, with reluctance, Wilson wrote up warrants for all of the men in the McSween house, including Billy.

But no one stepped forward to serve the papers.

The Shield children hadn't really slept in days. Elizabeth tried covering their heads with blankets and stuffing cotton in their ears, but nothing could quell the constant barrage of gunfire.

It's why they didn't hear Jesse Evans and John Kinney approaching.

It's why they didn't stop the men from placing logs and dry brush under their window.

"This must all end," Susan told her husband. But Alex McSween didn't respond. As the days had worn on, he had retreated further and further into himself. Now he was sitting in his chair in the living room, a rifle leaning between his legs. The rifle hadn't been touched for hours.

Billy wasn't even sure it was loaded anymore. *Maybe it's better if it isn't.*

Elizabeth Shield burst into the room.

"They have bad intentions," Elizabeth began.

"Was it the cavalry that tipped you off?" Billy asked. "Or the three gangs of outlaws surrounding the house?"

"They've stacked dry brush and wood under our bedroom window."

"Kindling," Billy realized. "They're gonna smoke us out."

"If you're not going to save us, I will," Susan said to her husband, who didn't flinch. Alex continued staring at the wall.

"What are you planning to do?" Billy asked.

"I'm going to talk to Colonel Dudley, remind him of his duty."

"I've heard better plans, ma'am."

"What choice do I have? Let my home be burned to the ground? Let them riddle us with bullets until we're dead in the ground too?"

"They might riddle you all the same if you go out there," the Kid replied.

Susan couldn't be talked out of it. She got down on her belly and had Billy open the door.

"I aim to exit the house. I'm a woman, and I'm alone!" she called to the men outside.

Billy heard the snickering from Dolan's men, and some of the soldiers too.

"Anyone takes a shot at this woman, snuffing you out will become my sole purpose in life!" Billy said.

The Dolan men stopped shooting long enough for Susan to crawl down the front walkway.

"Slithering around like a snake," Kinney said to more cackling.

Susan stood, brushed herself off, and marched up to Colonel Dudley.

"Why are you here, Colonel?"

"To protect the innocent women and children of Lincoln," he replied.

"Then why are you not protecting me? My sister and her children? My house?"

Dudley sneered. "I said *innocent* women and children."

"So you'll sit here on your high horse looking the other way while they murder us all."

"Who do you have in there, Lady McSween? 'Cause I heard Billy Bonney's voice. And I see Big Jim French sticking his head out that window from time to time. They aren't innocent and neither is anyone who safeguards them."

"You're just another appendage of Dolan, Peppin, and the whole goddamn Santa Fe Ring," she spat at him.

"If your husband is using you and your kin as aegis, I suggest you take it up with him."

Susan McSween went back into her home.

Then the shooting continued.

Bob Beckwith wasn't confident in the plan.

"We'll cover you," Kinney assured him.

"Can't we get the dummy to do it?" Beckwith asked.

"He can help, sure, but you found the coal oil, you get to be the hero."

"Stridin' up to the house and dousing all that kindling inches from their window—that don't seem like the sort of thing I'll come back from."

"They'll build statues of you," Evans replied. "Bob Beckwith of the Seven Rivers Warriors, the man who ended the Lincoln County dispute and restored justice for all."

Beckwith knew they were full of shit, but he'd been the one to find the coal oil. And if he succeeded, a lot of powerful people would owe him a debt of gratitude. "Fine, but Long and the dummy are coming too."

"Why do I have to go?" Deputy Long asked.

"Because," Sheriff Peppin replied, "I could take that star from you, and then you're just another rustlin' thief who the courts'll deal with."

The dummy was a local man who hung around the Dolan faction, mainly acting as their court jester. He didn't take convincing. He wasn't smart enough to see the downside.

Beckwith, Long, and the dummy took the same path Evans and Kinney had, leading to the window of the Shield bedroom. The dummy doused the logs and brush with the coal oil while Beckwith and Long kept their rifles trained on the window, lest Chávez poke his head out.

He didn't. No one did.

Deputy Long lit the match. The fire started slow, then a gust of wind blew across Lincoln, and the woodpile went ablaze.

As the men retreated, Billy and the Regulators opened fire. Beckwith, in the lead, made it through the hail of bullets, back to the safety of Dudley's camp.

George Coe, Henry Brown, and "Tiger" Sam Smith were in the Tunstall store next door. They, too, opened fire, cutting off Long and the dummy's path. Caught in a cross fire between the McSween house and Tunstall store, Long and the dummy took refuge in the one place they could: the outhouse.

Long and the dummy barreled into the confined privy. Bullets splintered and shredded the wooden walls. They had only one choice: they dove down into the shithole.

Inside the McSween home, Billy and the Regulators were trying to extinguish the fire. Elizabeth Shield had two full buckets of water in the bedroom for the children. She doused the flames beneath the window, to no avail.

Susan found sawdust and dumped it outside, but the fire still grew.

The wind was blowing, and the flames soon latched onto the walls. It would burn slow, but move room to room, spreading throughout the house.

"Jesus, Billy, we're in it now," O'Folliard said.

"Well, we could always surrender," Billy replied in between bursts of gunfire.

"You got a plan though, right?"

"Tom, I ain't ever planned my next meal, let alone what to do in a situation like this."

Billy looked at McSween. Alex was still in his chair, gazing into the distance, seemingly impervious to the hail of bullets, shattered windows, and the smoke now permeating the house. Just as Billy turned back to the street, he heard a vicious *slap*.

Susan was standing over her husband, whose cheek was now bright red. "Inaction is not an option!" she said. "We have to do *something*."

Alex slowly shifted his eyes to his wife. His lips parted, the words itching to come out; then he closed his mouth and said nothing. Susan began to cry.

Billy gently escorted Susan away from her husband.

"He's just doing his thinking," Billy said, trying to cover for McSween.

"Hogwash. He led us to slaughter and now he's paralyzed with fear. I've hitched my wagon to a blustering blowhard, and a spineless one at that." She looked Billy in the eyes. "We both have."

"Naw, Alex is smart. He'll come up with something."

"Billy, I say this with all the fondness I have for you. It's time to save yourself."

"Sorry, ma'am. I just can't do that. Weren't how I was raised."

"Me and Elizabeth and the children will be fine. Not even John Kinney or Jesse Evans dare shoot us in front of Colonel Dudley."

Billy knew the answer but had to ask. "What about Alex?"

They both turned and looked at McSween, sitting motionless.

"Alex has made his choices in life. Now we must make ours."

The explosion shook the house and knocked Billy and Susan to the floor.

The fire had reached the kitchen and the keg of gunpowder.

"Are you okay?"

Susan nodded. Billy helped her to her feet. She surveyed her home. The entire west wing was gone. So was the kitchen on the other side of the U-shaped home.

Elizabeth Shield came into the room with her children. "I love you, sister, but I can no longer—"

Susan hugged her deep and hard. "I know. We're going."

Dolan watched as the front door of the house opened. A hand jutted out and waved a white handkerchief.

"Tell your men to cease fire," Colonel Dudley said.

James Dolan had no intention of giving that order. "She's no innocent. If she catches a stray—"

"Do it, or when I'm done with Billy Bonney and his Regulators, I'll hang you in the middle of the street."

Dolan reluctantly told his men to hold fire.

Susan, Elizabeth, and the children walked out. Susan approached Dolan and spat in his face. Dolan reached back to slap her, but Dudley gabbed his arm.

"Let it be." He turned to Appel. "Lieutenant . . ."

Lieutenant Appel escorted Susan, Elizabeth, and the children out of Lincoln.

Dolan looked at Dudley, who nodded.

Then the firing began again.

This time in a fervor that wouldn't let up until it was all over.

"What's wrong with him?" O'Folliard asked.

"Ain't you ever see a man's spirit crushed?" Big Jim French replied.

Billy looked at McSween. Alex now had his head in his hands, and he was mumbling to himself. Billy took a knee and inched his ear to Alex's lips.

"Fritz . . . Emil . . . Insurance . . . Fritz . . . Emil . . . Insurance . . ."

"Alex," Billy said softly. "We could use your help."

But Alex just kept repeating those three words over and over into the night.

He's gone, Billy thought. First Tunstall, now McSween.

The sun fell into the horizon.

The shooting continued.

The Regulators were tired and hungry.

The front of the house was now engulfed in flames, joining the entire west wing. The Regulators were cornered into the only area that remained, a small room just off the east wing.

They'd been able to move Alex by half carrying him room to room as the fire spread. He continued muttering, "Fritz . . . Emil . . . Insurance . . ."

Billy sat back against a wall. He took in their surroundings. The fire swallowing the rest of the home, the smoke billowing in, their despondent boss, and his friends.

Josie. He wondered what his brother was doing right then, at that very moment. Was he still working at the Orleans?

Had he gotten off the pipe? Was he happy? Had he met a girl? *Girls.*

His thoughts drifted to Abigail. The look in her eyes, the venom in her voice, the last time they spoke, when he revealed he'd been the one to kill Buck.

And Isadora. The sweet, young muchacha. He'd been with other girls before and since, but she was the only one he'd wanted to *stay* with. And he hadn't. He'd been swept up into this life, first with Jesse Evans and the Boys, then the other side. And what had it gotten him? He was sitting on the floor while the world burned around him.

But he was still alive. Untouched by the flames or the law. Still *free.*

He began singing. Lightly at first, then louder, until all the men were listening:

> Darling, I am growing old,
> Silver threads among the gold,
> Shine upon my brow today,
> Life is fading fast away.

He closed his eyes and thought about his dream. *The horse. The dense forest. Each time riding farther and farther into the blackness . . .*

> But, my darling, you will be,
> Always young and fair to me,
> Yes, my darling, you will be
> Always young and fair to me.

The other Regulators looked at each other. Was Billy cracking up too?

He snapped his eyes open.

"Time to go."

"*Get to*? Going out last is the most dangerous position," Billy said. "Between the night and the fire, it'll take their eyes a minute to adjust, then another minute for their eyes to tell their brains what's happening. First man out the door, hell, he's got a cake-walk. It's the last fella out who's gonna get his hide burned."

"Or shot," O'Folliard said.

"Gentleman, see you on the other side, whatever that may be," Billy said.

Harvey Morris was first out the door, followed by Big Jim French, O'Folliard, Chávez, then Billy. They headed east, hoping to draw attention away so McSween, Francisco Zamora, Vincente Romero, and young Yginio Salazar could escape north to the Rio Bonito.

Billy's group made it five steps before a hail of bullets rained down on them.

They returned fire and kept running. They just needed to reach the large adobe wall behind Tunstall & Co.

Harvey Morris got one foot over the wall when the bullet hit him in the skull. He slumped to the ground, dead.

As John Kinney reloaded his rifle, Billy stopped.

He took careful aim and fired.

The bullet went through Kinney's mouth and out his cheek.

Billy, French, and Chávez kept running.

O'Folliard stopped over Morris's body.

"Tom!" Billy cried out.

The ground at O'Folliard's feet was sprayed with more gun-fire, shredding Morris's body.

O'Folliard snapped to and raced after Billy, French, and Chávez.

A bullet thumped into Chávez's shoulder. He dropped to a knee, but Billy caught him.

Billy pulled him upright, and they kept running.

George Coe, Henry Brown, and "Tiger" Sam Smith watched from the window next door as Billy and the Regulators drew fire. They escaped the Tunstall store and ran for the Rio Bonito.

Yginio Salazar, Zamora, and Romero dragged McSween out of the house.

Jesse Evans, Bob Beckwith, Deputy Long, and the dummy were posted up behind McSween's home, waiting.

Eight bullets ripped through Zamora.

Vincente Romero took five shots to the gut and head.

Both men fell dead.

Fourteen-year-old Yginio Salazar felt the bullet enter his back, above his shoulder blade, and he, too, fell.

McSween froze and threw his hands up. "I surrender!"

"Well, well," Bob Beckwith said, striding confidently toward McSween. "We got you now, you sonofa—"

The bullet burst into Beckwith's eye and never came out.

Evans and the rest started shooting in the direction the shot came from, but in the pitch-black of night, they were firing blind.

"Come on, Billy! We have to go!" O'Folliard said.

Billy'd gotten Beckwith.

But he wanted Evans.

The fire was illuminating McSween. But the Dolan men were cloaked in the darkness beyond the light of the flames.

Billy watched as McSween had his hands in the air, surrendering. More Dolan men and cavalry were beginning to flood in behind the house.

"Jesse!"

The roar of the fire was deafening, but Billy's voice rose above it. Evans stepped into the light, and Billy locked eyes with him.

Evans's pistol was already out and raised. As he extended his arm, Billy pulled his Colt from his holster in one swift move. Both men fired at the same time.

Billy heard the bullet whiz past his head.

He saw his bullet pierce Evans's shoulder.

Evans fell, disappearing behind the fire.

More Dolan men now surrounded McSween.

"You can't kill them all," Big Jim French said, placing a hand gently on Billy's shoulder.

God help you, Alex, Billy thought.

Then the Dolan men unloaded everything they had into McSween.

Billy watched Alex twist in anguish as the bullets riddled his body. His face tilted upward for a moment, as if looking to the heavens, then he crumpled to the dirt, dead.

Billy dropped his head and took a deep breath. There was sorrow, there was regret.

But no tears.

Those days were done.

So was the Lincoln County War.

Billy vanished into the darkness beyond the Rio Bonito.

Chapter 36

July 14, 1881

Billy woke just after midnight. His stomach was growling.

Three years had passed since that fateful night in Lincoln.

He'd befriended Pat Garrett.

And now Pat Garrett was hunting him too.

Boss Catron hadn't forgotten Billy had stolen from him. That miser Chisum too. They'd teamed up and hired Pat to track Billy down and bring him to justice—*by any means necessary.*

Billy had been jailed again, twice. And he'd escaped again, twice.

He'd killed more men. And been blamed for killing even more than he had.

He'd watched Charlie Bowdre and Tom O'Folliard murdered right before his very eyes.

He'd grown older.

But not wiser.

He'd been urged to run. To get out of New Mexico, start a

new life somewhere else, as someone else, but he just couldn't bring himself to do it.

He'd already changed his name twice. He wouldn't do it again.

Billy looked over at the señorita sleeping next to him. So beautiful. So lively.

So very optimistic for their future.

Paulita Maxwell had grown up since the first time he saw her in Fort Sumner. He was fond of her. *Cared* about her. Maybe even more than he had ever cared about Isadora.

Was it love? He wasn't sure. He didn't even know what that meant anymore.

Some thought Paulita was the reason Billy refused to leave New Mexico, but he knew that wasn't true. And it wasn't fair to her.

He'd stayed in New Mexico because he had nowhere else to go. No one else to go with.

No one to call *family*.

He'd lost track of his little brother. Heard he'd moved to California. When the timing was right, he'd go find Josie. He'd been saying that for five years. And he'd meant it for five years.

Billy climbed out of bed, slipped on his britches, and pulled his suspenders over his shoulders.

They still called him "the Kid." But he wasn't a kid anymore. He was a man. Twenty-two.

And he had the scars to prove it.

It was late. No one else would be awake. No need for his shirt.

He took a bite off the peach on the nightstand. The last bite. He wiped his mouth and set it back down. Maybe he'd grab more from the orchard outside. The peaches were good. Succulent.

No, he needed something with more substance. Pete Maxwell, Paulita's older brother, always kept a fresh slab of meat hanging in the main house. A cut of beef would do the trick and have Billy back to sleep in no time.

He grabbed the knife off the nightstand and pulled it from its sheath. He looked at the six-shooter next to it.

He just needed something to eat. Fort Sumner was safe. The people here loved him. Protected him. Except for Pete Maxwell, who always looked at him with an air of skepticism.

Billy'd be back in a minute. He let the gun be.

Billy crossed the courtyard. The moon was high and illuminated the peach orchard off the side of the bungalow. The orchard where he'd had it out with Abigail.

That was a long time ago. Another lifetime.

Pete will learn to love me, Billy thought. *Just as his sister has.*

Billy climbed the steps to the main house.

He stopped. Something was wrong. *Someone* was wrong.

Off in the dark, at the end of the long porch, two silhouettes, still as statues.

"*¿Quién es?*" Billy whispered.

No reply.

His senses tingled. He felt for his gun, but it was back in the room, next to the sleeping Paulita.

Billy tiptoed backward into the nearest bedroom—Pete's bedroom.

It was pitch-black.

"*¿Quién es, Pedro?*" *Who's out there?*

Billy turned toward Pete's bed.

It didn't hurt at first, the thunderous blow to his chest from Pat Garrett's Colt Single Action Army revolver that knocked Billy off his feet. Then he felt it. The white-hot heat and burning pain that made his whole body sweat.

Darling, I am growing old,
Silver threads among the gold,

Each breath shallower and shallower.
There wasn't enough air. There wasn't enough time.

Shine upon my brow today,
Life is fading fast away.

He could feel the life being sucked out of him. He saw his mother's face. Not how she was at the end, hollow and frail, but when he was a child. So vibrant, so beautiful, so full of life.

But, my darling, you will be,
Always young and fair to me.

Henry McCarty, best known as Billy the Kid, gasped and looked out the open door, at the bright moon hanging high above . . .

Yes, my darling, you will be
Always young and fair to me.

. . . and wondered what Josie was doing right then.

Author's note

Since his death almost 150 years ago, much has been written about Billy the Kid. Was he a cold-blooded killer? Did he murder twenty-one men? Was he really killed by Pat Garrett on that fateful night in Fort Sumner, New Mexico?

I was eight years old when I first saw *Young Guns*. My friend Peter and I went home and immediately tried to write our own western movie (the excursion lasted an hour before we went outside to play football). But my fascination with Billy the Kid remained, and over the years I would devour any book, film, or article I could.

The shootouts, multiple escapes from prison, and his final demise are well covered. But less so is *how did he become the young man to do all these things?*

Everyone arrives at a crossroads at some point, where a life-altering decision must be made. Billy's moment came the night he decided to escape prison for the first time.

He was only fifteen when he was arrested for aiding a local thief. But to Billy, he was simply holding on to blankets for a friend. Billy's mother had just died. His stepfather wanted nothing to do with him or his little brother. Billy was in desperate need of a family. And now here he was, orphaned and in jail, with no one to turn to for help.

So he made a fateful decision. Billy squeezed his small frame up and out the chimney and left town for good. That one choice would alter his life forever.

What takes this incident from fateful to tragic is not only the eventual outcome—being gunned down at the age of twenty-two—but also the fact that local authorities had no intention of putting the Kid on trial, much less sending him to prison. They were simply trying to teach him a lesson and were going to release him the next day.

I read about this fork-in-the-road moment some twenty years ago, and ever since I have been obsessing over the idea of how this one choice in his young life forever altered not only his destiny but folklore surrounding the Wild West as a whole, and how events across the West shaped his life.

After his self-liberation, Billy found himself in the midst of a swirling political climate of corruption, graft, and murder. He was in search of a family. Of community. Of a proper life.

What he found was Lincoln County.

Everyone knows how Billy the Kid's legendary story ends.

Here is how it began.

Thank you, and I sincerely hope you have as much fun reading the story as I did writing it.

—Ryan Coleman
Los Angeles, 2024

Acknowledgments

Apologies for the length here—you never know when you're going to have the chance to write a second book.

As always, my everlasting adoration and gratitude to my wife, Cassie, for her love, support, and her ability to understand me better than I maybe even understand myself—and for putting up with my incessant discussing of the story, and the maps and timelines spread throughout our home. And for editing these acknowledgments.

To my mom and dad, Nancy and Ron Coleman, who have always been there for me, always encouraged me, and gave me the foundation to believe in myself and pursue my passions. I know Mom is looking down with a big smile, bending the ears of Grandma, Grandpa, Aunt Mary, and Uncle Terry. "Yes, yes, we get it, Nanny. We're proud of him too."

I want to thank my (much shorter) sister, Krista Coleman, the yang to my yin. There's a special bond between siblings who are so close, and being able to share with you my excitement over this dream becoming a reality means everything.

I also want to thank my aunt and godmother extraordinaire,

ACKNOWLEDGMENTS

Betty Lou Lutterman, for always being there with sage advice, a sympathetic ear, or a laugh. You're the absolute best.

I also want to acknowledge and thank Sandi and Bill Capps, the greatest in-laws a guy could ever hope for. Thank you for welcoming me into your home and becoming family. And Sandi, thank you for giving me the most poignant line in the novel, which everyone else will have to figure out for themselves. And thank you to Jason Capps, Stephanie Osimiri, and Cameron Capps. I can't wait to hear what Cam thinks of the book—when he's old enough to read it!

And a big heartfelt thank-you to Josh and Stephanie Stanton for taking a chance on an unknown author when it was just a kernel of an idea and they didn't have to. I will be forever grateful and am so, so proud to publish this book with you and Blackstone.

And to the rest of the Blackstone team: Anthony Goff, Rachel Sanders, Greg Boguslawski, Becca Malzahn, Sarah Bonamino, Sean Thomas, Bryan Barney, Isabella Bedoya, David Baker, Candice Roditi, and especially Josie Woodbridge . . . it takes a village, and what a village this is. Thank you for all the hard work and dedication you put in to make this book a reality.

Thank you to the wonderful editor Diana Gill, who knew just the right areas to trim, expand, and expound upon to help me get out of my own way. This book is infinitely better thanks to you.

To some of the fellow authors I've met along the way who, whether they knew it or not, were a giant inspiration not only to the story but to me. First, the master, Don Winslow, for his incredible guidance in the early stages of the book and taking time away from writing masterpieces just to help a rube like me. To Steve Hamilton, someone I've been fortunate enough to get to know well and call a friend. As gifted of a writer as he is—and wow, is he gifted—he's an even better person. Thank you for the friendship and letting me bend your ear whenever I needed to, day or night. A big hearty thank-you to T. J. Newman, for her wisdom in helping me navigate my first novel and also not revealing some of my deepest, darkest secrets—mainly movies you'd be surprised I love. After what you did to me with *Drowning*, I hope I can elicit at least one single tear from you with this book. To the other authors at the Story Factory—Meg Gardiner, Adrian McKinty, Lou Berney, Reed Farrel Coleman, Eric Rickstad, Stayton Bonner, Greg Harden, Karina Kilmore, Ruth McIver, Siobhan MacDonald—your talent and creativity are an inspiration every single day. Thank you for letting me in.

Thank you to Deborah Randall. The unheralded—and heroic—work you put in behind the scenes is so very appreciated.

And finally, to my pal, accomplice, and a man who I often drive crazy, Shane Salerno. You asked me what I wanted to do, and when I replied write a story about Billy the Kid, you didn't blink; you just made it happen. And when I wasn't sure if I could even write a novel, you saw the potential in me and convinced me I could. And through your determination, fortitude, and tireless energy, you made this project a reality. Your love of books and the work you put in on behalf of your authors is awe-inspiring, and we're fortunate to have you on our side. You've changed so many lives, and we're all so grateful. Thank you, thank you, thank you, my friend.